COLD PRINCES

M.P. STARKWEATHER

Phoenix Eclipse Publishing

I want to dedicate this book to my two biggest fans, my husband Josh and my son Thom, who will probably never read any of my books. Thanks for pushing me to chase my dream. I love you both to the moon and back.

ACKNOWLEDGMENTS

I would like to thank:

My author besties, who encourage me to keep writing, even when it's hard;

My amazing PA, Gwen, who is my twinsie;

My Alpha Team who tries hard to keep me on track;

My Editing Team who does their best to make sure my books make sense and have as few typos as possible;

My Cover Artist, who's responsible for the gorgeous images on the front of this book

and My ARC Team, who catch some of the things the rest of us miss.

CONTENTS

CHAPTER ONE

DESIRES AND DEATH WISHES

VANESSA

Jarek pulls me closer, his hold on my wrists tight and unyielding. I can feel his alpha power radiating from him. His scent surrounds me—whiskey and cedar. It triggers my pheromones to respond, filling the room with honeysuckle and rain. The only indication that he notices is the slight change in his pupils. His expression remains stoic, his grip like a vice. He's obviously done this before and knows how to control his reaction to an omega. It's a handy skill for an alpha to have. And there is no doubt Jarek is all alpha. "No one is coming to save you, doll. You belong to me now."

I cringe at him calling me doll as if I was his plaything. "You're lying. My family will come." Even though I insist he's wrong, I know the truth. I've been here for nearly a week. My family found the body that was staged to look like me. Jarek had even pulled one of my teeth and planted it on the burned remains to make it more realistic. My family believes I'm dead.

The world believes I'm dead. Even Milo thinks I'm dead. Jarek is right. They'll never look for me now. None of them.

His chuckle sends chills down my spine. "You'll give me what I want. Just wait and see. We can do this the easy way or the hard way. Your choice, doll."

"I won't give you anything. I'll never help you."

I fight against him, trying to break free. The action is like trying to tear my arm off. There's no point. All I manage to do is rub myself all over his rapidly growing cock. Is the interrogation turning him on, or is it the proximity to me that caused it? I desperately want to know. I shouldn't care, just like I shouldn't want to turn him on, but the urge claws at me.

Hatred is carved into his features, along with something else. Desire, maybe? Could he be feeling this attraction too? "You will tell me where it is."

I spit in his face. "Never." The only reason I'm able to resist him is that I have no idea what he's talking about. He doesn't believe me, so he keeps pushing.

His free hand wipes my saliva away, then he leans closer until his face is a whisper away from mine. My heart races at his closeness. Sweat drips down my back. I want to hate him. I'm supposed to hate him, but I can feel my traitorous pussy dripping at his closeness. It practically begs for his touch. I know that he can smell my desire as well. I can feel his breath on my lips. If either of us move, our lips will touch. I hold my breath to stop myself from giving in to my basest desire. After a week of this, I'm beginning to wonder if what I'm feeling is biology or if I actually like him.

"You will, doll. And then you'll beg me to fuck you."

He shoves me away and leaves. I hate that I know he's right. I had nearly begged for it. If he'd stayed another five minutes, I probably would have. When I land on the floor, I drag myself up and straighten my clothes. *Come on, Ness, there's no reason to give up. You've gotten yourself out of worse scrapes than this. Focus.* I know I'm lying to myself, but I have to get some motivation somewhere.

The room is dark with no windows. It's basically a jail cell with an exposed toilet in the corner next to a small sink. The bulb above it is the only light in the room. Soft white rays glint off the mirror, catching my attention. I glance at my reflection and wince. Jarek's men had done a number on me. The cuts have scabbed over and the bruises are turning from dark purple to green. I look rough, and I don't like it. I'm not used to being man-handled by thugs. Father's men have always protected me from that.

I spend way too much time staring at my face in the mirror. My dark hair is tangled and the bruises on my face accentuate the blue in my eyes. I need a spa day to reverse all this damage. But that's not going to happen. I'm a prisoner here, and I'll never get to go to Bailey's Spa again. I might as well be dead. I fight against the tears that fill my eyes. I'll be damned if Jarek will see me cry.

The door opens, dragging me away from my reflection. For a moment, I think Jarek has come back. A shiver runs down my spine. Then I see it's him—the betrayer. Rafael has a plate balanced on top of a cup in one hand and holds the door with the other. "Are you hungry?" The tenderness in his voice almost gets a reaction from me. But if he really cared about me, he wouldn't have helped Jarek kidnap me and convince my parents that I'm dead.

"Go away," I growl. "I don't want you here."

"We both know that's not true," he laughs and closes the door. Then the asshole has the nerve to walk over to me and offer the plate and cup. I hate that he's right. I've missed him, and I'm starving.

"What is it?" I ask, not taking my eyes off his face. I won't be fooled by those chocolate eyes again. I can't let myself care about him. He'll only hurt me again.

"Pizza and soda," he says simply. It smells heavenly and I remember how long it's been since I've had anything to eat or drink.

"Water would have been better." I couldn't let him know that I'd noticed the smell of my favorite soda, or the pepperoni from my favorite pizza joint. After taking the plate and cup from him, I walk over to the mattress on the floor. I sit on my bed, placing the cup on the floor next to me and start to eat the pizza. I'm not really worried about being drugged again.

At this point, what more could they really do to me? I have no way to know they haven't already raped me when I was knocked out before. Except that something about Jarek tells me he wouldn't allow that. He makes it a point to tell me that I'll submit to him, even though he could easily overpower me and take what he wants. Force seems to be his style with some things, but not this. Maybe he does care about me. Either way, I can't trust any of them.

"I know, but this is what we had. Jarek wanted to let you starve after you spit in his face. You know you can't do that, tesoro. You need to tell him what he wants to know. That will make this so much easier for you." I winced at Raf's pet name for me. While he was with my family, he told me that I was his treasure, tesoro, in Italian. At one time, I thought it was sweet, but now it just rubs me the wrong way.

"We're not friends, Rafael. I don't know why you think you're helping me. I'm not going to give Jarek anything that he wants," I insist, with a mouth full of pizza. As much as I want to resist and refuse the food, I'm starving. He watches me as I eat, and for some reason it slows me down. I would have wolfed down the single slice and probably gotten sick after, but his attention on me makes me self-conscious about it.

JAREK

It takes every ounce of self-control not to pull Ness into my arms and kiss her. I have to get out of this room. Her scent calls to me. It makes me want to do things, bad things. I already do bad things, but she makes me want to burn the world down to protect her. I hate that she's so pissed at me. I want to tell her everything, but I can't. Not yet. I need her to hate me for just a little while longer. I can't protect her if I let her distract me.

She can't know that I've watched her for years. Not yet. She's not ready to know the truth. But soon, Ness will discover that things aren't always as they seem. Then I'll have my chance.

After I leave her, I head straight for the loading dock where I know the guys who brought her in will be. "Mario, Luigi, get over here. We need to have a chat." I watch as the two thugs put down their cards and slowly get to their feet. "Move it!" I yell, turning and walking into my office. I want privacy for what's about to happen. I should have handled this earlier, but after seeing her injuries darken and start to fade, I can't control my temper anymore.

"You wanted to see us, Boss?" Mario asks as Luigi closes the door. The betas line up in front of my desk and stand at attention.

"I just came from Ms. Dragonetti's cell. Would either of you like to explain to me how those bruises and cuts got on her face?" I took a deep breath to get my anger under control. I wanted to reach across the desk and rip their faces off for harming her. I had given specific instructions that she was to be taken, not roughed up.

They look at each other, trying to figure out what answer they can give that won't get them killed. The panic on their faces makes me laugh.

"Look, boys, I know that this racket is hard. Especially when you have to grab a broad quickly. I just want an answer. That's all. We're having a conversation," I assure them, refusing to look at the Colt .45 that lay on my desk. I don't need them freaking out just yet.

Neither of them speaks, and I start to shake with anger. I want to destroy them both. I train my expression so they can't see what I'm feeling. Then I walk over and sucker punch Luigi in the gut, doubling him over. I turn to Mario and clock him in the eye. "One of you is gonna talk, or you'll both be swimming," I threaten.

"It was him, Boss," Luigi offers. I can tell that it's only half the truth. I stare him down until he cracks. "I'm sorry, please don't kill me. I only hit her a couple of times. He started the whole thing." His insistence that his pal had been the one to hurt Ness first gets to me.

"Is this true?" I ask, turning to glare at Mario. He shakes his head, but refuses to say a word. "Are you too scared to speak? Good. You both should be terrified. If I send you to pick up something or someone, I expect the package to make it back to me unharmed. Do you understand?" I take a step around the desk and they both start to shake. Fear could be a great motivator in my line of work.

I pick up the gun and aim it at Mario. He winces, but doesn't argue or beg. He knows me well enough to realize that it won't help his situation at all anyway. I walk over to him and press the barrel to the center of his forehead. "If you ever disobey me like this again, you'll be at the bottom of the river. Got it?" He closes his eyes and nods feverishly. I smack him in the face with the butt of the gun, then I lower it and shoot him in the left foot.

He screams and drops to the floor, holding what's left of his foot and crying. I turn to his pal. "As for you, give me one good reason why I shouldn't put a bullet in your skull right now. You know we don't like snitches here."

To his credit, Luigi stares into my eyes while I threaten him. He doesn't flinch, even when the tears start falling and he pisses his pants. My alpha scent permeates the room, filling it with whiskey and cedar. I pull the Colt up and rest it against his right temple. "One good reason."

"I, I, I would never disrespect you like that. I don't deserve to live," he stammers. I agree with him, but I don't want to waste my time cleaning blood off everything in my office again.

"Good. I want you to remember your words. You don't deserve to live. But I don't feel like dealing with the mess right now, so I'm going to let you take your boy and get him patched up. Then the two of you are going to go wait in the parking garage across the street until I tell you to come back."

"But it's barely above freezing tonight and the temperature is supposed to drop," he whines. I crack him in the nose with the gun and laugh when he cries out.

"You should have thought of that before you pissed me off," I reply. "Now get out of here before I change my mind and splatter your brains all over the place."

"Crazy bastard," Mario mutters under his breath as he turns toward the door.

"What the fuck did you just say?" I grab him and spin him to face me.

"I didn't say anything, Boss," he whines. But their faces show me the lie. Besides, I know what I heard. I just want to see if he'll admit it.

My fists are on him before he can block or defend himself. I slam them into his face over and over, feeling the warm trickle of his blood coat my hands and drip to the floor. I'm vaguely aware of Luigi stepping back and trying to hide behind a file cabinet. This isn't about him, though. It really isn't even about me. It's about her, but I can't tell them that.

"I won't be disrespected. Do you understand me?" I growl as my fists and feet beat Mario into submission. He's curled in a ball on the floor, barely moving. I kick him in the spine, relishing the satisfying crack that comes with the contact of my boot.

I stomp on his injured foot, causing his hands to leave his face. Damn, I thought I had severed his spine. I'll have to try harder. My boot catches one of his hands and crunches it against the thin carpet. My lips curl into a smile when I feel the bones crunch. I want him to hurt. No one disrespects me. And no one touches what's mine. He should have known better.

He can't do anything but grunt and whimper. I can smell my anger fill the room with whiskey and cedar, but it doesn't smell the way it did with Ness. This is colder, darker, and smells burnt. I'm feeling almost feral as I let the fury take me. I let my hands and feet do as they wish, continuing to beat Mario until there's no way he could possibly survive. His head is twisted at an unnatural angle, and back is bent into almost a ninety-degree angle. His eyes are swollen shut. His face is a black and blue mess. The sudden silence in the room hits me, pulling me from my fury-filled haze.

That's when I turn to Luigi. "Get him the fuck out of here. Or you'll join him. Do what I told you to, and don't disrespect me again." He nods, keeping his eyes on the floor.

Luigi grabs Mario and drags him out of my office. He runs away like a terrified child, struggling to pull his dead friend behind him. I don't care if he freezes to death out there. I just want him out of my face. I walk behind my desk and sit down, picking up the phone to have someone clean that asshole's blood off the floor.

I have to get a handle on what I'm feeling for Ness, or I'll take out my entire crew. Then who will protect her?

RAFAEL

I hate how angry Ness is with me. Yes, I lied. Yes, I am part of the family that opposes hers and is currently trying to take her father out. I helped to kidnap her and lock her up here. But come on, there has to be a way to make her forgive me. It's not like she knows the whole story. There's more to this situation than meets the eye. She deserves the truth; I just can't be the one to tell her.

"Look, Ness, I know you're mad. I get it. But can't we talk about it?" I ask, strolling across the room to sit next to her on the futon mattress. I hate that we can't give her a better place to sleep. The idea of her lying on this thin excuse of a mattress to sleep on the cold concrete hurts me in a way I hadn't expected.

"No, Raf, we can't talk about it. You lied to me and now I can't trust you. You're working for my family's enemy. Please take me home," she counters. I almost give in, but I can't. It's not safe for her there, even if she doesn't know it yet. We saved her life by faking her death.

"I can't do that. Not until you tell Jarek what he wants to know," I insist. The proximity to her starts to set me off. I can smell her fragrance, honeysuckle and rain. I know that no matter how much she fights it, she's attracted to Jarek. And to me, or so I thought. My scent wafts over me; toasted marshmallow fills the air. All I want is to pull her into my arms and kiss her until she forgives me. If only she would give in, we could be a pack—we could be happy. But she's so stubborn.

"I already told you, just like I told him. I'm not giving anything up. So, if you're actually gonna kill me, you might as well get it over with," she growls. Where did she get the idea that we'd kill her? Jarek and I are half in love with her already, and we've only held her captive for a week. Granted, I had infiltrated her family for months and gotten close to her before the job, but still.

I stand and walk to the door, not wanting her to see how badly her words hurt me. "We're not the bad guys, Ness. You'll see in time." I glance over my shoulder to see her staring after me. I want to turn around and drag her off that mattress, or better yet, drop myself onto her and kiss her into submission. This isn't the time for it, though. She will have to realize that we've done this for her, not just against her father.

I stroll into Jarek's office, my jaw clenched like my fists. "She's not budging. What the fuck happened here?" I gesture to the dark red stain on his carpet. "Did you kill someone again?"

He laughs and gestures for me to pull up a chair. "Mario crossed a line. Those assholes put their hands on her and I will not stand for that. They have to learn."

"I've been wondering who'd done it. I would have hunted them down myself if you hadn't figured it out first," I said as I dropped into the chair. He didn't have to tell me which assholes he was talking about, as the twins who'd been nicknamed for the video game characters were the only ones not outside his door. Mario and Luigi were two of the dumbest guys we had working for us.

"I know she's not happy about this, but if we could get her to listen, she'd understand. It'll take time, that's all. Now we have to keep the FBI off our tail until we get to the safehouse." Jarek believes that the FBI is always following us. Normally, I'd call him paranoid, but this time he may be right.

"I thought I saw Milo yesterday when I went to grab food," I offer. Jarek nods. Milo is the agent who's been chasing us for years. So far, we've avoided him, but he keeps getting closer. We've been lucky. He's also the guy who was dating Ness until we took her. I wonder if Jarek knows that little tidbit. I refuse to be the one to tell him, though. I'll play dumb when it comes out.

"He's not really after us, you know. He just wants to use us to get to Dragonetti. I oughta just tell him what he needs to take the bastard down," Jarek threatens. I know he's not actually going to snitch, but the idea is amusing. I also suspect that Milo is working for Ness' dad, but I'm not sharing that either. I can't let Jarek have all the power. My secrets will come out when it's time. Then I'll be the top alpha here, and everyone will bow to me instead of Jarek. My cousin needs to learn some respect, as much as he insists everyone show it for him.

MILO

"Look, Dave, I've been on this op for years. You can't replace me. I started it. I'm close to a break," I insist, glaring at my replacement.

"Milo, I'm just telling you what Sarge told me. The FBI is being taken off the op. We're taking over. You'll have to talk to him. I've told you everything I know," he says while taking a step back from the desk I've been occupying at the 9th Precinct.

"I'm going to talk to him, then. I've worked too hard on this case to be pulled from it now," I growl as I stalk to the sergeant's office. I knock and wait for Sarge to answer. He takes his time to come to the door. I'm certain it's because he knows it's me. Dave probably messaged him to let him know I'm pissed.

The moment the door opens, I lay into him. "I don't know what you think you're doing, but you can't just take the FBI off a case. You don't have that kind of jurisdiction."

A figure steps forward, motioning for me to enter the office. Shit. I didn't realize my boss was here. "Executive Assistant Director Smith, I didn't expect to see you here," I stammer.

"I'm aware of that, Spezia. I don't want to be here any more than you want me here. But there have been complaints. You're too close to this one. We're removing you from the case." Her words are sharp, cutting through me.

"Ma'am, please. You can't do this," I insist. I don't want to resort to begging, but I will. I have to finish this. For my family. For my brother.

She shakes her head. "It's already been decided. Take a few days off to clear your head, then report back to me in DC." She shakes Sarge's hand and walks away before I can try to argue any further.

At this point, there's nothing else I can do but to gather my things and leave. I pack my notes slowly under Dave's watchful eye. He's there to make sure I don't take anything I'm not supposed to have. Lucky for me, he doesn't know about the copies I have at the hotel.

I leave the station and head back to the hotel. I should stop for dinner, but I'm too distracted. I know I'm getting close to breaking this one. How can I do that if I'm off the case and back in DC? I need to think. There has to be a way that I can keep working this instead of going home.

I start by calling Ma. I don't want her to hear about this from someone else. "Hey, Ma. How's it goin?"

"You know I worry about you. All that crime. Why you gotta be in the middle of it?" Ma always starts with that. Every phone call is the same. She wants me out of the FBI and back home in Jersey with her.

"I know you worry. That's why I'm calling. I'm fine, Ma. Just checkin in. I'll have this wrapped up soon and be up to visit," I lie. I can't tell her they've pulled me from the case. She needs justice for Jeremy as bad as I do.

"Marcy says that they're not gonna find proof and you're gonna have to come home soon. Is that true?" She sounds excited at the prospect of me coming home, even if that means Jeremy's killer gets to go free. I know that's not how she means it, though. I've been there on the nights she cries herself to sleep and asks her god why he let her baby die.

"No, Ma. Marcy doesn't know what she's talking about. I'm gonna find proof. I get closer every day. Look, I gotta go. The delivery guy is here with my dinner. I'll call soon. Love you." I hang up the phone before she argues with me. I hate calling, but I have to make sure she doesn't find out I've been pulled from the case.

I turn on the TV and flop onto the couch. I should think about dinner, but I'm not hungry. I'm irritated. And food won't fix that. I grab the paper box with my file copies and spread the sheets across my coffee table. For once, I'm glad I'm springing for a suite. It's expensive, but it allows me to do my work in peace.

I sift through the pages again, looking for anything I missed the first time. There has to be a connection. Something in my gut screams that the charcoal body the unies found wasn't actually the Dragonetti girl. If I'm right, she's out there somewhere. Could D'Angelo and his guys have taken her? Was there actually a mole in the department? That would explain why I got pulled from the case.

I think I'm getting closer to a new lead every day. If I'm right, and there's a mole, then that's why I got the boot tonight. I grab the bottle of whiskey that sits next to the couch. It's not dinner, but it's what I want right now. Maybe if I let things get a little fuzzy, everything will make sense.

I tip the bottle up, downing a third of it, then sit and stare at her picture. I feel like she's the missing piece of everything. If I find her, I'll get what I need. I know that I should leave it alone for tonight, but I can't. I pull the burner phone out of my pocket and dial.

"Kid, I told you not to call me here for a while," he answers.

"I know, but I need to talk to you. It wasn't her. She's still out there. And they took me off the case," I start before he cuts me off.

"I understand that you loved her. But she's dead. The coroner says it's her. That means it's her. Just because the two of you had a thing—"

I cut him off before he can bury his point any further. "Not loved, love. I love her, sir. And I will find her. I'll prove to you that she's still alive. I just need to disappear for a little while. Please. I need your help, Mr. Dragonetti."

The voice on the other end sighs and I know I've got him. "Fine, kid. But this is the last time. I'll send a package in the morning. Destroy this phone. I'll have a new one for you in the package. You're gonna be disappointed, son, and I'm sorry for that. She's gone and nothing will bring her back." The head of the Dragonetti family hangs up before I have a chance to argue with him. The sorrow in his voice is laced with something else. Satisfaction? But why would he be glad she's gone? He has nothing to gain from her death. Besides, she's not dead. I know it.

I refuse to admit that he might be right. Especially when he's wrong about so many other things. Ness and I are in love. We've been planning to run away together. Someone took her and I will find out who. I will get her back. It's been nearly impossible to keep my emotions in check with this case. It's probably better that I'm off it now. I can do things my way, and finally get results.

The burner phone crunches between my fingers as I curl them into a fist. Well, that's done. Hopefully, Dragonetti will deliver with the package and I can focus on finding Ness. She's all that matters.

CHAPTER TWO

GIVE IN OR FIGHT?

VANESSA

I'm losing track of how many days I've been locked away. The sun rose and set without my knowledge, since I'm in a room with no windows. All I know for sure is that the two guys who kidnapped me haven't been back in a few days. Raf is the one bringing me meals, and Jarek is the one trying to intimidate me into telling him my father's secrets. I don't mind the change. Those two guys who brought me here are complete dicks. The kind who has no problem hitting a woman. I would know.

What Jarek doesn't realize is that I can't tell him what I don't know. Daddy doesn't trust me, so I'm not allowed to know anything about his business. I'm just a stupid girl, and an omega to boot. That makes me weak and worthless, until he makes a deal to breed me. Maybe being locked up here isn't so bad after all. I don't have to play the ditzy socialite or date any of the losers Daddy keeps sending my way. Maybe if I stop fighting against Jarek, I can get a better room.

But how do I know I can trust him? I don't. I need a plan. I can't just stay here, waiting for someone to save me. Everyone I know believes I'm dead. How can I possibly survive this? I know my heat is coming. Once it gets here, I'll be completely at Jarek's mercy. I barely make it through his questioning now without begging him to fuck me. I can't let myself become bonded with him or his pack. I have to fight and find a way out of here. Then I can prove to Daddy that I'm good enough to be his heir; that he doesn't need a son to follow in his footsteps.

My cell door opens and I know it's Jarek. His smooth whiskey and cedar scent fills my room. My breath hitches as the door clicks. We're locked in here until he's done with me. That thought brings forward the fantasies I've been indulging in at night. I know the moment he scents me, because Jarek tenses and his pupils go wide. The honeysuckle and rain mixes with the whiskey and cedar. I have to admit, it's a mouthwatering combination.

I let myself have a moment with my eyes closed to think about it. His voice pulls me back to the present. "Are you okay, doll? You're not usually this quiet when I come to see you." Is Jarek actually worried about me? I shake the thought away. It's not possible. He can't care about me. His family is my family's enemy. People don't just go against that. This isn't Romeo and Juliet; this is real life.

"I guess I'm just realizing that there's no way for me to get out of here," I respond without looking at him. I know if I let my eyes meet his, he'll know exactly what I was thinking. I take a deep breath and step away from him.

From behind me, I hear the faint clink of the tray he must have brought being placed on the table he'd brought me a day or so ago. Everything is starting to run together, so I'm not even sure how long I've been here anymore. I feel as if I haven't slept in days, lying awake thinking about my family and my desires. Maybe I should just give in and make a move on Jarek. My heat will be here soon, and I will need an alpha to get me through it.

I rub my hands over my face and turn around, only to bump into Jarek, who had apparently been standing as close to me as possible without touching. "I wish you could see that we're not the enemy. I know you were raised to think we are, but it's not true. Raf and I have your best interests in mind, I promise." The admission catches me off guard. My breath hitches and I feel my eyes fill with tears. I force myself to tilt my head so I can look in his eyes.

Jarek's hand cups my cheek and he wipes away my tears with his thumb. "If you're so interested in what's best for me, why did you kidnap me and fake my death?" I hate how vulnerable the question makes me feel, but I have to ask.

"Because we need to protect you," he whispers, staring at my lips.

"From what? I've never been in danger before. My father's guys have always kept me safe," I argue, flicking my tongue along my lips slowly, enjoying the fact that he's so close.

"You don't understand." Jarek pushes me away and turns his back on me. I take a deep breath to steady myself. I can't believe how badly I want him. This urge to throw myself into his arms is nearly overwhelming. At the same time, his refusal to tell me what's actually going on is driving me crazy. I've spent as much time trying to figure it out as I have fantasizing.

"Then tell me," I insist, anger growing in me with every moment.

I give in to it and shove him. The only reason he moves is that he doesn't see it coming. Rage fills his eyes when he turns to face me. "Doll, watch it. You're walking a thin line here."

"I'm not scared of you. What are you going to do to me anyway?" I glare at him, refusing to show any fear. Jarek stalks back to me, forcing me to step back without even touching me. I stop when my back hits the wall. I can't break eye contact with him or he'll know that I'm scared as well as turned on.

Jarek smirks and wraps his hand around my throat, holding me against the wall. I gasp and lick my lips. Is this the moment he gives in and takes what he wants? Part of me desperately hopes so. He leans in, stopping when his lips are almost touching mine. "I'm going to make you beg for it."

I wince at the whimper that comes from me. Jarek laughs. He shifts so his lips are against my ear. "You want me, don't you, doll? Just say the word and I'll take good care of you." I shiver in response, not trusting myself to speak.

"I'm not going to hurt you. And I won't force myself on you, either. I'm not even going to kiss you until you ask me to," he whispers before releasing my throat and stepping back. I struggle to remain standing. My legs want to buckle beneath me, and I hate that he sees the effect he has on me. I hate it more that I miss his hand around my throat.

"Then you'll be waiting for a long time, Jarek. I'll never beg you to touch me. And I'll never ask you to kiss me. If you want it, you'll have to take it from me. Because I'll never be willing," I lie, hoping he can't see through my false bravado. Part of me hopes that he will take what he wants, because that would be really hot.

His laughter tells me that I'm not as convincing as I'd hoped. "We'll see how long you hold out when your heat hits. It shouldn't be too long now, should it?"

How does he know my heat is coming soon? The only people who knew that were me and my family. Raf. That bastard. He must have spied on my doctor visits too. "I won't give in to you. I'll let someone else take care of me when my heat comes on."

Jarek takes a step closer and lifts my chin with his finger. He gently presses his lips to mine. "No one else would dare touch what's mine."

I swat his hand away and sidestep to put space between us. I know he's right. None of his guys will defy him if they know he's already staked a claim on me. Fuck. "I'm not yours." I know there is no way he'll believe me, since my own body keeps giving away my true feelings. But I insist on doing the dance anyway. I won't give in to him until I absolutely have to.

If I could withstand my heat alone, that would make me the strongest omega that has ever existed.

I know it won't happen, but it's my life goal at the moment. "We'll see, doll." The door clicks closed behind him, leaving me alone with my tears. I consider everything Jarek said, and a few things stick in my memory.

To protect you. What do I need protection from? My father's thugs are the ones who protect me. Although, they didn't do a very good job if I'm being honest right now. Jarek's henchmen had no trouble snatching me right under my protectors' noses. I wonder how my father took the news. Then I remember that as far as he knows, I'm dead. I need to accept the fact that I'm not going home. One way or another, I'm stuck here.

I can either give in to Jarek's demands and become his woman, helping him take down my father, or I can let him kill me. I'm not sure which sounds worse right now. Would he kill me though? "I should hate him. I need to hate him. Damn it, why can't I hate him?" I mumble to myself as I pace the floor.

I can feel the changes happening in my body as it prepares to go into heat. I know that I won't survive without an alpha to knot with me. From my studies, I know that I'll be better off with more than one. It seems like Jarek is game to help me out, as long as I cooperate with his request to get dirt on my family. But who else would I be able to turn to?

Raf is a definite no, and Milo doesn't even know I'm alive. So that leaves Jarek. Just Jarek. The one man in the entire world who should want to see me dead. Yet, for some reason, he's protecting me. It doesn't make sense. He could have killed me when they staged the body. Instead, he kept me from seeing anything that would have stayed with me and made sleeping harder. All I know about the whole thing is what Raf tells me when he comes to visit.

Maybe I need to push Raf a little and see if he'll talk. Manipulation can work both ways, right? Maybe I can find out exactly what Jarek thinks I know, then decide if I want to tell him. It doesn't take long to find out, since Raf shows up a little while after Jarek walks away. I wonder if they each know that the other is trying to persuade me. Is it all a plan that they've concocted together? Or do they both want me but not know that the other is interested?

Raf opens the door and walks in carrying a to go bag. We must be near some fast food places, because he brings in a different type every day. I haven't had the same thing since they've been holding me. Today's meal is a salad and a milkshake. "Here you go, tesoro. I hope you enjoy it."

I greedily tear into the salad, secretly loving that he remembers how much I love to mix ranch and Catalina dressings. I glance over at the tray Jarek left behind, relieved to see that it held snacks I can eat later. "What do you want?" I ask between bites. I have to start a conversation somehow, and this seems to work the best.

"I've told you before, I want to prove that I'm on your side," he insists. Good, that's exactly the response I was hoping for.

"Okay. Then answer some questions for me. Unless you want to continue our usual conversation where I tell you to leave and you insist that you love me?" I stare at him as I speak, wondering what he's about to say.

Raf takes a minute and rubs his hands over his face. "You're going to get me killed, you know that, right?" He pauses, then drops onto the mattress next to me. "What do you want to know?"

"What exactly does Jarek think I know? He keeps asking me about where something is, but I have no idea what he's looking for." I hate showing him my hand like this, but it's the only way.

He stares at me. "What's in it for me if I tell you?"

"What do you want?" I'm scared of where this might go, but at the same time, I want answers. I need to know what I'm dealing with.

"A kiss," he says simply.

"No," I shake my head violently. I can't do it. I won't.

"Then I guess you'll just have to figure it out yourself," he taunts.

Damn you, Raf. I set the salad down and grab his shirt, pulling him close. My lips barely touch his, and he sighs. "Tell me first." I'll get the info out of him one way or another.

RAFAEL

I suspect that Ness is playing me, but I really want that kiss. That little tease she offered was just too much to resist. Besides, what can it hurt to tell her what Jarek is looking for? If she does know, she'll be more likely to tell him, or she'll slip up and tell me. If she doesn't, then I can let him know and we'll find it another way. But will she help him?

I pull her against me, soaking in her sweet honeysuckle and rain scent. She's still gripping my shirt, and I know that she wants to kiss me. I'm certain that she wants more than that, but I won't push her. Not yet. Her heat will come soon enough, then I'll make my move, and she'll be mine.

My cock jumps at her closeness, and I want to climb on top of her and ravish that delicious pussy. For a moment, I regret lying to her when I was undercover for Jarek, but I don't regret getting close to her. That was what allowed us to learn about her father's plot, and save her life.

"Ness, you know I can't tell you. Jarek will kill me," I lie, even though I know I'll tell her anyway. But maybe I'll play with her a bit before I let her win.

"Raf, you're a dick. You know that, right," she sighs against my lips. "I hate you." Then Ness shifts her weight and kisses me hard. Her lips feel like velvet. I lose myself in the sensation. I've missed this so much since she's been pissed at me.

On a groan, I deepen the kiss and push her back on to the bed. I expect her to fight me, but she doesn't. Instead, she embraces me tighter, as if she can't stand to be away from me anymore. Our tongues dance against each other and the room fills with the earthy scent of rain-soaked honeysuckle and pine. Her lust feeds my own until we're a tangled mess of want and need.

Part of me wants to fuck her so badly that my dick aches. But I won't push her for it. She doesn't believe me, but I love her and want what's best for her. That's why I convinced Jarek that kidnapping her and faking her death was a good idea. I even managed to make him think he'd come up with it.

I scrape my teeth along her neck and squeeze her full breasts through her shirt. Ness arches her back and whispers, "Oh, Raf." That's all the encouragement I need to slip my hand under her shirt. I fumble for a minute with the front clasp of her bra, but then I manage to free her from the cloth prison. I push the shirt up and stare at her for a moment. Perfection.

Mine. I lean down and take her taut nipple into my mouth, flicking it with my tongue.

She starts to purr and I moan. "Ugh, Ness, you're killing me." She fists her hands in my hair and pulls me back up to meet her mouth for another hungry kiss.

"Then you should do something about it, Raf," she orders. From her scent, I know she's already soaked in her slick. I growl and nip her neck, then lean back so I can rip her leggings off. "What the fuck, Raf?! I don't have anything else to wear, you jerk!"

"I'll bring you something after. Don't worry about it. Whatever you want, it's yours." I tower over her for a moment, waiting for her to meet my eyes. I can still see the desire in hers, even with the annoyance. She reaches for me and I kiss her again, desperate for her to accept me instead of pushing me away. I help her remove the ripped fabric that traps her legs, and she wraps them around me. There was so much more I had planned for her, but desire takes over and I rub my cock against her slick opening. Ness whimpers and I sheath myself in her. She lifts her hips to meet me, and we set a rhythm. I can't let myself come before she does, so I hold back. I think about baseball and hockey. When that isn't working, I think about how badly I hurt Ness by lying all that time and how I have to find a way to make it up to her. Controlling my thrusts, I slide in and out of her tight pussy until I finally slip a hand between us and stroke her clit. That sends her over the edge and she cries out my name as she comes. Her breathy tone sets off my own orgasm and my knot swells to hold us together while my seed spills inside of her.

I gently rock back and forth on top of her, careful not to put my full weight on her. "Oh, Ness," I whisper in her ear. "I love you." I realize the mistake the second the words leave my mouth.

"What? No. You can't. You don't," she stammers. I'd held off too long in telling her, and now she won't believe me, no matter how many times I tell her. One more thing added to the list of mistakes to make up for.

"I do, though. Don't worry, tesoro, you don't have to say it back. Just know that it's true. I want you to be mine forever." I expect her to balk at my declaration, but tears fill her eyes instead. I'm not sure what I did wrong to make her cry. "I'm sorry, Ness. Please forgive me."

She shakes her head, then rocks her hips and I realize that I've stopped moving. "Don't give up on me now, Raf," she orders, changing the subject. I guess I'll have to accept just the sex for now. It's not enough, but I think I have a chance now.

JAREK

I'm not sure what pulls me back toward Ness' cell, but I can't stop myself from making my way across the building to see her. I hate keeping her locked up, but I know that she's not going to understand that it's more for her safety than to make sure she doesn't run away. If only she could see the truth.

I stop outside her room. Should I knock, or just enter? I don't want her to think I've gone soft, so I throw the door open and freeze. What the fuck is Raf doing in here? Is he fucking Ness? I growl possessively and he jumps away from her. "What are you doing?" I don't point the question at either of them. I feel myself start to shake with rage. I know that I can't let myself lose control.

"Oh, uh, Jarek, I didn't know you were stopping by. I was just dropping off some food for Ness," Raf fumbles over his hasty explanation.

"I can see that. I hope she got her fill." Sarcasm rolls off me in waves. My whiskey and cedar scent turns burnt and wafts into the room. Raf's eyes go wide in anticipation. He knows that I want Ness for myself. I watch as she tries to cover herself.

I'm disgusted and annoyed. Who am I kidding? I'm pissed—at Raf, at Ness—mostly at myself. If I had handled things differently, it might have been him walking in on me. Well, if I've ruined my chances already, there was no point in playing nice.

"Raf, you're needed downtown. My dad wants a word. I suggest you get moving so he's not waiting any longer than necessary." I'm not exactly lying, but I could send anyone to meet with the head of our clan. It doesn't have to be my second in command. I just want Ness to myself for a while. I want to make sure that he didn't force himself on her. That would be unacceptable.

I'm not the most ethical man, but rape is where I draw the line. I will not condone any of my guys forcing themselves on any woman. And I know that because of my feelings for Ness, if he did, I'll kill him. It doesn't matter that he's my cousin, and my father will be pissed over the loss of his sister's kid. I love Raf like a brother, but I will not put up with anyone stepping across that line. I just need a moment with Ness to be sure. Because Raf wouldn't do that, right?

"I'm on it." Raf pauses at the door and looks at Ness, who is staring daggers at him. "Hey, Jarek," he starts. I look at him expectantly. "Would you get Ness another pair of pants? If I gotta meet Uncle Joe, I won't have time." He glances at her apologetically for a second, and she growls. I stifle a laugh.

"I'll take care of it," I agree, nodding toward the door to get him out of the room. As soon as I hear the click of the lock, I turn to my guest.

"Please just get me some clothes. I don't want to talk about it," she sighs and rolls over, pulling the blanket up further to cover herself.

"Ness, I need to know," I start to say, but she turns over and glares at me.

"You need to know what, Jarek? That's how all this started anyway. Because you need to know something that no one will tell me. I ended up fucking Raf because I was trying to get him to tell me what it is you've been asking me for. If you would just tell me, I could answer your questions," she blurts in a rush of words. Her cheeks flush and she looks away, as if she expects me to yell and throw things. In the past, I would have.

"I'll be right back," I mutter, turning toward the door. If we're going to have this conversation, I prefer her to be dressed. "Take a shower while I'm gone." I slam the door and storm down the hall. In the supply closet, I grab the bag of ladies' clothes Raf and I bought for Ness, then lean against the door while I compose myself. I can't let her see how much she gets under my skin. I need to focus or I'm going to fuck this whole thing up.

A couple of calming breaths later, I return to her room with the bag. For a moment, I worry that she ignored my request that she shower. I don't think I can handle smelling her pheromones mixed with Raf's without losing it to my possessive side. Honeysuckle and fresh rain hit my nose the moment I walk through the door. Before I can stop myself, I take in a deep breath, losing myself to the fragrance.

"Did you bring me something to wear?" Ness stands across the room from me, wrapped in a towel that barely covers her. I groan internally. What I wouldn't give for her to drop that towel.

I hold out the bag without speaking. She stomps over and grabs it, but I don't let go right away. I pull her closer to me. "I need you to tell me. I can't assume." I'm barely containing my rage at the thought that my cousin might have done something out of line. "Did he force you?"

She laughs. Ness actually laughs in my face. "Was that what you were trying to ask me before?" I nod, unable to respond with words. "So, now you're worried about my virtue? Not that it's your business, but no, Raf did not force me to do anything. I'm not thrilled about what happened, but it was good, and exactly what I needed."

I stare at her. I know she's telling the truth and it relaxes me a little. I let go of the bag and turn my back so she can get dressed. "I see. Good. I don't like when men take what they want from women without permission." I say the words more harshly than I intend to, and she gasps. Everything in me screams to pull her into my arms and kiss her breathless. I can't do that, though. Ness hates me, as she should. Because of that, I can't tell her that I've been in love with her for years, or that I would happily share her with my cousin if that was what would make her happy.

VANESSA

Jarek's attitude about me fucking Raf shocks me. He seems genuinely concerned about his henchman getting consent. I know now that they're cousins, which may complicate things more. I need to get a handle on my desires. I can't keep giving in to what these men want, even if I've only done so with Jarek in my dreams. And what dreams they are! If only I could get him and Raf to cooperate, I'd be on cloud nine.

No, Vanessa, you need to focus. Stop thinking about their scents and how they smell so yummy you want their cocks in your mouth. Easier said than done. I take a steadying breath and slip into a sweater and a pair of leggings from the bag.

While I'm getting dressed, he growls about men taking what they want from women. I can't help but gasp at his statement. It seems so out of line with what I know about him. Jarek D'Angelo is a force to be reckoned with. He's not a sweet, caring alpha who protects omegas. He takes what he wants and the world be damned. Or so I thought. Perhaps I shouldn't have judged him so harshly without giving him a chance.

"Why is it your business who I sleep with anyway?" I know I'm baiting him, but I want to see if he'll admit that he's attracted to me. This can't be one-sided, can it?

"It's not my business who you sleep with. But Raf works for me, and he's my cousin. So that makes it my business to find out if he's crossing that line." I can't help deflating a little at his words. I'm staring at his back, watching the muscles in his shoulders tense and relax. I don't want to tell him that I'm already dressed. I was hoping for a different answer, but clearly, Jarek doesn't think about me that way.

"Well, I'm dressed. What do you want? To ask more questions that don't make sense, I'm sure." I roll my eyes when he turns around. I swear he's checking me out, even though he pretends not to. Am I ever going to figure this man out?

"I have questions, yes. Stop pretending like you don't know the answers, and this will go a lot easier for you. If you tell me what I want to know, maybe we can find you a more comfortable room," he offers.

"Wait. Are you serious? If I tell you what you want to know, I can have a more comfortable room? That seems kind of strange," I reply. If Raf had just told me what I wanted to know, I might have answers.

Jarek steps closer, towering over me. "I don't lie. I can make your stay with us quite pleasant, doll. You just have to play nice."

A shiver runs over me at his words and the possible double meaning behind them. Why do I want him to be hitting on me right now? *Ugh, Ness, get it under control.* "What do you want to know?"

"Where is it? Don't pretend like you don't know. Just tell me, and we can make this situation better for you."

I throw my arms in the air. "Where is *what?* I don't know what you're talking about, Jarek. How am I supposed to tell you *where* something is, when I don't know *what* that something is?" I'm exasperated and annoyed. I know that he thinks I'm more involved with my father's seedier practices, and that thought amuses me. I laugh and Jarek steps closer, caging me against the wall.

"What are you laughing about?" he growls, and I shudder. At this point, I know my panties are wet and I just want to reach up and kiss him. But I can't do that. Jarek is my enemy, not my lover. Fucking Raf was a mistake and I can't afford to repeat it.

"The fact that you think I know anything about my father's business dealings. He has kept me away from all of that. I'm not allowed to know where things are or how things are done." Jarek's face softens a little at my admission. Does he feel sorry for me?

"So, you don't know where it is? Or are you lying to me to protect that bastard?" Jarek leans closer and I can feel his hot breath on my neck and ear. My hand comes up involuntarily and rests on his chest, over his racing heart. I can't tell if it's pounding so hard because he's this close to me, or if he's getting angry because I won't tell him something I don't know.

"Jarek, listen to me. I don't know what you're looking for. Tell me what it is, and if I know where it is, I'll tell you. I would never lie to protect my bastard father. He has henchmen to do that." I tilt my head to look in his eyes, and for a moment, I think he's going to kiss me. He turns his head a little, and his lips almost brush mine.

"I can't tell you what we're looking for. If you find a way out of here, you'll tell your father and he'll hide it somewhere else. But if you don't know anything, I'm not sure how long I'll be able to protect you."

Chapter Three

What Aren't You Telling Me?

JAREK

Ness is practically begging me to tell her what we're looking for. I wish I could. I'm dying to trust her, but I can't be sure what side she's on yet. My veiled threat is just an effort to get her to talk. She can't know that I would give my life for her. Not yet.

She laughs. "This is protecting me? I'd hate to see how you treat prisoners, then. I'm not a guest here, Jarek, and we both know it."

"But you are," I respond. Ness makes a face and I step away from her. "You're not a prisoner here. We're just trying to protect you." I know I shouldn't tell her, but I can't help myself.

"What are you protecting me from? Showering in a real bathroom? Sleeping in a comfortable bed? Freedom?" Her sarcastic questions shoot at me and I wince. I never wanted her to feel like she was a prisoner, although I understand why she does.

"Ness, please. I can see why you think you're a prisoner, but you aren't. We can't have you running home to your dad. He has to think you're dead. It's the only way you'll be safe." *Just stop, Jarek, you can't tell her. She's not ready. Not yet.*

"You're making it sound like my father is out to get me," she says, making a face. Her eyes meet mine and her smirk falls. "Are you serious? You think my father is trying to kill me. Why? I'm not even in any of his business. I'm not allowed to be." She's inching toward panic, and I can't let that happen. I have to talk her down.

"Ness, take a breath," I step closer again and pull her into my arms. In her anxious state, my alpha pheromones calm her. I want to do more than that, but I know I can't. I preach consent to my guys, and I will not do anything that crosses that line. She starts to hyperventilate, and I rub small circles on her back to regulate her breathing.

Once she seems calmer, I tilt her chin up so her eyes meet mine again. "You aren't a prisoner here. I just need to know that you won't try to run. It's not safe for you out there. If you believe nothing else that I tell you, please believe this. There's a contract out for your life. Since everyone thinks you're dead, it's been voided. But how long do you think it will take to be reinstated if someone finds you alive?" I need her to understand. I want her to choose me—to choose us, if she insists on having Raf too.

Ness looks at me, staring into my eyes as if she can force the truth out of me. Who knows, maybe she can? After a moment, she opens her mouth to speak, but no words come out. Tears slip from her eyes and roll down her cheeks. I can't handle her crying. I'll have to kill someone. Unfortunately, I can't get to the guy who caused all of this. But I will.

Against my better judgment, I lean down and press my lips to hers gently. That whisper of skin against skin sends a jolt through me and solidifies what I already knew. I will do anything for this woman. It doesn't matter to me that she's younger than me. I don't care that she's my enemy's daughter. I pull away before I can push things too far. I will not take advantage of her like this. "I'm sorry. I shouldn't have done that."

I turn to leave, but she grabs my arm before I can reach the door. "It's okay. I feel trapped here. You're right, though. You and Raf haven't done anything to hurt me. And I haven't seen the two guys who roughed me up in a while." I look away, unable to meet her eyes. "You took care of them, didn't you?" she asks quietly.

I know she's going to think I'm a monster, but I can't lie to her. I nod, turning to look at her. There's no fear in her eyes. No hate. No judgment. It's as if she understands that I'm trying to protect her. "They knew better, and did what they wanted. It won't happen again."

"So, where do we go from here? Right now, I'm locked in a room alone all day. I see you or Raf, but I don't get to leave this room. It doesn't exactly scream welcomed guest." The look on her face melts me. She's scolding me for locking her up while telling me she's lonely.

I deserve to feel the guilt that starts to eat at me. There was no way she would have listened when we brought her here. She was too angry. But now, I see other emotions in her eyes. The anger is still there, simmering just below the surface. "Where we go from here depends on you. No matter which room you're in, it'll have to be locked." She starts to protest, but I hold up a hand. "I have to know that you're safe. None of my guys will have access to you. Ever. So, the doors stay locked. But if you're willing to cooperate, we can move you to a different room where you'll be more comfortable."

"You talk like this is a hotel and you have several rooms to choose from." She laughs, and it's the sweetest sound I've ever heard. If I wasn't already in love with her, that sound would have pushed me over the edge.

"It's not a hotel, but it's not a prison, either. Come on, I'll show you. But only if you promise not to try an escape." I hold out my hand and wait while she thinks over my proposal. Will she decide that she can trust me?

Her hand slides hesitantly into mine. "I give you my word, I will not try to escape today. I can't promise any further than that. But for now, I feel safe, and that's enough."

VANESSA

The moment I slide my hand into Jarek's, I know my heart is a goner. I'm falling hard for him. I love the overprotective alpha type, and he fits the bill perfectly. It doesn't matter to me that he's closer to my father's age than mine. His salt and pepper hair is sexy, especially since I can tell it's been a while since he's had a haircut. Jarek's hair hangs almost to his shoulders, curling just a little at the ends. I want to reach out and fist my hand in it while I pull him down for another kiss. But I don't. Instead, I simply hold his hand and let him escort me out of my prison cell.

"This is the apartment side of the warehouse. The whole thing has been redone on the interior to fit our needs. From the outside, it still looks like an abandoned warehouse. On the inside, state of the art apartments for me and my crew.

Would you like to see one?" Jarek's excitement about housing is adorable, and almost contagious.

"I'd love to. Thank you," I force myself to remain calm and polite. Inside, I'm casing the place, looking for any and all exits. I told him I won't run away today. I still haven't decided about tomorrow.

We walk down the hall and stop in front of an elevator. He pushes a button and scans a key card. I try to get a look at the card, but he palms it so I can't see. So, this is how he plans to keep me. I bet there are key card locks on the stairwell doors too. The elevator opens and he gestures for me to enter. Then he follows me in and the doors close behind us. As soon as the elevator starts to move, I realize how close he's standing to me. I can feel his body heat warming up the small space.

It's cold in the small metal box, but I feel sweat trickle down the back of my neck. I know it's from Jarek's closeness. I should step away, but I can't. He's still holding my hand, and his body is pressing up against me. The elevator screeches to a halt, jarring as it stops. I can't hold back the squeal and grip his hand harder.

Jarek pulls me into his arms and rubs my back to calm me. Without realizing what I'm doing, I fist my hands in his shirt and lean into him. Then I start to purr. I don't usually purr like that.

I jerk back in surprise to find him staring down at me. I know he's taller than I am, but this position emphasizes the height difference. Jarek's arms don't release me, and his eyes stay locked with mine for a long minute. The intensity of the moment overwhelms me and I hyperventilate. I can't breathe. The walls seem to move and close in on me. Luckily, Jarek recognizes my panic attack and moves us out of the small space as soon as the doors open. He scoops me up and carries me bride style down the long hallway.

When he stops, I expect him to put me down, but he doesn't. Instead, he pulls out a key and unlocks a door, then carries me over the threshold. If we were dating, it would be sweet. Since he's my captor, I'm not sure if I should be excited or scared. I suddenly realize just how isolated I am here. Jarek could do anything to me and no one would know. My family thinks I'm dead already. Something about him makes me trust that he won't actually hurt me. Not intentionally, anyway.

I'm paying more attention to him than the apartment we walk into. Jarek lowers me to my feet gently. "Do you need some water? How about fresh air?" I get the impression that he doesn't really know how to be nurturing, but he's trying.

"Water and fresh air would be great. I thought you said no one lives in this one," I ask. Turning to look at the room, it's larger than I expected. The living room is decorated in a modern minimalist style, with a couch, an oversized recliner, and an oversized chair. They're focused around a fireplace that I'm sure is gas or electric, because there's no outlet for smoke. The wall in front of me has two large picture windows, which seems strange to me after his talk of the building looking like a warehouse on the outside.

"Here," he says, handing me a cold bottle of water. I watch as he strolls over to one of the windows and opens it, letting a soft spring breeze in. "No one lives here. Raf and I decorated this apartment for you. We had hoped that you would understand we were protecting you, and that you'd want to be closer to us."

I raise an eyebrow. "Closer to you?" How is this apartment closer to them? I can't help but wonder what he's talking about.

"Raf is across the hall, and I'm next door on the right. This one is at the end of the hall, so you'd be between us." I nod at his explanation, and consider his offer.

"And if I agree, I'm still a prisoner," I quip. He tilts his head and furrows his brow.

"Not a prisoner. You'll be able to come and go as you please within the warehouse as long as one of us is with you. I can even find some guards if you want some space from us." I roll my eyes and pace the floor. Was this better than being locked up downstairs? Definitely. Could I commit to staying here? I have no idea.

"What happens if I agree, then try to run?" Jarek's arms fall away from me as he takes a step back.

"Where do you think you'd go? Everyone thinks you're dead. It has to stay that way. There are things you don't know," he begins, then stops himself before he can say more. Now I really want to know what he's hiding from me.

"I don't understand what I'm doing here. You guys kidnap me, then act like you're protecting me from some unknown threat. Why can't you just be honest with me?" I turn my back to him and stare out the window at the city below. It wouldn't take much to get someone's attention and let the outside world know I'm here.

There's something about the way Jarek is acting toward me today. It's like he wants to tell me the truth, but is scared I won't believe him. Honestly, I probably won't. "The problem is that we don't trust each other," I say without realizing I'd put my thoughts into words.

"You're right. We don't. What can I do to make you trust me?" I feel his breath on my neck as he says the words. I draw in a surprised breath. I hadn't seen or heard him move. I turn to face him and shrug. I have no idea how either of us can make the other trust. He's always going to expect me to run, and I'm always going to expect him to hurt me.

"If I knew that, we'd be there already."

"Maybe this will be a start. Come on, check out the rest of the apartment." Jarek steps away from me again and walks into another room. I glance longingly toward the door for a moment, then decide to follow him. If I try to run, he'll catch me and I'll end up in that basement room again. At least here, I'll have sunlight and a little bit of privacy. Besides, I promised.

"How is this apartment supposed to..." I trail off as I walk into the next room. It's the biggest personal library I've ever seen. Oh, this is definitely something I could get used to.

"What? How? Why?" I can't form a complete thought, stuttering the single word questions at him as I spin in a circle looking at all the books.

"I'm somewhat of a collector. I haven't read them all, but I'm working on it. Please don't tell anyone. I have a reputation to maintain." His candor catches me off guard and I chuckle as if we've just shared a joke. Jarek D'Angelo is a fellow book nerd. What kind of twisted world have I been sucked into? I walk around the room, checking out the shelves.

Without staring or getting too close, I can tell he has a wide variety of books here. There are classics like Shakespeare, expensive first editions that are nearly as old, and even some smut by my favorite authors. I mean, I didn't expect a man, especially one who was a mafia enforcer, to read Moran or Loreweaver. I guess looks can be deceiving. "All of these are yours? Even these?" I gesture to my two favorite authors' books, sitting side by side on a shelf.

"Don't judge me until you've read them. Yes, it's romance, but it's way more than that. You don't like vampires? Or magic? Really?" he asks, shocked by the idea that I think less of him for his reading habits.

"Hold on. I love these authors. I never said any different. I'm just a little surprised that you, of all people, would enjoy their books. Most men I know stay away from reverse harem and ménage." I watch his cheeks turn a little pink with my words, then he picks up one of the books and hands it to me.

"This one is my favorite. You should read it." The book he hands me is pink with a guitar on the cover. I turn it over curiously. *Jameson.* Hmm, I haven't read this author yet, but the book screams small town romance. Who would have thought such a big guy would be a softie for romance novels?

"Thanks, I'll definitely do that." I place the book on the table to remind me that I want to start it before bed tonight. That is, if he lets me stay here. "So, does that mean you're moving me here?"

"If you don't mind being a prisoner up here instead of down there," he says. I wince at his words, then notice his smirk. The fucker is teasing me. My shoulders relax and I laugh at his sarcasm.

"I thought you said I wouldn't be a prisoner," I toss back at him.

JAREK

At first, I'm not sure how to respond. I don't want to keep Ness a prisoner, but I can't let her go back to her family. It's not safe. Why can't I just tell her that her father is the one who tried to kill her? That Raf and I only kidnapped her to keep her from dying. I should tell her, but I can't. Not yet. I know she won't believe me when I do tell her. Her reaction earlier when I implied it was enough to tell me that I have to have proof first.

I have to know why Dragonetti decided that his only child was so much in the way that she had to be killed. Does she know something? Or does he have more sinister motives? Most omegas are just sold to the highest bidder. I'm shocked he didn't try to do that. Unless he did, but for some reason they didn't want her. Who wouldn't want Ness? She's perfect.

I realize that I'm standing there, staring at her, instead of answering her. *Shit.* "I don't want you to be a prisoner. I want you to decide to stay." Damn, I almost told her I wanted her to stay with me. Nope. I can't go there. Not yet. Maybe not ever. Sure, I want Ness more than I want to breathe, but I won't force her into it.

I'm thrilled at her response to the library. I suspected that she liked to read and had even selected some of the books with her in mind. I can't believe I revealed my guilty pleasure to her, though. No one knows that I love to read smut. But if it helps me get Ness on my side, I'll deal with it.

"I don't know," she answers quietly. I expect nothing less. She's honest to a fault. At least she's not spitting in my face today. Baby steps are still progress, right?

"How about a trial run? You can stay here tonight and we'll take things day by day." I have no idea why I make the offer. It's not as if she can just leave if she decides things aren't working out.

"So, I'll be locked up here instead of in the dungeon?" she muses, then laughs. "Fine. This is better. Can I see the bedroom and the bathroom? And what about clothes?" I point toward the master bedroom and she bounces off as if I gave her a gift. Baby steps.

"If you want something specific, just make me a list. I'll get whatever you want. And yeah, we'll have to keep the door locked. But Raf and I will be the only ones with a key. Unless you want me to find another bodyguard. I need you to feel safe here."

I follow her into the bedroom, staying in the doorway. This is her space, and I won't intrude. I watch her as she inspects the room. Ness looks more relaxed than she has since we brought her here. She disappears into the bathroom and I hear her delighted squeal. Good, she likes it. "Ness? Are you okay?" I walk across the room and lean in the door.

"Oh, my. Jarek, this room is amazing. I tell you what—if you can get me some decent clothes and if I can have some privacy here, I won't even think about running for at least a week." Her face lights up when she makes the offer. I can't refuse her.

"There's a notebook and pen in the nightstand. Make me a list. I'll go get us some lunch. I'm taking a chance and leaving you here alone. Anything special you want to eat?" I know I shouldn't leave her, but I feel like it's the only way I can be sure she won't try to run. She doesn't need to know I'm going to send one of my guys out for lunch. I'll be right next door the whole time.

"Oh! I'd love a meatball sub from Carmine's. Extra onions, don't forget the parm," she blurts out, then covers her mouth with her hand. For just a moment, she forgets our situation and gives me her lunch order. I laugh and nod.

"Got it. Drink?" I enjoy her being silly and letting me in. I want to know everything about her. I can't push, though.

"Snapple orange mango for lunch, peach tea and mango madness for later, unless that's too much trouble. I know Carmine doesn't have those." Ness plays with the hem of her shirt. It seems odd to me that she's not used to telling people what she wants.

"If you want it, we'll get it for you. When you make the clothing list, write down anything else you need or want too. I'll make sure you get it." I shouldn't make promises, but my heart won't let me stop.

RAFAEL

I stop to check on Ness on my way back from the little errand Jarek sent me on. Uncle Joe hadn't really wanted to see me. He just wanted updates. And my cousin knew that. I stop short when I realize the cell door is standing open. I peek inside, but it's empty. Where is Ness? I pull out my phone and call Jarek.

"Yeah," he responds.

"Where's Ness?" I ask in a panic. If someone took her, I will hunt them down and tear them apart.

"Upstairs. The apartment we set up for her. I sent Dave to get lunch and I'm waiting in my apartment to see what she'll do while she's alone."

"What if she tries to run?" I head toward the elevator before jogging back to the cell to get the bags of clothes that were left behind. Ness would need something to change into if she was going to stay in the apartment. No doubt she'd want a shower, too. I wonder if Jarek fully stocked her room before taking her up there.

If not, I'll just run out and get what she needs. I press the button for the elevator and wait. Everything seems to be going so slowly today, and I find myself getting annoyed over nothing. Just as the doors open, Dave walks up. "I got everything Jarek asked for." He hands the bags to me and holds the doors open so I can get inside.

"Thanks," I reply as the doors close, and I fumble my key card out of my pocket. I scan the card and punch the button that causes the metal box to lurch upward. When the doors finally open, Jarek is standing there, waiting to take the bags from me. Dave must have let him know that he gave me the food.

"What is all of this?" I ask, gesturing to the bags Jarek takes from me.

"Lunch. I had Dave get you something too. Come on, we'll go eat with Ness and talk about a schedule. I told her we'll be keeping her company if she stays up here."

"And she agreed?" I ask in shock. How did he get Ness to agree not to run in the few short hours I was gone?

"I may have made some promises," he replies with a grin. Bribery. Why does that not surprise me? Jarek always finds a way to get what he wants. I'm not sure if it's good or bad that he wants Ness.

"Great," I say, stopping in front of the door. "Anything I need to be worried about?" He grabs my hand as I slide the key in and start to open the door.

"You can't just walk in. She needs to feel safe here. I told her we're the only ones with keys, but you have to knock and let her know who's coming in." I'm shocked. It's the most respectful thing Jarek has ever said. Maybe there's more to his desire for Ness than I thought. She might just be the one who can change him for the better. I pull my hand away from the key and knock lightly.

"Ness, it's Raf and Jarek. We have food. Is it okay to come in?" I glance at my cousin and notice the satisfied smirk. This girl is definitely getting under his skin. The door rattles as she fights with the knob, but it won't open.

"I can't open the door from in here," Ness shoots back at me. I take that as permission and turn the key, swinging the door open slowly. I half expect her to be holding a lamp or something as a weapon.

Instead, she's leaning against the wall with her arms crossed over her chest. She looks slightly annoyed, as if she didn't know she'd been locked in with no way out. Jarek obviously hadn't pointed out that a key was needed to enter and exit, then. That should make lunch a fun time. I've dealt with Ness when she's pissed before, and it's not really pleasant.

Then I notice that she's glaring at him, not me. "How was your meeting?" she asks sweetly. I'm caught like a deer in headlights when she grabs my arm and pulls me down for a kiss.

Not how I want to win her over, but I'll take any affection I can get at this point. I barely care that I know she's using me to irritate Jarek. He deserves it, after all. I lose myself in the kiss for a minute, then pull back to find him staring. I shrug and he stomps away.

"You know that pissed him off," I whisper. Ness grins and follows him into the kitchen where Jarek is setting the food out.

"What's all this? Are we seriously having a family lunch? You know we're not family, right, Jarek?" she scoffs at him before taking her sandwich and drink to the living room and settling on the couch. So much for a cozy lunch where the three of us could talk through things.

"Yeah, I know," he mutters under his breath, "at least not yet." His admission makes me smile as he hands me my lunch, and I follow Ness' example. Jarek isn't far behind, and soon we're all sitting in the living room around the coffee table.

"I thought we could talk about some things and set some ground rules for you living up here." Jarek started talking before opening his lunch.

"What's there to discuss? I'm a prisoner either way. At least up here, I have a decent shower and a tiny bit of privacy." Ness' words are like daggers to my heart. I want nothing more than to be with her. I can't make her see that we saved her, though. Not yet. Maybe she'll be ready to listen soon.

Jarek just looks at her. "Your privacy, for one. We're going to be here to protect you. That doesn't mean you won't have privacy. We can stay outside the door if that's what you want. Or we can come in and spend some time with you. With the exception of being able to leave whenever you want, you'll be in complete control."

Ness and I exchange a glance and she laughs. My eyes go wide and I watch to see how pissed he gets at her laughing at him. "I'll be in complete control. Yeah, right. You're never going to let me be in control. I haven't been here that long and I already know how it's going to go. You'll do what you want and I'll have to deal with it."

"That's not true. As long as you listen and cooperate, we won't have any problems." I raise an eyebrow at him, wondering what he's trying to do here. It seems like this conversation would have been better if I hadn't been a witness to it.

"Do you really think I'm just gonna roll over and take orders from you? I don't even take orders from my father. I don't understand why you're trying to make it sound like you're protecting me when clearly you just want to have me at your disposal. And why is that? What do you think I'm going to do for you?" She stands up and walks the few steps, stopping in front of him.

"I want to protect you and keep you safe. There are things going on that you don't understand. Just agree to cooperate and we'll be fine." She laughs again and straddles him. The chair he's in is barely big enough for him, much less with her on his lap. "What are you doing?"

"I'm giving you what you really want. Then maybe you'll stop lying to me about why you kidnapped me." Ness leans in and captures his lips with hers. I watch as she kisses him. I should be jealous, but oddly, I'm not. Instead, I'm turned on by watching her make out with my cousin.

I wonder if Ness will ever get to a point where she'll actually want both of us. The idea invades my fantasies, and I know exactly how I'll handle that later. I don't have time to dwell on the idea of pleasuring myself to thoughts of sharing Ness with Jarek, because he stands up and places her gently on the couch.

"You don't know what I want. I'm not going to let you manipulate me into answering your questions. It won't work."

Chapter Four

SECRETS AND LIES

MILO

As promised, Dragonetti's package is right on time. I barely repress a growl as I jerk it from the bell hop's hands and slam the door in his face without giving him a tip. I can't get the thought out of my head of Ness being out there somewhere, alone, while everyone thinks she's dead. There was no ransom, so she must not have been kidnapped, right?

I flop back down on the couch and tear the box open. There's no return address, but I didn't expect one. Ness' father is smart enough to prevent any connection to me. Otherwise, he would be in prison. I know that I should have focused more on catching him and proving that he was the one running the drug ring that killed my brother. For some reason, I'm always more concerned with his daughter.

I sift through the contents of the box, sorting everything out on the table in front of me. I know from the last time exactly what to expect. Burner phone, check. Cash, looks like a cool ten grand, check. A fake ID that I can use or not, check.

I pull everything out of the box and nearly miss the small, handwritten note tucked in the bottom.

I unfold the paper, shocked at what's inside.

When I said this is the last time, Milo, I meant it. You have twenty-four hours to get out of my city. If my guys find you after that, you'll wish they hadn't.

Shit. I have to find Ness fast. And I won't be using that fake ID, either. I probably shouldn't use the phone or cash. Damn. Well, I guess I'm burning that bridge earlier than I wanted. I tell myself it doesn't matter. I was going to find a way to turn him in once I found Ness anyway. Okay, if I only have one day to do this, I need to figure out the best place to start.

We've been watching the north side, searching for a connection between Dragonetti and the drug ring there. I have no other leads, so I guess I'll start there. I take a swig from the whiskey bottle, then head to the bathroom to shower and get dressed. I can't get much done in my underwear.

The water is too hot, but I don't care. I have to get out of here fast. I dry myself and throw on clothes, then toss everything I want to keep into a duffel. I put the money into a paper bag. I'll stop at the bank and deposit it under my alias on my way to the north side.

I stop at the door and take one last look around the hotel room that has been my home for the past few months. I can't say why, but I know I'm going to miss it. Just like I miss sneaking away from my partner to meet Ness after I found out who her father was. I shake the thought off and head downstairs.

After making a couple of stops, I head north until the buildings show a little more wear and a little less upkeep. I slow the sedan, my eyes searching for the specific place I need to be. Three streets later, I'm parking and going over it all again on foot. I don't have an exact address, so I can't just punch it in my GPS. I have to find one of Dragonetti's vehicles. It's not an easy task, since I'm certain that some of them are stolen. I finally see some guys who look familiar going into what appears to be an abandoned radio station.

I duck into a convenience store across the street and browse while I watch. Sure enough, the guys I saw carried black duffel bags into the building from the alley. No one in this area even seemed to notice. I will have to find a way inside. I need some leverage to protect me from Dragonetti's wrath. It seems odd to me that he's willing to kill me just because I asked for help. Or is it because I'm searching for his daughter?

The whole situation has me questioning things that had been happening before Ness' disappearance. She'd had a couple of close calls even though her father claimed that he kept her out of the business. I can't forgive myself for taking those two jobs for him. He'd told me that she was in danger, and it was the only way to help her. Then someone had tried to kill her anyway.

I wonder how much of what he told me was a lie. Probably all of it. I hate throwing my career away, but I know that Ness is out there somewhere. She could be scared and alone. I can't let that happen. I have to find her.

I grab a soda and candy bar and pay at the counter before walking outside and heading up the street. I can't just cross and try to waltz right inside. That's a sure-fire way to get myself killed. When I'm sure no one is following me, I turn and head back toward my target.

I'm half a block away when a car pulls out of the alley. Hmm. I wonder if they left anyone behind to guard the place. I keep my pace casual so I don't draw attention. A quick glance around gives me the impression that I'm not being watched or followed. I duck into the alley and hide in the shadows for a minute until I'm sure. Then I creep toward the door. I know it won't be unlocked, but I've been trained for this kind of situation. I make quick work of picking the lock and let myself inside.

Once inside, I lock the door back, so it won't be obvious that someone has broken in. The mid-morning sun streams through the rips in the window coverings, illuminating the hall. I steel myself against the feeling that I'm throwing away my career even more by breaking and entering Dragonetti's property. I'm definitely leaning into the gray on this, but Ness is in trouble, and I need to find her.

I creep down the hall, checking each door as I pass. None of them are locked, and there's no one around. The whole place is a little creepy. There's no indication that any of the unoccupied rooms have been used in a long while. Everything has a thick layer of dust on it, which tells me that this floor is a bust. I move further down the hall and find a staircase. If I run into someone, I'll have to fight my way out. My hand instantly grips the gun tucked into the back of my pants. *No, Milo, you can't shoot anyone. It'll attract too much attention.* My fingers relax and I drop my hand by my side again. Fists, it is, then.

I slowly open the door to the staircase, noticing the fluorescent lighting that isn't present in the hall on the main floor lights my way now. I pause to listen, deciding which direction is best to go. I don't hear anything coming from above or below. I start to descend the stairs, opting to begin at the bottom and work my way up until I find something useful.

My heart is racing as I head deeper into this building. I stop at the next floor and carefully open the door. Lights illuminate the hallway, but it seems to be deserted. Slipping through the heavy metal door, I ease it closed with barely a click. I stop to listen again, shocked at the silence. Is Dragonetti really so smug that he doesn't think anyone would dare to break into one of his properties?

I try the nearest door, finding it unlocked. Footsteps sound on the floor behind me, echoing down the empty hall. I duck inside the room and lean against the door. The footsteps continue past the door until they're so faint, I can barely hear them. So, it's not deserted after all. I'll have to be more careful in my inspection, so I don't get caught.

It can't hurt to check out this room, since I'm already here. I flip the light on and turn to survey the space. Hmm, an office, that's promising. I slide my hands into a pair of latex gloves to keep from leaving fingerprints. Then I proceed to search the room carefully, making sure to put things back where they were before I touched them. I can't let anyone know I was here. I don't want to hamper the FBI's investigation, but I need insurance. I have to protect myself and find Ness.

As I riffle thorough the desk drawers, I come across a small leather-bound journal. I flip it open and realize that it's not a journal, but a ledger. It has names, dollar amounts, and dates. This might be just what I need. I pocket the book and keep looking, bumping the mouse and waking the computer. Wow, this is some crazy shit. Who doesn't lock their computer in this day and age?

Lucky for me, whoever it belongs to didn't bother. I sit down in the chair and scroll through files. My hand freezes when my scan leads me to an email. There's no way. I rush to dig through my pockets, hunting for a flash drive. I need to copy as much of this as I can. Then I have to find Ness, immediately. Because I know I've fucked up.

I insisted to Dragonetti that his daughter was still alive. Even when he argued that she's dead. What if I'm the one putting her in danger? It would be my fault if anything did happen to her. How was I supposed to know her father had been the one to put the hit out on her? If it was his guys who'd taken her out, he would know if she was dead, wouldn't he? Fuck. I find the flash drive and get to work copying every file and email that I can. I have to figure out who I can go to with this. I can't take it to the FBI. It'll get thrown out of court for being illegally obtained. And I'll end up in jail with a bunch of guys I put there. Not my idea of a good time.

Fuck. D'Angelo may be my only chance. But can I get him to trust me? I don't know. If I can convince him to check out the files before he makes a decision, maybe. With the ledger tucked in my pocket and the now full flash drive accompanying it, I stand and right the desk before walking to the door and flipping the light off again.

I press my ear to the door and listen for footsteps. I'm close to the stairwell, but I have no idea where that thug went earlier. Easing the door open, I peek into the hall and listen closer. It's now or never. I pull my hood up to cover my face, just in case I get caught. Then I drag the door open and dash for the stairwell.

The door clicks closed behind me and I run up the stairs. "Hey, who the fuck are you?" The voice stops me momentarily. I can't afford to get caught here. Ness needs me. I pick up my pace and shove the figure out of my way, then rush through the door to the ground floor. Footsteps echo behind me, and I know if I stop, I'll be caught. Then the torture will start until they find out who I am and kill me.

VANESSA

Jarek pushing me away makes me angry. I should be grateful that he's not trying to take advantage of me, but instead, I'm pissed. "How could I possibly know what you want when you keep switching from hot to cold every five seconds? Either you want me or you don't. You need to make up your mind."

I shock myself with the outburst. I don't want him to know that I'm attracted to him. But I've just spilled those beans, and there's no way to take it back. Raf stares at me, and we both wait for Jarek to respond.

"I already told you, doll, you'll have to beg for it. But if you think for a second that I don't want you, then you aren't as smart as I thought." His calm response pushes my buttons. I jump from the couch where he deposited me and stalk over to him. He glares at me, even as my hand shoots out to slap him.

When my palm connects with his cheek, he grabs my wrist and pulls me back on his lap. I can feel his huge cock straining against his jeans. Well, that answers that question. I know he wants control, and I don't want to give it to him. His whiskey and cedar scent makes me want to beg, but I can't. If he has that kind of control, if I give that to him, I'll lose myself. I can't do that.

"This is becoming a habit, doll. You keep spitting on me and hitting me, and I'm starting to get a complex. Do you want me to think you don't like me?" His smirk enrages me again. But I can't physically hurt him. He's nearly three times my size. So, I do what I can. Sitting on his lap, I start to squirm, rubbing my ass against his cock. I know it's driving him crazy because his scent gives him away. I'm fully aware that he can smell my attraction, but after my declaration, there's no way to hide that anymore.

"I'm not going to beg you for anything. So, you can just forget that little fantasy." I fight my way free of his grip, stomp to my bedroom, and slam the door. I lean against the door, sliding down it until I'm sitting on the floor. Hot tears fill my eyes. I'd been trying to get information out of him using seduction, and it had backfired so fiercely that I was left feeling rejected. I shake my head to clear it, wipe my eyes, and stand up. I will not give him that kind of power over me. Omega or not, he isn't going to treat me like some toy he can play with and toss away.

After all, I'm Vanessa Fucking Dragonetti. Whether my father likes it or not, I'm the heiress to the Dragonetti fortune and the number one feared crime family in our city. I'm a God damned princess, and I need to start acting like it. Jarek will bow at my feet before I give him another moment of my time. My brain understands my thoughts, but my heart refuses to listen. I have no option but to avoid him until I can get out of here.

A knock at the door pulls me from my musing. "Go away. I don't want to talk to you anymore, Jarek." I force the words to come out without emotion.

"It's Raf. Can I come in? I just want to make sure you're okay." The sincerity in his voice has me opening the door.

"Fine, but I don't want *him* in here." I make sure to emphasize the word him loud enough that Jarek can hear. And I ignore his scoff in response, closing the door harder than I intend. "What do you want?" I turn on Raf as soon as the door clicks shut.

"I told you; I just want to make sure you're okay," he says, reaching for me. I push his hands away and step back.

"I'm fine. I just don't want to be around him right now. That doesn't mean I'll just fall into your arms, either. You two have some nerve, honestly. You don't own me, and neither does he. The sooner you learn that the better off we'll be."

Raf stares at me with his jaw open. "But, Ness, earlier..." He trails off, apparently unsure what to say next. Good. That puts me at an advantage, which is what I want.

"What, Raf? We fucked. Yeah, I know. I was there, or did you forget, in your lame attempt to force me to submit to you?" I'm being a bitch, but I don't care. They both keep pissing me off today, and I'm not going to just fall in line and let them get away with it.

"Will you at least let me bring your sandwich to you? I don't want you to go without food because we've upset you." Holy shit, does he actually care? Come on, Ness, don't fall for it. He's just trying to get you to let down your guard so he can claim you or some shit like that. Of course, if he really wanted to control me, he'd just use his alpha command and force me to submit. Why doesn't he?

I roll my eyes at him. "As if you care. But yeah, I'd like to eat my sandwich before it gets cold. Just don't let that asshole in here when you bring it back. And don't forget my mango." I assume he'll know that I want the juice, not the tea. We'll see how much attention he was paying while he pretended to be my bodyguard.

I know that's not fair, because he really did protect me while he was apparently undercover for D'Angelo. I'm more upset with him because he lied to me than that he's Jarek's cousin. I wish he could have just told the truth. Then I wouldn't have to punish him by withholding affection. Because no matter how hard I try to deny it, I know I'm in love with the jerk. I'm already half in love with Jarek too, but I refuse to let that information out. Honestly, if Milo somehow showed up, I would be able to make this my home.

I watch as Raf rushes out to grab my sandwich and drink, stopping the door from closing completely. Jarek is still sitting in the chair where I left him, facing away from my room. I wonder if he'll sit there all day. Part of me hopes that he does. I want to know that I have that kind of power over him, that this isn't completely one-sided. My heat is coming, and I'm terrified of what will happen if I can't figure out where I stand with these men.

They're my only hope of surviving it with my sanity intact. Raf's earthy pine scent lingers in my room. It makes me want to bury myself in his arms and push my worries away. But I can't yet. I have to know that I'm in control. I spent my entire life being controlled by my father—it's my turn now. I'm taking my life back, and no one is going to stop me. If these two want to be part of it, they'll get onboard with me being the one calling the shots here. If not, I guess I'll figure out how to get out of here and find Milo.

MILO

I have to make a split-second decision here, so I take a deep breath and run toward the exit. Luckily, the guy chasing me is trying to keep from drawing attention to the fact that this abandoned building isn't actually abandoned. That gives me enough time to get across the street and down another alley before he comes outside. I watch as he looks around before turning back and sneaking into the building. That was close. Too close.

I can't take a risk like that again. I have to find Ness and protect her from her father. As much as I hate it, I'll have to sneak into D'Angelo's hideout and convince him to help me. I'll offer him whatever it takes to make it happen. Although, that was how I got mixed up with Dragonetti in the first place. That offer can't be made lightly this time. All I wanted before was a chance to work in the FBI. Ness' dad had arranged everything for me, and that left me in his debt. And when I'd tried to get out from under his thumb, he convinced me that Ness needed my protection. I kick myself for falling for his tricks now, but at the time, I was a naïve kid who didn't know any better.

I can't go back to that. But what choice do I have? Ness needs me, and I need Jarek. Fuck. I steel myself against what I know I must do. Then I make my way, slowly, carefully, to the opposite side of town. I leave my car in a long-term parking lot in neutral territory to keep Dragonetti from figuring out that I'm going to ask Jarek for help. With any luck, he'll think I left it there when I ran. I pull my hood up and walk slowly but with purpose, thankful for the light rain that has started to fall.

Three blocks later, I'm in D'Angelo territory. I know where his hideout is, because I've been staking it out for months. Dragonetti wanted me to take out his competition, and like a good little lap dog, I was going to. So, I know exactly where to find Jarek pretty much any time of the day.

I stroll down the street, as if I have nowhere to be. I don't want to draw attention to myself, especially in this neighborhood. I keep my head down as I walk, happy to have the rain as cover. I stop and look in store windows as I pass, trying hard to be inconspicuous. I'm so close to Jarek's secret headquarters that I'm getting nervous. Will he give me a chance to explain? Or will he just shoot me and end it that way? I have no idea, but I push forward because I need his help.

A quick glance over my shoulder and I slip inside the building. I can hear people ahead, so I duck into a supply closet and wait. I have no idea what I'll do if I get caught. I don't have time to consider my options when the door opens, and I'm face to face with a very surprised man. He growls and I throw my fist out to punch him in the throat. I don't want to kill this guy, especially if I'm trying to get Jarek to help me. I can't see a way around it, though, as he attacks me again.

I dodge his next punch, then feel his nose crack when my fist connects with his face. He shoves me against the wall and tries to wrap his hands around my throat. I block and grab his hand. As much as I don't want to hurt him, I can't let him take me out. I snap his hand back, breaking his wrist. "I don't want to do this, man." I know that telling him won't change my actions.

While he's choking in pain because he can't scream, I grab a rag from the shelf and wrap it around his throat, pulling it as tightly as I can. I feel his nails scraping against my arms and hands. He's only using his left hand, because it's the one I didn't break. I hold the rag tightly with one hand while I twist his right hand again, causing him to collapse in pain. At this point, he curls into a ball, holding his wrist. I know that I should just walk away, but I can't risk it.

I grab the sides of his head and jerk it sideways, easing him to the ground as his life fades. This won't go over well with Jarek, but I have no choice. I have to live so I can protect Ness. I check the dead man's pockets for anything that will help me. He has a key card and some cash. He won't need either now, so I help myself.

I peek out of the closet and check the hall. It's empty for now, and I know I have to move.

JAREK

I refuse to be manipulated. I won't let that happen again. Ness thinks she can use her body to get what she wants, but she's wrong. I know that I'm no good for her, even though I want to grab her and never let go. It doesn't matter how badly I desire her; I can't let myself have her. She'll end up broken or worse. I have to keep being an asshole and push her away. It's for her own good.

I can't stop myself from flirting with her. And I know if she actually begs for it, I won't say no. But I have to put some distance between us. I can't get attached again. Not like that. I refuse to give my heart away.

It doesn't surprise me when she storms off after I plop her on the couch. I've been cruel and I know it. But it's all intentional. I know exactly what I'm doing. The door slams behind me and I don't even flinch.

"Why are you so hateful to her?" Raf growls. I know he's in love with her; I knew before we kidnapped her. I mean, it was honestly more of a rescue situation, but I'm not sure she sees it that way yet. And I can't just tell her that her father is the asshole who's been trying to have her killed. She'll never believe me. It's unfortunate that her FBI boyfriend isn't around to tell her what I know.

"Because I'm not going to let her manipulate and control me. You know as well as I do, that's what she was trying to do. She was going to use her body to get what she wanted."

"So? What's so wrong with getting what you want too? Just don't tell her anything," he reasons.

"You want me to lie to the woman you're in love with? I knew you'd fuck this up somehow." I laugh at my cousin as his face turns red and he tries to think of a comeback. I don't budge when he goes to check on her, choosing instead to eat my lunch. If she wants hers, she can come out and eat like a normal person. Just because I wounded her pride, that doesn't mean she can hide away.

I listen intently to their conversation, overhearing that Raf wants to bring her lunch to her in the bedroom. Oh, no, doll. You wanna eat, you have to eat with me. He saunters around the couch and picks up her meal. "Put it down," I order quietly.

"But Ness is hungry," he defends.

"Then she can come out here and eat with us, as planned," I counter. I glare at Raf, daring him to defy me. I am next in line for the D'Angelo family business. If he goes against me, he'll have to deal with my father, and his own. Neither will let insubordination stand.

"Come on, Jarek. Don't be that way," he nearly begs. I shake my head and he returns to the doorway where Ness is waiting.

"Where's my food?" I hear her ask. I almost turn around to see her face when he delivers my ultimatum.

"Jarek says if you're hungry, you have to come eat with us," he informs her flatly. I know he's sympathetic to her needs and desires, but I can't let them run the show here. I have to assert my dominance and keep control of my own operation.

"Are you serious? Fine, I won't eat." She slams the door in Raf's face. I only know because he grunts as it hits him. I know that she's hungry, because she hasn't had much to eat today. Raf storms over and flops into his seat.

"I hope you're happy," he growls, picking up his own sandwich. He silently returns to eating his lunch.

I can't stop the smirk that crosses my face. It doesn't matter that they're both angry with me. Now they know that I'm in charge and they can't counter it. "I am, actually," I admit before turning toward the closed door. "Hey, doll, if you don't come eat this, I'm going to. And if you don't eat lunch with me, you'll have to eat every single meal from here on out with me. Your choice."

She screams, then the door bangs open and she stalks over to the couch. Ness picks up the sandwich and stomps over to Raf, who's sitting the furthest away from me. "Move," she orders.

He jumps and does as she wants. I see how this is going to go. Next meal, I'll add more restrictions. Before it's over, she'll be eating on my lap.

"Oh, good. You've decided to join us. Enjoy your sandwich," I say with a sleezy smile on my face. I want to make this easy on her, but I can't since she decided to use my desire against me. Honeysuckle and rain wafts toward me. Wait, is she getting aroused by me bossing her around?

That's an interesting theory, and one I'll have to look more into later. For now, I focus all my attention on finishing my lunch. Or that's how I make it look. I'm really staring at Ness, watching her every move. I'm waiting for her to blow up at me and demand her freedom again. But she doesn't. Not yet.

CHAPTER FIVE

ONCOMING HEAT

VANESSA

Jarek's insistence that I eat with him annoys me. I wish I could just avoid him altogether. That would make the sting of rejection a little easier to bear. I was certain that he wanted me, but I must be wrong. Why would he act so hateful? Is it because Raf is here? Shit. I'm not trying to cause conflict between them. Omegas need affection; we crave an alpha's touch.

Well, if he's not interested, I guess I should fall back on my original plan. I have to get out of here. But how? I need to convince Jarek that I'm willing to help him. That's not happening until I get over being pissed about being rejected. So, I guess I'm stuck here for the time being. I'm a prisoner of the men who hate my father. If that's true, then why do I feel so safe with them?

With the exception of the men who brought me here, no one has touched me. Those two were pretty rough, but they haven't been around since. I wonder if Jarek or Raf did something to them for hurting me. Nah, that's probably just my imagination. They wouldn't really kill someone for hurting me, would they? But Jarek did tell me that they'd been taken care of. So maybe they would.

I let that thought settle as I slouch in my seat. While I scarf down my sandwich—no dainty bites for me—I watch Jarek through my eyelashes. I don't want him to know that I'm staring, but I can't resist. The idea that he would kill someone for hitting me sends a shiver down my spine. I should let it go, but I can't.

"Hey, Jarek. What ever happened to those two guys who brought me to your dungeon?" I watch as he and Raf exchange a look. Holy shit. Something did happen. But was it because of me? I'm dying to know. "What?"

Jarek stares at me. He looks pissed. "You should mind your own business so you don't share their fate."

"I just asked a question. I haven't seen them since they tossed me in that cage downstairs after they slapped me around a little. I was curious, that's all." More than that; I want revenge. I hate that those assholes hit me while I was still drugged and couldn't fight back.

"To answer your question, they've been dealt with. And I can personally guarantee that after Jarek's conversation with them, you'll never have a problem with them again," Raf answers with a smirk. Shit. He killed them. Otherwise, why would Raf answer that way?

I turn to Jarek, suddenly desperate to know the truth. "Did you kill them?"

"Would it upset you if I did?" I could swear his eyes show something akin to lust, but he blinks and it's gone.

"I don't think it would. They were both horrible to me. And beating up a woman while she's drugged and can't fight back is cruel, no matter who you work for. I would have expected better from your men," I admit. Why did I tell him all that?

"One is dead; the other is terrified that I'm coming after him next. Is there something specific you'd like to happen to him?" Jarek's tone is completely stoic. He's all business.

"Which one did you kill?" What is wrong with me? I'm over here imagining how hot it would have been to watch Jarek snuff out a life just because they offended me. Maybe I am mafia princess material after all.

"The short one," he chuckles. I can see on his face that he's remembering exactly how he did it. But I'm more upset that it wasn't the one who was cruel to me.

I can't stop the growl that escapes my lips. Hate fills my eyes and I raise them to meet Jarek's. "I want the other one."

"What do you mean, Ness?" Raf tries to play peacemaker, but I ignore him, staring intensely into Jarek's eyes.

"You wanna kill him, doll?" Jarek asks. His mouth quirks up into a small smile, as if he's impressed with my desire for blood.

"He was the one who hit me the most. The other guy just held me still for him. The tall one was the one who hit me, over and over, until the short guy made him stop. Yeah, they were both guilty, but the tall one was the one who started it all." I can feel the tears well up as I talk. I don't want to tell Jarek what happened, but I can't stop myself.

He clenches his jaw as I speak, and when I'm done, a low growl erupts from him. "You think you can torture and kill him? Are you that tough?"

Raf interrupts again. "Ness, you don't have to do this. You can't kill someone. You don't know how. Your father kept you away from the business, remember?"

"Don't tell me what I can and can't do, Raf." I turn to Jarek. "I want his blood on my hands. Are you going to let me do it or not?"

He stares at me for a long while, as if measuring my ability by the way I hold myself. I refuse to back down. I want to be the one to take his life. It doesn't matter to me that my father tried to shelter me and keep me out of the business. I know more about what he has going on than I'm supposed to.

It's about time I start using that to my advantage. All thoughts of escape or being angry with Jarek leave me with the prospect of revenge. "Okay, doll. Make me a list of what you need, and what type of space you want to do it in. I won't let you do it alone, but I will let you be the one to take him out. We can even drug him and tie him up, if that suits you." I feel a purr rumble in my chest. I can tell the noise surprises Jarek and Raf too.

RAFAEL

Ness' request to kill Luigi makes me balk. I would never expect her to be okay with what we do to the people who cross us, much less for her to want to take part. I guess my girl has a dark side after all. "Are you sure you want to do this, Ness?" I try again to convince her to let us handle it. I can tell from her face that it's not going to work. All I want is to keep her safe and away from the business. But it looks like she's going to dive right in.

"Of course, I'm sure. I want him to know that no one can treat me that way and get by with it. I want him to suffer more than he made me hurt when he hit me." Her cold tone sent a shiver down my back. I'm not sure if it's lust or fear. Maybe a little of both.

"Okay. Tell me what you need me to do. I don't want you to do this alone." I hope that I'll be able to talk her into letting one of us actually off the guy, but that look in her eyes tells me it's not gonna happen. Either way, the thought of her torturing a man then killing him is making my dick hard.

"So, you guys are just okay with me killing one of your henchmen. Why do I find that hard to believe?" Ness' question catches me off guard. I'm not expecting her to want to know why we handle things the way we do. There's a hierarchy. It's just our way.

I turn to Jarek, reveling in letting my head alpha answer her question. He looks a little uncomfortable, and I have to stifle a laugh. Turning to her, he answers, "Disrespect will not be tolerated. I handled half the problem for you. I should have asked you what you wanted done and how. It won't happen again." His vow to her hits me harder than her question did. That's a family response, not something promised to outsiders. Is he planning to keep her?

Wondering if Jarek could possibly have feelings for Ness, I get quiet. I can't compete against my cousin. There's no way. He has all the power and influence. I'm his second in command, because I can't beat him in a fight. I've tried. Could we form a pack together? I hate bowing to him, but I would do it for her, no matter how much it grates my alpha nature.

"I mean it; make me a list of what you need and the type of space. I'll make it happen. You wanna use water? We have a room for that. Electricity? Fire? You name it, and I can get it for you." Jarek's insistence is putting me on edge. What would happen if Ness took things too far and attacked one of us? Would he be so helpful and understanding then?

"Aren't you worried that I'll come after one of you while I have access to weapons?" Apparently, Ness is thinking the same thing I was. That means I won't have to wait to talk to Jarek about it later. Good.

"You won't." His reply is quiet with authority. I balk at his answer. He can't know that she won't do it.

"And why is that?" I wonder what will happen if she keeps challenging him like this. He's not a patient guy, and I can tell he's getting annoyed from the way he clenches his jaw.

"Because even if you somehow managed to kill both of us, you'd be locked in whatever room we put you in with no way out. And since everyone but us thinks you're dead, no one will come to save you. Wouldn't it make more sense to respect the men who are taking care of you, so that you get to live longer?"

"I guess that's a valid point. I'll take it into consideration," she quips. I laugh at her flippancy. "What's so funny? He has a good argument. It's like a dog biting the hand that feeds it."

"I know. I just didn't expect you to back down so easily. I figured I would get stabbed first or something," I admit, still chuckling to myself. I can picture her attacking me, and it gets me hot. Part of me hopes that torture and murder turn her on as much as they do me. Don't get me wrong, sex with Ness has always been hot. But the thought of fucking her while she's covered in someone else's blood nearly sends me over the edge.

No matter what she puts on the list for Jarek, I need to make sure there's at least one knife in the mix.

With Jarek's eyes on me, I can't risk adjusting my cock, which is even harder than it was before. So, I sit back and cross my legs, propping my right ankle on my left knee. Ness doesn't seem to notice that I'm uncomfortable, and that's a relief. I glance at my cousin and see he's having a similar problem, but isn't trying to hide it. I wonder again what will happen when Ness goes into heat.

"You know, we have other things to discuss, too," I offer, looking from Jarek to Ness and back again.

"Like what?" they say in unison.

"Well," I start, turning to face Ness again, "You're an omega. That means at some point you'll go into heat. I've heard those are miserable to suffer through alone. I just wondered if you'd thought about that at all."

I can tell from the way her face turns red that she has thought about it. But will she tell us about those thoughts? I have no idea.

"What are you suggesting, Raf? That I submit to you as my alpha so I don't have to go crazy with need during my heat?" Sarcasm drips from her words.

MILO

It's hard to keep a low profile when you're sneaking through a building owned by one of the toughest mafia families in the city. I know that if I get caught again, I may not be so lucky as I was last time. I can take out one guy easily, but if a group jumps me, I'm screwed. And I have to make it to Jarek so I can find Ness.

She's probably trapped somewhere, scared out of her mind. She needs me. And I'm not going to let her down. I keep my head on a swivel and climb the stairs. I freeze at a noise behind me, turning slowly to meet my fate. I may not survive this adventure after all. Sorry, Ma.

I glance around, not seeing anything. Then I hear the noise again. It's scraping against the stairs. What the fuck? Where is that noise coming from? The stairwell echoes and it's hard to tell. I shake it off and keep going. I have to find Jarek, so I can get help finding Ness. I repeat it to myself over and over. That's all that matters.

I stop at a landing and listen at the door before opening it and checking the hall. I don't see anyone, so I slip thorough the door and start walking to the left. The hair on the back of my neck starts to stand up and I get the feeling I'm being watched. Shit. Cameras. I check the corners of the hall and don't see anything, then turn around. I almost miss the fist coming for my temple before it connects.

When I come to, my head is throbbing. I look down and see my hands tied to a chair. Leaning a little further, I notice my ankles are bound to it as well. Fuck. *Well, Milo, this is your own fault. You know better than to ignore those feelings.* Now I have to find a way out. A quick glance around the room and I realize that I probably have a concussion. The room is spinning and I feel sick. I try again, slower this time. On my left is a table which has tools spread across it. This could end badly for me.

On my right, there's another table, but it has my jacket and its contents spread across it. Fuck, the ledger. I have to get free and grab my stuff. I have to find Jarek and convince him to help me find Ness. Ness. Oh, if there's a God, please let her be okay. I can't handle the thought of her out there somewhere—alone and scared. That's the thought that pushes me forward. I have to save her.

Dragonetti probably has men scouring the city by now, searching for her. I can't give up. No matter how screwed I am. I have to focus. The spinning is better for a second. I try to check out the room for an exit and end up moving too fast again. I lean over the arm of the chair and empty the contents of my stomach. Great, that's just what I need.

The door opens and I slouch a little as if I'm still out. I know they won't believe it since I just threw up. But maybe I can fake submission and get the drop on them. "This bitch got sick. I'm not cleaning that up."

"You'll have to, or someone will tell D'Angelo. You don't want him sending his son over here again. We barely survived the last visit from that psychopath."

Wait, this isn't Jarek's hideout? Fuck, my intel was bad. Now what am I going to do? I've avoided his father because the old man is crazier than his son. But if these guys are more afraid of him than his dad, maybe I can use this in my favor.

"If you're so scared of Jarek, you should let me go. I'm working for him." The lie falls easily off my tongue, and for a moment, I think they believe it. At least there are only two of them.

"Oh, yeah? If you're working for him, why'd you break in here and kill Max?" The two men are standing in the shadows, the bright light from the hall making it hard to see their faces.

"I was sent to test you and report back. Max was in the wrong place at the wrong time. Anyway, I got the answers Jarek wanted. You can let me go now and I'll head back to tell him." Another lie, but I think I'm on a roll here.

They both step into the room and one closes the door. The other flips a switch and bright light fills the small space. The fluorescent light is harsher than the lamp that was illuminating the space before. "Doesn't that figure? The psychopath sent one of his goons to try and trip us up. I bet he's trying to get the old man to take us out so he can have this building too."

The other man scoffs. "As if Seventh Street isn't enough for him. Greedy bastard. Maybe we should send him a message." I blink a few times to adjust my eyes to the burning light. Now that I can see clearly, I wish I'd kept my mouth shut. These guys are huge, and obviously don't like Jarek. My idea of convincing them to let me go flies out the window as they stalk toward me.

"Guys, you don't have to do this. I'm just an errand boy. I'll tell Jarek that you've got this place locked down. You have my word. We have to stick together, right?" Maybe another tactic will work.

I realize my mistake the moment the first guy stops in front of me. I stare at him for a moment, memorizing his features. If I make it out of this, I'll come back to finish these two off. He's tall with blond spiked hair. I glance at the other guy. He's shorter, with a shaved head and muscles twice the size of the first guy.

JAREK

Ness' admission that she wants Luigi dead excites me. I want to give her the chance to take her aggression out on him. She retrieves a pen and notebook to make me a list of torture implements she'll need, and I take that moment to adjust my hard cock in my pants. I've never wanted a woman more than I do right now. But I know that I can never have her. Even if Raf keeps trying to convince her that she should submit to us for her heat.

How would that even work? She's so stubborn and argumentative. There's no way she'll ever truly submit. The question is, would I want her if she did? Probably not. Honestly, the fight in her is what draws me to her. She's gorgeous, but that's not what does it for me. I want a woman who can stand up to me. I want something to break and reshape to suit me.

I crave the violence of it as much as I crave Ness. I lose myself to these thoughts for a minute, then realize that Raf is staring at me. I follow his eyes and realize I've got my hand down my pants, gripping my cock. Shit. I wink at him like it was intentional and glance at Ness to make sure she didn't notice.

Satisfied that she's engrossed in her new mission, I stand and stretch. Nodding to Raf, I walk into the kitchen and wait for him to follow. "I want you to go grab our guy. Tell him we have a special mission for him, and take him to the dungeons. Make sure he gets an empty room. I don't want him to even have a bed, or any weapons if he figures out what's happening."

"What about Ness?" he asks, clearly irritated that I'm sending him away.

"I'll stay with her until the list is done. Then I'll lock the apartment and the floor down so that only our keys work. No one else will have access, and I'll only leave her alone long enough to get the supplies. Besides, you can come back after he's secure." I can tell from his face that this appeases him.

"Okay, I'll be back." He rushes from the room and I hear him talking to Ness. "I'm going to get your guest of honor set up, okay? I'll be back up in a little while."

"Is Jarek going with you?" I wonder what she's going to say when he tells her that I'm staying.

"He's gonna wait for your list, then go get supplies. So, you'll be alone for a little while. But don't worry. He and I have the only keys to your apartment and this floor. No one else can get up here."

"Good. I have a few things to discuss with him. I'll see you later." She dismisses him like she's the alpha and he's her submissive. But he doesn't argue, instead, he heads out, waving to me as he walks out the door.

I walk back to the living room and drop into the chair I've used since lunch. I'll give her a minute to let me know she has something to say before I bring it up myself. "Oh, you're back. Did you have a nice, private chat with Raf?" She glares at me with her words.

"I did. I had to get him moving on your plan. Unless you've changed your mind?" I tease. I know she hasn't and won't. She wants revenge more than she wants to breathe right now. I'm too familiar with that feeling.

"He said you're going to get what I've written on the list. So, am I stuck in this apartment while you're gone? Or are you going to actually let me have a tiny bit of that freedom you keep promising?" She's baiting me, and I know it, but I have to give her some resistance. I can't let her know that I'm fighting feelings for her.

"I was planning to lock you in the apartment. Did you have something else in mind?" I'm anticipating her words as she considers them.

"I want to be able to go anywhere on this floor, since you can lock it up where only you and Raf can come in. And before you argue, it shouldn't matter if you guys aren't hiding anything. I'm tired of staring at these walls already. I want to walk around and trick myself into thinking I have a choice here." Ness almost looks like she's going to cry. I can't let myself think about that. Her tears have the ability to bring me to my knees and I know it.

"So, you want to be able to snoop through my apartment and Raf's? Why? Planning to grab some weapons?" I can't help prodding her. I don't know why she's so intent on nosing through our private spaces.

"I just need to explore. I'm going crazy here. Unless you'd rather I start tearing the place apart because I'm bored?" She bats her eyes at me. Damn, she knows that she's got me.

"You're gonna be the death of me." I shake my head and close my eyes for a minute. All of my weapons are locked up with a fingerprint scanner. I know she can't get into them. But Raf's? That's a totally different story. He's got things on display, and who knows what tucked away in hidey holes throughout his apartment.

"Is that what you're scared of? That I'll kill you in your sleep if you give me any freedom?" She laughs at the thought.

It's not exactly what I'm worried about, but probably better to let her think that than to tell her the truth. "What if I am? If you manage to find weapons, are you really telling me you wouldn't use them to get away from us?"

VANESSA

"Of course, not. I have nowhere to go, as you keep reminding me. What good would it do to kill you? It seems to me that you're the only thing standing between me and your men, who made it very clear what they think an omega is good for."

I didn't want to tell Jarek how disrespectful his men were. I'm just sick of everyone treating me like I'm a walking baby factory. There is more to me than that and I will do whatever it takes to prove it. Even if that means killing a man who terrifies me more than Jarek ever could. The things that guy told his friend that he wanted to do to me while he hit me—I can't even think about it.

So, I'll put on a brave face and torture the man before I end him. I'll let them all know that I can't be treated that way. I won't rely on a man to do it for me. Even though I'm sure Raf or even Jarek would. They both went a bit feral when I told them about who'd actually been the one to hit me. Jarek's reaction tells me that the man lied to him. The fact that he lied to Jarek tells me that there is no shred of decency in him.

"More than just those two idiots? Because I'll take care of that. No one will ever talk to you that way again. If they do, they'll deal with me. That's a promise, doll." There's more tenderness in Jarek's voice than I expect, and it nearly knocks down my walls. A single tear slides down my cheek and he catches it.

I can't speak, so I hand him the list and turn away. I refuse to cry in front of him. "I'll lock the floor down and make sure you can get into our apartments. I'm not opening the empty ones, though. There's nothing in them. Raf and I will be back as soon as we can. Be ready." He speaks softer than I've ever heard him. Is he going to be tender with me now? That will be extremely awkward.

I wait a while after he leaves before I go exploring. I don't want him to know that I'm mentally mapping the place. I may not have anywhere to go, but that's not going to stop me from trying. I'm also feeling extra needy and emotional right now, so I definitely want to check out their rooms and see if I can find something to calm me down.

I head across the hall to Raf's apartment first. After spending time with him at my father's compound, I have an idea of what to expect when I open the door. Jarek is more of a mystery. The living area looks sparse, with just a couch, side table and huge TV. The kitchen is cleaner than I had expected, but it doesn't look like he eats here much. I bet they both have more takeout than they'd want to admit. It isn't like they have a woman around to cook for them. Or did they? I have no idea what kind of arrangements they had before I got here or even still have now.

Shit, here I am acting like they're mine. What the fuck is wrong with me? It has to be my heat. What day is it? I have absolutely no idea. But maybe Raf is right. My heat is coming whether I want it to or not. The thought freaks me out for a minute, and I find myself crawling into Raf's bed, snuggling in with his scent surrounding me. And it calms me down more than I want to admit. At least they're not here to see this.

I'm so focused on his scent that I don't pay much attention to the bedroom furnishings or décor. I just curl up in his bed and let his scent calm me. I hate being so emotional. I can't stop the tears that start to fall. Why do I feel so weak? What is it about these men that has me so hooked that I completely forgot I was looking for a way out?

I can't help but cry myself to sleep in Raf's bed, curling around his pillow with his sheet and blanket wrapping me in a cocoon of his earthy pine scent. And that is exactly how he finds me when he returns from his errand. I hear Jarek and Raf yelling for me, as if I had somehow managed to run away.

They sound so far away, though, and I don't want to leave the comfort of my hiding place. I wait here until I hear him getting closer. He's in his apartment now, tearing through the place. Still yelling, but he sounds more scared than pissed. Is he worried about me? I try to call out for him, but my voice is nearly gone.

Raf slams the bedroom door open and rushes toward the bathroom, ignoring the bed. To be fair, it was a mess when I found it. "Raf?" I say softly.

"Yeah, Ness. What's up?" he asks absently, still searching. The bathroom, the closet, under the bed. Then our eyes meet and he stops. "Ness! We've been searching for you for almost half an hour! Is this where you've been hiding?" I can see the tears he's been holding back. He thought I was gone. And it hurt him. That's new information, and I don't know how to process it.

"I'm fine. I just got overwhelmed and your scent calmed me down. I guess I fell asleep. I'm sorry. I didn't mean to upset you. Or Jarek," I admit, even though it costs me. Jarek rushes in the room and kneels on the opposite side of the bed from Raf.

"Ness. Are you okay? What happened? Were you hiding from someone?" The words rush out of him, and I can hear the panic in his voice. They are both still terrified for me.

Chapter Six

AN ALPHA'S WILL

MILO

With two nearly lumberjack sized men stalking toward me, I don't have many options. I should have expected them to hate Jarek before I opened my big mouth. I've been trained better. I know to assess the situation first, then finalize my cover. I'm really fucked this time. "Can I ask you something before you get started?" I hear myself talking and try pointlessly to shut myself up. At this point, I'm a passenger on my own crazy train, being driven by the desire to live long enough to make sure Ness is safe.

Both men stop and stare at me. No one has ever done this during one of their "meetings". I can tell from their faces. "What?" the shorter one asks.

"I actually have two questions, if you don't mind. First, what are your names? It doesn't make sense to 'send a message' if the recipient doesn't know who it's from, ya know?" I pause and wait to see if they'll answer.

The blond one responds, "Not that it matters, but I'm Mateo and this is Jayron."

"What's your other question?" the dark-haired man, Jayron, asks.

"Are you gonna kill me, or just rough me up? I gotta know whether to pray or just let it happen." What the actual fuck am I doing? *Shut up, Milo! Stop talking right now. You're making it worse, asshole.*

"This guy is hilarious," Mateo says to Jayron before turning back to me. "You don't think dropping your corpse at Jarek's door will be enough of a message?" Shit. I need a backup plan here. How can I get them to at least cut me loose so I have a chance?

"You make a solid point. But hear me out...wouldn't it be more satisfying to be able to say you beat the shit out of one of Jarek's top guys in a fight? Or do you really want to do it while I'm tied up? That seems like a bitch move to me." I know I should shut up, but I can't.

Mateo's fist jerks my head sideways as it connects with my cheek. Fuck, that hurt. I writhe against the restraints. If I can get my hands free, I can at least block.

"Mat, he's got a point. It might be better if we untie him. Besides, there's two of us, and only one of him. There's no way he can get the drop on us." Oh, Jayron, you idiot. Of course, you'd be the one to fall for my prodding. Relief washes over me for a moment. I may survive this after all. Just as I relax, Mateo punches me again, this time in the gut. I double over with an oof.

"Fine, but I'm not taking any chances. I'm gonna rough him up a bit first. Nobody said torture had to be fair play." Fucking Mateo. What a dick. The thought runs through my head as his fists and feet continue to attack me.

He doesn't stop until I'm on the verge of passing out, and Jayron steps in. "Mat, that's enough. As it is, we'll have to wait to fight him because you beat him too much." I feel my eye swelling shut as blood drips from my lip onto the floor. I can hear the echo as it falls. My ribs are cracked—I know because I've been in fights before. Never where I'm tied to a chair and someone whales on me, but I've been hurt before.

I take mental stock of my injuries. This asshole even made sure to break my fingers so I can't make a fist. Fucker. I'll find a way to kill him. For now, I'll have to trust that I've gotten through to Jayron and they won't kill me if I pass out. It's not like I have a choice. I'm tied to a chair and Mateo beat me senseless. That's my last thought as the world goes dark.

I come to with Jayron standing over me, apparently tending to my wounds. "Hold still. I'm stitching these cuts. If you want a fighting chance, you'll let me finish."

"You coulda stopped him sooner," I pant. I expect him to hit me for it, but he doesn't.

"I could have, yeah. I also could have let him finish you off. But I didn't do either one, did I? Just shut up and hold still. We agreed to let you rest for a few hours before we beat the shit out of you again. That should be enough."

I wonder how he convinced his friend to give me time to recover some strength. I must look worse than I expect. If the work he's doing to my face is any indication, I'll have some pretty bad scarring by the time I find Ness. If I find her. No, I have to find her. I can't give up now.

After he's finished sewing me up, he brings me a sandwich and a drink. "I'm going to cut one hand loose so you can eat. No funny business though, or I'll kill you myself. Understood?" I nod at him and hold very still as he cuts the rope binding my left arm to the chair.

With my arm free, I stretch a little, groaning, and he eyes me suspiciously. "I'm not attacking, just needed to stretch a little. Let me eat and rest, then I'll fight." He nods and walks away, leaving me to it. I look around the room slowly, but there's still no way for me to get ahold of anything that will help me get free. I'm stuck here, and I'll have to fight my way out. For Ness.

An hour later, the door opens again, and both men step inside. This is it. My one chance to get out of here alive depends on me being able to beat these two up in a two on one fight. Can I do it? I sure hope so.

RAFAEL

Jarek and I get back to the floor at the same time. It was easier to find Luigi than I had hoped. That fucker wasn't expecting Jarek to come after him. His shocked expression when I tackled him and tossed him in that room was priceless. "You're back quick. Did you get him?" Jarek asks me. I grin in response.

"Of course, I did. He's such a dumbass that he thought he'd gotten away with it. He was just hanging out downstairs." We leave the elevator together, and the first thing I notice is Ness' door standing open. I rush down the hall before Jarek calls to me.

"I let her have the floor. She wanted to nose around in our spaces. I'm sure she's just enjoying not being locked in." His admission relaxes me a little. But if that's what happened, where is she? Wouldn't she run out to greet us? Unless she found something she didn't like.

"Something feels off about it. I don't know." I have a feeling that something is wrong, and I need to find her fast.

"You check her apartment and I'll start on mine, since those are the open doors. Don't freak out yet. I'm sure she's here somewhere." Jarek heads into his apartment, so I turn to hers. I start in the bedroom, but it's empty. After checking every room, I start calling out to her. She doesn't answer. I can't help panicking a bit. We took her to protect her and now she's disappeared.

"Ness! Come on, this isn't funny. Where are you?" I call out. I've searched everywhere in her apartment. I can hear Jarek calling to her as well. That means he's searched his as well. Maybe she's hiding in my apartment for some reason, trying to see how we'll react.

I stalk in carefully, just in case there are clues. If someone did break in and take her from us, I want to be able to find her. She needs us to protect her. I can tell that she's been here, because certain things have been moved, but only slightly. It looks like she picked things up to get a closer look, then put them back slightly off from where I had them. I know my mess, what can I say?

There's no sign of her hiding in the kitchen or living room, so I head to my bedroom. The bed is a mess, but I leave it that way on purpose. I search the bathroom, calling to her. She's not there. I dig through the closet to make sure she's not tucked behind something in there. Then I check under the bed. "Raf?" I can hear her in my head. I'm going crazy.

"Yeah, Ness. What's up?" I ask absently, still searching. The bathroom, the closet, under the bed. Then our eyes meet and I stop. "Ness! We've been searching for you for almost half an hour! Is this where you've been hiding?" I feel the tears I've been holding back. I thought she was gone. And it hurt. Why did it hurt so much?

"I'm fine. I just got overwhelmed and your scent calmed me down. I guess I fell asleep. I'm sorry. I didn't mean to upset you. Or Jarek," she admits. Jarek rushes in the room and kneels on the opposite side of the bed from me.

"Ness. Are you okay? What happened? Were you hiding from someone?" The words rush out of him, and I can hear the panic in his voice. He's as scared as I was. We should probably talk about this later when Ness is occupied. If he wants her as badly as I do, we might be able to work something out. Who knows? Maybe I'll actually get to be head alpha if we form a new pack.

"I'm fine, really. I was exploring and got overwhelmed. Damned omega sensibilities, I guess." She laughs it off, but the pain in her eyes is still there. I want desperately to kiss it away, but I know she won't allow that.

"Well, if you're good, we should get ready to handle your guest. He's waiting in a cell downstairs. I brought you a new outfit for the occasion." Jarek seriously went clothes shopping while he was picking up supplies? Who does that?

"I hope it's black to hide the blood," she says with a smirk. He nods and holds out a hand to help her from my bed. I follow them silently, watching how gentle he is with her. It's so unlike him. I want to say something, but I don't want to ruin it for her. This is way better than how hateful he was when we brought her here. Ness may be getting under his skin.

I wonder if she finally realized how close her heat is, and that's what set her off. I would ask, but she got really upset the last time I brought it up. I'll just have to stay close so I'm here when it happens.

I sit in the living room with Jarek while Ness goes into her bedroom to change. "What else did you bring her? That bag was full."

"Just some necessities. Make up, hair stuff, the usual." He shrugged it off like the gesture wasn't a big deal.

"So, she's getting to you, huh?" I smirk at my cousin. I know it'll bug the hell out of him. He swings at me and I jump out of the way.

"I do one nice thing and suddenly you've decided that I'm falling. That's ridiculous. She needed these things to feel better about herself, especially since she's going to face that bastard who beat her up. It doesn't mean I've gone soft." He growls the words at me and I know he's lying to us both. He's falling hard for our girl.

"We're going to have to have a talk about this before her heat, you know," I suggest.

"What do you mean?" he asks, glancing at the bedroom door to make sure Ness isn't walking into our conversation.

"If you want her too, that's fine. I don't care to share. But I want the chance to be head alpha for the pack we create," I insist.

"I'll never bow to you," he growls.

The door slams open and Ness stalks out. "Neither of you get to decide my fate. Who I bond with is *my* choice, not yours. Now, are we going to torture a man, or would you rather finish your pissing contest first?"

VANESSA

I storm out of the room, stopping at the elevator. I can't get any further without one of them and it pisses me off even more. I can't believe those assholes were discussing forming a pack with me without even asking me if it's what I want. I know that If I don't stay mad, I'll crumble, so I hold the anger as tightly as I can. I want to punch someone, but I don't want them to lock me away again. So, I'll take it all out on the man who used me as a punching bag while telling his friend all the depraved things he wanted to do to me.

Instead of focusing on my upcoming heat, I turn my attention to thoughts of what I'm going to do to the man downstairs. I plan to make him cry, worse than he did to me. And when I'm finished with everything, I'll take him right to the brink of death. Only then will I repeat the things he said about me. Only then will Jarek and Raf know why he has to die. And only then, will I slit his throat and watch his life fade.

I'm a little shocked at myself to be honest. I didn't expect to *want* to torture and murder someone. Maybe Daddy was wrong about me when he said I don't have what it takes to be his heir. Perhaps when I finally escape, I'll be able to toss this in his face.

But, do I really *want* to escape? I don't know. I mean, I feel like I'm finally getting through to Jarek, and Raf seems like he actually cares for me. Seriously, if I could get them to kidnap Milo, I'd be perfectly happy staying here with them. Of course, that would mean that they'd have to give me some freedom. And let the world know I'm still alive. I'm not sure they'll go for that.

Unless I convince them that it's the only way. I need to prove that I'm an asset and make them want to give in to what I ask for. I'll start with doing the thing my father thinks I'm too weak for. I hold my head high as Jarek and Raf join me at the elevator. We step inside, and neither of them says a word as we descend.

"Are you ready?" Jarek asks when the elevator stops. I nod as the doors open. Jarek walks in front of me and Raf walks behind. A few of their men line the corridor. Some of them start to whisper as we pass. Both men growl in different directions and the whispers stop. I can't help the smirk that crosses my lips in satisfaction. Maybe I should stay.

The door at the end of the hall swings open and we walk inside together. Jarek and Raf check the room out and inspect the chains holding my victim in place on the wall. His arms are chained above his head, and his feet are chained apart. He's pretty much spread eagle for me. Someone has stripped him down to a pair of ratty jeans.

I stroll over to the table beside him and run a hand across all the shiny tools laying out on it. Jarek got everything I asked for and then some. How sweet. He wants to please me. I let the thought bolster me for what I'm about to do. Because I find that I want to please him as well. Perhaps this can be a bridge to mutual understanding.

"I know how worthless omegas are in your opinion. Too bad I'm the one holding your life in my hands this time. I'm likely to be less kind than you were to me," I sneer at him with my words, speaking low to keep this conversation between us. "But don't worry, they don't know what you said to me. Yet." I smile sweetly and turn back toward Jarek and Raf.

"Are you boys sticking around?"

They both nod. Raf pulls over a chair, and Jarek leans against the wall with his arms crossed. It looks as if they're relaxing, but I can tell they're braced to intervene if needed. By the time I'm done with this asshole, they'll be begging me to let them kill him. And I'll deny them, because this is my right. I'll prove I'm strong enough to be their omega.

Woah. Did I really just think that? Is that what this is about? Perhaps I need to rethink things. Well, it's too late now to stop this, so I guess I'll think it through after. "Now that we know we have an audience, I'm gonna need you to scream extra loud for me, okay?" I smirk at him as I pick up a knife from the table.

His eyes open wide, and he starts to hyperventilate. I should be worried about scaring the poor beta to death, but I'm not. "Wait, you don't have to do this. I'll apologize. I'll do whatever you want. Please don't hurt me." He looks from me to his boss. "Stop her. I've been loyal to you. Please."

I press the blade to his throat. "I'm tired of listening to you whine. Instead, we're going to play a game. You're going to do exactly what I tell you to, and if you refuse, I'm going to cut you. Where and how deep will be up to you."

"Okay, okay. I'll play. Tell me what to do."

I turn to the two alphas watching. I can't stop my eyes from flitting to their cocks. I hope neither of them noticed. It's too dark in here to tell if they're aroused. Damn. I was hoping that watching me would turn them on. I guess I'll have to try harder.

I pull the knife away from the man's neck. "First, you're going to tell them what you did to me when you took me from the van to the holding cell."

He shakes his head violently. "No. I can't. I won't do that."

"I was hoping you'd say that." I laugh. "Where should the first cut be? I'll give you a choice. Which would you rather lose—a finger, or a toe?" I watch the fear play across his face.

He's not convinced that I'll actually do this. To be honest, I'm not either. But we're about to find out.

"What? That's crazy. Neither." He focuses past me again. "Please stop this. She's crazy."

I glance at Raf, then back at my prisoner. "What's your point?"

Then I look at Jarek. "I believe the lady asked you a question. You'd better answer it before one of us decides for you."

Oh, that's a great idea! If he doesn't choose, I'll let one of them decide. This game just got more interesting. My eyes light up with anticipation. I'd been concerned that I would chicken out and not be able to do this. Instead, I'm actually getting turned on by the idea of it.

"You heard the man. You can choose, or I can let them choose." I wait impatiently for him to consider his choices. "Fine, if you won't give me an answer, I'll let Jarek decide where the first cut should be." I turn back to the sexy alpha, who's staring at me intently.

"Start with a finger." His words send a chill down my spine. I lick my lips and turn back to the table full of implements. Even I know I can't cut off a finger with this knife. But...could I make him beg for me to cut it off if I started with this knife? Nah, I'll save that for later. I pick up a pair of pruning shears and turn back to my prisoner.

"I guess we're gonna start with a finger. Okay?" I'm shocked at the bubbly excitement in my voice. I hear Raf chuckle, but I don't turn. I can't get distracted here. I tighten my grip on the shears and grab Luigi's hand. He starts to fight me. "You sure you wanna do it the hard way?" I ask. He stops for a second and I use that pause to snip his pinky finger off his left hand.

Blood spurts and oozes from the stump. My eyes open wide and I realize just how much this is getting me going.

JAREK

Watching Ness torture this guy is seriously hot. I'm standing close enough that I can smell her arousal. Who would have thought the naïve little princess would be turned on by snipping off a man's finger? Not me, that's for sure.

"Now the toe," I say quietly, watching Ness' reaction while keeping an eye on the man who's chained up in front of her. He understands now where he fucked up, and I have no doubt he regrets his decision to lay hands on what's mine. But it's too late for him, and I have no sympathy.

Ness squeals with delight as she kneels down in front of him and grabs his right foot. She looks up at him and giggles again, then in one solid move, takes off not one, but two of his toes. "Omega." I use the word as a warning.

She drops the toes, stands up and places the shears on the table. Then she bounces over to me. His blood is smeared on her, but she doesn't care. She's enjoying this so much. "Yes, Alpha." She giggles again. It's the sweetest sound I've ever heard.

"I said one toe. Not two. You have to be careful. I know it's exciting because this is your first time, but you don't want to kill him too quickly, doll. Why don't we switch to the branding iron for a bit?" I nearly melt at how intently she's watching me, hanging on every single word. I brush my hand over her cheek, smearing the blood instead of wiping it away. She closes her eyes and purrs at my touch. Damn, resisting her is going to be harder than I realized.

"You look stunning with a man's blood on you," I whisper before gesturing for her to go back to work. She smiles at the compliment and bounces back to the table.

A look of concern furrows her brow. "Alpha?" she asks timidly, turning back to face me.

"Yes, Omega? What's wrong?" I stare directly at Luigi, who's crying about the lost digits and muttering apologies.

"I want him to tell you what he said about me to his friend. But I don't know how to make him do it." Her pout is adorable. She would be almost child-like if she weren't talking about torturing information out of a man. My dick stands at attention, harder than it was five minutes ago.

"Do you want us to help you get the information? Or do you want us to talk you through doing it yourself?" I offer. I don't want to step in, but I'll give her the choice. I'm not forcing her into anything.

"I want to do it. Will you or Raf talk me through it?" Her smile returns when I nod. What is this woman doing to me?

I walk over to guide her in the next part. She picks up the heated iron from the small furnace beside the table. "Let me show you where to poke him first. Put that back so it stays nice and hot, okay?"

Ness grumbles at me, but does as I request. I point out places she can jab him with the burning hot metal that won't instantly kill him. She seems satisfied with my suggestions and reaches for the rod again. This time I don't stop her. We're completely tuning out Luigi's cries and pleading. Right now, it's just Ness and me. Two souls bonding through torture.

"I'll give you a chance. If you tell them what you said about me, I'll kill you quickly. If you still won't talk, I'm going to make it hurt." My cock twitches at her threat, and I wait to see what he will do.

I turn to look at Raf, who's moved closer to get a better view. I'm certain he's as turned on as I am.

"I didn't say anything," he insists. Ness jabs the red-hot iron into his side, in the exact spot I showed her. The smell of burning flesh fills the air, mingling with her honeysuckle and rain. His screams are ecstasy. Her reaction to them is even better.

I watch her come undone with every poke. When I slip my hand over hers to take the iron from her, she jumps a little, then turns to look at me. "We have to give him a break. Remember, you're not trying to kill him yet. You want him to talk." I put the end of the metal back into the furnace to get it hot again.

Then I gently place my hand on Ness' back and guide her over to the chair Raf is sitting in. He stands and eases her into it before squatting next to her. "You're doing a great job, Ness." He brushes her hair off her face and kisses her cheek.

She turns her attention to him and smiles. "I didn't know how good this would feel. I wanna make him bleed again." I may have created a monster by letting her explore this. It's not like Raf or I care that our little omega is a little blood thirsty.

"I'm impressed, doll. I didn't think you'd be able to do it." She glares at me for a moment, then smiles.

"I know. Neither did I. So, how long does he need to rest before I can make him bleed? We already know he's not going to tell you."

I kneel next to her and take her hand. "What are you trying to get him to tell us? We already know that he was the one who beat you. What more is there? Did he sexually assault you?" I growl the words out, knowing that if she so much as nods her head, I'll walk over and rip his head from his shoulders with my bare hands.

She shakes her head. "No, but the things he said were nearly that bad. I want him to tell you. Then I want to end him." The fierceness in her is making me crazy. I want to tear him apart as badly as she does.

VANESSA

Jarek and Raf try to entertain me while we wait for Luigi to recover a little from what I've done to him so far. I ask a few questions about where I can stab him without killing him right away, and they explain everything clearly and concisely, as if I'd asked for the best way to get to the other end of the city. The whole situation is laughable, but I'm glad they're treating this like a learning experience instead of just leaving me to it.

If Jarek hadn't stopped me earlier, the man would be dead and I would have gotten zero satisfaction from it. I want him to suffer. I want him to regret every word he said about me that day. Those words are branded on my brain, just like all the marks I left on him with the iron.

I find myself soaking up their knowledge of torture. And wondering what having sex with the two of them together would be like. Would they agree to it? I picture the three of us tangled up together, covered in Luigi's blood. I know my pupils are blown with desire.

Raf says something, but I don't hear him. I'm lost in my fantasy. Jarek leans over, putting his face in front of mine. Without thinking, I jerk forward and press my lips to his, hard. His arms wrap around me, pulling me out of the chair as he stands up. I wind my legs around his waist and grip his shoulders, melting into the kiss. This is what I expected to happen earlier when I kissed him. This is what I crave.

He breaks contact way too quickly, turning my face to meet Raf's. His lips capture mine in a relentless explosion of emotion. Suddenly, I believe every word he said to me after we had sex the last time. He really does love me. How could I have not seen it?

The three of us belong together. I know there will be a lot to discuss after this, but I don't care. I lose myself in the emotions that swirl around me. But Raf pulls away too soon as well. I whimper, but Jarek shushes me.

"You have work to do, doll. Then we can play." As much as I want to argue, I know he's right. I have to finish this, or I'll never have peace. No amount of sex or love will make this pain go away. I need revenge. Or justice, depending on how you look at it.

I nod, and he sets me on my feet. I stalk back over to the man chained to the wall. He's awake now, and staring at me with fear. "Are you going to tell them what you said to your friend while you beat me? Or do you want me to slice you open slowly and watch you bleed?" I pick up a knife and touch it to his throat.

"Fine! I told Mario that omegas like you need to be put in their place. You have to be forced into submission with a strong hand. And that you, specifically, deserved to be beaten and raped daily until you knew who your master was."

I slice the knife down his chest as he screams. "That's not exactly what you said," I reprimand. A glance over my shoulder tells me that it was enough, though. Jarek and Raf are pissed and barely holding themselves back. They want me to finish this. So, I will. I stab the knife into Luigi over and over, his blood splashing me with every stroke. I laugh at his screams as he begs for his life. I sink the knife into his chest, burying it in his heart. Before he takes his last breath, I jerk it out and slide it across his throat, his blood spraying across me as he dies.

A strange thought hits me as his life drains away. I never even knew if Luigi was his real name, or just something they called him.

CHAPTER SEVEN

A REALLY BAD DAY

JAREK

When our prisoner finally starts talking, it takes everything I have not to rush over and tear his head off his body. How dare he say those things about Ness. I will not stand for that kind of disrespect inside my organization. Especially not directed at my woman. If she wasn't killing him right now, I would. Wait, am I thinking about her as mine?

There's no way she's really attracted to me. I can come up with so many reasons why it would never work out. Maybe she doesn't really care about me being older after all. We might have to sit down and have a serious talk about all of this before her heat hits.

Ness turns back to face us once the deed is done. The man hanging from the wall behind her is limp and lifeless. For a moment, I think she's going to break from the weight of what she's done. I can see the shadow of guilt across her face. Our eyes meet and it disappears. She just killed a man, and feels no remorse for it. This woman is amazing.

I want to ask her why her father wants her dead, but I understand that might hurt her. I push the thought away in favor of something less morbid. "Come here, Omega." I wonder if it annoys her that I call her doll or Omega instead of her name. She walks to me slowly, as if she knows that she's about to get into trouble.

Ness stops in front of me, just out of reach. She bows her head and replies quietly, "Yes, Alpha." It hurts my heart to hear the defeat in her tone. I didn't even use a command on her, and she sounds broken.

"Do you think you're in trouble, Omega?" I step forward to see if she backs away. Ness doesn't move.

"Yes, Alpha." Shit. This isn't what I wanted.

"Why are you in trouble?" I ask the question gently and wait while she fidgets before answering.

"Because I didn't tell you earlier what he said about me, and you're angry that you didn't get to kill him for it." Her simple words melt my heart. All of my doubts fade and I know I'm standing in front of the only omega I will ever claim again. Now I just have to convince her.

"Do you think you should be in trouble for that?" I glance at Raf and can see that he's struggling not to pull her into his arms, the same as I am.

"Yes, Alpha. I should have told you. But I was scared and didn't know if you actually cared about me." I lift her chin with my index finger, forcing her to look at me. The tears in her eyes are my undoing.

I tilt her head back a little more, then I lean down and press my lips to hers. The kiss is sweet and quick, with no heat. This isn't the time for passion. Tenderness is what she needs. "My sweet Omega, I'm sorry I made you feel like you were in trouble. Yes, I am upset that you didn't trust me enough to tell me about this. But I'm so proud of you for fighting your monster."

She smiles through her tears. I press my palm to her cheek and she nuzzles against it. Then she turns to face Raf, who is patiently waiting for her attention. "Are you angry with me too?"

Raf grins at her. "I'm pissed as hell—not at you, but you already killed the bastard, so there's nothing I can do about it. Come here and let me kiss you." He holds a hand out to her and she lets him pull her into his arms.

Ness glances at me to see if I'm okay with it. She wants us both, but isn't sure how we feel about sharing. I can understand that. After all, we were fighting earlier about how I'd never bow to Raf. I nod to her and she faces him again. I watch as he kisses her tenderly, taking a cue from me. Good. Maybe I'll get him to submit after all. Because I will not bow to my baby cousin. It won't happen.

When she pulls away from him, I take control of the situation. "I know everyone is excited about our afternoon entertainment. But I think we need to discuss a few things before we get carried away. There's no point in giving in to our desires if we can't agree on how things will work in the future."

"Okay," Ness agrees easily. It's strange, because she's normally arguing with everything I say.

Raf cocks an eyebrow at me. "You're suggesting we talk instead of fuck? Really?"

"Yes, I am. This is bigger than sex. This is potential bonding. We need to get it right."

MILO

Jayron cuts the ropes that bind me to the chair. I know that I should attack, but I wait. He steps back and gives me some room. I carefully push out of the chair, stretching and working out kinks in my muscles. It's been a while since I fought, especially against two men.

I roll my neck and pop my fingers. With more than half of them broken, it hurts, but I can't let that stop me. I close my eyes for a second to mentally prepare for the pain that I know is coming. When I can't stall anymore, I put my fists up and nod. "Okay, I'm ready. Thanks for giving me a sporting chance."

The two men stalk toward me, hate in their eyes. Good. The angrier they are, the more likely they are to make mistakes. I can use those in my favor. I'll take any distractions at this point to give myself a level playing field.

Mateo swings first and I barely duck in time. If I can get them angled just right, I think I can get them to hit each other. I work on getting them maneuvered around with some half-hearted punches and kicks. They don't seem to catch what I'm doing, and fall into place perfectly.

I dodge a few more punches, before taking one to the kidney. The pain nearly brings me to my knees. But I have to keep moving them into position. I don't have time for pain right now. Ness needs me and I have to get away from here so I can find her.

I step closer to Jayron, and sure enough, Mateo follows, blocking me in. I watch as Mateo draws back his fist, then turn to see Jayron doing the same. They plan to hit me at the same time. It's a good idea, but I've trained for this. I wait until both start swinging forward and drop to the floor. Rolling out of the way, I watch as their fists connect with each other's faces. I can't help but chuckle. Then I jump up and grab a knife from the table next to my chair, keeping it behind me so they can't see it.

"You fucker. I'm gonna kill you." Mateo races toward me, and I let him tackle me, shifting the knife in front of me just in time to sink it into his chest. I fall back, letting Jayron think that his friend has me pinned. I shift his weight, groaning as if I'm fighting him, while I slide the knife from his heart.

Mateo is a big guy, but I let him fall on me in a way that I could flip him off when Jayron got close enough. I bide my time, waiting patiently for the other man to check things out.

I hear him walking over, but wait until I can see him to shove Mateo off me and jump to my feet, sliding the knife across Jayron's throat in one fluid motion. He falls to the floor with a pool of blood under him.

I wait a few minutes before I leave, just to make sure they're both dead. I grab my jacket and everything that was in the pockets before they went through it. I even keep the knife I just used on the two men. You never know when you'll need another weapon. I holster my gun and slide Jayron's gun into the inside pocket of my jacket.

Then I look through their pockets, taking their cash and anything else that might help me. I'll count it later and see exactly what I end up with. I find a cell phone and scroll through the contacts. Jarek's number is right here. I pocket the phone, not worrying that it'll be traced. These guys are probably using burners too.

Now to find out where Jarek's hideout really is. One of these dicks said where it was earlier, but I don't remember. I stumble out the door and into a hallway. I have to be careful that I don't get caught again. I'm not sure I'll be as lucky a second time. I head out the emergency door at the end of the stairwell, sounding the fire alarm as I go. That should buy me some cover, and then whoever is in charge here will have to talk to the fire department about it as well.

The distraction works, and I manage to get out of the building safely. I have an idea, and I figure it can't hurt to try. Worst case, they'll realize someone has one of those bozos' phone. I pick a number at random and dial it.

"Yeah, J, what you need?" the voice answers.

"Boss wants you to pick up one of Jarek's guys and take him back where he belongs. You know how to get there?" I try to sound as much like him as I can, coughing to cover up anything that might give me away.

"Yeah, J, the hideout on Seventh Street, right?" Could it be that easy?

"If that's where Jarek is, then yeah. That's what I said, isn't it?" I try to play the tough guy, even though I'm not sure how Jayron would have talked to this man.

"Where do I need to pick him up?" Then I realize how stupid this plan is. I can't let one of D'Angelo's guys see my face. I disconnect the call and drop the phone into a dumpster as I hobble toward Seventh Street, and hopefully, my next ally. I keep to the alleys as much as I can, then duck into a convenience store to clean up a little.

The clerk looks at me funny, but doesn't ask what happened, probably because of what part of the city we're in. It doesn't matter why, I'm just glad the kid doesn't seem too concerned. I don't want him calling the cops. I'd rather get this all done before anyone knows I've been here. I get the key to the bathroom and clean up the best I can. On my way out, I grab a soda and a candy bar.

VANESSA

Jarek and Raf escort me back to our apartments, leaving my victim to be cleaned up by someone else. My mind is racing as the elevator climbs. I can't say for sure, but it feels like both of them have made their intentions pretty clear. I don't know if I'm excited or terrified at the thought of being their omega. It looks like I'll have to make a decision soon. Will I stay and bond with them, or will I try to follow through on my original plan and run? I honestly don't know. I'm too quiet on the ride, and Raf pulls me into his arms again. He's not pushing for anything, just holding me. I don't want to admit how much I like the way it feels. His scent, fresh and earthy, surrounds me.

Jarek reacts to my rain-soaked honeysuckle scent, mixing his whiskey and cedar with it. The three scents mingling triggers me in the best way. I'm covered in blood and my panties are soaked. I want nothing more than to fuck these two alphas in this elevator, but I know it's not happening. Jarek was clear. He wants to talk first. I'm willing to hear him out. Besides, maybe if we come to an understanding, I'll be able to get them out of their pants.

What the fuck is wrong with me? I just killed a man for disrespecting me, and now I'm scheming to get two alphas into my bed. I'm even considering bonding with them. All while I'm covered in a dead man's blood. I'm shocked that I'm not disgusted by the idea. While he was pretending to be one of my father's henchmen, Raf told me that he had a list of all the dirty things he wanted to do to me. Now I find my self wondering what could possibly be on it.

The elevator stops on our floor, and Raf passes me to Jarek so he can step out first. I don't understand why he has to clear the floor before we can get out of the elevator. Are there really people working for Jarek who want to hurt him? Would they even stand a chance? I doubt it. He can be practically feral, and his moods seem to turn on a dime.

I'm surprised with how comfortable I am in his arms, especially after how cold and blunt he's been with me for the past couple of weeks. Has it been weeks already since they faked my death? Wow, I've lost track of what day it is. I wonder how Milo is, and suddenly my mood goes sour. I miss him. That doesn't mean I'm not looking forward to this talk with Jarek and Raf about possibly forming a pack, it just means that I'll never feel whole until Milo is back at my side.

Jarek must notice the change in me, because he pulls me closer and kisses the top of my head. Raf nods to him, indicating that it's safe. Jarek scoops me up and carries me. I'm expecting us to enter my apartment, but he takes me into his instead. Oh, good. I didn't get a chance to explore here yet. I perk up when he sets me on the couch. "I'm a mess! I'll ruin your couch." But it's too late, he's already carefully placed me on the pale amber material.

"It'll clean up. And if not, I'll buy another. This is more important than that." I relax a little at his insistence. Maybe he's right. My heat is coming soon, and I don't want to go through it alone. I'm sick of feeling so empty. If I'm being honest, I'll admit that even when I had relationships with Milo and Raf, I still felt that something was missing. Could that have been Jarek? Was this gruff, salt-and-pepper haired man the answer to my loneliness?

Raf brings me a drink, but doesn't sit next to me. I can't stop my pout at the fact that neither of them sits close enough to touch. "It's for the best, Ness. We need space so that we'll actually talk."

"Fine," I say with a sigh. "Then talk. What exactly is it that you think we need to discuss?" I play dumb, and poorly. I just want to hear them say the words. I want them to tell me how much they want me. The thought of those words send a shiver through my core. Both men groan, and I know that I've perfumed again. Damn.

"Okay, let's get through this as quickly as possible, since our girl can't seem to wait for her reward," Jarek begins. My pussy pulses at the thought of what my reward might be. He takes a deep breath in, smelling my arousal, then continues. "We should start by declaring our intentions and asking Ness what she wants."

He turns to Raf, who immediately drops to his knees in front of me. "Ness, you know that I love you. All I want is the chance to be with you. To take care of you. To claim you as my omega."

I lick my lips and turn to Jarek, wondering if he'll tell me that he wants me or if he'll make it sound like he's doing me a favor. I wipe a tear from the corner of my eye as Raf returns to his seat across the room.

Jarek takes his place at my feet, pulling my hands into his. "Omega, you test me to no end. You try my patience and make me want to spank you constantly. You're frustrating and difficult."

I wonder where this is going, because it doesn't sound like he wants to bond with me at all. "Oh," I start before he holds up a hand to stop me.

"You're also gorgeous and smell delicious. All of that is why I want to make you mine. I want to claim you, to mark you as mine. Then I want to scream from the rooftops that you're mine and dare the world to do something about it."

"What? That makes no sense. You want me because I'm infuriating?" I scoff at his words. I suspect that with him, I'll never get poetry. I wonder if I can be okay with that. Even with my mock disapproval, I know the answer. He admitted that he wants me, and that's enough.

"I can't give you sweet words like Raf. I'm not that guy. If you don't want me because of that or how much older I am, I understand. I won't hold it against either of you." He sounds so defeated. I expect him to be cocky, not vulnerable. And I don't expect him to give up so easily.

I lean forward and put my hands on either side of his face. "Jarek, my beautiful beast. Please don't sell yourself short. Your age doesn't matter to me. I'm not as shallow as you think. And I don't care if you give me sweet words. I just want you to be honest with me about your feelings. This is the closest we've come to that since we met." I press my lips to his gently, and he comes undone. Jarek pulls me into his arms and I wrap my legs around his waist. He deepens the kiss, and our tongues tangle. He tastes as amazing as he smells.

RAFAEL

I watch in amazement as Ness shows Jarek the tenderness he can't seem to give anyone. I wonder if this is going to work out or if it'll just be a huge mess. There's a reason he's never been bonded—he came close once, but we don't talk about that. People call him a beast, and rightly so. He can't be tamed, not even by Ness. She doesn't seem to mind, though. I can't take my eyes off them as they pour their hearts into that kiss.

Jarek's phone vibrates on the table, but he doesn't make a move to check it. He's too wrapped up in our girl. And now I'm certain that she's ours. Everything else is just details. She's claiming us as much as we're claiming her. When his phone stops vibrating, I jump at mine starting. This has to be bad, if whoever was calling him is calling me now.

"This is Raf," I answer, turning away from Ness and Jarek. I can't focus if I'm watching them.

"Jarek didn't answer," the panicked voice tells me.

"He's busy. What do you want?" I'm not trying to be gruff, but honestly, this guy is interrupting our moment.

"Our guys from Twelfth Street got jumped. It's bad. We need backup."

Fuck. Twelfth is our best squad. If someone got the jump on them, it's really bad. "We'll be there as soon as we can. I'm getting Jarek now." I hang up the phone and turn to see both Jarek and Ness staring at me.

"Twelfth is in trouble. We need to go. Now." I cross the room, stopping to press a quick kiss to Ness' cheek before I walk out. I need to get my weapons from my apartment. I hear him telling her that everything is okay, but she'll have to stay here without us for a bit.

I'm sure she's not happy about it, but it's part of this life. We're not bankers, and we don't get weekends off. The people who attacked our guys don't care that it's Saturday and we're spending time with our girl.

I tear through my weapons stash. Three knives, two guns, extra clips of ammo. What else? Shit, I'm usually the calm one. Ness has me all messed up inside. I know what was about to happen, and now we'll be set back again. She may not decide to bond with us after all. No, I can't think like that. I shake my head to clear my thoughts.

I hear Jarek stomp up behind me. "How bad is it?"

"The kid said it was bad. I'm not sure which one he was. Hector's little cousin, maybe. I know the voice, just can't connect the name. He sounded scared."

Jarek rubs his hands over his face, then starts grabbing weapons from my stash. Between the two of us, we have enough for six men. But if it's as bad as I expect, we'll need it. He pulls out his phone and sends a text. "Backup."

I understand what he means, and nod. "That's a good idea. Who could have surprised Twelfth? They're the best we have."

He shakes his head. "I don't know, but we need to get moving. I don't want to leave Ness alone any longer than we have to. We were just getting somewhere."

"Agreed. Let's move."

We head down the elevator, leaving Ness in Jarek's apartment. "Aren't you worried that she'll try to escape?" I can't stop myself from asking. "I know we all just talked about forming a pack, but what if that was just an act?" I hate doubting her, but I also know how angry and vindictive she can be.

"How would she get out? We're the only ones who have access to that floor. No one can get in or out without one of us. There's nothing to worry about except for her getting lonely and being pissed that we were gone too long." He explains as if he's not concerned at all with the possibility that Ness could be playing us.

"Okay, I hope you're right. I love her, but I'm not sure if she can be trusted. I witnessed her dark side before today, and it's kinda scary." I admit that, knowing I'm opening myself up to ridicule for being scared of an omega who's half my size.

Jarek smirks. "I should have known that's how she has you wrapped around her little finger already. Here I thought her pussy was that good."

VANESSA

That phone call messes up my entire day. I was riding the high of torture and murder, looking forward to claiming my men. Then they just leave. I understand why they have to go, but I don't have to like it. I want them here with me. Of course, Jarek just had to order me to stay put. As if I was planning to run away. Where would I even go? We were finally getting along. Fuck.

After they leave, I pout and stomp my feet for a minute. Then I realize why this is bothering me so much. They're out there, without me. More specifically, without my mark, showing the world that they're mine. Any other omega could try to claim them, and there would be nothing I could do about it. Do I honestly believe either of them would let another omega claim them? No, but that's not the point. They're mine.

Shit, am I already falling in love with them? How was this happening so fast? I mean, I've known Raf for over a year, so that's not completely shocking. But Jarek...I've only known him for a couple of weeks. Of course, his reputation precedes him, so I know tons of things about him. I wonder if any of it is actually true. I hope I have the chance to find out.

Tears spill down my cheeks before I realize I'm crying. I'm scared that something will happen to them. As if on autopilot, I find myself digging through Jarek's laundry, sniffing shirts and choosing which ones to take. I do the same in Raf's apartment, taking my treasures back to my apartment and hiding them in my closet, where I cuddle up and wait for my men to come back.

While I'm laying in my closet, breathing in the scents of Raf and Jarek, I realize that something is missing. Milo. I'm dying to call him and let him know that I'm okay. And that I miss him. But I know Jarek will never allow that.

I asked once about calling my mother to let her know that I was okay, and he had a fit. "It's not safe. You can never call anyone from your past." He growled the response and locked me in my apartment for a full day. Just when I'd thought we were getting somewhere, we jumped back a few steps. It drives me crazy when he's like that.

But maybe he really is just trying to protect me. I don't know why that extends to my family, though. They can't be the ones who are after me, can they? That thought sticks in my head for some reason. I feel like I heard something odd before I was kidnapped. What was it?

I think back to the night I was taken. Raf and I were waiting for Milo to arrive. We'd planned a dinner date, and of course, my father insisted that Raf go everywhere I went.

I sniff his shirt again, letting the scent take me back to the memory. I went to get my coat, and heard Alan talking to Father behind closed doors. "I need it taken care of tonight. No loose ends. Understood?" My father's voice was cold and harsh.

Something about Alan's response had stuck with me. "Are you sure, Sir? She's your daughter."

"She's ruined and worthless. I can't even sell her anymore. And she's no good to me if she can't make money."

I remember running down the hall to Raf, and telling him what I'd heard. It had scared me, but he handled it calmly. He told me to call Milo and tell him to meet us at the restaurant. Then he put me in the car while he made a call. I couldn't hear his conversation, but it must have been to Jarek. Holy shit. Raf and Jarek had saved my life. How did I not know that my father was trying to kill me?

What had he meant when he'd said I was ruined and worthless? I mean, I wasn't a virgin, but most omegas my age aren't. Was he angry because I'd wanted to be with Milo? Or because I'd been flirting with Raf?

I can feel myself sinking into the grip of panic. I know that I'm safe here. I've known it all along, even when that dirty plumber-looking guy had beat me up. Part of me knew that Raf or Jarek would take care of it. Instead, they gave me the chance to do it myself. That means something. I have to hold onto that.

I take deep breaths, holding Jarek and Raf's shirts up to my face to calm myself. When that doesn't work, I leave the comfort of my soon-to-be nest and head back to Jarek's apartment in search of a phone. Maybe I can call or text them and one of them will come back.

I know it's pointless. Neither of them would leave their phone behind. I would have to talk to them about giving me a phone. It's not like I would call anyone at this point. I have no way to know who else was involved in my father's plan. I'm on the verge of hyperventilating as I dig through drawers and search shelves in Jarek's place. I need to find a way to contact him.

Fuck. I can't find anything in his apartment. I realize I should clean up, but I just can't right now. I have to find a way to get them to come back to me. Figuring out who's out to get me messes with my head and I can't deal with it alone.

With little hope of finding anything, I head to Raf's apartment and start searching there. How do these men survive without computers or phones? I know they each have a cell, but that does me no good right now.

I stop, holding the drawer I just dumped on the floor. I have to breathe. Then I have to think carefully about this. They wouldn't just leave a computer out in the open. Not with the idea that they can't trust me. Where would they hide it?

Chapter Eight

FINDING NESS

MILO

After cleaning up, I work my way toward the location I'd been given. This would have been easier if I'd convinced the guy to give me a ride, but I can't risk any of Jarek's men realizing who I am before I have a chance to pitch my idea to him. If he refuses to help me, I'll be back to square one. But I will find Ness, and I will protect her from her father. Or I'll die trying.

I stop short when I hear conversation coming closer. Two guys just exited a building talking quietly. Wait, is that Jarek? And what is Ness' guard doing with him? Shit. There's more to this story than I thought. Maybe walking up to him on the street is not the best option...especially when he looks pissed. I watch as they climb into a sports car and race off.

Now I just have to get into the building and wait for Jarek to return. That should be easy, right? Fuck. How did my life turn into this mess? All I wanted was to be with Ness. And since I'm sure she wants to be with me, there shouldn't be an issue. If only I hadn't asked her father for permission to marry her, maybe none of this would be happening. I hope when I find her that she'll forgive me.

Before I can worry about that, I have to find her. And to do that, I need Jarek's help. So, back to the task at hand. How do I sneak inside? I watch the building from the alley for a while, hiding in the shadows. Then I cross the street and stake things out from there. Hours later, they still haven't returned. When I see four guys leaving, I know this is my chance. Once they turn the corner, I jog across the street. I've played out different scenarios in my head, and decide that best option is to act like I belong here. The only way that won't work is if someone recognizes me.

I'm hoping for the best as I enter the building. From the lobby, it looks like a standard apartment building. Now I just have to figure out where Jarek will go when he comes back. I duck into a storage closet when I hear footsteps.

"Just make sure you have the food delivery ready exactly on time. I know it's crazy, but no one else has access to the boss' floor. He or Raf will pick it up. All I know is he said to have it ready at six. It's not like you won't get paid if they don't show."

Hmm…no one else has access to the boss' floor. Interesting. So, he doesn't trust his guys with his property. That's good to know. But which floor is it? And how do I get there? The elevator is probably wired for sound and images so that's out. I step out of the closet, careful to keep an eye out for people and cameras.

I find the stairwell quickly, and notice the pattern of the cameras. They sweep a specific area in one direction, then back to their starting position. I time my move carefully, then dash through the door. I've watched long enough to realize that no one takes the stairs. I don't blame them. I'd rather do the elevator too. Okay, now I just have to figure out which floor I'm heading to. I glance around the stairwell, locating the camera. Fuck.

Luckily, I've had my hood pulled up the whole time, so I'm pretty sure they haven't got my face on camera yet. I just have to play it off like I belong here. Keeping my head down, I climb the stairs. It's easy to figure out which floor is Jarek's, since there's only one with a keycard access lock. I fumble a few times before I manage to crack it. I'm hoping there isn't a tamper alarm, since I don't have access to my usual Federal assistance.

It's too late to worry about that now. The door opens silently, and I realize that there have to be cameras on this floor too. Shit, I hope there isn't someone monitoring from nearby. I need to find a place to hide until Jarek gets back. I guess I'll find out soon if someone is watching.

I sneak down the hall, scanning for cameras. If there are any, they're very well hidden. I can't find them. As I walk, I check doors to see if any are unlocked. This floor has five doors, which makes me think the apartments are quite large. The first two doors are locked. I'll come back and pick them later if I need to. The next door I come to is ajar. That seems odd, so I instantly perk up. I have to be focused so I don't get surprised.

I ease the door open and peek in. I don't see anything, but I can hear someone rifling through cabinets and drawers. Have I stumbled upon a break in? I chuckle to myself. Well, if I've caught someone breaking into Jarek's apartment, maybe he'll be more likely to hear me out instead of killing me on sight.

Walking silently, I creep up on whoever is trashing the place. As soon as they're in my sights, I freeze. "Ness?" She jumps and turns around in a flash.

"Milo? What are you doing here?" She starts to rush into my arms, but stops suddenly. She moves behind the couch, like she's trying to put space between us. "Did my father send you?"

So, she already knows. I shake my head. "No, Ness. He's convinced that you're dead. I didn't believe it, so I had to find you. But I screwed up. He knows that I found evidence that you're alive. I was terrified that he was going to find you before I could."

Her expression changed from fear to relief.

VANESSA

The moment I see Milo, I know my life is over. Father must have sent him to kill me. But how did he see through Jarek's perfectly executed fake of my death? After Milo explains that my father has no idea he's here, and only suspects that I'm alive, I relax a little. I'm still in danger, just not from Milo

"So, you're really not here to kill me?" I ask, keeping the couch between us as I scan Raf's living room for a weapon. I don't want to mistrust Milo, but the timing of it seems odd. Jarek and Raf get called away and then Milo shows up? That sounds staged to me.

"Ness, my love, I would never. I've been searching for you ever since they found the body. I knew that wasn't you. I couldn't give up on you. Your father tried to convince me that you were gone, but I didn't believe it. But I found proof that he's the one who was out to get you. We can use it to take him down."

"Then what are you doing here? How did you find me?"

He looked at me sheepishly. "By accident. I came here to talk Jarek into helping me find you and take your father out. I had no idea you were here. Is he holding you hostage? Has he hurt you?" At this point, I'm sure he can see the fading bruises from the plumber wannabe.

"Not exactly, and no, Jarek has not hurt me. One of his men got handsy, but I took care of it. You're telling me that my father is still after me, even though everyone thinks I'm dead?" Fear creeps back in and I struggle to breathe. It's insane that my father, my own family, is the one who was out to hurt me the whole time. I can't believe that Raf and Jarek protected me. I didn't even know Jarek before this.

Milo stares at me with his jaw dropped. "What do you mean, 'not exactly'? You're not exactly a prisoner here?" I know he'll have trouble understanding, but I grin anyway.

"I mean, it's complicated. Jarek, Raf, and I…well, we've just started discussing forming a pack." I watch his face fall at my admission. "But now that you're here, you can join us. I've been wishing for you to find me for weeks now. I'm thrilled that you're here."

He continues to stare at me, dumbfounded. "Jarek could kill me when he returns. You know that, right? Especially since I used to work for your father. Fuck, I should not have come here." He turns as if to leave. I can't let him go.

I race around the sofa and launch myself at him, catching him off guard and knocking him to the floor. Once I have him pinned, I lay over him and press my lips to his. Milo squirms at first, trying to get away. I understand his reaction. Jarek is terrifying, and if he's claiming me, another man won't want to get in the way of that. But I want Milo too. And if Jarek can't accept that, we'll be through before we even get started.

I thread my fingers through Milo's hair and massage his scalp. He starts to relax and flips me over on my back. I let him take control and deepen the kiss. His growing erection presses into my core. As his lips and tongue assault mine, I let my hands wander across his body.

"Ness, we can't," he pants in my ear. I don't want to stop, but he sounds terrified. I push myself up on my elbows and look at him.

"What's the problem?" I ask, completely oblivious to what his problem is.

"I can't fuck you in Jarek's house. He'll kill me."

I can't stifle the laugh that bubbles up. "This isn't Jarek's apartment. This is Raf's." I push him off me, and he helps me to my feet.

"It's still another man's home. I can't. Especially if they've claimed you." What was it with these men only hearing part of what I tell them?

"We had a conversation. No one has claimed me. I understand that Jarek is a beast and everyone is scared of him, but come on, Milo." I tut my disappointment at him before I stroll away, heading back to my own apartment. I only realize he's following me when I catch his sea water scent surrounding me.

I'm getting tired of the run around, and wonder if Milo wants me at all. I turn to face him. "What do you want, Milo?"

"To protect you from your father," he responds quietly.

I shake my head. "No, Milo." I gesture between us. "What do you want?"

He takes a minute to think about what I'm asking. I leave him with his thoughts and grab a drink from the fridge before settling on the couch and picking up the novel I've been reading. If he wants to talk, I'm here. If not, I'll get lost in smut. A few minutes later, the couch dips as he sits beside me. I glance at him and raise an eyebrow, but don't speak.

"I want you, Ness. I've always wanted you. I just don't know how to fix this." His admission touches me. It's so unlike the possessive alpha I'm used to. When I spent time with him before, he was very much in charge and in control. It's strange to see this side of him. I wasn't sure if it was fear of Jarek, or of my father that made him hesitate.

I put the book face down on the table, open to the page I was reading. Then I turned to face Milo again. "I don't know how to deal with an uncertain alpha. I can fight back against demands, but this feels more like rejection. I know you said you want me, but you pushed me away."

MILO

I don't know how to react to Ness' statement. I want her more than I want to breathe, but I know I'm no match for Jarek and his army. "Come with me. Let's get out of here. I can take you away and protect you."

Ness raises an eyebrow at me. "No. You can stay if you want. But I'm not leaving here. It's not safe for me out there, and I want to see where things go with Raf and Jarek. Honestly, Milo, I want you to stay, but not if you're gonna be spineless and scared of Jarek. I deserve more than that."

When did Ness get so decisive and tough? What has she been through here? I wish we could go back to a month ago, when everything was good between us. I feel like I'm screwing it all up here, and don't know how to fix it.

"Babe, please. Give me a chance. Let me take you somewhere safe." At this point, I'm begging her, and I don't care. I just want to get out of here before Jarek comes back. I've already fought enough today. I don't need to go toe to toe with him right now.

"I told you, Milo. I'm not leaving. I'm staying here with Jarek and Raf. They'll protect me from my father. Maybe we'll even go after him first. I'm not the same innocent little girl I was a month ago. If you can't handle that, you should leave. I'm done playing games." Ness picks up her book and goes back to reading as if I'm no longer sitting beside her. What the fuck did these guys do to my girl?

"Vanessa, you have to listen to me. I'm not leaving without you. If that means Jarek kills me, then so be it. I can't give up what we had so easily. You want me to stay and fight for you, fine. I'll stay and fight. But give me something worth fighting for."

I see the tear slide down her cheek as she does her best to ignore me. I'm not giving up. Even if Raf and Jarek can keep her safe, she needs me. When I got here, she said she'd been hoping I would find her. There's a reason for that. And I'm sticking around until I find out what it is.

"Then stay. I won't beg, and I won't fight you if you decide to leave. It doesn't matter if you have all the pretty words for me, or if you love me. I deserve more. Can you handle that?" She doesn't even look at me as she speaks. My insides are Jell-O, jiggling around with the thought that she's going to dismiss me. How did we get from planning a wedding to this?

I bowed to her father, that's how. I was stupid and let Dragonetti take advantage of my desire to spend time with his daughter. I couldn't see it at the time, but I let him interfere and ruin our relationship, pushing her into our enemies' arms. Wait, is Jarek the enemy here?

Everything is too much, and I can't think straight. It may be the blows to the head earlier. The room is spinning and I lean my head back. I have to get through to her somehow. I need her to believe me that I'm here to protect her. I want her to trust me like she used to.

With my head resting on the couch, I speak to her without opening my eyes. "Ness? Do you think I'm still working for your father? Is that why you were scared when I found you?"

I can feel her shift on the sofa next to me. "I wasn't sure until you told me that my father had ordered a hit on me. If he had sent you to kill me, you wouldn't have told me. I don't understand what you're so afraid of, but I don't think you're here to hurt me. Not intentionally anyway." Her words sting, but I deserve it. I've been whiney and scared since I got here. I need to stop it. I have to prove to her that I can take care of her. I want a place at her side in whatever pack she chooses. If that means I have to play nice with Jarek and Raf, I guess that's what I'll do.

"How can I prove to you that I want to be with you? I understand that you don't want the words. But what can I do?" I hate the idea of begging her, but I can't stand losing her either. I know that I'll do whatever it takes to convince her that I'm the alpha for her.

"I gave you that chance, but you didn't want to disrespect Jarek, remember? Or have you already forgotten what just happened?" I know she's pissed at me, but I'm hoping she can sympathize with my situation.

"You just told me that you and Jarek were talking about bonding. How can I fuck you behind his back knowing that? Ness, I want you more than anything. But it's not worth ruining my relationship with a potential packmate. Surely you can see that." Trying to reason with her may be a mistake, but it's all I've got.

"Wait, you're serious. Are you planning on asking Jarek if you can stay? I still don't understand what you came here for."

I turn to look at her. "I plan to do whatever it takes to be with you and prove that I can take care of you. If that means asking Jarek to join his crew, I guess that's what I'll do." Part of me wants to tell her that her father threatened to kill me if I don't leave town, but I don't want to make things worse there. She just found out he was trying to kill her; I can't imagine how she'd react to learning he wants to kill me too.

She sighs and walks away. I don't move from the couch, because I can't figure out what I've done to piss her off this time. "Fuck." I lean my head back on the sofa again. My head is killing me. I have no idea how bad my injuries really are. I cleaned up at the convenience store, but can feel dampness seeping through my shirt again.

I stay like that until Ness returns a few minutes later. The pressure of her sinking onto my lap makes me jump. "Hold still. You're bleeding. Why didn't you tell me that you were hurt?"

"Well, I was more focused on finding you than what I had to do to get here," I admit with a wince. She grabs my jacket and pulls it off me before dragging my shirt over my head.

The moment my shirt is off, she sucks in a sharp breath. "Oh, Milo. This is bad. How did this happen?"

VANESSA

Milo's chest is a mess of black and blue, with cuts and scrapes, with two spots bandaged. He's bleeding from what appears to be a stab wound. I stare at him until he answers me.

"I got in a little fight. Or two," he says flippantly. Fucker. How can he be so calm when he's bleeding? And those bruises have got to hurt.

"Don't fuck with me, Milo. You'd better start talking. Before I get the wrong idea and have to go after my father myself." With what I've learned today about him, and the memories I recovered earlier, I wouldn't put it past my father to be behind this, especially if he thought Milo knew where I was hiding. That son of a bitch. I didn't even know I was hiding until earlier today.

It feels weird to know that I went from a kidnapping victim to a rescued mark in less than a day. I've spent all this time beating myself up about being attracted to my kidnappers, and in reality, I was only attracted to my heroes. Although I'm sure that Jarek and Raf would balk at that idea.

I shake the thought away and focus on Milo again. He still isn't talking. "Please tell me what happened. You know there's no judgement here." I grab the supplies I brought and start cleaning his wounds. I carefully peel the blood-soaked bandages off and nearly start to cry. How many times had he been stabbed? And yet he still fought his way back to me.

I'm not letting him go, no matter what Jarek says. But first, I have to fix him up and figure out exactly how to work all this out. I'm careful as I wipe the blood and grime from his wounds before gently placing clean bandages over and taping them down.

"I was looking for Jarek. I ended up in the wrong hideout, and got caught. Somehow, I convinced the two thugs who nabbed me that a fair fight was a more honorable way to die. So, after they beat the shit out of me, they turned me loose, and I managed to take them out."

His explanation is so matter-of-fact, as if he's telling me about a day at the office instead of about killing two men. Because I'm certain he had to kill them to escape. D'Angelo's men don't play around. "You took on two of D'Angelo's men and killed them? That is impressive."

Milo looks at me in shock. "You've changed, Ness. I like it. You're different than you were the last time we were together."

I nod my agreement. I know that I've changed, and I'm glad Milo is okay with it.

"I have. I don't need protection. I can handle myself." I hold up a hand to stop his protests. "That doesn't mean I won't let you big, strong men take care of me. It just means you have to respect the fact that I can take care of myself, too." I scoot off his lap and grab one of Jarek's shirts from my closet. I bring it to him, and Milo looks at me for a minute before pulling it over his head.

Can any of them really do that? Will they accept that I can take care of myself? Or will they fight each other for dominance and try to control me the way my father did? I won't let that happen again, no matter how badly I want to be with them. I can't give up.

Not if I want my freedom. And I'm sick of being used, so I will fight to be my own person. I need to be sure that I'm strong enough to fight. Maybe Jarek will train me if I ask. I know it'll be tough, but I need to be able to keep myself safe. I can't always depend on them to take care of it.

I notice that Milo is staring at me. "What?"

"You're concentrating on something really hard. I'm just wondering what's got you worried," he said softly. His tenderness surprises me, even though it's a very Milo thing. He never was an alphahole when we dated, so I'm not sure why I expect him to be now. I'm struggling with my emotions and he knows it.

"I'm just trying to figure out how to be tough enough to survive. I know that I'm getting there, but I don't think I'm there just yet. I'll probably need help." I hate admitting that, but if Milo is going to be one of my mates, he needs to know what he's getting himself into.

He takes my hand and strokes it gently. "Ness, I've got you. Whatever you need. And you'll see, Jarek and Raf will accept me, somehow."

"None of you are safe if my father is after me. Shit, that's what I was doing. I need to call Jarek or Raf and get them back here. They need to know what's going on. Give me your phone," I demand. I can feel the panic starting to race through me.

"I don't have one." He looks at me earnestly, then squeezes my hand. "There are things I need to tell you, but I don't want you to freak out about anything. Okay?"

Sure, because that didn't sound ominous at all, I think to myself. "Okay, I can try." It's the best I can give him. I can't promise not to panic, since I'm already panicking. I brace myself for whatever Milo has been hiding.

"I fucked up, Ness. I asked your father for favors while we were dating, and I've done things for him when he called those favors back in. He helped me get to where I was in the Bureau, but at a cost. I've destroyed evidence and hidden his involvement in things. But the last time I called him, I fucked up big time. I told him that I knew you were alive. That I had evidence. And now he's after me, too. If he finds us, we're dead.

That's why I was so intent on finding you." His grip on my hand tightens, and I wince.

He tries to pull away, but I hold him in place. "It wasn't that. I can't believe he would use you like that." I pause for a second, then continue. "This isn't your fault. How would you have known that he was an evil bastard? It's not like I knew it either until just before all of this happened." I kick myself mentally for not seeing it sooner. Of everyone who should know that the head of the Dragonetti crime family is a psychopath, his daughter tops the list. But I spent my life in the dark, far away from most of it.

"Ness, everyone knows he's crazy. I knew better than to get involved with him," Milo admits. I know why he did, and I love him for it.

"You only got involved with him because of me. We both know it, so don't bother trying to deny it. The day we met, you decided that you could bend your morals to spend more time with me. Even if I was supposed to be an informant." He looks at me, raising an eyebrow. "I'm not as naïve as you think. Just because I don't say anything, that doesn't mean I don't know anything. That was my father's biggest issue. He thought he was hiding things from me, when in reality, I know about all of it. I was just a little slow to realize that he was the one making attempts on my life."

Milo caresses my cheek with his hand. "I hate this. All of it. A father should protect his daughter, not try to kill her. I don't even know why he's after you. I'm the agent, I should be able to figure this stuff out. But I'm lost and it scares me."

A tear trails down my cheek. "Sweet Milo. He's after me because he realizes I have evidence that he's been framing D'Angelo's boys for things he's been doing. Well, I had evidence. Now I guess that's gone. Since I don't have my computer or access to any of my accounts. Fuck. I hate that he's winning this. I want to confront him, but that would nullify everything Jarek has done to keep me safe."

"Wait, what are you talking about? Are you saying that Jarek is behind your faked death? I thought maybe he saved you from your father's attempt." Milo looks confused. I completely understand. This is a complex situation, and I'm not sure I understand it all myself.

"Jarek and Raf kidnapped me. They faked my death and held me captive for a couple of weeks before we actually talked about what he's looking for. I'm still not sure exactly what it is. But Jarek is convinced that I know where it is. I just can't figure out what it is."

Milo grabs his jacket and pulls out a small leather-bound book. "Could it be this? I found this in your father's crack house—the manufacturing one." He hands me the book and I flip through it.

My eyes widen in surprise. This is the physical copy of everything I'd been collecting for the past two years. "Milo, I could kiss you!"

MILO

"I mean, who am I to deny your desires, love?" I can't help flirting with Ness, even as her eyes fill with tears. I hope they are tears of relief or even joy, but I don't dare ask.

She leans over and presses her lips to mine for a brief moment, and the world feels right. I need to hold onto this feeling for as long as I can. How will I convince Jarek and Raf to accept me as one of her packmates? I can't lose Ness again. I won't.

"So, what exactly is in that book? I didn't have a chance to really read through it." I should have taken the time to know what I was giving her, but I'd forgotten about the book until she started talking.

Ness smiles at me, and I no longer feel any of my pain. "It's his ledger; his record of every transaction his drug operation has done in the last two years. It looks like it even has his loan shark info in it. Who's borrowed money and who hasn't made their payments. Some of these people have come up missing recently, and I'm betting dear old dad had something to do with every one of them." Her smile is contagious, and I find my mood lightening.

"I'm glad to know it was worth what I went through to get it. I nearly died." I say it lightly, but I see the shadow cross her face as she considers my words. "Ness, baby, I'm fine. Honestly. There were moments when I didn't think I would be, but I am. I found you. That's all that matters."

I brush her tears away, and she leans into my arms, letting me hold her. It feels like coming home. I want nothing more than to stay like this forever, but I know we can't. We have to talk about other things.

"Ness, love, can we talk?" I ask gently, not wanting her to move from where her head lays on my chest.

"About what?" she responds hesitantly. I know she's not looking forward to this, but I have to know what she wants before I can plan what I'm going to do.

"Do you want me to be part of your pack?" There's no sense in beating around the bush, so I spit the question out. My hand trails gently up and down her arm while I wait for her response. I can feel her hesitation, and I worry that I've fucked this up more than I originally thought.

"Milo," she begins, sitting up and breaking our connection. This is it. Ness is going to tell me that she no longer wants me. I'm going to be broken, but I'll still protect her. No matter what, I'll keep Ness safe. Even if she doesn't want me.

I look away, unable to hide my disappointment. I don't want to change her mind with guilt. Instead, I focus on the corner, away from her face, and the rejection she's about to hand me.

Ness touches my face, trying to turn me toward her. I don't move at first, unable to fight the emotions that are racing through me. "Milo, look at me. Please," she requests gently. So, she wants to look me in the eye when she turns me down. Okay, I can do this.

I let her turn my face until it's inches from hers. "You don't have to say it. I understand. It's okay, you don't have to feel guilty about it. You can't help how you feel."

"Would you shut up already? I can't tell you how I feel because you've already decided that I'm rejecting you. When if you'd shut the fuck up for two seconds, you'd see that I'm not." She pauses to make sure I'm still paying attention. "I'm not rejecting you, Milo. I want you to be part of this pack. I'm just trying to figure out how to get Jarek to accept that. Raf is easy—he'll do whatever I ask. But Jarek is, well, he's older and somewhat set in his ways. He'll want to dominate you. Are you okay with that? I can't ask you to do that for me. It has to be your choice."

Fuck, I hadn't thought of that. Can I relent some of my alpha power if it means being with Ness? That's stupid. I've already done that with her dad. Of course, I can let Jarek be in control if that's what it takes.

"I would do anything for you. But I understand how this is a big thing. Giving up control to another alpha isn't easy for any of us. If we can convince him to accept me, I can bow to him. Especially if he has your best interest at heart." I search her face with my eyes. "Does this mean you'll accept me as part of the pack as long as he does?"

Ness nods. "I would accept you even if he didn't. I was wishing you'd show up, and then you did. I think we're connected, Milo. We're meant to be together. I just have a connection with Raf and even Jarek, too. I can't help it."

"I understand how omegas work, Ness. You have nothing to apologize for. It's in your nature to need more than one alpha. We can make this work. I can't say it'll be easy, especially since Jarek and I have been on opposite sides of the law for years. But I'm not an agent anymore, so it shouldn't be an issue."

"What? You quit? Why?" Ness looks shocked and confused.

"I actually got fired. For being, uh, too involved with your family. I'm pretty sure your father was behind that too," I admit.

Chapter Nine

DRAGONETTI, WHO?

VANESSA

Fuck. Of course, my father would get Milo fired the second he suggested I might be alive. That just seals the fact that daddy dearest is the one behind all of this. I know at some point I'm going to come up against him. He'll know that he didn't manage to take me out. I just hope that when that happens, I'm strong enough to win. With Milo, Jarek, and Raf at my side, I know I will be.

"I would apologize, but I know you'll say it's not my fault, even though it is. I can't get your job back for you. I can, and will, take him down. I promise you that." I'm shaking with fury as I make the vow. I won't let my father win.

Milo pulls me into his lap, wrapping his arms around me. "Breathe. This is not your responsibility." His fresh sea water scent surrounds me, calming my rage. "We can go after him together, but I do not want you to try on your own. Promise me that." He presses his lips to mine, not giving me a chance to respond. He knows I won't let this go.

"Now, give me the words. I want to hear you say it." He's pushing me to promise. I don't want to, because my family is my responsibility and I should be the one to take my father down. But I know that no matter how hard I insist or push, Milo will never let me do it alone. It's the only reason I agree.

"I promise I will not go after the big, evil bastard on my own. I'll bring my three even bigger, stronger men with me. But I will take him down." I refuse to concede that fact. They will not shield me from this. "Now I guess we just have to wait for Jarek and Raf to get back."

I hate that I can't call them and get them to come back. But having Milo here with me, at least I feel safer than I had when I was alone.

"Where did they go, anyway? I saw them leaving and they looked pissed." It figures Milo would pass them on their way out and still somehow manage to get up here with me.

"Someone called and said a group of their guys was being attacked. It sounded bad. Raf was upset and Jarek was pissed. I'm a little worried because they've been gone a while. I guess I expected them to come back faster than this." I snuggle into Milo's arms and relax. He leans over, grabbing the remote and turning on the TV.

"Well, let's just settle in here and wait for them to get back. Then maybe I'll get to talk to Jarek before he kills me," he jokes. I shift a little so I can watch as he flips channels, looking for something to watch.

"What about that show?" I offer, gesturing to the screen. It's the practical joke show where a group of friends try to embarrass each other just for fun. "Remember when we were almost on there? That was the funniest date ever. I wish they had let us have the tape."

"Your father would have shit bricks if we'd let that go on air. And I would be at the bottom of the river. But those guys are hilarious. We can watch this if you want." He sets the remote down on the couch beside us and we settle in for a while.

"Do you need a drink? Or a snack?" I ask after a bit. I'm already laughing so hard; I'll need to use the bathroom soon.

Milo must be having the same issue. "Yeah, a drink and snack sound good. Where's the bathroom?" I point toward my bedroom as I stand up to go to the kitchen. He walks through my room as I hunt down something for us to snack on.

He sneaks up on me while I'm digging through the cabinet. "Damn, you scared me!" I can't quite reach the cheese crackers, and nearly fall when he surprises me. Somehow, Milo manages to catch me and grab the box at the same time.

"I'll get this." He nods toward the bathroom as if he knows that I have to go too. It's crazy how in sync we are already. I race off and do my business, checking my hair and makeup before I return. In my absence, Milo has our snack laid out on the table in front of the couch.

Cheese crackers, peanut butter, and apple slices, plus a mango drink for me and a tea for him. How did he do all of this so fast? "Thank you, this looks amazing."

I sit down next to him and we return to watching the show while we snack. The show is funny, and takes the edge off my worry. It's like Milo can read me and knows exactly what I need. I guess that's an alpha thing. Maybe this situation won't be as bad as I originally thought. With Milo here, I feel complete. I'm sure that we'll convince Jarek to let him stay. If they ever get back from that emergency.

My heart is racing and I'm fidgeting again. I need to stop worrying about them. I know that Jarek and Raf can take care of themselves and each other. But for some reason my omega side just will not let it go. Milo pushes his scent at me again to calm my obvious nerves, and I feel myself relax a little bit.

I can't stop glancing at Milo as we watch the show. This is so much like our afternoons before this mess happened. I lay my hand on his, and he threads our finger together before leaning over and pressing his lips to mine. I hear the door creak, and know what's coming next. If Jarek's growl is any indication, things are about to get loud.

JAREK

The door to Ness' apartment is ajar, just like mine and Raf's. It seems odd to me, so I nudge him toward his, and I head toward hers. If she listened to me, she'll be in mine anyway. Of course, I know she didn't listen. Ness doesn't do what she's told. It's one of the things I love about her.

I step through her door just in time to see Milo lean over and press his lips to hers. How the fuck did he get in here? And is he wearing one of my shirts? I can't stop the growl that escapes my throat at him being near my omega. Milo jumps up and backs away from Ness, holding his hands up to stop me from attacking.

"It's not what it looks like, really," he insists.

I glance at Ness, and she rolls her eyes. Obviously, he wasn't forcing himself on her. She would have fought back. But how did he get past my security? I turn back to him. "How did you get in here? This floor is locked down and only two people have access."

"Uh, I, well," he stammers. Ness openly laughs at him.

"Fuck, Milo, just tell him you picked the lock. It's not rocket science, and he's gonna figure it out anyway."

I fist my hand in his shirt, picking him up off the ground. "Wait, please don't kill me. I didn't mean to do anything wrong. I saw a pretty girl and couldn't help myself. I came here looking for you."

His words filter through my anger and I wonder what the fuck he was looking for me about. An FBI agent wouldn't usually keep company with mobsters, but I already know that Milo was working for Dragonetti as a way to get close to Ness.

"You're telling me you don't know her?" I ask him with my eyebrows raised.

"I, uh, no, I don't know her." His terrified response warrants a chuckle from Ness.

"What's so funny?" I ask her.

She rolls her eyes and laughs again. "You two and this pissing match. Milo, he knows who you are. And he knows that you know me. There's no point in lying about it now. Besides, I'm pretty sure he saw us kissing, and that's what has his panties in a twist."

I glare at Ness. How dare she speak to me that way? Just for that, I'm going to teach lover boy a lesson. "You broke into my home, and now you try to lie to me about it? Big mistake, Fed boy." I drop him at the same time I swing my fist and catch his jaw.

Ness gasps and stands up. "Stay out of it, Ness," Raf warns her. Good, I want him to be part of this too. Milo is holding his jaw and backing away from me. I stalk toward him and punch him in the gut, doubling him over. I nod to Raf, and he flies over, tackling Milo to the floor.

"Now, Milo, there's two ways we can handle this. You can tell me the truth, or I can kill you and drop you on Dragonetti's doorstep. Which is it gonna be?" I stand over him as Raf holds him down.

Ness stomps over and gets between us. "Stop this right now. Milo is mine, just like you two are. I will not have my pack fighting."

Raf and I turn to her. "Did he claim you?" I ask, hearing my own growl mingle with my cousin's. She shakes her head.

"No, he didn't. But neither did you or Raf. I get to decide who's in my pack. Remember? We were talking about this earlier? Well, if you kill Milo, I won't bond with either of you. He came to find you so you could help him find me. If you'd stop acting like an ape, I could tell you exactly what's going on here." Ness shoves Raf off of Milo and helps him to his feet, putting herself between us and him.

Fuck. I don't want to back down. My alpha side is itching to put her in her place and make her beg for mercy. But I also don't want to lose the chance to bond with her, either. "Fine.

We won't kill him. But I'm not going to just agree to allow him into the pack because you said so."

"Oh my God. You are such a baby. Milo isn't going to challenge you for head alpha status. And since Raf agreed to let you have it, nobody is taking your place. You big, dumb oaf. Everyone sit down so we can talk this out." Ness stares at us, waiting to see if we'll give in. Of course, Raf strolls over to the couch and sits down, turning off the TV. Fucker.

With the three of them staring me down, I have no choice but to comply. I don't want to, but I stomp over to the chair and flop down. Ness and Milo take the opposite end of the couch, where she can stay between us. "There now, isn't that better?"

"Not really. I was having fun pounding the new guy," I growl. Milo's eyes go wide, and I know that he's scared of me. I like that. Maybe I'll let him stay after all.

"You're impossible, you know that, right?" she scoffs at me. I want to pull her into my arms and spank her for being so disrespectful.

"Look, I don't want any trouble." Milo holds up his hands in surrender. "I came here to ask you to help me find Ness and save her from her father. It seems you've already done that. Now I'm asking if I can stay. I want Ness as badly as the two of you do. And she wants the three of us, so we should try to make it work, to keep our omega happy."

I growl at his words. I don't want to share her with either of them, but it looks like I won't have a choice.

VANESSA

Just when I'm about to give up on the whole situation, Raf stands up. "I'm in. If Milo is what Ness needs to feel complete and settle here, I fully support it."

Jarek stands and gets in his face. "Who said you get a vote?"

"You dumb fuck. All three of us are in love with her. Don't you think that means something? And if she's willing to form a pack with the three of us, why would you stop that? Are you that scared of your own happiness?" Raf challenges his cousin, not backing down. I've seen them fight, but I've never seen Raf go full alpha on Jarek before. Not gonna lie, it's totally hot.

And they can all tell because of the flood of my rain-soaked honeysuckle scent that fills the room. Fuck. There are moments when I love being an omega, and other times when I hate it. This is a hate time. I don't need them knowing that their stupid fight has me hot and bothered, imagining the three of them all over me. Who knows, maybe I can even get Milo and Raf to make out for me. Damn. I have to stop thinking about that.

Three growls indicate that my arousal has not gone unnoticed. Suddenly I'm surrounded by whiskey and cedar, earthy pine, and fresh sea water as the three of them respond to my scent release.

"Are you guys done yet? I can't take this fighting." I try to cover it all up, but get knowing smirks in response.

"Oh, I can tell exactly what you think of the fighting, doll. You can pretend that you don't like it, but we know better. Don't we, boys?" Jarek looks at Raf and Milo for their agreement. Both men nod. Fuck me.

"So, all I had to do to get you to behave is get turned on by Raf standing up to you? I wish I'd known that earlier." I watch Jarek's face as I explain exactly what got me going. The disappointment is apparent, but I don't back down. "If you want to do something to turn me on, you'll apologize to Milo for punching first instead of letting us explain the situation."

He looks at me, then Milo, then turns to Raf. I laugh when Raf shrugs. "She has a point. There's nothing hotter than a man who can say he's sorry for being wrong." Jarek growls, but doesn't attack him. Well, we're making progress. Everyone sits back down and I sigh.

"We need to figure this out before my heat hits. I need to know who's going to be here to take care of me. And I won't put up with you guys fighting each other. You're supposed to protect me, not try to isolate me." I hope I can get through to Jarek. I want this to work so badly.

"I mean what I said. If you want Milo, I'm good with that. As long as I get to be part of your pack." Raf's reassurance makes me smile. I'm glad I was right about him.

"Thank you. And Milo already said he wants to stick around, so I guess that just leaves Jarek. Are you in or out?" I hate feeling like this is an ultimatum, because I know how he'll react to that. But I have to know what he's thinking. "Or do we need to discuss it in private?" Maybe giving him some reassurance will help the situation.

Without a word, Jarek stands up and walks into my bedroom. Not exactly what I had in mind, but it works. I turn to the other two. "I'll be back in just a bit. Wish me luck."

I follow Jarek into my room, closing the door behind me. I pause and take a deep breath. *I am not going to fight him. I am going to convince him to give this a chance.* When I turn around, he's sitting on the bed, staring at me.

"Look, I don't want to fight about this. And I'm not going to force this. But I care about all three of you. Please don't make me choose. I don't know how to live without all the parts of myself." Perhaps honesty is the way to go here.

He sighs and holds out a hand for me to come to him. I don't hesitate, taking his hand and sitting down beside him on the bed. "I know that. And I understand. Thank you for telling me. But I can't come across as weak here. I can't bow to you or anyone. I have to be the head alpha. There is no compromise on it." His tender tone shocks me nearly as much as his honesty does.

"No one is challenging you for head alpha. Milo told me that he'll bow to you. And I'm pretty sure Raf agreed to that earlier, too. So, what's the problem? Talk to me." I don't want to beg, but I will if I have to.

"You drive me crazy. So much so that I can't focus. I hate being around you as much as I hate being away from you. I don't like being soft or vulnerable. It pisses me off."

I huff a laugh at him. "Are you kidding me? You're pissed off because you care about me? For real? That is the craziest thing I've ever heard. You know that, right?" I can't believe what he's just told me. It's ridiculous, but I can see from his face that it's the truth.

"I'm being honest. I'll accept Milo into the pack if that will make you happy. As much as it grates on my nerves, I'd do anything to make you happy and keep you safe." I can see the tears forming in his eyes. I lean closer and press my lips to his.

"Thank you. I thought you would, but I understand you have to be a macho alpha about it. I don't want to miss what we could have because you're being stubborn." I stand up and step in front of him, standing between his legs.

"I don't want to share you at all. But I know an omega needs more than one mate, and more than one alpha. I can't be as thrilled about the situation as the other two are. I'm too old for this shit. I just want to settle down with you and have some babies. I don't want drama." He wraps his hands around my waist and pulls me close, until his face is inches away from my neck.

"I don't want drama either. So, stop being dramatic and kiss me already," I breathe in his ear. He turns his head and captures my lips with his.

RAFAEL

With Ness and Jarek in the next room, Milo and I sit on the couch and stare awkwardly at each other. "I guess we should get to know each other, since we're gonna be family," I offer.

"I used to be an FBI agent. Ness and I were dating when you were her bodyguard. Does this mean you were a plant the whole time?" Milo asks with a shrug.

I nod at him. "Yeah. I was there to see if I could get intel on Dragonetti and his business. Ended up falling for his daughter. Then I couldn't resist snatching her when I found out about the plot to have her killed. Jarek is my cousin. Mom's brother is his dad."

"Oh. Okay. And you just took her? Jarek was okay with that?" He cocks an eyebrow at me. This guy is actually kind of cute. I wonder how Ness would feel about a little exploration. With her involved, of course.

"Nah, I had to call him and explain everything first. I would never bring someone back to our hideout without checking with him first. I asked him what I should do about it, and he told me to bring her back here. Then we faked her death and figured that would get her old man off her trail for a while. At the very least, he won't know it was us who took her." Part of me wonders why I'm explaining everything to this man who, until today, would have been my enemy. But the rest of me understands that things change at the drop of a hat.

Adapt or perish, that's my motto. Or at least, it should be. "Wow. So, the whole thing was his idea? That seems odd to me, but I don't know him." Milo stares at the window.

"Is he hunting you down too?" I'm not sure how I know, but I do. Milo's nod doesn't surprise me. Now I have two people to keep safe instead of just one. Three if you count Jarek. But more people are scared of him than not, so he should be okay.

"Don't worry about it. We'll keep you hidden."

"You seem awfully sure that he'll accept me into the pack. Do you know something I don't?" I can sense his worry. I understand why, but I know my cousin, and I can see how he feels about Ness. There is no way Jarek will send Milo away.

"I know Jarek. He won't send you away. Ness wants you; Ness will have you. It's that easy. Seriously, man, don't sweat it. You'll be fine." He has no reason to trust me, but I can see that he wants to. And for some reason, I want him to.

I turn the TV on because we need a distraction from his nerves and my curiosity about what may be happening behind that closed door. Just my luck, I flip a couple of channels and the most famous space movie ever is on. That should work. I glance at Milo and he nods at me. Then he goes to the fridge and grabs a couple of beers. I'm glad he's feeling more comfortable now.

The movie gives me a chance to decompress and relax. I let my mind wander to thoughts of Ness' heat coming. With the three of us, that will lead to some interesting sex. I can't wait to see what Milo is up for. I've always been bi-curious, but I'm not about to try things with my cousin. That's just wrong. And I kill people for a living.

But Milo is fair game. As long as Ness is into it. I find myself imagining a heat scenario where Ness is encouraging us to explore. I know my cock is getting hard, but I don't even try to hide it. This movie isn't exactly sexual, but Milo isn't paying attention to me anyway. Besides, he wouldn't know I was thinking about him, would he? Nah, there's no way.

I wonder how big he is. And if he's into making out, would he be into taking things further? In my imagination, he's totally into it, and Ness cheers us on. Of course, Jarek is only interested in Ness, even in my imagination. Though it would be hot to watch him with Milo while I fuck Ness. Maybe she can convince him to play nice. I almost laugh at the thought.

Before I can give the thought anymore of my time, the bedroom door opens and Ness walks out. "Jarek wants to talk to you," she says, glancing at my raging boner. "You might want to adjust that first." She chuckles and drops onto the couch next to Milo.

I fix my dick so it's not as obvious, then get up and walk into her room. This seems odd to me, but I guess it's all part of the process.

Jarek is waiting for me, leaning against the wall. "What's up?" I ask.

"We need to figure out how this is going to work if we let him stay," he responds, running a hand through his hair. I know he's already decided to accept Milo, otherwise we'd be having a completely different conversation.

"What's there to figure out? He stays, it makes Ness happy. He leaves, it makes Ness unhappy. It's not complicated," I spit back.

"I get that, but I need to make sure that I'm still the head alpha." Oh, my God. Not this again. What an insecure dick.

"Look, princess, nobody is going to take your title from you. I wanted it, but not enough to make Ness suffer. Milo has no problem bowing to you. He, and I, just want to be with Ness. We'll go along with whatever you tell us to. And I think he'll be an asset to the team. The Bureau fired him because he was involved with Dragonetti." I should not be the one explaining this to him, but since my cousin seems dead set on not talking to Milo, I'll handle it.

I seem to be doing a lot of go-between work lately. I hope it doesn't become permanent. I'm not a fan. I'd still like to know what Ness did to convince him to cooperate. But I guess I'll have to get that info from her later.

"Really? That is interesting. Why didn't he tell us that?"

I stare at my cousin in disbelief. "Seriously? You started beating his ass the second you walked in the door. It's not like he had a chance."

"You helped," he defends.

"I tackled him. I never hit him. There's a difference," I insist. I know it's ridiculous, and I probably should have apologized to him, but it's too late now. "So, what is this really about?"

"We're gonna have to set him up in one of the open apartments, and get him a key card to access the floor."

MILO

The moment Jarek summons Raf to Ness' room, I start to sweat. Either he's planning to accept me, or he wants Raf's opinion, or he wants Raf to take me out. I have to be prepared for anything here. My mind starts planning my escape route as Ness drops onto the couch next to me.

"Are you okay? I know Jarek attacked you pretty hard earlier. Do you need anything?" she asks, threading her fingers through mine as if it's the most natural thing ever.

"I'm fine. Raf and I talked and had a beer. This is weird, Ness. It feels like I'm waiting for my execution. I don't like it." Admitting that to her is painful, but I don't want to lie to her.

"Milo, babe, there's nothing to worry about. Jarek will accept you. He just has to play tough guy and make you sweat first. And see what Raf thinks of you. It's all gonna work out, I promise." Her reassurance does little to calm my rising panic.

As an alpha, I have two options when faced with a larger, stronger alpha. Submit or fight. I offered to submit, but I may have to fight my way out of this one. And I don't know if I can win. Jarek is not only bigger and stronger than me, he's crazy. I've dealt with crazy before, but it was on my side. I'm not sure how to fight against his type of insanity.

I sit there, holding Ness' hand and waiting for my sentence to be passed down. I know that the second that door opens I'll have one moment to react to whatever Jarek says. Am I fast enough to get away? Where would I go if I could? Fuck, this situation sucks. In an instant, Dragonetti ruined my life so badly that I have nowhere to go.

Just as I start pondering that, the bedroom door opens and Raf walks out. He nods at me and stops to kiss Ness before he leaves. Oh, shit. This is bad. Where is he going? Before I can process that thought, Jarek stands in front of me. His hulking body towers over us as we sit on the sofa. I can't help but swallow my nerves as he stares me down.

"Stand up," he commands. Ness rolls her eyes at him, but I jump to do as I'm told. This is it. I'm about to learn my fate. What is it about this man that terrifies me so much? "I am the head alpha here. I make the decisions about who stays and who goes. Do you understand that?" His growl halts Ness' chuckle. He's serious, and I know it.

I drop to one knee and present my neck. "Yes, sir." It's all I can do to stop the trembling of my body. I can't show weakness, but must show respect. It's the only way I'll survive this.

"Good. Now get up. Raf will take care of your apartment and key card. I'll figure out what you can do to be useful to me. And we'll both be watching you very closely, Fed. Don't screw this up. Ness is rather attached to you, and I'd hate to have to hurt her by killing you."

My eyes widen and I nod. "Understood. Thank you."

His shoulders start to shake, and I'm certain he's holding back laughter. I steal a glance at Ness and she's glaring at him. Suddenly a laugh breaks free and he holds a hand out to me. "It's okay, man. I just had to do it. I couldn't resist. And honestly, I mean every word. But this isn't that kind of family."

"Wait, you were messing with me?" I stare at Jarek as he laughs openly. Ness scoffs, but she's smiling too. "Were you in on this too?" I accuse her. She rolls her eyes again and shrugs. Damn these people. Why do I want to be here?

"You're lucky that's all he did. He wanted to beat you to a pulp as an initiation, but I told him if he did that, I'd never bond with him." Ness grins and I can't help but laugh too.

"I bet that was pretty funny, watching me grovel in front of the head alpha. Don't worry, Jarek, I'm not here to steal your power. I just want to be with Ness and help protect her. That's it."

He gestures for me to sit down before taking the seat I've decided is his next to the couch. "I was hoping we could discuss some things after you're settled in. I do have some work for you if you're interested. If we're forming a pack with Ness, each of us will have access to the family bank account, so there won't be payment. We have enough money to buy whatever we want, so that's not an issue. And if you choose not to work with us, we won't do anything to you. Except maybe give you shit for being a mooch."

Well, this is going way better than I expected. Maybe Ness will be the one to tame the beast. I guess I'll find out.

"I'm definitely interested in hearing what you have in mind." I lean forward, expecting him to explain now.

"We'll talk about it once you're settled in. I'll give you a few days. Then we'll talk about it. For now, I think it's best for you to stay inside the hideout. Ness said that her father is after you too. I can't have something happen to my newest pack member." He turns to Ness. "You know we have a few things left to discuss as a group before we can make this pack official, right?"

Ness nods. "I do. And I know what you're worried about. Worst case, we don't become an official pack until he's dealt with. It won't bother me after my heat when we've all claimed and been claimed." She smirks at her own words.

Chapter Ten

AN OFFER HE CAN'T REFUSE

VANESSA

The next few days pass quickly. Milo is settling in nicely, and Jarek is actually playing nice for a change. I watch with interest as Raf flirts with Milo, and neither man looks put off by the idea. As expected, Jarek is worried about making our pack official, because we'll have to file paperwork with the city. And that will out me as alive. Which will alert my father, and put all of us in danger.

After Jarek is sure Milo is settled, he asks us to help with an interrogation. Milo looks at me and I smile. I know exactly what this means, and I'm excited to do it. I enjoy embracing my darkness, especially when it helps one of my men get information. I'm looking forward to learning more techniques to inflict pain without the release of death.

"Are you sure you want to do this, Ness? I can take care of it for you. It's okay, really. I don't mind. You don't have to witness this," Milo tries desperately to talk me out of participating.

Bless his heart, he has no idea what he's gotten himself into by falling in love with me. Now I'm getting nervous that he won't want me after he sees what I'm capable of. Raf picks up on my nerves and takes my hand. "It'll be okay. Once he sees how strong and fierce you are, he'll want you even more." He winks before turning toward the elevator that will take us to our prey.

"What did he mean by that?" Milo asks. He seems hesitant to follow us.

It's my turn to make an offer. "You know that you don't have to do this, right? I can handle it, and Jarek can find you something else to do." He scoffs at my words. "Good, then stop doing that to me."

I've made my point, and am satisfied that he'll stop trying to talk me out of this. I follow Raf to the elevator, where Jarek is waiting. "Come on, doll, get your boy toy in check. We have matters to handle."

I smirk at Jarek's words, then grab Milo's hand and drag him with me. I watch the metal doors close, locking me in with these three dangerous men. And I feel myself already starting to get turned on. Maybe they'll all fuck me while I'm covered in my victim's blood. That would be hot.

"Doll, I need you to get your desire under control. I don't want this guy to want you while you kill him." I start to protest, but Jarek holds up a hand. "As amusing as it would be, that's not what I want to do here. Also, if we get in there and you can't handle it, just tell me."

I wonder what he means. I've been looking forward to this all day. Why wouldn't I be able to participate? Fuck, he's as bad as Milo. They're all trying to protect me. Fuck that, I'll protect myself. "I'll be fine."

The elevator doors open to the dimly lit hallway, and we all follow Jarek to the cell where our subject is. I keep my eyes on the floor until we're inside with the door closed and locked behind us. The four of us face the man who's chained to the wall.

I lift my face to see who I'm dealing with, and any trace of desire leaves me in an instant. Hanging there, on the wall, in chains and looking beat up, is my cousin. "Jimmy? What's he doing here?" I turn back to Jarek.

"I thought you said you can handle it," he responds in a low voice.

"You didn't tell me it was family," I insist. "Why him?" I push, knowing that I'll likely be punished for it later. I don't care right now. I want to know why he expects me to torture my own family.

"He's the one who led the attack on Twelfth Street. We've had him down here for a little while. But he's not talking to us. I thought maybe you could convince him that a quick death was preferable to torture." Jarek's response halts my breath for a second. He seriously expects me to torture and possibly kill my own cousin.

If Jimmy led the attack on Twelfth Street, he deserves to die. My father's men didn't just go after D'Angelo's men. They killed innocent children in addition to the men and women who were working or living in the area. I have trouble equating my cousin, who I grew up with, as being the man responsible for the deaths of children.

"Ness, you don't have to do this. I can do it for you," Milo offers. Jarek glares at him, and he almost backs down.

I grab Milo's hand and squeeze for a moment before letting go. "I'm okay. I can do this." I walk past him to the table next to Jimmy. The tools are laid out much like the last time. I can do this. Almost too easily. And it scares me. I want to hurt him for what he's done. After selecting the right knife to start with, I take the three steps to where my cousin is chained to the wall.

"Hi, Jimmy. How are ya?" I ask cheerfully as I stare him down. I can tell he's fighting through whatever they gave him. It takes him a minute or two to realize that I'm there.

"Vanessa? But you're dead. Did I die? Is this hell?" he asks as tears fall down his cheeks.

I shake my head. "Not yet, dear cousin. I'm very much alive. As are you, though you won't be for long unless you start talking." I show him the knife I hold in my hand. "I'm not afraid to hurt you if you don't talk."

"I, I can't. I don't know anything." The falter in his voice tells me that he does.

JAREK

Watching Ness interrogate someone is like watching her come into her own. Gone is the timid omega; a fierce warrior taking her place. And I know that I can take over in a moment's notice, so I'm not worried about this guy being her cousin. He wasn't worried about the kids he ordered his men to kill, so why should I be?

While she tries to convince him to talk to me, I turn to Milo. It's time to pump him for information too. "So, you ready for that mission we talked about?"

He looks at me for a second before nodding. "I thought this was it, but sure. What did you have in mind?"

"I need to know everything you know about Dragonetti and his operation." I can see his demeanor shift. This makes him uncomfortable, and I'm not sure why.

"I don't know anything. All I did for him was hiding evidence and redirecting investigations away from his organization," he insists. I believe him, but I still think he's hiding something.

I want to push him for answers, but Ness is putting off nervous omega vibes. Her scent fills the room, but it's not the usual sweet smell. This is acrid with a hint of burning. "Omega." The one-word command has her dropping the knife on the table and walking over to stand in front of me.

"Yes, Alpha," she answers when she's in place. And she thinks she's in trouble again. Fuck. I have to get her past that. I'd rather deal with my brat that the subservient version of my girl.

"Doll, are you okay? If you can't do this, no one will think less of you. I just need to know," I offer quietly, whispering my words in her ear.

"I can do it. I'm just struggling to focus with him crying about when we were kids. I want to do this. Please, Alpha." I can hear the determination in her voice.

"Then get back over there and slap him around when he starts to cry. Show him that he can't get to you that way. Otherwise, he's never going to talk. He thinks you won't hurt him. Prove him wrong. If you can't use the knife, take the hammer to his fingers and toes. Punch him in the gut or face."

"Yes, Alpha. Thank you," she responds quietly before turning around and holding her head high. We watch her stalk over to Jimmy and smack him hard in the face.

"Now, back to what we were discussing." I refocus my attention to Milo. "I know you have something on him, or you wouldn't think you can protect Ness on your own."

Milo shakes his head. Raf steps closer, but I shake my head at him. As if being dismissed, he walks over to watch Ness. He knows what information I need, and will be fine handling that. "Milo, I can't let this go. I know you know more than you're telling. If you can't help us, we might start to think you're against us. You don't want that, do you?"

"I don't know anything. I can't help you. No amount of torture is going to change that. I can't give you what I don't have."

I step forward, leaning down to get in his face. "I could pound you to a pulp right here, right now. And you still won't talk?"

"Like I said, I can't give you what I don't have." His insistence that he knows nothing makes me want to swing my fists into him until he admits the truth. You can't work for Dragonetti for that long without learning something.

"Besides, you don't want Ness to turn around and see you beating me. You agreed that wouldn't happen. Do you really want to risk what you could have with her?" He makes a good point, but I'm past caring about that right now. I need answers.

I glance at Ness and see that she's finally making some head-way with her cousin. He's talking and Raf is recording it. We may get answers after all. I draw my fist back and punch Milo in the gut. To his credit, he doesn't yell.

"That's for threatening me. I don't take kindly to snitches. Of course, I don't want to risk what Ness and I are building. But I need to know how to take her father out. And since you worked for him, you should have the answers I need." I glare at him again. "If you won't talk, I'll strap you to the wall and let them handle it."

I don't realize that my voice is louder than I intend it to be. Ness' head whips around and she races to Milo's side. "Are you okay?" she asks him as she crouches down next to him. Raf shakes his head at me.

"I'm good," Milo says. "But Jarek wants info on your father. He thinks I have it. I tried to explain, but he won't listen."

She stands up and stalks over to me. "Look, Jarek. This isn't going to work if you beat the shit out of Milo every time my back is turned. Maybe forming a pack with you is a bad idea. As a matter of fact, if you ever hurt Milo again, I will never be yours. I'll fuck him in front of you, then kill you myself."

Her anger is sexy as hell. But I believe she'd do it, so I just nod. "Fine. But I know he has intel on Dragonetti, and we can't take him down without it."

Ness' expression changes as if she just remembered something. "Fuck. The ledger. Milo gave me Father's ledger and I forgot to tell you. It has everything in it that the FBI would need to take him down. But that doesn't excuse your treatment of Milo. Apologize. Now." Her demand smacks me in the cock. I want to bend her over and spank her, but instead I turn to Milo.

"I'm sorry."

MILO

Jarek's apology shocks me. I don't think it's sincere, but I accept it anyway. Then Ness steps away to finish interrogating her cousin. I don't want to think about her torturing the man. I stare in shock as she jabs the knife into his arm. She wasn't kidding when she told me she'd changed. The Ness I knew would never be able to do this to anyone, much less family.

This Ness seems to enjoy inflicting pain, no matter who is on the receiving end. It's seriously hot, but also completely disturbing. I wonder if it will haunt her afterward.

"She's fine, you know. It takes talent to bring someone to the brink of death while holding back. I think she enjoys it too. Watch how good she is," Jarek whispers to me. He's done a complete one-eighty from his attitude toward me a few minutes ago.

Maybe they're all crazy. I watch as Raf instructs her just where to slide the knife to do the most damage without killing the man. They almost seem like they're getting off on it. There's so much blood, and the poor guy isn't talking anymore anyway.

"I don't understand the purpose of this. He's not telling you anything. What good does it do to kill him in the most painful way possible if you're not getting answers?" I can't help asking the question.

Jarek shakes his head at me before walking toward his cousin. A moment later, Raf is standing beside me and Jarek is giving instruction. Ness is eating up the attention and trying her best to perform for them. It seems off to me somehow. Maybe I'll ask her about it later and see if she'll talk to me.

"He's not so bad, you know. And he does care about her. I think you should give us a chance." Raf's suggestion catches me off guard. *I should give them a chance?* That's a little backward, but okay.

"I'm not sure what you mean. How am I not giving you all a chance?" I can't help but ask the question.

"You claim to want to be with Ness, but even I can see that this part grosses you out. I'm not saying you need to enjoy torture, but you shouldn't be so obvious about your disapproval. Ness can sense it, and it's making her self-conscious. She's usually her most relaxed here, but today, it's like she knows something is off."

I hadn't realized that I was messing up her vibe. I guess I should be more accepting of their hobbies. "This just isn't anything I've ever been part of. I don't really know how to react."

"You should also probably at least consider joining us in our plan to take Dragonetti down. If you don't, Jarek won't feel like he can trust you. And that will make things difficult for you. I understand that you don't want to be on the wrong side of this, but you already are. We aren't on the same side as that man. Not after what he's done to Ness. I don't think we know all of it yet, either." His words slam into me. I've never considered what Ness went through with her father. I know it's bad, but she doesn't ever want to talk about it, so I don't push the issue.

Does this mean she's told them what her father did to her? Why wouldn't she? They support her in anything she does, even in choosing me for a packmate. Fuck me. "Okay, I'll do what I can to help you guys take him out. But I meant what I said to Jarek earlier. I don't know anything. I did find that journal, but I don't even know what's in it. Ness understands it, though. I'll help however I can." I make the vow with no malice toward Raf or Jarek. These men are my family now, and I have to start acting like it.

The cell phone in my pocket feels heavy against my leg. I should call my mother and let her know I'm alive. But if Dragonetti has her phone bugged, it would be a bad idea. I'd be tipping him off to my location and daring him to come find me. I really don't want that. Besides, I don't think Jarek would replace the phone so soon after buying it. No matter how rich he claims to be.

"Good. We can all talk about it after this. I think Ness is about to break him. It's always harder when they're family, you know?" I stare at Raf. He's tortured his family before? That's some sick shit. Okay, I have to be less judgmental here.

"I feel like I'm learning more about you guys every day," I say in response.

"That's good. We're becoming family. Just in time for her heat to hit." How does he know so much about her heat? I shake the thought away and focus on the interrogation that's happening across the room. If you can even call this blood bath that. We all know the guy is dead as soon as Jarek gets what he needs from him.

The poor guy only gets a few more minutes before Ness slits his throat and stands in the spray of blood. It's disgusting, but somehow kind of hot. I'm starting to see what Raf and Jarek were trying to tell me about this.

Ness bounces over to me after hugging both Jarek and Raf. Neither of them seems to care that their clothes are covered in blood now. When in Rome, right? I hold my arms out to her, and she launches herself at me. I barely catch her before her lips are on mine. The taste of her is different with someone else's blood covering her. I can feel my pants start to constrict against my growing desire. Who knew I'd be into blood play?

RAFAEL

I can see that Milo isn't into the torture at first. But by the time Ness slits Jimmy's throat, Milo is starting to come around. He may not realize it, but he's one of us. I know it's not easy to give up everything you're used to. I watched Ness struggle with trying to change things until she finally accepted that this wasn't her old life.

Since she accepted that, she's been happy here. She's embracing the new adventure that is being our mate. Fuck, I can't wait until her heat hits. I know Jarek is as amped about the thought of putting a baby in her as I am. We haven't talked about that possibility yet. I wonder if she even wants kids, especially knowing that her father is after her.

Maybe we should have a pack meeting before her heat hits and talk everything through. I'll have to make the suggestion to Jarek so he can feel like it's his idea. I may not be head alpha, but I certainly know how to get my cousin to do what I want. It's not hard when you understand people's motivations.

When Ness is finished with our guest, Jarek and I usher Ness and Milo back to the elevator. It's time to clean up, then get ready for dinner. It's Jarek's turn to cook, so I know he'll send someone out for takeout. His mama would be so disappointed that he didn't pick up any of her skill in the kitchen. But at least he got her charm.

I stand at the back of the elevator, watching the three of them interact for a minute. It doesn't take Ness long to realize I'm lost in thought. She slips from between them to wrap her arms around me. I hold her for a moment before I meet her gaze.

"What's wrong?" she asks quietly.

"Nothing, love. I was just thinking about dinner," I tease. I'm sure she knows that isn't exactly what I was thinking, but it's close enough to the truth for her to drop the issue. Or at least I hope so.

"It's Jarek's night to cook," she says, her eyes going wide. I can't help but laugh at that response.

"Wait, what does that mean?" Milo asks. I'm amused because he hasn't noticed yet that we trade off on dinners. Probably because I've been taking his nights.

"We have a schedule. You'll understand soon enough," I tell him casually. Jarek glares at us all. "And you'll learn really quickly that Jarek can't cook."

He growls in response. "No, I can't, but I can order pizza." Ness and I laugh, but Milo looks lost. That makes us laugh harder.

"Don't worry about it, Milo. You'll be fine. He'll send someone out to get the pizza. And we'll have time to clean up first." I'm trying to reassure him, but he still looks worried. I wonder if he's thinking about pizza or the fact that we're hungry so soon after killing a man.

I decide to change the subject. "We should have some fun tonight. Just the four of us." I wiggle my eyebrows at Ness and she starts to laugh.

"What did you have in mind?"

I lean down and press my lips to hers before pulling her closer so she can feel my growing erection. "Oh, I have things in mind. I'm just not telling any of you yet."

Ness' laughter lightens the mood. And she doesn't say no. After all, if we're going to be a pack, we will have to share her. I wonder if we can start tonight. I look to Jarek to see his response. He gives a slight nod, then we both look at Milo.

He shrugs a little and I want to laugh. Leave it to the new guy to be less committed than the rest of us. "What do you say, Ness? Are you ready to take on the three of us together?"

A shiver washes over her and she purrs in my arms. My cock jumps and I'm certain all three men in the elevator have the same issue. Desire fills the small space, accentuated with our scents. I pull her even closer, grabbing her ass and urging her to wrap her legs around my waist. She does, letting out a moan when her core slides along my dick.

I want nothing more than to fuck her in this elevator, but I haven't gotten a straight answer from her on whether she's ready for that or not. So, I'll be content with using her body to stroke myself until we get back to our floor. I can feel Milo and Jarek watching us, but I don't care. I'm dying to tear our clothes off and sheath myself in Ness' tight, hot pussy. I hear growls before I realize it's coming from me.

My eyes widen and I look at her. She's grinning at me, as if she enjoys pushing me to the point of craziness. "We could take a shower together, if you want," she offers. "I do need to clean up a little."

I barely suppress the groan that forms in my chest at her idea. "All of us, or just you and me?" I force the words out and glance at Milo, then Jarek. Both of them are watching us as if hoping for an invitation to whatever is going on here.

"Do we have a shower big enough for everyone?" she asks innocently. Fuck me. This woman will be the death of me. I know it. Yet here I am, practically begging for the killing blow.

I look at Jarek. "Yeah, there's a pack suite on our floor that has a bed large enough for the four of us, and a shower that's big enough for eight people. That doesn't mean you can invite four friends." He smirks, and I chuckle at his attempt to joke with our omega.

Ness purrs again, rubbing herself on me.

JAREK

I can tell from the change in Ness that she's going into heat. I don't think she's had time to create her nest. There is no good way to ask, so I don't. We'll make one in the family suite that I've been preparing for her. "Raf, it's time. Take Ness to her room and help her shower. Milo and I will get things set up in the suite."

Understanding my meaning, my cousin nods and carries Ness to her door. Once they disappear inside, I turn to Milo. "Have you ever gone through a heat with an omega?" I ask, gesturing for him to follow me. I walk into my apartment and head straight for my hamper.

"No, but that won't matter, will it?" he responds, understanding what I'm doing, and helping me by grabbing the blankets and pillows from my bed as I get a few shirts, both dirty and clean.

"I don't think you can truly know what to expect until you've seen it firsthand." I glance over my shoulder at him.

His eyes go wide. "Ness is going into heat now? Oh, shit. What do we do?"

"We're already doing it. Here, put this on." I toss him a clean shirt, so we can get rid of the bloody ones. Although, with her heat being here, I'm not sure Ness will care about a little blood. After pulling on a clean one myself, I pick up the shirts I was carrying and nod toward the door, leaving the bloody shirts on the bathroom floor.

I stop at Raf's apartment on my way to the new room. Milo and I do the same in here as we did in mine, collecting blankets, pillows, and shirts that smell like Raf. "Have you been through a heat with an omega before?" he asks me quietly as we walk into his apartment to gather clothing and bedding. I don't want to answer his question, so I let it hang a little too long before I respond without looking at him.

"I have. It was a long time ago. She was taken from me way too soon, along with the rest of the pack we'd begun to form. I never thought I'd have this chance again. I know I'm not the nicest guy to be around, but I appreciate you being here and helping us take care of Ness." I know that I should say more, but feelings aren't my thing. He needs to know that if he's going to stick around.

"Do you think we'll complete the bond tonight?" More questions. That's what I get for telling him I know what I'm doing.

"Probably. I wish we'd talked about it and clarified that this heat is when she wants to do it. But it may be too late for talking. When Raf brings her to the suite, we'll have to see if she's feverish. If so, we'll play everything by ear. If it feels right in the moment, we'll do it. If not, or if she says no, we won't. Understood?" I stop in the hall and face him.

"Yes, Alpha." He exposes his neck to me and I smile. This one learns quickly. I'm not a complete dick, but I do like to be respected. Okay, maybe I am a complete dick. But that's beside the point.

"Good. Let's get this nest set up before they get done with the shower, shall we?" I continue down the hall to the apartment that will be ours as a pack. Once the bond is complete, we'll all be living here together. I hope we're ready for it.

I lead Milo into the apartment and hear his gasp at the sheer size of it. This one takes up most of the building on the same side as my apartment. "It's definitely big enough for all of us," he marvels.

"I'm glad you think so. Raf and I designed and built it ourselves. Of course, he wanted me to be the one to tell Ness about it." For some reason, Raf thinks I need to be the good guy in her eyes. I'm not comfortable telling Milo that, though.

"If you guys did the work together, I can see why he'd want you to take credit. He seems to think you're too hard on everyone. Doing nice things for them makes you appear more approachable." His explanation makes perfect sense, and I nod in understanding.

I show him the nest, and we carefully place the pillows and blankets around the circular mattress that's sunk into the floor. Once those are in place, we go back through and tuck the dirty shirts we collected in random spots, so our scents fill the space. I put the stack of clean shirts in the bedroom. I'm not sure we'll need them, but want to be prepared just in case.

We work in silence to finish setting up the nest while we wait for Raf and Ness to arrive. When we finish, I turn to Milo. "Do you want a beer?"

He nods and follows me to the kitchen. "You already have it stocked?" He seems shocked by this.

"Why wouldn't I? I mean, we knew Ness' heat was coming, and we'd already talked about forming a pack. It seemed like the thing to do." Why am I justifying my actions to him?

"That's awesome. I never would have thought to do all of this for her. I'm glad you're here," Milo admits to me. I can see that he's going to be a good fit here.

"Before they get here, I have to ask. Are you going to help me take Dragonetti down? I'm not making threats or anything. I'm asking, man to man. Will you, as part of my pack, help me take down the monster that's coming for two of my pack-mates?" The look on his face tells me that he will, and that he knows I've figured out that Ness' dad is after him too.

He holds out his hand to shake mine. "Gladly."

Chapter Eleven

AN OMEGA'S CHOICE

VANESSA

This day has me so riled up that I'm drowning in desire. It's all I can do to not jump all three of my men in the elevator. Luckily, Jarek has a 'family suite' ready for us. It sounds like he was saving it for when my heat hit. I'm glad we don't have to wait. I've been spending time with each of them individually, so I'm kind of nervous for our first group time.

I'm excited to see what comes of Milo and Raf's flirtations. It seems as if they're both into the possibility. I wonder if I can get them to explore while I watch. Hmm, that gets me going even more. I'm soaked with slick, and it's only getting worse. I know my heat is coming soon, and that's causing my sex drive to rev up.

This isn't the best timing, but I can't help feeling like this will be when I claim my pack. It seems odd to me that Jarek tells Raf to take me to my room to clean up. I thought we were all going to shower together. A wave of nausea hits me and I feel flushed. Maybe it's for the best that we aren't all going to be together. It'll be bad enough if one of them sees me get sick, I don't need them all staring at me.

Raf carries me into my apartment and heads straight for the shower, without even taking clothes off. "What are you doing?" I ask as he sets me on my feet under the spray. "I'm fully dressed!" He kneels in front of me and starts stripping my blood-soaked clothes off.

"I know, babe, but I don't think you realize what's happening right now. You feel warm, right? Kind of dizzy, a little sick? And super horny...am I right?" His questions don't make sense. How can Raf know exactly how I'm feeling?

I nod slowly, trying to connect the dots. What is he trying to say? None of it lines up with any illness I've heard of. "Raf, I don't understand. Just tell me whatever it is. Why did you toss me in here fully dressed when I wanted to go to the big suite with all of you?" I feel stupid asking, but I really don't know what he's hinting at.

He steps back after taking my clothes off and strips himself down in front of me. I nearly lose all ability to think with him standing naked in front of me. Raf waves a hand and motions toward his face. "My eyes are up here," he jokes before stepping into the shower with me.

"Let me take care of you. Jarek and Milo are getting the suite ready for us. I have no idea how you don't know, but your heat is coming on. Right now. It seems early to me, but my math may be off a bit. Or stress is pushing things ahead a little. Either way, you have nothing to worry about. We'll take care of you."

He presses a kiss to my forehead before grabbing the shampoo bottle and motioning for me to get my hair wet.

I purr at him as he washes and conditions my hair for me. Raf massages my scalp and rakes his fingers through my dark waves to make sure there aren't any tangles. It should be the sweetest thing anyone has ever done for me, but instead, it's super erotic. All I can think about is getting his knot inside of me.

Maybe he's onto something here. I guess that could be a sign that my heat is here. I just thought I was feeling revved up from torturing and killing my cousin. Or it could be a bit of both, I suppose. Either way, what he's doing feels so good that I'm struggling not to jump him.

"Mmmm, Raf, that feels so good," I purr as he rinses my hair. I can't believe I'm purring at him. It's the oddest thing. Before these men, I wasn't even sure omegas could actually purr. Now, I seem to do it all the time.

"You think that feels good, just wait." He squeezes the excess water from my hair and eases me away from the spray. Before I realize what he's doing, he has me pressed against the wall with one leg over his shoulder.

I gasp as he bites my thigh, near my center. I can feel my slick increasing as I get more and more heated. Raf runs his tongue across my entrance, flicking my clit. I shudder and grab his shoulder to steady myself, even though he has me pinned. I can't move even if I wanted to. Not that I want to. I'm perfectly happy letting Raf and his extremely talented tongue have their way with me right now.

He licks again, then snatches my clit between his teeth and flicks it with his tongue. I'm getting close to coming undone, but he doesn't relent. Raf sucks the little nub into his mouth and pushes a finger into my soaking pussy. More, I need more.

"You'll get more, babe. I'm not done with you yet," he pulls back and answers before continuing his torture. I hadn't realized I'd said the words out loud. The words repeat in my head, over and over, as I move closer and closer to the edge. I know he's trying to make me come so I'll get some relief from the symptoms of my heat. I wonder for a second if I've felt the full brunt of them yet, or if it'll get worse before it gets better.

I don't have time to consider that thought, because Raf, his tongue, and his fingers push me over that edge into bliss. I cry out with the orgasm that tears through me. "Good girl, now let's do it again," Raf growls the words into my mound before clamping down on my clit again.

RAFAEL

I'm pissed at myself because Jarek realized Ness was going in heat before I did. I should have known from how her scent changed while I watched her interrogate her cousin. If I'd been doubting her loyalty or her choosing us, at that moment, she proved herself. She was ruthless with him. My cock jumps at the thought. It was already at attention because I'm in the shower with my face buried between Ness' legs.

I know that she tastes just like she smells, but the honeysuckle is different now. It has a warmth to it, as if I'm sucking it straight from flowers that have been in the sun all day. My own scent mingles with hers; earthy pine and rain-soaked honeysuckle fill the room. I'm glad I restrained myself enough to clean her up before I started to take care of her in other ways.

She cries out with her release and I ease her to her feet. Making sure to turn off the shower, I grab a towel and dry her off before doing the same to myself. I feel her eyes on me, but she's trying to control her urges. It's amusing that she didn't realize her heat was here, but I've known omegas who had different experiences every time.

Some hate being needy messes, and I suspect Ness will feel that way too. She likes to be in control, even if she is an omega who craves our touch. I love watching her at war with her two sides. We still need to have a conversation about kids. I don't want to force something on her that she may not want. Especially with who her father is and what he'll do to us for claiming his only child. But I'm not scared of him. I'll tear him in half for what he put my girl through.

I wrap the towel around my waist before snuggling Ness into her fluffy robe. I wonder why she never uses this thing. It's the softest material I've ever felt. Stubbornness. Because I bought it for her, and she's been mad at me. I smile at the thought.

At her whimper, I scoop her up and carry her down the hall. "Ready or not, it's time to stop fighting this." I look at her in my arms. "I have to ask, though, do you want the bonds? I don't know if we'll be able to resist claiming you in the moment. It'll be better if we know before we start."

When she raises her eyes to meet mine, I see so much love that it throws me off for a minute. "I want the three of you to claim me at the same time, then I want to claim each of you. And yes, that's my decision, not my heat making it for me. I've given it a lot of thought." A shiver runs through me at her words. She's actually considered this and made the decision before now. I can tell from the way she emphasizes the words. That will make Jarek feel better. I know he's been worried about how mad she'll be if we claim her prematurely.

I kiss the top of her head and open the door. The apartment is beautiful, but I don't give Ness a chance to look around. Once inside, I head straight for the nest. This towel is starting to slip, and I don't exactly want to be in the middle of the apartment with my dick out. Not that it would matter, because the four of us are the only ones who have access, but it's the idea of it.

I nod to Jarek and Milo as we pass them. Ness reaches over my shoulder for them, and I'm sure they follow us to the nest. I don't slow or stop until I can lay her in the center of the inset mattress that's piled up with all of our bedding and some shirts that carry our scent. I kiss Ness gently. "I need to talk to the guys for a minute, then we'll come take care of you, okay? Can you give us just a minute, love?" She grimaces, and I know she's in pain, but she nods anyway.

"Hurry, please." Her words urge me on, and I turn from her, grabbing the other two by their shirts and pulling them out the door with me.

Jarek looks offended, and Milo confused. "What's going on?" Milo asks.

"Before we get taken over by hormones, I wanted to tell you what Ness told me," I say.

"So, she's suffering while you have story time?" Jarek growls. I punch him in the arm and continue.

"Trust me, you're gonna want to hear this. She wants us to claim her all together today. Then she wants to claim each of us. I figured you'd be worried about it, so I wanted to address it before the moment comes up. Stop being a dick, and let's go take care of our omega."

Jarek glares at me, then his expression softens. I'm glad he finally realizes how much he loves her. And I know that claiming her without permission would weigh on him tremendously. So, I don't regret pulling them away for a moment. Before anyone can say anything else, we hear Ness cry out.

Without waiting for them, I race back into the room. Ness is writhing on the nest, clearly suffering. We need to ease her pain, so that the fever will ebb. I drop on the bed next to her, pulling Ness into my arms. "It's okay, baby, we've got you." I press my lips to hers, and feel her relax into the kiss.

I hear the other two approach, just as Ness flips me onto my back and climbs on top of me. "Oh, you think it's gonna be that easy, do you, doll?" Jarek grabs her and pulls her off me and into his arms. He captures her lips with his and kisses her fiercely. It takes me a moment to realize that both he and Milo are naked now, just like Ness and me.

VANESSA

I should feel self-conscious, being naked in front of Jarek for the first time. Instead, I'm excited. I want to stare at him, but before I even fully register that he's not wearing clothes, his lips are on mine. The kiss is searing and passionate. I can feel Raf and Milo watching, and it just feels right. This fire inside of me is threatening to burn me alive, but I trust these three to keep me safe.

I let myself drown in his kiss, taking every bit of passion that he's giving me and matching it with my own. When did I fall in love with him? It doesn't even matter now. I know that's what happened, and my heart is full from it. These men are my pack. All that's left is the claiming.

That thought has me pulling away from him slightly. I wonder for a second how he'll react, but don't let myself chicken out. Jarek looks down at me, loosening his grip as I push against him. I can see on his face that he thinks I've changed my mind. Before he can turn away, I pull him down to me. I trail my lips along his jaw before sliding my tongue down his neck to his shoulder. I draw a deep breath of his whiskey-soaked cedar scent, right at the gland, before I bite down as hard as I can. I feel his reaction, and hear him take a shallow breath in. He isn't expecting that, and I'm way too satisfied with myself for catching him off guard.

"Mine," I growl as I pull back. "Always."

Jarek's eyes meet mine and I can see the sheen of tears. Even with my words, he still hadn't believed that I wanted him. Damn. I want to know who did this to him. Who made him feel like he didn't deserve to be loved? But that was a topic for later. Right now, I need to claim my other two mates. As if he understands, Jarek passes me to Milo, who's watching intently.

I don't even bother to kiss him first, instead, going straight for his gland. I lick it and sniff deeply of his intoxicating sea water scent. Then I bite down just like I did with Jarek. Milo's intake of breath tells me that he wasn't completely ready either. Why do these men doubt my love? With him claimed, I turn my face to his and kiss him deeply. Two down, one to go. I growl at him as well. "Mine."

Milo understands what I'm thinking and shifts me toward Raf. Fucking Raf. This dick who lied to me for more than a year while pretending to be my bodyguard. But he did actually protect me, better than any of my father's men ever had. I hate that I love him. I'm still angry about everything, but I can't deny my desire to claim him. His eyes meet mine, and he kneels to make it easier for me to get to his neck. It feels different with him. He's the only one who doesn't doubt me. That thought touches me in a way I never expected.

Tears fill my eyes as I breathe in his earthy pine scent before I bite down on the spot where my mark will remain for the rest of his life. He doesn't react the way the other two did. His arms wrap around me and he hugs me tightly, groaning at the feeling of my teeth on him. Before I can kiss him, he growls at me. "Yours. Forever." I shiver at his words. I'm already soaked with slick and dying to fuck them all, but somehow, he makes it more intense. "Forever," I growl back as I take his lips in a desperate kiss. I want these men to fuck me, to claim me, to love me.

I pull away from Raf to face the three of them. There's no trace of jealousy or doubt on any of their faces. "I figured that would be the only way you'd believe Raf that I want you all to claim me."

"You knew that's what I wanted to talk to them about?" he laughs.

I nod. "You're pretty easy to read, now that I can tell when you're lying," I tease. He grabs me and hugs me tightly. I relax into the embrace for a moment, then slide my hand down to lightly stroke his cock. He releases a growl and holds me tighter. "Ease up, big guy. I'm sure you all have ideas of how this is going to go, but I want something specific for my claiming." I pause for a minute as a wave of intense pain rushes over me.

I hold up a hand as Jarek steps forward. "I'm okay. Please, just let me tell you what I want." Raf loosens his grip and I lean over for a minute to catch my breath. When the pain passes, I stand again and look at them. "Jarek, I want your knot so bad I can't stand it. The other two can fight it out for my other holes." I know the blunt statement catches the three of them off guard. It's not something I would normally say.

But I'm determined to get what I want here, especially if they're all going to bite me and claim me together. Raf and Milo look at each other for a second, then Raf nods. Somehow, they make a decision without a word. I can't wait to see what they do.

Jarek reaches for me and I practically jump into his arms. He moans my name as his hands roam my body. There were so many times over the past few weeks that I have imagined this moment. I wonder if it will live up to my fantasies.

JAREK

I can't believe Ness claimed me. Somehow, I still expect her to reject me and push me away. Except she can't. She claimed me. All I have to do is claim her back and we'll be tied together for the rest of our lives. The thought excites and terrifies me. I've fantasized about this moment for weeks; longer if I'm being honest.

Not even Raf knows about that, though. And I refuse to tell him. Or her. No one needs to know how I've pined for this girl since she was far too young for me. I can't forget that moment. It's burned into my brain.

My nana was coming out of a store with bags in her hands when some asshole knocked them out of her hands. I wasn't fast enough to get to her before it happened. Ness was a teenager then, and strolled right up to my nana. Ness picked up the spilled groceries and refused to let her carry the bags.

Of course, I helped Nana into the car and took the bags from the girl. It was the sweetest thing I'd ever seen. I spent days searching until I found out who she was. Imagine my surprise when I found out that the girl I had a crush on was my father's enemy's daughter.

I shake my head to push the thought away. This isn't the time to get nostalgic. Now is the moment I'll claim my mate, my omega, my other half. Most alphas don't get a second chance if they lose their omega. I know better than to take this for granted.

My hands roam across Ness' skin, cooling the warmth while pushing her for more. I know that this time won't be as rough as I'd like, but I can try to give her tenderness. There will be plenty of time to explore kinks later. For now, I need to make sure she's ready to take my knot.

I pull her close to me and ease us down onto the mattress. I can't stop running my hands over her, caressing every inch I can reach. I press my lips to hers and nip at her lip to get her to open for my tongue. I deepen the kiss, letting my tongue tangle with hers. I nearly forget that Milo and Raf are watching as I slide my hands down her body again.

Ness' breath hitches when I stop just above her core. She wraps her arms around my neck and tries to pull me down on her. I don't let it happen. I stay there, just out of reach, as she bucks her hips at me. It's intoxicating to see how much she wants me. I need a minute or I'll be done before I even start. I trail kisses down her jaw and neck, breathing in her scent.

My lungs fill with rain-soaked honeysuckle, and it's the most beautiful thing I've ever smelled.

My fingers massage her hips, moving toward her thighs, as she continues to thrust her hips at me. I know what she wants, and I refuse to give it to her until I'm satisfied that I'll be able to make her feel good.

I continue trailing kisses down her shoulders and chest before pulling a taut nipple into my mouth. She sucks in a sharp breath as I gently bite down on it, stroking my tongue across the tip. She threads her fingers through my hair and holds me there, refusing to let me stop. Her moans are enough to keep me going. I need this woman like I need air. I have no idea how I've managed so long without her.

I slide a hand between her legs, barely touching her mound. She whimpers, and I can't handle torturing either of us anymore. I stroke my fingers along her slit, then dip one inside. She's dripping slick, and my finger slides in easily. I insert another, testing her, but she stretches to accommodate with little resistance. I feel a tremor of pleasure from her as she relaxes her grip on my hair. I kiss my way back to her lips, greedy and desperate for more.

I fuck her with my fingers as she continues to buck her hips, begging for more. Hovering over her, I stroke my cock over her opening, coating it with her slick. She whines again, and I start to ease the tip into her. I can tell that she wants more, but I'm determined to take this slow. It's torture for both of us, in the best way.

Once the tip is inside her, I pull out and rub my dick around in her slick more. She growls against my mouth, biting my lower lip. I guess she's done playing games. In one quick move, I sheath myself in her. When I'm buried to my balls, she groans. "Oh, Ness. Your pussy is so tight. It feels so good." I'm not sure how she'll react to the words, but I can't help expressing myself.

"Then fuck me, Jarek. Stop torturing us both and fuck me harder." I freeze. My jaw drops and I stare at her for a moment. My sweet, seemingly innocent Ness is a dirty girl after all.

"Are you sure you can handle it, doll?" I ask, still frozen in place.

"Jarek, if you don't fuck me hard, I'm going to kick you in the balls. Then I'll make you watch while I fuck Milo and Raf for the rest of my heat and you don't get to participate." I have no idea if she means the threat or not, but it's enough to jump start me into motion.

I growl at her, but start pumping my hips, thrusting into her harder and faster. "You wouldn't dare," I pant. But I know she would do it, just to spite me. So, like a whipped puppy, I do as she commands, fucking her harder and faster with each thrust.

VANESSA

Just when I think I'm going to have to push Jarek over and fuck him myself, he finally cooperates. While he thrusts into me over and over, I try to motion to Raf and Milo to come join the fun. They're just staring at us. It's weird, but I guess since I've already slept with both of them, they want to let Jarek have his moment. I'm dying for more. I feel so empty, even with Jarek's larger than expected dick inside of me.

"Please," I pant, "I need more." Apparently, that admission is the only thing they were waiting for. In a flash, Milo is next to us, and Jarek is rolling over with me on top of him. I don't have to wonder why; I know how badly Milo has been dying to fuck my ass.

I feel his hand reach between Jarek and me, cupping slick to coat himself with. I'm surprised that Jarek doesn't punch him for touching his dick. Hmm, maybe they won't be so hard to convince that sharing doesn't have to be exclusive to me.

I don't have time to ponder that idea. Milo slides his cock into my rosebud, slowly inching inside until he's fully inserted. I moan at how amazing it feels. After a moment, he and Jarek start moving in tandem, one thrusting when the other pulls back. The rush of sensation is almost too much for me. I start to collapse onto Jarek's chest, but Milo wraps an arm around my waist to hold me up.

I turn my head and kiss him deeply as I race toward my release. Before I get there, I want Raf to get involved. When I release Milo's lips, I reach for Raf. He kneels in front of me with very little encouragement, already knowing what I want.

His dick is hard and ready, pointing at my face when he settles close enough for me to reach. I grab the base with one hand and lick it before sucking him down as far as I can. How did I manage to find three men who are sized well above average? I mean, that is the norm for romance novels, not real life. Humming my contentment around his cock, I feel him jump at the sensation.

I pump myself on his dick a few times, willing him to understand exactly what I want. My eyes meet his and I nod slightly. Then I relax as he takes over fucking my mouth as Jarek pounds my pussy and Milo thrusts into my ass. In this moment, I feel so full. Relief washes over me as the pain goes away, being replaced with the pleasure of being cooperatively fucked by my three mates at the same time.

They push me toward orgasm after orgasm, until I feel as if I'll explode if I have another. I flick my tongue around Raf's dick, knowing exactly what will set him off. I want him to come first, so he can bite me with the other two when they come. I have to push him further to get him there first.

Once I start stroking him with my tongue, he eases up on his thrusts, letting me take over. Within a minute, he's shooting his release down my throat. I swallow before releasing him from my mouth with an audible pop. "I'm so close. I need you three to claim me together, when I come."

They grunt their understanding. Jarek keeps bouncing himself up into me, while Milo has slowed down, obviously getting close himself. Raf reaches between Jarek and me, then starts stroking my clit. I cry out with my orgasm, and feel three sets of teeth on my neck and shoulders. Jarek bites me on my scent gland, Milo on the opposite shoulder, and Raf goes straight for my neck on the same side as Milo. I wonder if they discussed it before. The whole thing goes smoother than I ever would have expected.

The moment they all pull away from me, I collapse onto Jarek's chest. Milo slides out of me, reaching his release when they pushed me into mine. Jarek's knot is the only thing holding us together. I lay there, panting, while Jarek rocks gently against me. Milo and Raf rub their hands down my back and over my hair.

"Look at you, being a good girl." I'm not sure which one of them says it. The other one says, "Such a good girl, taking that knot." I purr at them, even though I can't tell which one is which right now. I'm nearly comatose with bliss from so many orgasms and being claimed.

I can feel Jarek's release, his cock twitching as his knot finally releases us. I know that I'm going to pass out soon, because my body needs to rest. Before I can, Milo is next to me with a warm, damp rag. He cleans me up and holds me. Then I realize that Jarek is no longer holding me. I try to lift my head, but I'm too exhausted.

I whimper, hoping the sound will make him come back. Instead, Raf appears next to me and holds a straw up to my lips. "It's water. You need to hydrate." I start with a small sip. The ice-cold water tastes like the best thing I've ever had. I drink deeply until the cup is empty.

A shiver rushes through me, and I realize that I'm covered in sweat, even after Milo cleaned me up. One of them wraps a soft blanket around me. Just when I feel like Jarek is never coming back, his face pops up in front of me. He holds a candy bar up and I manage to nod. My stomach growls, and I realize that I don't know how long we've been occupied here.

I scarf down the candy bar, then Milo insists that I need more than just sugar. I let him feed me a protein bar and some fruit before I'm just too tired to stay awake.

NOW WHAT?

MILO

Ness's heat lasts for thirty-six hours. During that time, we each take turns knotting with her, cleaning up after, and making sure she eats before she passes out again. After three days straight of taking turns knotting our girl, we're all exhausted. I'm awake before the others, and take my time making breakfast. I have no idea if we'll all stay in this family suite or go back to our separate spaces. I know that Ness' heat is finished because her fever is gone and she slept all night. Even being inexperienced with omega heats, I can tell the difference.

I find bacon in the fridge and pancake mix in the pantry. That should be a good enough breakfast for everyone. I expect today to be pretty chill, giving us all time to relax and recover. That thought is shot down as soon as Jarek stomps into the room.

"You okay?" I ask, holding out a cup of coffee.

He growls but takes the cup from me. I think he'll feel better once he gets some caffeine in him, but it doesn't seem to help.

I notice that he's dressed, so he knows Ness' heat is finished too. Jarek pulls out his phone, taps a few buttons, then curses under his breath. A moment later, he walks away. I think for a second that he's going back to the nest, but he turns and leaves the apartment.

Fuck, I wonder what that's about. By the time I'm finished cooking breakfast, Raf and Ness appear. They've obviously showered and are dressed in clean clothes. I set the food down on the table and make sure I've turned off the stove.

"Good morning, sunshine," I say to Ness as I kiss her cheek.

"You made all this?" she asks in return. I nod and gesture for them to sit. I bring three cups of coffee and the syrup to the table.

"I did. Jarek had coffee, but didn't stick around for food." I want to ask if something happened, but I can already see from Ness' expression that it did.

"Well, that's his loss, then." I decide from her words that I'm not going to push the issue. I can ask Raf about it later.

We sit down and eat in amiable silence, never discussing the missing pack member or his attitude this morning. When we finish, Raf stands and starts clearing plates. "I'll clean up. You should go find Jarek. He has a job for you." I'm curious now, so I ask what I know I shouldn't.

"Is that what he was so pissed about earlier? And what he fought with Ness about?" I know I should direct the question to her, but he's the one talking to me right now.

"Yes, the dick thinks you have to prove your loyalty to him. As if you're just some random thug off the street and can't be trusted," she growls.

Raf holds up his hands in defeat. "You know he has to protect the family, and the pack. It's not like he's singling Milo out. Everyone has to prove their loyalty, even me."

"I didn't. Or is he going to give me a task as well?" Venom drips off her words. Would he make her prove herself? After we claimed her and she claimed us, that seems ridiculous to me. But I don't know him that well, so I guess anything is possible.

"Ness, come on. You know he's not going to make you prove your loyalty. It's not the same thing. Milo was a Fed. Jarek has to be sure he's not still working with them to take us down. Look, Milo isn't offended by it. Are you, Milo?" Raf turns the end of his justification toward me.

"I get it. I'll do whatever I need to. It's okay, Ness. Nothing to be upset about." I try to defend Jarek, but can tell from her face that it's not going to help the situation. I kiss her cheek again, and turn toward the door. "I'm gonna go find Jarek. Good Luck, Raf. I'll see you two later."

I can hear them start yelling the moment I get to the door. My day has to go better than his will. I wonder what Jarek has in mind for me, and hope it's not anything too bad. I'm not even sure I want to get mixed up in his mafia family. I just want to be with Ness.

I'm not sure where I'm supposed to meet him, so I go to Jarek's apartment and knock. The door swings open and I can hear the shower running. Probably best to wait for him. Inside or out? I decide that it's safer to wait in his living room than to stay in the hall, just in case Ness and Raf move to a different apartment. I wouldn't put it past her to try and get away from him if he's still defending Jarek.

I understand why she's pissed, but I expected him to test me in some way. I wonder if she knows what he has in mind. That could be what pissed her off. Or it could just be that she's feeling protective of me and doesn't like him testing me at all. I won't know until he tells me my task. I sit on the couch and wait for him to finish his shower.

The moment I hear the water shut off; I call out to him. "Jarek? Raf said you have a job for me. I'm waiting out here. I didn't want to surprise you."

I hear him grunt his response, but that lets me know he heard me. I hate Ness being upset, but I want to stay here with her, and it seems like the only way to do that is by completing whatever task Jarek gives me and proving he can trust me.

VANESSA

I am beyond pissed that Jarek feels like Milo has to prove his loyalty. And I'm furious that Raf just keeps defending him. But when Milo joins in, I feel as if my feelings are being pushed away. It's just like being around my father. I will not stand for it. I leave Raf with the dishes and stomp to the shower. It doesn't matter that I've already showered once today, I'm taking another. I need the time to calm down. I would have been glad to have company today instead of being left alone while they worked, but knowing that Jarek thinks I need a babysitter sets me off too.

I do not need supervision. I'm not going anywhere. I wish he would believe me. Maybe I should ask for a job to prove it to him. Would that even convince him? Probably not. That fucker would believe I'd completed the job just to spite him. I can't win here.

I turn on the water, as hot as it will go. Once it's heated the room up, I strip down and step inside, letting the heat warm me. Somehow it helps to cool my anger. The longer I stand under the hot spray, the more I see the reasoning behind Jarek's plan. Logically, I know that Milo used to be a Fed, and that he could be secretly working for them to take down D'Angelo's operation. But it hurts my heart that Jarek can't trust Milo the way I do. I guess it would be different if they'd claimed each other too.

Maybe I can talk them into that at some point. I mean, it makes sense, right? We're all connected. Why not have the guys claim each other? At least claim Milo and let him claim them. Raf and Jarek claiming each other would be a little weird. And if it leads to a little sword crossing, I wouldn't complain. Again, unless Jarek and Raf were doing it. Of course, with those two, they'd probably take sword crossing to mean fencing with their cocks. That would be hilarious to watch.

My thoughts are getting away from me. I have no idea how long I've been in the shower, but the water stays hot. I hate feeling like I was irrational earlier. But it's not like I have to tell any of them that I understand. I can stick to being pissed about it and make them grovel for my forgiveness. That sounds like a plan.

With my newfound resolve to not admit I made a mistake in getting upset, I finish my shower, carefully combing the tangles out of my dark hair. Once I'm dried and dressed, I return to the living area of the new suite. I expect Raf to be gone, but to my surprise, he's relaxing on the couch with a movie. Well, at least he's obedient. No doubt, Jarek told him to make sure I'm not left alone.

It's not like I can leave, even if I want to. Which I don't. Not with my father scouring the city for me to make sure I'm dead. It's not safe anywhere but here. And the only reason I'm safe here is that no one knows I'm here. The two men who helped abduct me are dead, and the three who know about me are my mates. The rest of Jarek's men are kept in the dark. They only know that he had a "guest" but that they were dealt with and were no longer a concern.

I wonder if he'll actually apply for a pack certification now that we're bonded. It would involve admitting that I'm alive, which would open us up to attack from my father. I don't want to be his dirty little secret, but at the moment, I don't have a choice. It's just another thing to add to my sour mood.

"Hey, love. Do you want to watch a movie with me? I promise not to defend Jarek anymore." Raf's offer is too good to refuse. I don't really want to be alone; I just don't want to fight about Jarek and his asinine testing of Milo's loyalty.

"Fine. What are we watching?" I can see it's a cartoon, which would seem odd, but I know how much Raf loves those princess movies. Something about the underdog getting the girl always makes him happy.

"It's a classic. She's beautiful, he's a monster. They fall in love and everything is perfect." I can't help but smile at his enthusiasm. This man, who kills people as part of his job, is completely into cartoon movies. He even sings all the songs, which is adorable.

"You are such a child, Raf. But I love that about you." I make the admission begrudgingly, not wanting to fight with him, but not wanting to smooth things over yet either. I want to question him about Milo's assignment, but I know that even if he had an idea what Jarek sent Milo out to do, Raf would not tell me. At least, not without some sexual favors. And I'm not in the mood to bribe him right now, so, I'll have to wait for Milo to get back.

"Are we moving in here now, or just saving this place for my heats?" I don't know if anyone has asked, but if they did, it was when I wasn't around.

Raf shrugs. "Don't know. My guess is that Jarek will leave that up to you. If you want, I can help you move your stuff in here, then you can help me move mine. We'll let Milo and Jarek move their own stuff." His offer is sweet, and I consider it for a moment.

"Maybe after the movie." I don't feel like doing anything right now. My heart still hurts from Jarek's attitude and hateful words earlier. I drop onto the couch, as far away from Raf as possible. He glances at me before flopping over to lay his head in my lap. I guess that's what I get for trying to avoid making up with him.

JAREK

I know that I've pissed Ness off, and I expect Milo to have the same reaction. I can't stand to argue with him after he's cooked breakfast for all of us, so I slam back my coffee and leave. I make myself some toast and grumble for a bit before getting into the shower. I'll have to go back and get Milo in a while. There's no reason to ruin their breakfast, so it can wait. Even if he doesn't do the job today, it'll hold until tomorrow.

I wish Ness could see my side. He has to be tested. I have to know that I can trust him with my family's business. More than that, I have to know that I can trust him with her. Which is really what this is all about. I can't just accept him into our pack without knowing that he would sacrifice himself to protect her.

The moment I turn the shower off, I hear something. Wrapping the towel around my waist, I head for the door, then hear

Milo shout to me. Good, he's here. I guess I won't have to fight with Ness anymore today after all. Part of me is dying to go to her and apologize, begging her to forgive me, and promising to never do it again. But that part of me gets shoved down by the alpha who craves protecting his family.

If I could find Dragonetti's records, I could use that to garner favor with the Feds. That would get him out of my way. But killing him would be way more satisfactory. I'm itching to just walk up to the old man and put a bullet in his head. The more I learn about how he's treated Ness, the more I want to lock him in the basement and take him apart piece by piece. I can't decide which idea would cause him more suffering, though. Getting him locked up would result in him knowing that his daughter is mine now. And I can't get past that idea, either.

I shake the thought away as I walk out into the living room. Sure enough, Milo is sitting on my couch, waiting. At least he was considerate enough to close the door and not mess with any of my stuff. Everything is just as I left it.

"Raf tell you what you're here for?" I ask, wondering if I should expect an attack.

Milo stands, nodding. "Yeah. Ness is pissed." He pauses and holds out his hand to shake mine. "But I get it. You don't really know me. And you have a lot to protect here. What do I need to do?"

His complete lack of anger or animosity throws me off. I almost don't want to make him do the job now. But I know that if I don't, one of my guys will find out, and there will be hell to pay for showing favoritism to the former Fed. I think he can sense my hesitation, because he keeps talking after shaking my hand.

"Seriously, Jarek. I would think less of you if there wasn't something I had to do to prove myself. Ness will come around. She's just quick to defend those she loves. And I can see how she would view this as an attack against me. But I know it's not. It's a good leader, taking care of what's his. So, let's talk about what I have to do, shall we?"

"Thanks, man. I appreciate that you understand. I wasn't trying to piss anyone off. I tell ya what. I'll go with you, and we can move things along quicker." I can't believe I'm making the offer to be his driver, when normally I'd wait it out here and see how the new guy fared when he came back.

Milo laughs. "You don't have to do that. Unless you want to. I'm cool with it either way. Of course, if you're with me, there's less chance that Dragonetti can get to me. But really, I'm good either way. Just tell me what I have to do."

"Okay, here's the plan." We sit at the kitchenette and I go over the job with him. It's fairly simple, but if he gets caught, it'll be felony charges. Which would definitely tell me if he's still secretly a Fed. The more we talk, the less I believe he's going to betray us. After we go over the whole thing twice, discussing the timeline and maps, Milo nods.

"I've got it. Simple really. Get in, get the box, get out. The whole thing is a matter of timing." This man casually discussing robbing the evidence locker at the police station makes me laugh.

"It is, but you know if you get caught, you're toast. Unless your FBI contacts would bail you out." I raise an eyebrow and he laughs.

"No one will bail me out if I get caught. I can't even get Jackson to answer my calls, and he used to be my partner. Of course, I got rid of my phone, so he probably thinks it's some scammer calling. Doesn't matter. I'm in. You need that box, you'll have it." His determination impresses me. If he can actually pull this off, I'm buying him a steak dinner. Hell, if he gets the box and makes it out without anyone stopping him, I'd almost be tempted to suck his dick.

Almost. Maybe I'll get Ness to do it for me. And I'll take care of her while she takes care of him. Then she'll have to forgive me, right? Even I see how badly that suggestion would go over. I'll just keep that thought to myself. I do need to find a way to convince her to get over being mad at me. Maybe Milo will help me come up with something I can pick up for her that will help me out. It can't hurt to ask him on the way.

RAFAEL

I know that Ness is trying to stay pissed and that's why she sits at the end of the couch, as far away from me as she can get. That's also why I flop over and lay my head in her lap. I'm not about to let her stay mad at me for something Jarek did. Even if I agree with him, I'm not trying to fight with her. I want us to snuggle while we watch the movie.

I would love a nap, but I'm not sure how cooperative Ness is feeling. I know she can't get off this floor, but she could hide from me and make it hard for me to do what Jarek asked. All he wants is for her to be protected. Delaying my sleep is the least I can do. Besides, I understand that she's hurting. I want to kiss it and make it better, but I'm sure she's just as tired of sex as the rest of us after dealing with her heat.

I never thought I'd feel that way about sex. Especially sex with Ness. But today, comforting her is more important. I feel her tense when my head lands in her lap. It doesn't take long for her fingers to start running through my hair, though. Good. That tells me that she's not as mad as she wants me to believe.

We watch the movie in silence for a while. It drives me crazy to watch quietly instead of singing the songs. But I do it. Because I think it's what Ness needs. A little quiet and emotional space to process her feelings. I know she's mad at Jarek for not trusting Milo. I just don't think that's why he's forcing the issue.

I think it has more to do with saving face. If anyone under him found out that Milo didn't have to do a task to prove himself, they would lose respect for Jarek, and that would undermine our entire operation. Which is exactly what I want to tell her. But I can't because it would let her know that he really does care about what other people think, even though he pretends like he doesn't.

My cousin is a very complex man, and has many facets. The only reason I understand is that he told me as much when I had to complete my job. It isn't so much about proving yourself to Jarek as it is proving yourself to the crew. He should have told her that. Then she couldn't possibly argue about it being pointless.

I turn my face to look at Ness while her fingers stroke my hair. She's beautiful, and seems to be engrossed in the movie. It took her long enough to get there. Now I can just look at her. A few moments pass, then she looks down at me.

"What?" she asks, suddenly self-conscious at me staring.

"Nothing. I just like to look at you, that's all. You really are beautiful." I watch her cheeks turn pink.

"Shut up, Raf. That's stupid."

I growl at her and her eyes go wide. "Do not tell me it's stupid to think you're beautiful. It's stupid to argue about pointless things that won't change. It's not stupid to admire beauty."

"Okay. You win. I'm stupid." Her words are quiet, but I can feel the pain in them. She thinks I'm talking about her fight with Jarek.

"Ness, baby, that's not what I'm saying. I understand why you're mad at Jarek. I do. I also understand why he has to test Milo. Okay? We don't have to agree on it. I'm not even talking about that. I was saying that you'll never convince me that you're not beautiful, so there's no point in having that argument. That's all." I stare at her as she averts her eyes for a minute.

"I know. I'm trying so hard to stay mad. But I get it too. I don't want to, but I do. He has to do it. Otherwise, he'll lose respect, and that will lead to anarchy. We can't have that. But did he have to be such a dick about it?" Her quiet words make my heart jump. Exactly what I thought. He hurt her feelings. She wasn't really ever mad; she was hurt.

I sit up and pull her into my arms. "I thought that was the problem. It's okay to be upset that Jarek is being a dick. He's a dick most of the time. I promise I'll talk to him, and he will do better. But I need you to promise that you'll be honest about your feelings and not try to hide them behind anger." I tug her more until she lets me drag her into my lap. Her head rests on my chest and I know she's close to tears.

"He does make me angry, though, even when he hurts my feelings." Of course, she'd defend herself that way.

"Trust me, I know. He pisses me off too, especially when he hurts your feelings. But don't take it out on me for defending him. Or Milo. He's just trying to be accepted here. And he'll probably do whatever it takes just to be close to you. I know I would if I were in his situation." I explain carefully, not wanting to upset her further.

She reaches up and wipes tears from her eyes, and my heart melts. I can't handle tears. They will be my undoing. "Aww, baby, don't cry. It's okay. We'll tie him up later and you can punish him. Okay? I'll help by setting it up however you want. How would you punish him? Spanking? Knives? Tie him up and make him watch us have sex?" She laughs at my suggestions, and I know I'm on the path to cheering her up. It's a bonus if I get to watch her take Jarek down a notch or two at the same time.

VANESSA

I know that Raf is joking, but I can't help considering a punishment for Jarek. I'm pretty sure he would do the same for me, so why not? He deserves it, after all. "You'd really help me with that? Even knowing that he'll retaliate?" I can't believe that Raf may be serious.

He cocks an eyebrow at me. "Of course. He's my cousin. I'll hold him down and beat the shit out of him if it makes you smile."

Oh, shit. He's serious. Like really serious. "Well, in that case, maybe I will come up with a punishment for him." I realize at this moment that I have no idea what Jarek is into. I feel like he'd be a daddy type, but that's never been my thing. "Do you think he'd enjoy being spanked? I'm at a loss here. I have no idea what he would enjoy and what would actually be a punishment."

Raf's eyes light up at the thought that I need him to help me with this. "Well, I don't know a lot about his sex life either. Your heat was the closest we've come to anything like that. But I know that he isn't afraid of a little pain. So spanking or even knife play won't bother him as much as being tied down and forced to watch as we pleasure you would. I'm pretty sure that would be the worst form of torture for him, especially if you serviced him but he couldn't reciprocate."

I love Raf's idea. "Do we have a way to tie him up?" I can't imagine that my men just have those kinds of things lying around. But from Raf's face, I know that they do. "Seriously? You just have restraints lying around somewhere?"

"Not for sex purposes, but yeah. Have you forgotten about what we do here? We have all kinds of ways to tie people up. I think there are some leather cuffs downstairs. You wanna go with me to check?" Wait, Raf is offering to let me leave our secure floor? That's huge.

"Aren't you afraid someone will see me? Or that I'll try to escape?" I can't help but ask the questions as I stare at him in disbelief.

"Well, most of the guys are gone right now. And the ones that should still be here are pretty good at minding their own business. If it worries you, I can give you one of my hoodies and you can pull the hood up. As for escaping, I don't think you would. Or is that your little secret—that you're waiting until we trust you to run away?" I'm almost offended by his question, until I look at him and see that he's teasing me. Raf believes me that I wouldn't run away, and I didn't even have to tell him.

"I mean, we are bonded. That would make it a little hard for me to hide from you, wouldn't it?" I tease back. He bumps my shoulder with his and walks out of the apartment. I chase after him just to see where he's going. I run into his back when he stops at his door. "What the fuck, Raf?" I ask as he turns around and grabs me.

"See? You wouldn't leave. I know it. You're too crazy about me." He hugs me tightly before shoving me into his apartment. "Now, let's get you a hoodie so we can go get those cuffs." I follow him into his bedroom as he grabs a pull over hoodie from his closet. It's black and has a band logo on it.

"What band is this?" I ask as I pull it over my head and adjust the hood to cover my hair. I don't recognize the picture, but it looks like it's from a concert of some sort.

"Have you never heard of Tool?" he balks at me. "Well, I know what we're doing after we get the cuffs set up. I need to fix this hole in your musical education."

My eyes go wide for a minute before I realize he's teasing me again. I can't believe I briefly think he's angry because I don't know a band. That's ridiculous. Of course, my mate is not going to be angry with me for that. I laugh and shake my head at him.

"As long as I can punish Jarek, I'll listen to whatever you want me to," I tell him as we head for the elevator. "Also, this hoodie is so soft. I might just keep it."

He growls, but I glance at him and see his smile. He likes the idea that I want to keep his clothes. I'm pretty sure they all do. But I wouldn't be surprised if any of them had a favorite piece and refuse to share it with me.

"Well, it is my favorite, so maybe we can share?" I smile at his offer of a compromise.

"I'll think about it," I respond. Then I squeal as he grabs me and starts digging his fingers into my sides, tickling me as the elevator descends. I'm glad we've made up from our disagreement this morning. I hope that punishing Jarek makes me feel better about our fight. I would much rather get along with my men, but I need them to stop being stupid first. Otherwise, this will never work.

When we get downstairs, I can see that Raf was right. Most of their crew is gone. The ones who are around don't pay any attention to us. I'm not even sure any of them look my way. It's probably for the best. I'm sure they can tell we're bonded. That usually deters other alphas and betas from expressing too much interest in someone else's mate. I think it's a scent thing. Everyone who bonds has a slight change in their scent, indicating that they're taken, and making them not smell as good to potential suitors. I had forgotten about that when he offered to let me come with him.

CHAPTER THIRTEEN

MAKING A PLAN

JAREK

I sit in the car while Milo makes his way inside the police precinct headquarters. Guilt starts to eat at me as Ness' words echo in my head. *What if he gets caught? What if he gets hurt trying to prove himself?* Fuck, maybe she was right. I shouldn't have made him do this. But there was no other way to show the crew that he's not going to betray us. Besides, he understands that I have no choice here. Why can't she?

Maybe I should spank it into her. After all, she threw a huge fit and was extremely disrespectful. I should bend her over my knee as soon as we get back. And do it in front of the entire pack. Yeah, I know that's just Milo and Raf, but then she'll understand that she can't talk to me that way in front of them.

I can picture it. Milo and I walk into the family suite where Raf and Ness are waiting with dinner on the table. I walk past the food, grabbing her arm and dragging her to the couch. I sit and pull her onto my lap with her ass in the air. Then I rip off her leggings and thong, tossing them onto the floor. Milo and

Raf stand there with their mouths gaping open while slap her ass until it's red and raw. She'll cry and probably try to fight me, but I'm stronger, so I will be able to hold her off and make her take her punishment.

Of course, I know what will happen if I do that. They'll baby her and then it'll be three against one. Somehow, I'm the bad guy here and there's no way to win this time. I sigh deeply as I stare at the building and hope Milo is having better luck than I am.

My mind goes over every possible scenario with him as well. I see him walking into the building and immediately being arrested. When that happens, he doesn't have anyone to call, because he doesn't have anyone's numbers memorized. So, he has to call his mother and tell her. Then she's panicking and trying to figure out what happened to her successful FBI agent son to make him get arrested. What a way to find out your son is actually working for the mafia! I don't wish that on any mother who isn't already in the family.

Or even worse, he automatically dials Dragonetti, who then discovers that Milo has been with me and that we have Ness, who isn't actually dead at all. Fuck, there are at least a dozen ways this can go tits up on me here. Why did I have to choose this mission for him to prove his loyalty? Oh, yeah, because he was assigned to this precinct while he worked on the mafia taskforce. It's the only way I'll know for sure he's on our side.

At least the box he has to grab is small enough to fit inside his jacket. Provided he can get into the evidence locker to snatch it. I wonder how he'll play this off with the people who know him. With as long as he worked on the task force and was stationed at this particular building, it will be nearly impossible for him to get in and out without someone recognizing him.

There's almost no way he can get what I sent him in there for. It's virtually impossible. If he can find a way, he'll be a legend among the crew. Maybe that's what I was really thinking. Or what I should have been thinking, instead of how I didn't want anyone to think I went easy on him because of our pack. Not that anyone knows about that yet. But they will.

I'll have to make an announcement, and my guys will have to see what he's done to earn his place. Only then will they respect him enough to follow his orders. I hope someday Ness can understand that is the real reason I did things this way. It's not to hurt Milo or keep him from becoming one of us. It's a way for him to earn the crew's respect. They won't take kindly to being ordered around by a new guy, especially one who's a former Fed.

Maybe instead of spanking, I should sit down with the three of them and really talk to Ness about all of this. I'm not sure if she's been sheltered or not from the way she reacts to things. It seems as if her father has managed to keep a lot of our world away from his only child. Then other times, she understands and knows more than I thought she would. She's impossible to read.

Nearly as much so as this job is for Milo to complete. The longer I sit here, the more I think this is a mistake. What was

I thinking sending him into the center hub of the local police and asking him to steal for me? I should have listened to Ness. I should call him and tell him to forget the whole thing. There's no way he'll make it out of there without getting arrested. Then what am I going to do? Better yet, what will I say to Ness?

I'm so fucked here. If Milo gets arrested, I'll have to find a way to get him out. Then we'll be publicly connected. Maybe I can drop some cash off to his mother. If only I knew where she lived. Fuck. I slam my fist down on the steering wheel. I have to call it off. I pull my phone out of my pocket and dial Milo's number.

I hold it to my ear and listen to each ring, panic building with every moment that he doesn't answer. Fuck it, I'm going in.

MILO

With nothing more to go on than the size of the box and the file number it's attached to, I head into the police station. I know there's no chance of getting in and out easily, since so many of these officers know me. But I have an advantage that Jarek hasn't considered. I know exactly where the cameras are and what their rotations are as well. I know where to stand and when to walk without being noticed.

As long as I avoid the chief, I'll be just fine. I'm not even sweating at the prospect of getting caught. I'm pretty sure I can play it off as a test of security since I used to work here and know the officers who usually handle evidence.

I don't want to risk getting too cocky about it, though. Anything can go wrong, and usually does. I stroll past the front desk, walking casually into the bullpen as if I belong. That's the key aspect here, acting like I'm supposed to be here. I've got this. No problem.

I turn a corner to head toward the evidence storage area, and run straight into Jackson. "What the fuck are you doing here?" I ask without thinking.

My former FBI partner looks me up and down before responding. "I could ask you the same thing. At least I still have a job. What's going on?" He pulls me into an empty interrogation room and closes the door. "There are rumors that Dragonetti is after you. Somehow, you've double-crossed him? Is any of it true?"

I raise my eyebrows at him, avoiding his questions. "Where did you hear that?" Fuck, if Dragonetti has already put word out that he's after me, I'm not safe anywhere. I'm pretty sure a couple of the guys I used to work with are working for him too.

"Around. You know. I can't exactly tell you anything since you're no longer FBI. But you need to lay low. And don't let the chief see you. She's still pissed." I nod at Jackson's warning.

"I figured. Don't worry, I'm just in and out." I realize that he's waiting for me to explain further. Fuck. I need something quick. "I just need to pop down to the coroner and pick up a death certificate for the Dragonetti girl. There are some things that don't add up there, and I'm looking into it in a PI capacity."

Double fuck. He already knows that Dragonetti wouldn't put a hit on me and hire me for a job. Too late now, I'm going with it.

"If Dragonetti is after you, who hired you to look at the girl's death?" Yup, there's that pesky question. Nope, not a problem.

"You know I can't disclose that information. But I can say that the girl had more than one parent, if you know what I mean," I say, implying that Mrs. Dragonetti had been the one to hire me. I wonder for a moment if Jackson is going to let this go, or if I'll have to dig myself out of this hole.

"I got ya. Just keep out of the chief's sight and you'll be okay. You want me to go with you?" He looks hopeful, but I shoot him down.

"Nah, man. I'm good. I can't justify taking you away from your job just because someone's mom doesn't want to admit her baby is dead. But I'll give you a call and we can hang sometime." The false promise falls easily off my tongue and I nearly feel guilty for lying to my former partner. Nearly. I have a family to protect.

And now I have to go down to the basement and talk to the coroner so my story pans out. So much for in and out. I shake Jackson's hand and head down the hall to the elevator. Once inside, I push the button for the basement and act casual while it descends.

The doors open and I walk into the office. "Hey, Milo! I haven't seen you in a while. What's up? I thought you got canned?" Stacy is the bright spot of the whole situation, as always.

"I did. I'm doing some PI work now. Got hired to look into the Dragonetti girl's death. Can I get a copy of her certificate?" I wink at her, remembering just in time that I shouldn't be hung up on a dead girl.

"Give me about ten minutes, and I'll have it for you." She turns back to the computer to continue what she was doing before I came in.

"I'll be back. Gotta hit the men's room." I watch as she nods, not looking up from the computer. At least evidence is directly above us. With any luck, I'll be able to sneak in, get the box and be back within the ten minutes Stacy gave me.

I take the stairs, because they're closer to the men's room than the elevator. And they open directly at the door of the evidence storage area. I poke my head out the door and see that the officer on duty has stepped away to use the restroom himself. That gives me maybe three minutes to pick the lock and slip inside, while avoiding the cameras.

Okay, Milo, let's do this. I watch the camera move and as soon as it turns away from the door, I stroll up. I'm shocked to find it unlocked and slightly ajar. I slip my hands into the surgical gloves I brought and sneak inside.

Within less than a minute, I have the box secured in my pocket and am heading back downstairs. I manage to leave everything exactly as it was when I arrived. Stacy has the certificate ready for me when I return to her office, and I casually make my way out of the building.

Just as I walk out the door of the station, I see Jarek getting out of the car and heading my way.

VANESSA

The dungeon, as I've started to call it, is dark and smells of iron. I know it's from the bloodshed that happens here, and it doesn't phase me anymore. I long to be part of it all, standing beside my men as they tackle whatever is tossed in our way. Right now, that happens to be Jarek's punishment.

Since Raf's suggestion, I've been thinking about how I'm going to pull it off. I've got nearly every detail planned out now, in just the short time it's taken us to get downstairs. "Do you think just wrist cuffs will hold him? Or do you have ankle cuffs too? I think we might need both." I suggest as we leisurely stroll down the hall toward the torture rooms.

Raf is holding my hand, and I've let the hood fall back from my hair. It's hot, and no one is looking at me anyway. I'm still keeping the hoodie, though. It's soft and smells like him. There

I go getting distracted again. Okay, leather cuffs to hold Jarek in place. Yes, okay. I'm focused again.

"I'm gonna grab both. I'm sure he'll cooperate once you explain why he's being punished, but you can never be too careful. Also, don't talk about it too loudly. Just because they aren't looking doesn't mean they're not listening. We don't want to embarrass him in front of the crew." Raf's explanation sounds more like an admonishment, and I feel my cheeks turn pink at his words.

Tears fill my eyes at the thought that I might have done something to cause Jarek to lose the respect of his men. I vow to keep quiet until we're back on our floor. At least there, I know that no one can see or hear us.

Raf leads me into one of the torture rooms, then stops abruptly. "What?" I ask before looking around his shoulder to see the man hanging on the wall.

"I didn't realize this room was occupied. I just need to grab some supplies, then we'll be out of here." His words are directed at the man hanging on the wall. Raf steps in front of me, blocking me from view. "Hood up, baby," he whispers over his shoulder. I do as he says with no argument. I have no idea who this man is, but if there's a chance that he could recognize me and tell someone, I'm not taking it.

I want to run back to the safety of our floor, but I don't want to leave Raf. I also have no way to get the elevator to work without him, so I'm stuck. He turns me to face the door as he rummages around to find what we came for. This situation is making me more nervous as every moment ticks by. My heart starts to race, and my breathing is getting shallow.

I jump and squeal when Raf's hand touches my back. I'm not expecting the contact, and it scares me. "It's okay, baby. I got what we came for. We can go now." He eases me out the door and closes it behind us with a thud.

"Who was that man?" I didn't get a good look, but there was something familiar about him.

"One of the alphas your father tried to sell you to. I didn't realize which room he was in. We have a team taking care of him. But I don't need him seeing you. That would take away part of the fun of what they're doing to him."

I make a face at that. "You're posing the torture as punishment for my death?" It's just a guess, but I know I'm right when he looks at me and winks. "That's completely stupid. Why would you guys care if I'm dead?"

"Because we were planning to kidnap you and ransom you back to your father, of course. They're playing it off like we're pissed at losing out on the money. He may get to go home when we're done with him. He has no idea where we are or how he got here. As long as he doesn't see anything, he'll go home as soon as we have the cool mil we're extorting from his family."

I'm both impressed and appalled at Raf's explanation. "You're extorting a million dollars from his family? Are they actually going to pay that?"

"If they want to see their boy again, they will. And don't under value yourself. A million is really low for an omega." He winks at me again.

"I don't know what to say to that. It's brilliant and crazy. Were you guys really going to kidnap me and ransom me back to my father? Or is that just something you came up with to torture and extort this guy and his family?" I'm not sure I want the answer, but I can't stop myself from asking. The insanity of it all makes my head spin.

"Of course, we were. That is, until we found out he was trying to kill you. Then it became about protecting you. If my original plan had worked, we could have ransomed you and then kept you. It would have been great."

"You sound disappointed that it didn't work out that way. You know, if we took my father out, I could legally take over his business dealings and you'd have all of his money," I offer.

"Wait, you'd be into that?" he asks, stopping just outside of the elevator on our floor.

"Of course. I want to take him down as badly as you guys, now that I know he's trying to kill me. Please tell me that Jarek will let me help," I'm practically begging.

"We'll convince him that it's our best option. We've been talking about it since we took you. He's just not sure how to make it happen. So, if you have any ideas, you may want to pitch them while you have him tied up tonight."

RAFAEL

I help Ness set up the leather cuffs for Jarek's punishment. It's going to be the best thing I've ever been a part of, especially if she goes with my suggestion. Okay, I would totally hate it as a punishment, but I'm going to love being on the other side of it. And he deserves it for being a dick to her. He should have given her a logical explanation and she would have agreed to letting him test Milo's loyalty.

With the cuffs in place, Ness decides that we can snuggle up on the couch for a bit while we wait for them to get back. We talk for a while about her idea of how to get her father out of the way. Then we argue about it. In the end, we agree to let Jarek decide.

It's nice to just hold her, and I think we both doze for an hour or so. I jump at the door opening, then relax when I realize it's just Milo and Jarek. So, either Jarek changed his mind, or Milo proved himself. I can't wait to see which it is.

"Ness, baby. They're back," I whisper into her dark curls and her eyes flutter open.

"Already?" she asks, searching my face. "Both of them?" I nod and she sighs heavily. I watch the worry leave her eyes. "Good." She doesn't make a move to go to them, which surprises me. Then I realize it's because she's still mad at Jarek for making Milo do this. And she's probably mad at Milo for playing along. Well, that's better for me anyway. I like being the only one not on her shit list.

Jarek and Milo walk into the room, talking quietly. "I still can't believe you pulled that off. It's insane. You're going to be a legend around here."

A legend? What the fuck did Jarek have him do? Now I wish I'd paid more attention to what they were talking about earlier, when Jarek and Ness were fighting.

Milo shakes his head. "It was luck. I'm telling you; I got really lucky with the whole thing. It did help that I know the cameras and all that. But come on, the guy working evidence went to the bathroom and left it open. That's luck. I might not have made it if I'd had to pick that lock."

"What exactly did you have to do?" Ness asks, raising an eyebrow at them while snuggling closer to me.

"I had to walk into the precinct and take this," he offers, holding the small box up for her to see. What the fuck is in that box? I furrow my brow, considering what Jarek could have wanted from evidence storage.

"But what's in it?" Oh, please don't let this turn into the whole, *'what's in the box?'* thing that went around after that one movie came out. Hopefully it's not body parts or something. Of course, that box is pretty small. It fits in Milo's palm.

Milo looks at the box in his hand before holding it out to Jarek. "I don't know. It wasn't my job to look in it. I just had to steal it from the right evidence box." I'm impressed at his lack of curiosity. Personally, I'm dying to know what it is.

Jarek takes the lid off the box and pulls out a diamond and sapphire bracelet. I still don't understand what's going on. Why would he have Milo break into evidence and steal a bracelet? We have enough money to buy whatever we want. He kneels in front of Ness and drapes the bracelet over her left wrist.

"This was my grandmother's. She would have wanted you to have it. As it happens, the bracelet was stolen and ended up with some, unsavory types. It took me a while to track it down. Milo was kind enough to retrieve it for you." Jarek explains as he fastens the white gold band of gems on her wrist.

"It's gorgeous. But I'm confused. Why would your grandmother want me to have it?" Ness asks.

At this point, I'm looking at Jarek the same way Ness is. Grams would want her to have it? What don't I know? I'm about to ask when he takes her hand and starts explaining.

"You met her, you know. It was years ago, but she never forgot." He tells us the story of Grams going to the corner store and thugs knocking her groceries out of her hands. Ness rushed to help her pick things up, then refused to let Grams carry the bags to the car. Apparently, Jarek saw the whole thing, but Ness got there before he could. The entire situation sounds like a meet cute from a movie, but I remember Grams talking about the sweet girl who helped her and how she wished us boys could find an omega like her.

"That was your grandmother? She was so sweet, and tried to pay me for helping. I would never take money for being kind to someone. I hope you taught those unruly boys a lesson after I left." Her eyes twinkle with mischief.

"I can neither confirm nor deny that those boys got their asses kicked by a group of D'Angelo cousins," Jarek laughs in response.

Ness smiles. "Good. Now let's talk about your plan to get my father. I can help." I'm surprised that she shifts the subject like that, but I know that she's been dying to tell Jarek her idea. We've been over the whole thing a dozen times, with me trying to talk her out of it, but she won't listen.

"I don't want you involved. I'd rather just let him think you're dead until we can take him down," Jarek argues.

"I'm pretty sure he knows she's alive," Milo interjects. "I talked to him about not believing she was gone, and I think he may have agreed with me. I didn't know at the time that he was the one after her."

VANESSA

"It doesn't matter if he knows I'm alive or not. I should be the one to help take him down. I'm the one he's trying to kill, or tried to kill. Whatever. He's my father, and if I take him out, I'll be the one in charge of his empire. Wouldn't that be better than letting Lewis or Smith have it?"

I know I'm making a good point, and I'll keep pushing until Jarek agrees. I will not back down from this. I'm going to look into the old man's eyes as I ram a knife into his throat. Woah, where did that come from? I didn't realize I want to kill him until right now.

Three pair of eyes stare at me, and I know they've seen the shift in my expression. "What?" I ask, trying to sound innocent.

"You're plotting. Spill." Fucking Milo. He can read me like no one else.

"I was just thinking about how good it will feel once my father is no longer an issue," I offer. I don't know if he believes me or not, but then Raf speaks up.

"She was fantasizing about killing the bastard," he says. How the fuck did he know that? There's no way he could know what I was thinking.

"Ah, yeah, she does have that look about her, doesn't she?" Jarek agrees. Mother fuckers. They know me better than I thought.

"Okay, yes, the thought has crossed my mind. Would it be such a bad thing, though? If I kill him, he'll be out of the way, and I'll take over his empire. Then we'll be unstoppable." I can tell my argument is working. At this point, I'm more focused on getting them to agree to this, and nearly forget that I'm supposed to be punishing Jarek right now.

That can wait. This is more important. "I don't disagree with your idea. I just don't think you should be the one to do it. He won't go down easily. It'll be a fight, and I don't think you're ready." Jarek tempers his words with his tone, and I can tell he's not doubting my ability, just my resolve. It's hard to kill family, even the ones who've wronged you.

"I understand your concern. What if we compromise?" I ask, then continue. "Use me to lure him out, and then you guys can kill him. I promise that I'll cooperate and listen to your instructions. Just please let me do this." I know I'm dangerously close to begging, but I don't care. I want him to agree so badly that I would probably let him tie me up if I thought it would help.

"What if we just call and tell him we have something he wants? We don't have to be specific, and we can keep Ness safe in the car while we deal with him." Milo's suggestion sounds interesting, but I'm not sure I want to give up my idea yet.

"Why would she be in the car? Why not leave her here where she's safe?" Raf asks him.

"Because I know she wouldn't stay here alone while we went to do this. She'd be too worried about us and would find a way to go. It's safer if we take her with us," Jarek explains. Damn, they do know me.

"Fine. I can live with that. As long as I get to go and see it happen. But I can tell you right now, he won't come alone to a meeting, even if he says he will. There will be guys hiding somewhere waiting to take you out. I need you guys to be safe. I can't lose you." Tears fill my eyes and I brush them away. I don't want to be sappy and emotional right now. I want to kill my father.

Jarek pulls me into his arms and presses a kiss to my forehead. "We'll take care of it, doll. He will pay for what he's done." The idea that these men want to kill my father should hurt me, or piss me off, or something. But it doesn't. It makes me feel loved. I know I can count on these three to take care of me forever.

"Okay, so, I'll call and get the ball rolling. I know he's not going to talk to me right away. But I can plant the seed and hint at what I'm trying to tell him. Then we'll have to wait until he calls back and get him to meet us. It'll probably take a couple of days." Jarek walks away, pulling out his phone and making the call.

I look at Raf and Milo. "Do you think this will work? Will you guys be able to take him out?"

They exchange a glance. "He deserves to be in jail for everything he's done, but if it comes down to protecting you, I'll shoot the bastard myself," Milo promises.

"Are you going to get the FBI involved?" Raf asks Milo. "I don't know how we'd stay out of prison if that happened."

Milo smirks. Cocky fucker. "I have ways. But I'm not even sure they'll talk to me after everything I did to help Dragonetti. We'll have to play it by ear." That does not make me feel better about the situation. But I trust these three with my life, so I'm willing to tamp down the fear and panic that's trying to take hold.

"I need a distraction. I'm going to go crazy worrying until this meeting happens," I admit. They look at each other before turning their attention back to me. Jarek walks back in the room at that moment.

"I think we can help with that. What did you have in mind?" he asks, wrapping an arm around me and kissing me deeply.

"More of that," I answer before winding my arms around his neck and pulling him in for another searing kiss.

Chapter Fourteen

GOING AFTER DRAGONETTI

RAFAEL

I didn't realize when Ness and I set up the cuffs that she would change her mind and insist that we tie her up. To be fair, the idea sends chills down my spine and makes my dick jump. It's too fucking hot knowing that we have a girl who wants to try new things. Who knows, maybe she'll decide she wants to do a little blood play too.

I don't focus on that, though. We'll take baby steps to get there. Whatever it takes to make her feel safe and loved. "Are you sure you don't want to stick with the original plan?" I ask as I fasten one of the cuffs onto Ness' wrist. She's lying on her back in the center of the bed, completely naked.

"I'm sure. I trust you guys. Besides, you know he'll screw up again, and we can use it on him then," she offers. I nod and move to her ankle, making sure it's secure but not too tight. Milo takes care of the other side. I'm not sure where Jarek went.

With Ness secured, we take our time stripping in front of her, giving her the distraction that she needs to calm herself. More than anything, I want to take care of her. It's all I've wanted since I met her. I can't thank Jarek enough for sending me to infiltrate Dragonetti's team. If not for that, I never would have met the woman of my dreams.

Milo clears his throat and I realize that I've been staring off into space with my dick in my hand. While seeming to look directly at him. I laugh and shrug it off. "I got distracted."

He doesn't seem offended, so I just go with it. He and Ness have no idea what I was thinking about, and I'm not offering that info up.

She laughs. "If you guys want to, I wouldn't be opposed to watching." That's so fucking hot. And now we know exactly what she thinks about it. Not that Milo and I have ever talked about it. But I catch him looking at me almost as often as he catches me looking at him.

I can't read his expression, but it seems like he's considering something. I wonder if it's Ness' suggestion or if he's looking for a gentle way to turn me down. I'm not sure if I want to know. I shrug again and take a few steps toward him. Ness hums her approval.

Milo looks at her, then at me. I can't help but chuckle at his shrug before he closes the distance between us. "I take it you might be interested?" I ask, knowing it sounds cocky.

"Maybe," he replies. "I already know you are." How could he possibly know that? Oh, yeah, I've been flirting with him for weeks. It's good to know that he didn't miss that. I try to keep it subtle. I don't want to push anything.

I brush my hand on his cheek and my heart jumps as his eyes flutter closed. My hand wraps around the back of his neck and I pull him to me. My lips gently caress his, and I hear Ness' sharp intake of breath. I hum against his lips, tracing my tongue along the seam until he parts them and flicks his tongue along mine.

It's an intense sensation, but different than it is with Ness. I nip at his lip and deepen the kiss, drawing a moan from him. Our naked bodies are pressed together now as his arms wrap around my waist. The hand on his neck holds him in place as my other hand explores his back and shoulders. I knew before that I was attracted to men as well as women, but never expected this. Ness continues to encourage us, no doubt dripping wet from watching. What a dirty girl.

After a few minutes of exploration, I break the kiss. Ness pouts, but I did it for a reason. I slide my hand down Milo's back until I'm cupping his ass. I watch his face the whole time, feeling both of our cocks harden at the contact. I kiss his jaw before trailing my tongue down his neck, nipping and sucking. I trail my teeth over his scent gland and I'm rewarded with a wave of his sea water scent. I smell my own earthy pine mingling with it before realizing that Ness' rain-soaked honeysuckle is filling the room too.

I turn to her. "You like to watch, dirty girl?"

She licks her lips and nods. "Mmm, you two are so hot."

I look at Milo again. "She likes to watch. That's so dirty." He chuckles and pulls me close for another kiss, taking control this time. Everything about this feels right. I can't wait to see where this goes. I lose myself in the sensation of Milo's lips on mine and his body pressed against me until I hear Ness start to moan as if she's getting close to coming.

When we glance over, Jarek is between her legs with his face buried in her sweet pussy. Ness is bucking against the restraints, trying to get more from him, but her eyes are still locked on us. I watch her face as my hand trails down Milo's chest before wrapping around his cock.

She cries out as I begin to slowly pump him. His moan is drowned out by her orgasm. A moment later, his hand is gripping my dick and matching my strokes. We stand there, jerking each other, while we watch Jarek feast on our girl's delicious slick. It's almost enough to push me to come. But I don't want that yet. I want to enjoy these sensations with my mates for a while longer.

Ness starts fighting against the restraints more, and for a moment, I worry that she's going to hurt herself. "Our girl needs us, Milo. We'll have to continue exploring later." He nods and we go to opposite sides of the bed, settling in next to Ness.

VANESSA

I'm surprised that Raf and Milo finally start to explore each other. I could tell they both wanted to for a while, but neither would admit it. It's so hot watching them kiss. I feel like I'm going to explode when they start touching each other. Before I can feel left out, Jarek slips into the room and settles between my spread legs. I can't move even if I want to, but I'm excited to see what he has in mind. I relax into the softness of the mattress as he starts to lick along my folds.

I keep my eyes focused on Milo and Raf, but I can't help making noise as I get closer to falling over the edge into my climax. I don't want them to stop, but I need more. Jarek's tongue is teasing me to the edge, then backing off. I know he's doing it on purpose, and I want to force him to stop. I start pulling against the restraints. It does no good, and I realize that these probably will hold Jarek down for me when I'm ready for that.

But for now, I need this. I need the torture. The pleasure that borders on pain. My heart falls a little when I realize that I've interrupted Milo and Raf's exploration. Well, we have our whole lives for that, so I guess it's okay. They come to the bed, climbing on next to me.

With Jarek's mouth working me over, and my inability to move, all I can do is lay here while Raf and Milo each start playing with a nipple. They seem to be working in tandem, one being gentle while the other is rough, then alternating. Just when I think I can't take any more of either sensation, the three of them stop.

I whimper my displeasure, not able to form words. I thought the touching was too much, but the not touching is worse. My body screams for more. "Please," I beg. That's all it takes for Jarek to line his cock up and sheath himself in me. I want to wrap my hands around Milo and Raf's dicks, but I can't move. I look at Raf and lick my lips, nodding toward his engorged member. I hum as he moves closer and slips it in my mouth.

I suck him down as far as I can while Jarek pounds into my pussy like he's mad at it. After a minute of that, I pull back from Raf's cock. He understands what I want and eases away so I can be free for a moment. "Milo," I say, and his cock replaces Raf's. I know that one of them could easily slip under me and take my ass. As much as I want that, I would love to see them explore more first.

With Milo's dick sliding down my throat, I stare at Raf's. I know they're watching me, and hope that they come up with the idea before I have to tell them it's what I want. I glance at Milo and he groans. "You want to watch, don't you?" he asks. I open my eyes wide since I can't nod or speak. He grins at Raf, and I watch as they readjust to make it work.

Milo leans over me and sucks Raf's cock into his mouth. I hum my approval as Raf sucks in a sharp breath. Jarek is still pounding into my soaking wet pussy. Even he growls his approval. From this vantage point, I can see Milo working Raf over while I do the same to him.

I know that I'm getting close to coming again. I feel my pussy contracting against Jarek's cock as his knot swells inside me, locking us in place. I groan around Milo's dick and watch as he bobs up and down on Raf's, bringing him closer to the edge. I suck Milo harder, staring at him doing the same to Raf. I hope that we can all come together.

It's awkward that I can't use my hands at all. I can't move, so I just hold still and let Milo fuck my mouth as he sucks Raf at the same pace. It only takes him a few thrusts to shoot his load down my throat. I watch Raf tense as he comes. I wonder if Milo considered his options before now. He swallows, then kisses me deeply. I can taste Raf on him and it pushes me over the edge. Milo blocks my screams as I come undone. Jarek is still locked to me, thrusting a little as his seed spills inside of me.

Raf unfastens the cuffs, turning me loose. My arms and legs feel like jelly, and I sink into the bed. Milo and Raf start massaging my arms and legs to help me recover. I feel Jarek's knot release before he shoves the other two out of the way to kiss me. "That was hot," he whispers against my lips.

"So, you like to watch too?" I ask him breathlessly. He laughs.

"I like to watch you while you watch them. Who knows? Maybe Milo will want to explore with me some time," he says quietly. I never expected Jarek to be interested in men too. Even though I'm spent, I feel my core tighten at his words.

I look at him, then Milo. I don't want to push, but, damn. Jarek, still on top of me, turns his head to Milo. "What do you think? Maybe?"

Instead of answering, Milo leans over and presses his lips to Jarek's, kissing him gently. "Oh, fuck," I whisper, feeling a gush of slick. These men will be the death of me. But, death by orgasm, what a way to go.

Jarek only lets Milo have control for a moment before he raises up and dominates the kiss. While I watch, Raf slips his fingers inside of me to coax another orgasm out.

MILO

It's not hard to relax and let Jarek take control of the kiss. I can't believe that I kissed him! I never expected my attraction to be reciprocated, especially by him. Now it turns out I may have three mates instead of just one, and I find that idea to be fascinating. Especially since Ness seems to be fully on board.

Unfortunately for us, a phone rings before we can do anything but kiss. Raf must go to answer it. Jarek pulls away, but doesn't release me. He looks at me with a hunger I've only seen in his eyes for Ness. It's thrilling and intimidating at the same time. When Raf comes back, he clears his throat and Jarek releases me. We both sink to the bed on either side of Ness.

"That was Stevens. Dragonetti agreed to a meeting." Those words were all it took to kill anything that was left of the sexual tension that had filled the room moments before. I stand and hold a hand out to Ness to help her up.

"We should get cleaned up and then discuss," I offer, pulling her into the bathroom to the shower. I want to give Jarek and Raf a moment to talk. I know that Ness isn't going to just go along with anything, and we don't have time for another fight.

I turn on the water, then proceed to clean her up before tending to myself. I wash her hair and condition it, being careful to comb the tangles out and rinse it thoroughly. I know I'm keeping the others waiting, but I don't care. I will not skimp on Ness' care. She silently lets me take care of her needs, and I start to wonder if she's upset after all.

"Are you okay?"

She turns around and looks at me for a moment. "I am. That was beautiful, and my father nearly ruined it with that interruption. I want him taken care of. And I want to be the one to kill him."

"I understand your feelings. I want him taken care of too. And I would love to be the one to do it. But I understand there are bigger forces at play here. It may be better to get him locked up. You know that one of the guys he's crossed that's in prison would take care of it for us." I can tell from her expression that she hates that idea. "If we can grab him and take him to the dungeon, we will. Is that a good enough compromise?"

She nods reluctantly, and I'm glad I know her so well. If we have a chance to grab him, she's going to kill him before we get back here. I'll have to make sure Jarek knows. Though, he probably suspects as much. Once we're finished showering, I turn the water off and take my time drying her before tending to myself. I help Ness into her robe before wrapping a towel around my waist.

We join the others in the living room after I throw on a pair of pants. "He wants to meet tonight. My guys are getting everything ready for us. All we can do now is wait. Raf is making dinner." Jarek explains when his cousin ducks out of the room quickly.

"So, we're just supposed to wait here while someone else gets the car ready and everything?" Ness is appalled by the idea.

"Did you expect to do it yourself?" he asks, clearly amused by her reaction. "I trust the men I have on this particular job. They'll be our back up anyway."

"Oh, I hadn't considered back up. That makes sense. Sorry, I'm just on edge here. I want to confront him so badly." Jarek pulls Ness onto his lap on the couch and holds her close. It's a sweet moment, so I head into the kitchen to see if I can help with dinner.

In the kitchen, the scent of pasta sauce fills the air. Raf has a pot of boiling water on the stove and another with sauce in it. "Need help?" I ask. He jumps and turns toward me.

"If you want. Are they having a moment?" His response makes me laugh. I nod and he continues. "Good one or bad? I don't want to walk out there if it's bad."

"Good. I thought they were about to fight, but he managed to convince her that he wasn't completely incompetent." I laugh at my own words, and Raf joins in.

"That's a relief. I don't think he's going to let her be involved in this, even though he said he would. And when he double-crosses her, she's going to be pissed. It'll be left to you and me to keep her from killing him. Even though it'd be his own fault if she did."

He stirs the pasta before focusing on the sauce. "Do you really think he'll try to go back on his word?" I can't see Jarek doing that, even to an enemy.

"To keep her safe, he just might. I hope he doesn't, but there's no way to keep him from doing what he thinks is best."

Raf steps back and opens the oven, revealing a loaf of French bread that's been coated with garlic and butter. The scent is amazing and my mouth starts to water. "Everything smells so good."

"Thanks. Italian is my specialty. And Ness loves it, so Jarek wanted me to make it for her tonight. That's why I'm so certain he's going to betray her. Why else would he want me to make her favorites?"

I study Raf as he works, clearly not needing any help from me in the kitchen. He moves like a chef, even though I don't think he's ever been one. "How did you guys end up mixed up in all this anyway?" I can't help asking.

VANESSA

Jarek holds me for a while. It feels good, but I can tell he's hiding something. "What aren't you telling me?" I ask, staring up at him.

Guilt coats his features. "Nothing," he insists. But I know better. He's done something that he feels guilty about.

"Lies. Tell me the truth. What did you do?" I ask, pushing this time. "Don't lie to me, Jarek."

Before I can get an answer, Raf and Milo walk out of the kitchen carrying food. "Let's eat," Milo says, placing a plate of bread on the table. He quickly passes out place settings as Raf starts dishing out the best smelling spaghetti. My question is momentarily forgotten.

Once everyone has food and is sitting around the table, Raf turns to Milo. "To answer your question, we got roped into this because Jarek sent me on a job. I infiltrated Dragonetti's security team, and managed to get assigned to Ness." He stops talking for a minute to eat, gesturing for all of us to dig in as well.

We do, then he continues his tale. "Of course, she's gorgeous, and completely irresistible. But you know this, you were there at that point. Then after a while, I heard some things that were disturbing. When Ness came to me having heard something similar, I called Jarek and we got her out of there. That wasn't the original plan, but this one seems to have worked out better for all of us, hasn't it?"

"Go ahead, tell him what the original plan was. I wanna see his face," I say, motioning to Milo. I'm sure he'll freak out when Raf tells him. Instead, Raf glares daggers at me.

Jarek laughs. "Raf wanted to kidnap her and sell her back to Dragonetti. Or take the money from him and keep her. I doubt either would have worked."

Milo's jaw drops. Yup, clearly, he's freaking out. "You were gonna kidnap her and ransom her back to them? You would have handed her back to those monsters? So, all you wanted was money. That's what all of this is about?" I can tell Milo is getting pissed, and no amount of delicious spaghetti is going to fix it.

"Milo, honey, it's okay. Take a breath." I reach over and grab his hand. "Yes, before they met me, this was about money. But it's not about that now. They're not going to arrange this meeting just to sell me back to my father. There's no way they would have faked my death if that was the plan all along. Trust me. Please."

Milo relaxes a little at my words. I can see he's still upset, and I don't like it. But I have no idea how to make him understand. If being bonded to the three of them isn't enough, I don't know what would be.

He grips my hand and takes a deep breath. "Okay. I get it, really. It's just hard to hear that you were meant to be a payday for them. What changed?"

Jarek and Raf share a look. "I did, Milo. I changed. I realized that they hadn't actually done anything to hurt me. And they even helped me punish the guy who did hurt me. That helped too. And we talked. Communication is extremely important. I don't think people realize how important."

"I get that, and we're communicating now. I had no idea any of this was going on. You were her bodyguard for a year. How long were you waiting to execute this plan? It seems to me like you should have dropped the idea after a month or two tops." Milo's insistence is sweet, but I know he's not going to get anywhere with this conversation.

Before Raf can answer, Jarek's phone rings. "Yeah." I'm shocked. He never answers the phone at the table, much less in a room full of people. Maybe he senses the tension and is trying to help.

He listens for a minute, nodding. "Okay, we'll be ready in ten minutes." He pauses. "Yes, ten minutes. Tell them to wait." He hangs up without another word.

"Finish eating. We can argue about plans and shit later. We have to be in the garage in ten minutes." With that order given, he refocuses on his plate and eats. My stomach turns over and I run to the bathroom.

For a moment, I think I'll be sick. I break out in a cold sweat. Can I really face my father? Panic takes hold as I imagine what could happen if he defeats the men I love. There would be nothing standing between him killing me or worse, selling me to one of his allies. The thought of being tortured and raped makes my stomach flop again.

I should just stay here. But I can't. I have to go with them. I have to know that they're safe, and that they defeat him. I can't let them do this without me. *Pull yourself together, Vanessa. You are a fucking queen, and you will face the man who tried to kill you.*

I take a deep breath and look in the mirror. "You can do this. Bitch up and do it." Pep talk complete, I wash my face, fix my makeup and walk back into the living room.

"Are you okay, Ness?" Milo asks.

I nod. "I'm good. Let's get this over with." The three of them exchange a look and I know what's about to happen.

"We want you to stay here, Ness, where it's safe." Raf steps forward, taking charge. No doubt, Jarek is scared to piss me off.

"I can't do that. I have to face him." I won't beg, but I'm not backing down, either. Yes, I had a minor panic attack, but it's okay. I can do this.

Raf turns to Milo. "I'm not fighting with her. I agree with Jarek. She should be the one to take him out if there's a chance." I don't expect Milo to be the one trying to get me to stay here.

JAREK

I can see that Ness is upset with Milo. And he's upset with me. But that doesn't matter. "If we're going to defeat him, we have to do it together. You can all be mad at each other later. Right now, we need to focus."

Milo growls at me, and I step forward, getting in his face. I'm taller, so I have to lean down to do it. "Do you have a problem with me being the head alpha of this family?" I push a little bit of alpha influence into my question and watch as he squirms against it.

He lasts longer than I expect before he bares his neck and submits. "No, sir." His words are quiet and ashamed.

"Good." Then I turn to Ness. "And you will obey, do you understand, Omega?" The shock in her eyes nearly undoes me. But I have to maintain order in this family. I can't have their fight interfere with this mission. Otherwise, we'll always be looking over our shoulder for Dragonetti to come after us.

"Yes, Alpha." The words are reluctant, but immediate. I know that she'll do what I tell her to without issue. And that's exactly why I agree that she needs to be there when we deal with her father. She needs to show him that she's not the weak little omega he thinks. She's strong, with a loyal heart and fierce streak that he needs to see.

"Then let's load up," I order, waiting until they all walk out the door to follow. My heart is racing as I get them into the SUV that will take us to meet my greatest enemy. I can't let him get into my head, though. My father would tell me that's exactly what Dragonetti is counting on. He'll get into my head and I won't be able to kill him.

I won't let that happen, though. I will kill him. Or should I let him live so he suffers? It may be satisfying to watch his face when he realizes that I've claimed his daughter. After everything he took from me, he deserves to suffer. When we arrive at the rendezvous point, I pull Milo aside.

"I need you to call your FBI contacts. If we don't kill him, I want the bastard to rot in prison for everything he's done, especially to her."

Milo looks at me, confused. "I thought the plan was to kill him?"

"I think he deserves to live, knowing that his enemies have his daughter. I want him to fall asleep at night knowing that we're the ones taking care of her, cherishing her. I want him to know that his grandchildren will have my name. Once he's in prison, someone there will finish him off for sure. If they don't, we can always put a hit on him." I wonder how ethical it is to have this conversation with a former FBI agent, but at the moment, I don't care.

He nods, pulling out his phone. "The moment I make this call, they'll know I'm in with you. And I can't guarantee that we won't all go to prison. But I'll do everything I can to protect our family. Always."

"We still have some tricks that we can use to get out of any kind of trouble. Don't worry. Just get them here." I walk away, expecting him to do as I ask. I don't worry when I see him pocket his phone and walk around to lean on the back of the SUV. I'm sure he just needs some privacy for the call.

"What's up with Milo? Is he still mad at Ness?" Raf asks me when I return to the front of the car.

"No, he's more worried about Dragonetti and what's going to happen to us. He's scared for her. That's why he didn't want her to come with us. But I know she'd never forgive us if we don't let her see this through. I'm shocked she's staying in the car like I asked." I peek through the window to see her anxiously staring out the bullet-proof glass.

"All she wants is to make us happy. Well, that and to kill her father. Which is completely understandable if you think about it. We want to kill him too. I can't wait to see his face when he realizes what we've done." I laugh at Raf's statement.

"I have to make sure everyone is in place," I tell him before walking off to make a few calls. I need our back up to be hidden from sight while still having clear shots at the other side.

I dial the phone and wait for an answer. "Yeah, boss." Recognizing the voice immediately, I continue.

"You got everyone in place?" If not, I might have to come find you and pull your head from your ass. I don't tell him that, though.

"Yes, sir. Everyone is in place. You have snipers hidden in several areas with line of sight to where you expect Dragonetti to be and the ability to move quickly if something changes. We will be ready, sir." I like this kid. He's eager to please and has a way with the guys. I might make this a permanent change for him.

"You're not going to run when the shooting starts, are you?" I have to ask, even though I know the answer. This kid would never run away from bloodshed.

"The only running I'll do is into the fray, boss." I like the cocky answer. And it eases my mind that the kid is on our side. Travis is more than a little crazy.

"Okay, Trav. Just stay focused, and don't shoot until I give the signal. Got it?" I wait for him to respond affirmatively before cutting off the call. Now that everyone is in place, all that's left to do is wait for the old man to show up.

Chapter Fifteen

WAIT, YOU'RE NOT DEAD?!

MILO

I tell Jarek I'll call my contacts, but I can't. I stare at my phone for a minute, then put it away again. I can't call them. We'll all go to prison. And none of us would survive that. I check my gun to make sure it's ready to go. I'll take out Dragonetti myself if I have to.

There's no way I can bring the FBI down on Ness or the rest of my found family. Speaking of family, I still have to call mom and tell her about all of this. I need her to understand why I won't be there for Christmas or basically ever again.

But I have to take Dragonetti out for what he did to my brother. Mom deserves that justice at least. I hate myself for putting it off as long as I have. I should have killed the bastard the moment I realized he was the one responsible. I let my feelings for Ness get in the way, and I can't let that happen again. Once he used her as leverage to get what he wanted from me. Now I'll use her the same way, except I'll never let him have her.

I need to focus. I should not be operating a firearm with an anxious mind. I take a few deep breaths to calm myself down. Dragonetti will be here any time. I have to be ready. I clear my mind and meditate for a moment. I let thoughts and memories flash past without giving them any attention. I find myself recalling how I found this family. The bloodshed and pain were worth it to have what I have now.

I finally feel complete. And I know that revenge isn't always the answer, but this time, I think it'll do. I want the old man to hurt the way I do. But I can't do that through Ness. I won't use her to take him out.

What real chance at revenge do I have? I found the ledger, but I can't even decipher it. Ness has been working on it since I got here, but as far as I know, she hasn't found what I'm looking for yet. Of course, there's always a chance that he has no records of my brother and what exactly happened to him.

I'll face that possibility when it becomes relevant. Until then, I'm going to keep to the plan. Take him out before he can do anything else to hurt Ness. I won't leave it to someone else. If Jarek doesn't do it first, I will.

Raf walks up to me, glancing around. "Are you okay, man?"

"I'm good. Why?" Can he tell what I'm thinking just by looking at me? If so, I might be fucked with this plan.

"You seem jumpy. I know you're not thrilled about Jarek wanting Dragonetti to go to prison, but if we all testify, he should get put away for the rest of his life. You know that no matter how much Ness wants to kill him, she'd be broken if it happened. Right? There's a part of her that still loves him because he's her dad."

Raf's words tear through me, settling in my heart. Fuck. I can't kill him. I can't put her through that. But I can't call the FBI, either. We'd all go to prison, testimony or not. I'm so fucked here. "I understand. I won't kill him." I say the words, wondering if I really mean them.

He seems to have the same reaction. "You sure? Because you still look like a man possessed. Ness said you have reasons to hate her father. We all do. But for her sake, we have to be willing to let it go and focus on what's important. Ness is what's important. We can make it so he can never get to her again without killing him. And trust me, it's not what I want either. But I want her to be okay. And I think that killing him might not be what she needs." His words make sense, but I hate myself for wanting to disagree.

I think Ness would be better off without him, but I can't force the issue. I don't want to break her. I can't be responsible for that, no matter how badly I want his blood on my hands. I have to let this go somehow. I just hope I can.

For a moment, I consider giving Raf my gun, just so I can't possibly take the old man out. In the end, I decide I should keep it. If I need to defend myself, and don't have my gun, I'll be a sitting duck. I can't do that to Ness. I need to be the man she deserves. I will be the man she deserves.

But does that mean I should call Jackson? Fuck. I hate not knowing the right thing to do. I guess I should ask myself where my loyalties are. Because if I'm loyal to Jarek, Raf, and Ness, I should do what my head alpha asks without question. I'm relieved that he doesn't treat me that way, though. He doesn't stand over me to be sure I've done what he wants. He trusts me. Fuck, fuck, fuck.

I shoot a quick text off to Jackson. I hope this isn't a mistake.

Jackson, I need your help. I hope he doesn't ask too many questions. I can't give him answers to anything, and I know it.

Spezia, what's up? Here goes nothing. I type out my reply, explaining that I have evidence that can be used against Dragonetti, and I know where he'll be in a few minutes. I wait for a response.

How deep are you in this, Milo? Way too deep to answer that question, Jackson. I don't reply to his question. I simply send the address of the garage we're meeting in.

VANESSA

Whoever said that waiting is the hardest part was not wrong. I'm pissed at myself for agreeing to stay in the SUV while my loves are outside walking around like they're invincible. I should have insisted that I stay with them. I can't deal with the idea that someone could take them out. But I know the vehicle is bulletproof and it makes them feel better about me being here.

I stare out the window, watching as they make sure everyone is in place and double check everything. I know it should be getting close to the meeting time. I start picking at my nail polish nervously. I just want this over with. I want to go home with my men.

Maybe I should have stayed there instead of coming here. It's not like talking to my father will make a difference. I should have just let it go. But no, I insisted that these three men I love confront the man who emotionally tortured and abused me for my entire life before trying to have me killed. What was I thinking?

Regret washes over me in waves. I carefully dry my tears. I will not let my father see me cry. He doesn't deserve my tears. He doesn't deserve to live. As I sit there waiting for him to arrive, I think about the past. It wasn't always bad. Things didn't even get bad until he realized that my mother could never give him the son he wanted. I was ten when that announcement was made. Before that, he was mostly absent.

There was a time when he would hug me and tell me I was his princess. I was so little back then. No doubt, he had plans to sell me even then. It wouldn't have mattered that I was a child, or that he didn't know what my designation was. There were men in his circle who would have, and probably still would, pay him handsomely for the chance to own me.

Those men are monsters, who run child pornography rings and kidnap women to work in their brothels. They deserve to burn in hell for their crimes. I wonder if my father has ever been involved in any of those practices. I'll have to work on that ledger more to find out. I know there are parts of the business that he kept away from me because he thinks I'm too delicate.

When he arrives here, he'll find out just how delicate I really am. I can't wait to see his face when he learns that I'm not actually dead. I wonder if he'll get angry or scared. Perhaps both. Maybe he'll run. Would Jarek shoot him in the back? I doubt it.

One thing I can say for my men—no matter how ruthless they are, they are honorable. There's no way my cold princes would ever shoot a man in the back. Hmm, I like that description. My cold princes. That's exactly what they are. Cold and calculating to everyone but me. I get to see the side of them that's hidden from the rest of the world.

With me, they're warm and passionate, kind and considerate. It's amazing the complete change in them. But I'm glad they are exactly who they are. Both sides. I need them all. The cold, hard men to protect me, and the warm, kind men to care for me. They really are every omega's dream.

I'm getting tired of waiting. I want to get out of the car and stretch, but I know the second I open this door, one of my sweet, supportive men will shove me back inside and lock the doors. So, I stay put. I know they're worried about keeping me safe. And I know that my father can't be trusted.

I watch out the window until I'm so bored that I'm starting to fall asleep. I should have asked Raf to leave the car on so I could listen to the radio. As it is, the windows are barely cracked open, and I'm getting a little bit of a breeze. Movement catches my attention and I sit up straight. He's here.

A dark SUV pulls up across from the one I'm in. I watch as Jarek, Raf, and Milo tense. Of course, Jarek has Milo waiting behind the car. We can't let my father know everything at once, now, can we? I can imagine his sense of betrayal when he realizes that not only does Jarek have me, he has Milo too.

I know my father well enough to know that he will go into a rage when he finds out. And he'll try to kill me again. Probably Milo too. Especially if what Milo said was true, about calling and asking him for help to find me. I almost hope that somehow Milo misunderstood, even though I'm sure he didn't.

My father is a dark, uncaring man. I can see him treating Milo exactly as it was described. Sending his little bit of help along with a threat, sounds exactly like his style. I'm so proud of Milo for fighting back against it, though. He could have just moved back in with his mom and left me behind.

The realization of how much these men love me and are willing to go through for me makes me smile. I watch as my father climbs out of the SUV and walks a few steps to face off with Jarek. Raf stays closer to the car, probably to protect me.

I can't hear what they're saying, but my father looks pissed. Has he dropped the bomb yet? Fuck, I want to hear what is going on out there. Instead, I'm hiding in this bulletproof prison where I can't hear anything. I nearly growl in frustration, then realize that with the windows cracked, he might be able to hear me.

I take a quiet breath, calming my emotions again and refocus on watching the scene playing out before me.

RAFAEL

When Dragonetti pulls up, I stand next to the car, letting Jarek take point. Since he's head alpha, it would be disrespectful to do anything else unless he requests it. This should be a conversation between two family heads. Of course, Dragonetti doesn't know that Jarek is bonded now and that his father will give him half the business once all the paperwork is filed. And we can't file that paperwork until this man standing in front of us is dealt with. I want nothing more than to rush up to him and slit his throat. But I know that doing so is not the best way to handle things.

I watch as they exchange fake pleasantries, the whole *How are you?* and *How's business?* bullshit. I can tell from Jarek's posture that he's fighting his rage. I hope he wins against it. If not, things could get ugly. And we just decided that we weren't killing the bastard.

If Dragonetti dies today, it'll be at Jarek's or Ness' hand. I hope neither of them does it. I think that Jarek understands how bad it could be for her if we kill her father. Even if she hates him. I know that he asked Milo to call the Feds, but I have no idea if it actually happened. I'm not looking forward to what's coming next. I know in my soul that this isn't going to be as easy as we want. Dragonetti will never just give in and surrender.

I am looking forward to his reaction to learning that we faked Ness' death. That thought puts a smile on my face. I hear Dragonetti's asinine comment about it too.

"What's with him? That goofy smile pisses me off," he growls at Jarek.

"Who, him?" Jarek asks, pointing at me. "He's in love. It makes a man a little goofy. Get over it. You're dealing with me." His expression is hard and cold. He is the model of professionalism; minus the slight tick I can see in his jaw as he clenches it.

I appear relaxed against the SUV, but I'm on guard. My hand is inches from my gun and I'm ready to pull it any moment. I know that Jarek's arms crossed against his chest puts him in the same position to grab both of his guns if needed. As much as I want this meeting to go well, I know it won't. The moment Jarek mentions Ness, the mood will completely change. Dragonetti will lose his shit and bullets will start flying. It might be different if Dragonetti wasn't the one trying to have her killed.

That thought pisses me off again and I want to rage kill them all—Dragonetti and his men. But I can't. I have to focus on Ness and her needs. That's more important right now. I pull up the mental image of her strapped down while we all pleasured her last night. That was hot as fuck. Okay, gotta put that away now before I'm sporting wood at a gun fight. I can't let these assholes think I like them that much.

"What exactly do you want, Junior?" Dragonetti asks Jarek with a snarl.

"First of all, no one calls me Junior, old man. Second, I would expect a little more respect, given I found something you lost," Jarek deadpans back. I'm impressed at how well he's keeping his composure. I might have decked the old man by now.

"You may call me Mr. Dragonetti, child. And what exactly do you think you've found that belongs to me?" The old man is starting to lose composure, though. Things will start to go south soon. I have to be mentally ready.

"Then you may call me Mr. D'Angelo. Or son-in-law, which ever you prefer." Jarek smirks and waits for Dragonetti to figure out his meaning.

"What are you talking about?" Yeah, the old man has completely lost his edge. He's getting angry and won't be able to resist attacking.

"I'm talking about being mate bonded to your omega daughter. I just wanted to say thank you for trying to kill her and being so sloppy about it. That's the only reason I ended

up with her, and I'm thrilled with how things worked out."
I know that Jarek is being sincere, but the old man takes his
words as sarcasm.

"You do not have my daughter. My daughter is dead."

Before I can anticipate her move, Ness opens the SUV door
and steps out. I didn't even think she could hear what was being said, although Dragonetti had started talking louder when
Jarek brought Ness up.

"Am I dead, Father? Because I feel very much alive," she says
with a laugh. Her eyes show no amusement and I'm worried
she's going to try to kill him. Jarek glares at her, and I pull her
against my side.

"You see, old man, I don't lie. But what you don't know is
that she's ours now. We've mate bonded with her and you can
never touch her again."

"What? You're not dead?! Vanessa, get over her right now!"
he yells, his face turning red and his breathing ragged.

"Why, Father, so you can have Mickey kill me? Nah, I'm
good over here with my guys. Thanks, though. Without your
little plot to kill me, I never would have discovered my fated
mates. I can't wait for our pack to take you out." Ness shows
no fear, but her body trembles against mine. I don't like where
this is heading, and I want to shield Ness as much as I can.
Ideally, I'll convince her to get back into the SUV where it's
safer.

"You little bitch. After everything I did for you, this is how
you show your father respect? You'll all pay for this betrayal.

You boys should have brought her back to me the minute you found her." His words are intended to piss us off, and it works. I'm struggling to hold myself back from attacking.

JAREK

The old man keeps trying to get a rise out of me, but instead, I get one out of him. I can't help laughing at him as he blubbers about respect and returning his property. "You think we found her? No, asshole, we took her before your guys could even try to kill her. They were too busy talking about what they were going to do while not paying attention to who could hear them. That's how we took her."

I pause, then decide there's no reason not to tell him. "Also, that guy over there with the goofy grin and his arm around your daughter? That's my cousin. Raf might look familiar to you. He pretended to be one of your security operatives for a year and played bodyguard for her. Next time, you should probably make sure you know who you're hiring."

I watch his eyes go wide at the admission. He stares at Raf as if trying to place him. Is the old man losing his mind? Perhaps there's something else going on here after all. But it still doesn't explain why he wanted to kill his own daughter.

"What? How? I don't understand. How did you get a man into my organization? Much less your cousin." He spat the words at me angrily.

"It was easy. He made friends with one of your guys and that guy brought him right in. You hired him on the spot. Didn't even make him do anything to prove loyalty before handing over your daughter. Honestly, I struggled to figure out what the fuck you were thinking. I would never let anyone untested near my family." I nod at Raf and he snaps his fingers over his head.

Milo walks around the car to stand beside Ness, wrapping an arm around her, and sandwiching her between him and Raf. I watch the old man's face as it plays out and see the anger turn to fear. He knows that we have him now. I wonder if he'll try to negotiate or fight first. I'm not sure which I'm hoping for.

"I would never put my daughter in danger. Vanessa, surely you know that these accusations are just a way for him to keep you from me. Come with me now, and we'll go home. Then we can talk about this misguided attempt to extort me." I can see the fear in his eyes, and hear it in his voice.

"No one is trying to extort you, old man. None of us want your money. We want justice. You need to admit what you did and explain to your daughter exactly why you did it." I know I'm pushing and it's not likely to work the way I want it to.

Ness deserves the truth, and I'll do whatever it takes to get it for her. Even if that means killing Dragonetti's men until he talks.

"I won't admit anything. Because I have nothing to admit." He's sticking to his story. But his initial reaction to Ness being alive is all it takes for her to know he's lying.

"Father, you've already shown your true colors. You might as well admit that you contracted men to kill me. I heard them talking myself. It's not like I let someone else talk me into leaving. I ran to save myself. To get away from your men and you. Granted, there was a little more to it than that, but everything worked out in the end." I'm impressed with how well she's handling herself, facing her fear and forcing her father to admit his crimes.

"I told you, Vanessa, I have done nothing wrong. I will not admit to things I did not do," he insists, practically begging her to believe him. "You have to know that I would never let anyone hurt you. How could I ever put a hit out on you? That is ridiculous. I will not stand here and let you accuse me of these things. Get in the car so we can go home. Your mother will be thrilled that you're still alive."

Ness shakes her head. "No."

"What do you mean, 'no'? Get in the damn car, Vanessa. You will listen to me, or there will be consequences." So, when begging doesn't work, he's going to switch to threats. Good to know.

"Old man, you'd be wise not to threaten my omega like that again. I will not give a second warning," I growl the words into his face as I tower over him. I'm disgusted and intrigued; we're nearly the same age, but he looks at least ten years older than I do. Life has been rough on him.

"You were serious about all that mated and bonded shit? No. I do not approve. There will be no pack created. I'll fight it. As her father, I have the right to choose my daughter's mate or mates as I see fit. She will go to the Volantes. They know how to handle rogue omegas. She'll learn her place with them." The old man's words illicit a growl from my chest.

Before I realize what I'm doing, my hand wraps around his throat. "I gave you a warning. I will not repeat it. But I will tell you what will happen to you if you continue with this line of thinking. I will tear your throat out and feed you to my dogs. She's *my omega* now. You will have nothing else to do with her. Do you understand?"

Fear fills his eyes as he registers my threat. I can see that he believes me. He knows enough about me to know that I will kill him without a second thought. I want to, but I know that if I do, Ness will hurt for it. That's why I had Milo call his FBI friends. We're going to do this the right way. No excuses, no unnecessary murder. For once, I'm doing the right thing. For Ness.

VANESSA

The look on my father's face is priceless. I can't hear everything Jarek says to him, but I can see the old man's response. I hate that he's my father, and part of me wants Jarek to kill him. But I don't know if that's the answer. I thought it was, and I was prepared to do it myself. Now I wonder if he shouldn't spend whatever time he has left in prison and see what happens there.

I know that if he gets arrested, we'll all have to testify, and it'll take a lot to get him put away. But it may just be worth it. Especially if I never have to face my children and tell them that their mother or fathers killed their grandpa. A better story will be that gramps was a criminal and got himself arrested. Even if he gets killed in prison, it won't be by our hands.

I look at Milo. "Can you call Jackson and get him down here? I don't think I want any of us to kill him. I want him to answer for his crimes, though."

His eyes meet mine, and he stiffens for a second. "Jarek had me contact him already. I don't know if I can keep us out of jail, Ness. This isn't the best idea."

I press my lips to his cheek. "It's gonna be okay, Milo. Trust me. We have everything we need to get him put away for the rest of his life."

I turn my attention back to Jarek and my father. I can see that Jarek has released him, and my father is cowering in front of him. I wonder if Jarek talked him into surrendering. "Can you hear what they're saying?" I ask Raf, who is staring intently at the situation unfolding.

"Looks like your dear old dad is begging for his life. He wants to make a deal with Jarek, and use you as leverage. Of course, Jarek told him to fuck off. You aren't payment for anything, love, and he will not agree to use you that way. Hell, he didn't even want you as bait tonight. But he understood that you need to be here for this." Raf's explanation of Jarek's thoughts makes perfect sense. I suspected as much when the guys were fighting over letting me come with them or not. I just hadn't expected Jarek to be the one who understood my need for closure. I'm glad he did, because I would have snuck out and been here anyway.

At least this way, I'm more protected. I have my men with me and I actually feel safe, even knowing that my father's men are hiding just like ours are. They probably have high-powered rifles aimed at our heads right now. It's intimidating, but I trust my loves to keep me safe. They won't let anything happen to me. My father, on the other hand, could give the signal to take me out at any time.

I wonder if I should get back into the SUV so that the guys can focus on what they are doing here. I don't want to leave the warmth that I have standing between Raf and Milo, even if it would be safer. I want to see what Jarek does and how he handles my father. I want to be closer and hear what they're saying.

I guess if my heart would stop racing, I could maybe make out as much as Raf does. I take a calming breath, and try to focus.

My father still looks terrified, and I wonder if he's giving up. But he won't; I already know it. He will push Jarek to the edge in an attempt to get him to mess up and give my father an advantage. I hope that Jarek doesn't fall for it. Whatever happens will be what happens. I hate when people say that, but it's true. There is nothing I can do to change the course that this interaction is on. All I can do is ride out the storm and see my family safely on the other side of it. Hopefully this ends with my father behind bars and us free to live our lives.

There are no guarantees though, and I have no idea if we'll even make it out of this alive. If we don't, I'll be happy for the time we had together. For a brief time, I truly felt loved. These men are the best thing that ever happened to me, and I will go down fighting for them. I won't give up, no matter how bleak things seem.

Something feels off, and I automatically take a step forward. I can't tell if my father is trying to beg for his life or negotiate my return. Either way, I don't like it. I want him to leave us alone. With any luck, Jackson will get down here and this will all be over soon.

Panic starts to creep up my spine. Sweat drips from my hands, and my heart races. I feel like the air just got thick and I can't get enough into my lungs. Raf squeezes my hand and Milo wraps his arms around me. I know they're trying to ground me so I can breathe, but it's not working. I need to hear what's going on. I have no idea what lies my father is telling Jarek, and I'm worried that Jarek will believe him.

I watch, being held back by Milo and Raf, as Jarek glances over his shoulder. He must notice that I've moved closer, because he shakes his head and Raf pulls us back to the car. I want to get closer, though, so I struggle against them. I need to get to Jarek. Something is wrong, and I can't stand by while my father ruins everything.

"Baby, it's okay. Just breathe. Jarek has this under control," Milo whispers in my ear.

Chapter Sixteen

And the Truth Comes Out

JAREK

I know that Raf and Milo are having trouble holding Ness back, but I need her to stay as far away as possible. Her father is finally talking, trying to come up with something he can tell me to save his life.

"The truth is the only thing that will save you, old man," I sneer.

"Fine, you want the truth? I might as well tell you, since I'm going to kill you anyway." The confidence of this old man is almost admirable. Almost. "I promised to sell Vanessa to the Volantes, but her mother objected in a very violent way. They ended up refusing the trade. You see, I owed them a very large sum of money, and given that the product they supplied came up missing, I did not have said money. They were going to kill me, so I arranged for Vanessa to pay my debt in the only way I could figure out."

"You put a hit on your own daughter just to pay for drugs? That's cold." I grit my teeth and clench my fists to keep from punching him.

"Of course. She's my daughter, and an omega. That makes her my property, to do with as I please. I don't know what you're so upset about. She's damaged goods anyway. You know she wasn't a virgin when you got her, don't you? Shameful."

"You're not doing much to make me not want to kill you," I offer. He continues his story.

"At first, I thought I could auction her off and use that money to pay my debt. But then I discovered that she'd already been deflowered and was worthless for that purpose. I tried to sell her to different families for breeding purposes, but none of them wanted to deal with her stubborn and outspoken attitude. I can't say that I blame them, but both could be beaten out of her in time."

My open palm cracks against his cheek. I watch as his bodyguard finally starts to step forward, but he raises a hand to stop him.

"As I was saying, I couldn't find anyone to purchase her, and auctioning was out of the question. Who wants a used omega? Yuck. So, I considered faking her death, but then I would have had to find something to do with her. I decided that was too much work, so I put the hit out. Imagine my surprise when, two days later, she turned up dead, and no one asked for the fee. I thought I'd gotten lucky, or that whoever did it had been busted for something else and I would get a request later for the fees. I was totally prepared to pay."

I clench and unclench my fists. I want to hit him again, but I need to get these answers for Ness. I don't know if she can hear him right now or not, so I have to make sure that I remember everything he says. Not that I'll have a problem with that. This sick fuck's words are branding themselves onto my brain as he speaks.

"It would have been better if she'd just kept her pants on and not spread her legs for anything that moved. I could have at least made a profit and gotten an heir out of it. But no, the whore had to give the prize away before I could sell her. The whole thing pisses me off, honestly. I should sue her for it, but she doesn't have any money that's not already mine. And I don't know who she gave her virginity to, so I can't go after him."

The more he talks, the more I want to kill him. Even though I decided to let the FBI have him, the desire is still there and growing.

"You know I could kill you for all of that right now," I threaten.

"You could, but my snipers would kill her before my body hit the ground." Fuck. I knew that he had guys stationed, just like we do. I wonder if I can get a message to ours and have them silently take out the other side. I can't figure out a way to make Raf understand what I'm thinking. We need to work out better signals for things, so that this doesn't happen in the future.

I grab Dragonetti by the shirt and haul him off his feet. "If you're smart, you'll tell your shooters to back off. If anything happens to her, I will kill you. As it stands, I hadn't planned to do that today. Don't force my hand." It's a warning, or a threat, or a promise. I'm not really sure anymore. But if he does anything to hurt Ness, I will kill him without a second thought.

Honestly, I wish I'd never asked Milo to call his FBI buddies. If I hadn't done that, I could just snap this fucker's neck and be done with it. If I do that now, I'll be the one going to prison. Because there would be no way to explain it away when they finally arrived. I hope if they're coming, that they arrive before the shooting starts. It doesn't look like that will happen, though.

Fuck. This whole thing went about as well as I expected, but not as well as I had hoped. I want Dragonetti to apologize for treating Ness so badly, but I can see that he has no reason to believe he's done anything wrong. I still want to punch him in the face, and I might before this is over.

"I'm not doing anything, boy. I'm simply telling you what you asked of me. Is that not enough? Just because you don't like the answer, that doesn't mean I've done anything wrong." He smirks, and I know that he's egging me on. He wants me to start something, so his men can kill Ness.

MILO

I watch as Jarek and Dragonetti have a conversation. When Jarek slaps the old man, I put my hand on my gun. I'm expecting things to go south, but somehow, Jarek holds back and nothing happens. I need to get Ness into the car where she'll be safe. But how do I convince her of that?

"Ness, baby, you need to get back into the SUV. I have a feeling that things are going to get bad soon. You father isn't going to let Jarek get by with slapping him like that. You and I both know that he doesn't take kindly to disrespect." I don't want to force her into the car, but I will if I have to.

"I know, Milo. I just don't want to miss anything. I'll get in there in a minute, okay? Just let me watch Jarek put the bastard in his place, okay?" I can't argue with her, especially when I can hear the need in her voice. She needs to see this through and to know that he's been dealt with.

My phone vibrates and I pull it from my pocket. Jackson is calling me. I can't answer right now, because I fear that will jump start the shooting that I worry will happen at any moment. I click a button, sending the call to voicemail and pocket the phone.

Refocusing on Jarek and Dragonetti, I can see that they're talking again. Jarek looks as if he's getting pissed. The old man is pushing his buttons for sure. I'm amazed at the control Jarek shows over his emotions. I wouldn't know he was angry except for the set of his jaw. He looks as if he wants to bite Dragonetti's head off and spit it at his feet. That image makes me laugh. Ness looks at me like I'm crazy, and Raf cocks an eyebrow.

"Sorry, funny thought." I hope I can get myself under control. I can't stand here cracking up at stupid imaginary shit while we're about to be attacked by my former employer's men. I want to refocus my efforts on getting Ness into the car, but she refuses to cooperate.

I thread my fingers through hers and squeeze her hand. I wish I could make all of this go away. One shot is all it would take to end this. The old man would be dead, and Ness would be able to take over his empire. Then we would no longer have to worry about any of this bullshit. But if I do that, Ness will get upset with me. Would she be so pissed that she would never forgive me? Would that anger be enough for her to break our bond? I don't want to find out.

As tempting as it is to just take care of it, she asked me not to. I have to respect that. I can't just make decisions on my own anymore. That was the one benefit of being single and not having a pack leader to report to. What was I thinking committing myself to these people? I hate giving up my autonomy.

Ness seems to understand my thoughts and squeezes my hand again. "It's okay, Milo. Jarek has things under control. You'll see. My father will surrender and we'll take him down by legal means. No more unnecessary death." I wonder if she means that.

When she helped Raf and Jarek torture and kill her cousin, she seemed really into it. I'm still a little freaked out about it, even if it was pretty hot. I can see her taking a permanent role as executioner for the D'Angelo family.

Shit. I completely forgot about that. If we file the paperwork for this family to be an official pack, I'll be a D'Angelo. And so will Ness. I don't know how I feel about that. On one hand, it's not like I have anyone but my mother left, so that's not really an issue. On the other hand, that means that any children I have with Ness will have that last name instead of mine. But that last name would be mine. Fuck, why does all of this have to be so complicated?

I need to focus on what's going on. I can't get distracted and let my guard down. I have to protect Ness. That's been my only desire for so long now. And I have to make it up to her for fucking up and letting her father have proof that she's alive. Even if he didn't believe me. Of course, I'm not convinced that his surprise was real when she stepped out of the car. I think he knew exactly what he was walking into here.

"Get ready, it looks like he's trying to signal someone. I saw Jarek block his arm, but that won't stop him for long. His guys may start shooting because of that. We can't know until it starts." Raf directs his words at me. It's enough to push me to pay attention.

"Ness, you really should get back in the car," I insist. I know she won't do it, but I can't help asking.

"Not yet, Milo. I want to see what happens. It'll be okay, really. I trust you guys to keep me safe." She presses another kiss to my cheek before doing the same to Raf. I want to grab her by the shoulders and shake her, but that would involve taking my hand off my gun.

I won't do that. If I do, Dragonetti could get the drop on us. I wonder if Jarek has guys searching for Dragonetti's snipers to take them out. I would do that if I were in charge. But I don't know if he's ever done a meet like this, and I have no way to know how he normally handles these things.

All I can do right now is position myself in front of Ness while allowing her to see what's going on between Jarek and her father.

VANESSA

What the fuck could Jarek and my father be talking about for so long? I really expected this to devolve into a fist fight or bullet spray by now. I'm glad it hasn't, but I'm still expecting the worst. I want to go to Jarek and drag him out of here. Nothing good will come from negotiating with my father. That asshole will just try to take me away again and sell me.

I'm shocked that he hadn't managed to sell me before. Things seem tense between Jarek and daddy dearest. I flinch when Jarek slaps him. But my father, ever the weasel, just takes it and moves on. I wonder what he said that pissed Jarek off enough to hit him.

No doubt, it was something hateful about me. Honestly, I'm glad I ruined his plans for selling my virginity to the highest bidder. I've never been so grateful for a naïve bodyguard in my life. Kyle was easy to seduce, and being a beta, there was no chance that he could get me pregnant. Of course, I was already on birth control anyway, so I was double protected. But watching my father's face when he found out was priceless.

You can't sell something that doesn't exist. Unfortunately, that little tryst cost Kyle his life, and made mine hell, even though my father didn't know he was the one I'd fucked. As much as his death hurt me, it was worth it. I don't want anyone to die for me, but it saved me from being sold into a sex slave situation, so I can't feel guilty about it. It was him or me. And I chose me.

None of that matters right now. What matters is getting the four of us out of here without anyone getting hurt. I need to figure out a way to make that happen. I can't see any way to get Jarek away from my father, though.

"Can't we just leave?" I ask Raf. I know it sounds whiney, and I don't care. "I'm getting worried that this isn't going the way we'd hoped."

"It's okay, love. Jarek has it under control. If he didn't, he would have given the signal by now. Our guys are in position, and have your father and his men in their sights. Just breathe. And maybe think about getting back in the SUV." He raised his eyebrows at the suggestion that I hide.

I roll my eyes at him. "No. If you're out here, I'm out here. I will not hide from that monster anymore. I'm in this just as deep as you are. I can't leave you three to deal with my issues. No matter how much I want to. But I do love that you would do that for me."

I want to let them take care of it, but I know how guilty I would feel if anything happened to them. I need the three of them to take care of me. We're a family, and we need each other. I can't survive without them. And I don't want to try.

My father raises his voice again. "I don't know why you won't take my deal, D'Angelo. It's a good deal, and you can keep the whore."

Jarek's growl is low and makes my insides quiver. My damn pussy drips at the noise, and I shudder. Watching him argue with my father makes me wet, and I'm not sure I want to think about the kinks that involves. But I do wonder what my father would do if my guys just started fucking me in front of him. That would leave us way too vulnerable, so I won't suggest it.

"Baby, you're gonna need to get that under control," Milo says quietly.

"We'll take care of you when this is done, but he's right. You need to stop thinking about how hot we are and focus on why we're here. We can't take care of you if we're distracted. Keep focused, please. I can't take anymore of your pheromones right now. My dick is so hard it hurts." Raf's words snap me out of my thoughts. He's right. They're both right. I need to focus, and not be a distraction for them. I can't be the reason this goes bad.

"Sorry. It's just that growl. It gets me every time. I can't handle it." I offer the half-hearted apology, expecting it to be enough.

"Sorry isn't going to fix it. Just relax. Stop thinking dirty thoughts. Please," Milo orders. I hate that he's being forceful with me, but I understand why he's doing it.

"Got it." I decide to shut off my mind and stop thinking about anything that could distract them. I don't want to be the reason someone gets killed. I need to focus on what's going on in front of us and be ready to get back into the car when the fight starts. Maybe I should just give in and return to safety now.

But I don't want to do that. I want to stand with my men and show my father that I'm not scared of him anymore. He has no power over me, and I want to prove that so badly. I need to focus and pay attention so I can act accordingly.

I watch as they argue more. I wish I could hear what Jarek was saying to him, but my father looks scared again. "This is killing me. What are they saying?"

Raf glances down at me. "I can't get all of it, but your father keeps offering for us to join him and keep you as payment for becoming his lackeys. Jarek is trying really hard not to kill him for the insults. But I can't hear everything, because someone keeps breaking my focus."

I know he's irritated with me, but I don't care. I won't hide.

RAFAEL

I know she's not going to get back into the SUV unless one of us forces her to. I hate that she's out in the open like this, but I can't physically put her in the car without turning my back on Dragonetti's men. And that's not safe for any of us.

I can sense the fight coming, but everything seems to be moving in slow motion. It's like Dragonetti wants to taunt us into making the first move. Like he knows something we don't. I wonder if he's trying to bait us so he can have the FBI take us down.

Then I start to wonder if Jarek has thought about this possibility. My cousin is more ruthless than his opponent, so no way he hasn't already planned for this. It's probably why he asked Milo to get his buddies on the way. Even if Dragonetti has FBI or police in his pocket, it wouldn't be the same guys Milo has. Or would it? I really don't know.

"Is your guy coming?" I ask Milo quietly over Ness' head. I know she's already asked him if he called, but he didn't really give a straight answer.

"I don't know. He started asking questions I don't have time to answer, so I stopped talking to him. I had to be focused on what's going on here," he growls.

I understand his frustration. This is not going well, and there's nothing we can do to change that. "Let's hope he shows up. Otherwise, we may have to go back to the original plan." As much as I want Dragonetti dead, I don't want Ness involved. I would take his life myself with no hesitation, but he's her father, and I don't think she'd actually be okay with that, no matter what he did to her.

Deep down, I know she loves him. And I understand. Fathers can be assholes, and some can be really big assholes. But in this line of work, that's expected; even encouraged. Dragonetti wouldn't be a very effective mafia boss if he wasn't a complete and total asshole. That doesn't mean he couldn't have been a good father. But that is the usual issue we have as kids of mafia people.

There aren't many honorable men in this line of work anymore, and the women are nearly as bad. I'm surprised that Ness' mom didn't come with her dad to try and force her to cooperate. I'm glad he didn't bring her, though. I'd hate to see what he would do if she was here and Ness continued to disobey him. I don't want to know what will happen to her if he manages to escape us and get home to his wife.

Unfortunately, most mafia wives bear the brunt of their husbands' anger and disappointment. It's not an ideal situation, but it is more common than people want to admit. There are shelters everywhere that claim to help abused women, but the moment they find out that the woman in question belongs to one of our families, they are on their own. It makes me glad that we were able to claim Ness before she fell in with one of those types.

I hate the idea that her father wanted to sell her to known abusers. I fight those thoughts away and refocus on what's unfolding in front of me. Dragonetti actually throws a punch at Jarek. He misses, but I wonder what Jarek said to him to make the old man that angry. Milo chuckles, and I turn to ask him.

"Did you hear what Jarek said to cause that?"

"Something about how good Ness is in bed, I think. I didn't catch it all. I think he's trying to keep things between them so she can't hear." I nod at his response. It's what I would do. There's no reason for her to hear the nasty things her father is saying about her. I haven't even heard everything, but I've heard enough to know that it's been pretty ugly.

I'm glad that Jarek is the one handling this. I would have already killed the bastard for half the shit he's said about our girl. I imagine shoving my blade into his heart and watching his blood spill all over my hands. I would run my hands over Ness' body, covering her in his blood while forcing orgasms out of her with nothing more than my hands.

Then I imagine forcing my gun between his lips as I fuck his mouth with it before pulling the trigger and spraying his brains out the back of his head. As satisfying as that would be, I restrain myself from trying to fulfil the fantasy. I need to remain in control. I can't let him win. I have to do what Jarek asked and keep Ness safe. That means not getting lost in fantasies of killing the old man or fucking his daughter while coated in his blood. No matter how hot they are, I have to push those thoughts away.

There will be plenty of time to fuck Ness while we're coated in someone's blood after all of this is taken care of. The thought pushes me to pay more attention to Jarek and Dragonetti. I notice that Milo is standing half in front of Ness, and I reposition myself to cover her other side. If she won't get back into the car, she'll have to deal with a human shield for protection.

Even without hearing their conversation, it's easy to tell that things are getting heated between the two men facing off in front of us. Dragonetti's bodyguard has tried to step forward a few times, but been waved off by the old man. That in itself is a slap in the face to Jarek, implying that the old man can take care of Jarek on his own and doesn't need help. I know that my cousin could snap this mother fucker in half if he wanted.

JAREK

Dragonetti continues to tell me about how he was going to sell Ness to the highest bidder, and how much her death had helped him by giving him the insurance money to pay his debts. Once those were paid, he was able to expand his business and get himself into more debt.

He wants us to bow to him, and keep Ness in exchange for working his drug trade. I assure him that I will never work for him. He makes some snide comment about Ness being a whore and I slap him again. The fucker tries to punch me, but he's so old and fat that I can dodge the punch pretty easily. Okay, he's not actually that old, but he seems so much older than me.

And he has zero control over his anger. I've already pushed him over the edge too many times to count in the past few minutes. I can't wait to end this. A quick glance over my shoulder tells me that Ness is not getting back in the SUV like we agreed on. That makes me angry.

I'll have to punish her for that later. A good spanking should set her straight. Especially if she can't sit down for the rest of the day. Imagining her naked ass, red and throbbing from my hand, makes my dick hard. That's not ideal for what I'm dealing with right now. I have to force the thoughts from my head and push Dragonetti to finish this so I can deal with her.

"Look, we're not going to agree on this, ever. How about you stop being a bitch, and just give up. She's not going anywhere with you. I only asked you here so you would know that your daughter is still alive, and that she's being taken care of. If you want war, you'll get it. But you won't survive." I try to sound as menacing as possible, when really, I'm getting bored with this conversation. I'm sick of his incessant whining, and would prefer to just kill him and get it over with.

"How dare you speak to me that way? Don't you know who you're dealing with?" I can't help but chuckle at the level of offended he is. "You insolent child. You will pay for disrespecting me like this. I'll have your head on my wall. Or perhaps I'll send it to your father as an example of what I'm capable of." It's an honest threat; I can tell that he means it, but I'm not scared of him or his henchmen.

"I'm getting bored here, Dragonetti. You're never going to offer me something that will be worth giving her back to you. She's not yours anymore. I was just offering you the knowledge that she was alive before you hear it from someone else.

Because you will. We're going to file the official paperwork tomorrow for our bonding. There will be newspaper articles and maybe television spots about it. I was trying to show some respect by telling you in person. But if you want to drag this out, I'm just going to take my omega and walk away." I watch his face as I speak.

Anger melts into fear, and fear turns to annoyance. So, he's scared of me, but not that scared. "Look, I get it. A man comes in and takes your daughter away when you think she's dead. That wears on a man. But don't pretend like I didn't do you a favor. At least until the news gets the story that she's still alive. Then the insurance company will be coming after you for the money you got as a payout for her death. You should consider that."

Dragonetti growls and lunges at me. I sidestep and he falls on his face. I don't bother to stifle my laugh. "You son of a bitch," he spits as his bodyguard helps him to his feet.

My fist shoots out and connects with his nose. I feel it crack and smirk in satisfaction. "No one talks about my mama that way. Ever."

"You broke my nose. You'll pay for that," he whines before making a motion with his arm. I know that it's the signal we've been expecting as the bullets rain down on us. I turn toward the SUV, hoping that they've gotten Ness back inside. They're dodging bullets and starting to shoot back.

I grab Dragonetti, holding him in front of me as a human shield. When his bodyguard tries to attack me, I punch him with my free hand, knocking him out. I pull my gun and hold it to the old man's head. "Call your guys off," I growl in his ear, making sure to back myself up against his SUV for cover from the shooters.

"I can't," he replies. I can hear the fear in his voice. He knows he's not making it out of here alive.

My crew starts taking out Dragonetti's guys one by one. I watch as Raf and Milo cover Ness while shooting back at the snipers. A bullet hits the car beside me, and I pop a couple of shots off in the direction it came from. Interesting. That was where one of my guys was. I wonder if he's shooting at Dragonetti or me. Either way, that was too close for comfort, so I take him out.

"Call your guys off before they're all dead," I order again.

"I can't call them off. There is no signal for that. They'll keep shooting until you're all dead or you kill them." I hadn't expected that from Dragonetti, but if that was how he wanted to play it, that's what we'll do.

"Fine, we'll kill them all then. If that's what you really want," I spit at him. I pull him with me out into the open, where his guys are shooting.

Chapter Seventeen

CONSEQUENCES

VANESSA

I watch as Jarek uses my father as a shield against the snipers that are currently shooting at us. I don't have time to get back into the SUV. I know Jarek, Raf, and Milo are all going to be pissed at me about this. I'll be lucky if I make it out alive, just so they can spank me into submission. That would be the best punishment I could hope for. Worst case, they'd tie me up and leave me there with absolutely no orgasms for a week.

Fuck, that would be horrible. Maybe death would be preferable to that kind of punishment. A bullet whizzes past my head and I duck, realizing that death is not preferable. I have to find cover or I'm not going to make it out of this garage.

I watch as Raf and Milo start aiming for the spots where the shooters have to be. They're more skilled with weapons than I had expected, taking out their enemies efficiently. I'm glad they're not wasting ammo. I can't tell how many shooters my father brought, but I'm pretty sure that one of Jarek's guys just shot at him. Fucker. I'll have him in the dungeon as soon as we're done here.

Before I can even focus on how I want to take the man apart, I see Jarek fire in that direction and a sniper rifle falls from the rafters. Damn, these men can shoot. At least he's somewhat safe now. I know he's telling my father to call his forces off, and my father is refusing. But I can't hear them over the bullets flying past.

I crouch behind the SUV, almost under it, trying to get as much cover as I can. I can't make myself run, though. I need to see my men in action. I have to know that they're okay.

I watch in horror as Jarek steps into the line of fire, holding my father against him. The men who've been shooting at us adjust their shots to avoid their employer. That courtesy doesn't seem to extend to me as gunfire rains around the three of us.

Milo ducks behind the SUV for a minute, probably to reload. Raf is at the front, tucked under similar to how I am. I can hear the bullets pinging off the bullet-proof metal that covers the SUV. I know that I should go to the door and climb inside, but I can't make myself do it.

I watch as Milo comes back around the car, taking careful aim at one of the guys who's trying to kill me. I try to keep count of how many men my guys take out, but there are just too many. And it's not just my three guys shooting, either. Jarek has men stationed in different places overhead, who are defending us as well.

I close my eyes for a moment and cover my ears. Just when I think the noise is too much, everything goes silent. All the shooting has just stopped. What happened? I drop my hands from my ears and open my eyes.

I don't see Milo, and fear grips my heart. Logically, I know that if he's dead, I'll feel it through the mate bond. And I don't feel it, but that could just be because of the adrenaline. I crawl out from under the SUV and look around for him. Nothing.

I scan the room quickly for Jarek, and find him still holding my father. His gun is pressed to the old man's temple. That should keep him in line. I still don't see Milo, and now I realize that I don't see Raf either. My heart races, and I struggle to breathe.

I race around the car to see if they're hiding somewhere else. As I'm running, a single shot rings through the air. I feel the projectile tear through my right shoulder and I drop to the floor. Pain tears through me. It hurts so badly that I can't move. I can't scream or even speak.

I know that Jarek watched me get shot. No doubt, he's panicking himself right now. I can't even tell him that I'm okay. I wonder what he'll do, but the world starts to spin. I have to fight the darkness. I can't give up. I don't know how bad the wound is, but I can't risk passing out and bleeding to death.

I have to stay awake. Darkness grips my vision. I'm pretty sure that I'm still conscious, even though I can't see anything. I can still feel my feet and the fingers of my left hand. I wrap them around my bloody shoulder and try to stop the seeping. The pain is worse when I touch it, but I'm surprisingly calm.

It's eerie how calm I am. I know that I have to be in shock. There's no other explanation. *Stay awake, Ness. You will not go out this way. The old man will not win here today.* He wants me dead, so I refuse to die. I redouble my efforts to clear my head.

My vision comes back to me in waves, black turning to gray, then clearing for a moment. Then everything starts to spin again and I have to close my eyes. Okay, vertigo is not my friend right now. When is it ever, though?

With the dizzy feeling taking over, my stomach starts to roll. I know that I'm going to be sick. I'm also aware that someone is screaming, and bullets are flying again. There's nothing I can do but make myself as small as possible. I curl into as tight of a ball as I can, squeezing my eyes closed tightly and hoping I don't throw up all over myself.

I keep my left hand pressed tightly against my right shoulder while I use the concrete to stifle the blood flow on the back side. The pain is horrible, and I'm worried that I'll pass out before someone comes to help.

MILO

While Ness is safely under the SUV, I work my way around to where Raf is hiding. "We have to take out the last of the shooters. I'm going up there."

He nods at me and motions that he'll cover me. I sneak to the scaffolding that will take me up to find the men who are hiding. Once I'm at the top, I carefully work my way around until I find guys who aren't familiar. Opting for my knife instead of my gun, I quietly crawl up and slit the first one's throat. Blood sprays from his neck and his gun clatters to the floor below.

Fuck, that wasn't good. They'll be expecting me now. I glance over the edge and see Jarek holding Dragonetti in front of him like a shield. I don't see Raf, but when I look around the rafters, I can see that he's on the opposite side, working his way toward me. Good. We'll take out the shooters, then deal with Dragonetti.

The shooting stops, since there aren't any more targets below. That will make it harder to find the rest of the guys up here, but I won't let that stop me. I'm going to kill them all for thinking they could pin us down like this.

I make quick work of searching the alcoves and snapping necks where I can, while letting my knife do the work for me when I can't. I'm careful not to let any more guns fall from up here while I'm working.

When Raf and I meet in the middle, I'm certain we've taken care of all of Dragonetti's henchmen. I look over the edge to tell Jarek that we're clear when I see Ness moving from behind the car. "What is she doing?" I ask Raf.

He leans over and shakes his head. "She should be fine. As long as we got them all. I think she's looking for us. I'm going to head back down and meet her."

After he disappears, I watch Ness make her way around the car. I jump when a shot rings off to my left. Fuck, I missed one. Ness grabs her shoulder and drops to the ground. I will kill this mother fucker for shooting our girl. I can't get down to her safely from here, so I leave that to Raf. Jarek has his hands full with Dragonetti right now. I have to trust that the wound is not fatal.

I creep toward the area where the shot came from, careful to move slowly and quietly. I'm sure the guy isn't moving, and I don't want to spook him. I want to slit his throat and watch him bleed out. I can't believe how quickly I went from the FBI mindset of only killing as a last resort to I will fuck up a mo-fo for hurting my family. I guess what they say is true. You have no idea how far you'll go until you're put in that position.

I slow my breathing and listen. I've got you. I move to my left, keeping in the shadows. I see the guy laying on his stomach, trying to hide. He must know that Raf and I were up here hunting. Good. I hope he knows that I'm coming for him. And I hope he knows it's gonna hurt. I'll make sure of it.

I tackle the man, punching him in the face to start. "You shot my omega, you fucker. Now you're gonna die." I stab him in the kidneys, just because I feel like making him hurt. He cries out in pain and I let that push me harder. I want him to suffer. I sink my knife into his back, deflating one of his lungs. I can hear him struggling to breathe.

The whistle of his breath only pushes me to do more. I wish I could take my time and really work this guy over. But with Ness injured and no light up here, a man can only do so much. "You got lucky today, asshole." I tell him as I slide my knife along his throat slowly. Blood gushes from his neck, and I can't resist stabbing my knife into his neck over and over until his head is barely attached. I know I'm covered in the man's blood, but I think I'm starting to see what Ness enjoys about torture.

Ness! Fuck. I carefully work my way back to the scaffolding and climb down to see if she's okay. Jarek has passed Dragonetti along to Raf, and he's cradling Ness in his lap. "Is she okay?" I ask quietly.

"I don't know. It's her shoulder, so she should be. Help Raf with that dick, would you?" His pleading glance tells me that he won't let me check Ness out for myself anyway, so I do as he asks.

"I can't believe you'd do this to your own daughter," I say to Dragonetti before planting my fist in his face.

Raf laughs, but holds the man up. "We're supposed to keep him alive until the Feds get here, remember?"

"Oh, he'll be alive. More so than the asshole who shot Ness. I found him and took care of the problem," I report. Raf gives me an approving look. I know I've done what my family expects here, and I'm actually proud of myself. It's a strange feeling.

"I know we're not exactly in the clear here, but has anyone called an ambulance for her?" I can't help asking the question, even though I already know the answer.

"I've got a surgeon coming to check her out. He's one of ours, so there's no risk to her. He's the best surgeon I've ever met, and can take care of her out of a hospital. No one will know what happened here unless we want them to."

"Okay, that's good. We need to keep this out of the press as much as possible."

RAFAEL

When I race down to Ness, I find her alive but barely conscious. I can see the terror in Jarek's eyes. This is his past repeating itself. So, I go over and take hold of Dragonetti, so he can hold Ness and know that the wound isn't fatal. I fight against my own desire to comfort and care for her, because my cousin needs it more.

While he holds her, I keep a hand on the old man. I want to rip his head off for putting his daughter in this position in the first place. Instead, I pull out my phone and call Jim. He's the best surgeon in the city, and he usually works for us. I know it'll be kept quiet and he'll be here quickly. He should be able to patch Ness up before the FBI arrives. That is, if Milo actually called his pal.

I guess we'll find out about that soon enough. Dragonetti refuses to talk, instead smirking at us and laughing under his breath. I want to kick him, but I hold myself back. I can't afford to be holding a corpse when the Feds get here.

Milo must have found the shooter, because he isn't far behind me, rushing to Ness and Jarek. My cousin must ask him to help me, because he storms over, rage plastered across his face.

"I can't believe you'd do this to your own daughter," he says to Dragonetti before planting his fist in the old man's face.

I laugh, but hold the old man up. "We're supposed to keep him alive until the Feds get here, remember?"

"Oh, he'll be alive. More so than the asshole who shot Ness. I found him and took care of the problem," he reports. I give him an approving look. He did what we expect, and I can tell he's proud of himself.

"I know we're not exactly in the clear here, but has anyone called an ambulance for her?" he asks me, expecting the answer to be no.

"I've got a surgeon coming to check her out. He's one of ours, so there's no risk to her. He's the best surgeon I've ever met, and can take care of her out of a hospital. No one will know what happened here unless we want them to." I explain casually.

"Okay, that's good. We need to keep this out of the press as much as possible."

I nod, even though I know we'll be plastered across the front page for this. There will be no way to escape it, especially if we testify to help put the old man away. I've made peace with this idea. What's going to suck is the publicity Ness will get for coming back from the dead.

I want to shield her from that, but it's not possible. We never considered that she'd come back into society when we faked her death. There just wasn't time to think about every aspect of our actions. We acted quickly to save her life.

"You bastards will go down for this, you know," Dragonetti says quietly.

"How do you figure?" I ask, turning him to face me. Milo stands behind him with his gun in one hand and a rather hefty hunting knife in the other. I think it helps that the knife is still coated in blood. I watch the old man's eyes trail over it before focusing on me again.

"You kidnapped and raped my daughter, then shot her. Who do you think they're going to believe? Besides, I have half of them in my pocket already," he laughs.

"Which ones are in your pocket?" Milo jabs the knife into the old man's side, just enough to get his point across, but not enough to hurt him. Yet.

"Wouldn't you like to know? It's not like you were smart enough to figure it out when you worked at the precinct. Some FBI profiler you turned out to be. Can't even see what's right in front of you. Or should I say behind."

My head jerks around at the old man's words. I realize that his bodyguard is no longer sprawled out where we left him. Fuck. That means the bastard isn't dead after all. "Where did he go?"

Milo grabs Dragonetti by the throat, holding the knife to his jugular. "I've got him. If he has an 'accident' I'll just have to explain it. Or we'll just leave and torch the place before the Feds get here. Either way, find his guy."

I'm impressed with how Milo takes control, so I do as he asks. Gun in hand, I make my way around Dragonetti's SUV. Nothing. Fuck. I hope this guy hasn't made it up to the scaffolding. Before I can make my way over and climb up, I see movement beside our SUV. He's going after Jarek and Ness. Not on my watch.

I creep around the opposite side of the SUV, keeping low so the guy doesn't see me. Just as he's about to pounce on Jarek, I tackle him to the ground and punch him in the face. I want to keep him alive, but I can't trust that he won't attack us again. Milo pulls Dragonetti over by his throat and tosses me a pair of zip tie cuffs. "Tie him up. I'll get this dick."

Once the prisoners are tied up, we strap them to columns away from each other. They're still close enough that we can keep an eye on them, but they aren't close enough to help each other escape.

Milo watches the bodyguard and I keep my eyes on Dragonetti. Now we wait. "How long until your friends get here?"

"I don't even know if they're coming. Jackson didn't exactly say 'yeah, we'll be there at two pm.' We just have to wait and see if they show up."

I hate waiting, but if Milo didn't get a straight answer, I guess that's all we have.

VANESSA

I'm cold, and the darkness keeps trying to pull me under. I think I see Raf for a second, but I can't reach out to him. A moment later, Jarek pulls me into his arms and cradles me on his lap. He brushes my hair off my face and applies pressure to the wound with his jacket.

"It's okay, doll. Stay with me. We're going to take care of you." His sweet words encourage me to hold on. I don't know how much blood I've lost, but it can't be good for him to be openly sweet. He kisses my forehead and whispers in my ear. "Please don't leave me."

Oh, my sweet beast of a man, I don't plan to. But I can't get the words out. I try to open my eyes again. It's just too hard to keep them open. I want to sleep. I'm so tired. I hate this feeling. I don't recommend getting shot. It does not feel good.

I groan because I've laid on the cold, hard ground long enough that everything hurts. "Raf, Milo, give me your jackets. She's freezing." I hear Jarek's words, then feel the soft fabrics touch my skin as he drapes their jackets over me. I release a sigh, unsure if the noise is just in my head or if they can hear it.

"How long until Jim gets here?" Milo asks. Who is Jim and why do they need him? Is he a cleaner, who will take care of the mess here so we can go home? I hope so.

"He's coming in now," Raf answers. Looks like I might find out, if I can stay awake long enough.

"Raf, where is she? I brought everything I could for a mobile surgery unit. The guys will set it up and we'll get her taken care of." My eyes flutter at the new voice. I can't focus to see what he looks like. He sounds nice, though. What does he mean when he says he'll take care of me? Am I dying?

A minute or an hour later, I have no idea how long, I'm carefully extracted from Jarek's arms and placed on a stretcher. I shiver, because they've taken the jackets away. I don't have long to be cold, though, before I feel a warm blanket cover me. Another sigh escapes my lips and I relax. If Jarek let them take me away from him, I must be in good hands.

I don't fight against the doctors. I'm not sure I could if I wanted to. I feel the IV as they place it in my arm. Then I feel even more drowsy as they give me a sedative. No doubt so they can examine and repair my shoulder. I think the bullet went straight through, but I'm not really sure.

"Just relax, Vanessa. We've got you. Take a nap, and when you wake up, you'll be on the road to recovery with your mates." The doctor's voice, Jim, I guess, is pleasant and lulls me to sleep.

I wake up, groggy and disoriented, to Jarek's face about a foot away. At least he's giving me a little space. "Am I okay?" I'm surprised at how clearly the words come out.

"You're going to be just fine. Jim said the repair was pretty easy. The bullet was through and through. He fixed what he could, but that shoulder could still bother you for a while." Jarek brushes my hair from my forehead as he speaks.

"I know I should rest, but I want to see him. I want to tell him that he's lost. We've won. He can't ruin what we have with his hate." I try to sit up, but it's too hard right now. I have no energy, and pain shoots through me when I move my arm.

"Sorry, doll, you're not getting out of this bed right now. You'll get your chance to tell the asshole off, but it won't be today. We're still not sure if the Feds are coming or not. Milo can't get Jackson to answer now." Jarek looks concerned.

"What do we do if they don't?" I can't agree to letting my father go. There's no way we can do that. He has to pay for what he's done.

"If we have to, we'll load him up and drop him off ourselves. He will go to jail today. But it's gonna be a long day of answering questions and trying to figure out how to keep ourselves out of jail too," he admits. That had been the biggest concern for all of them, even while we were planning this confrontation.

Maybe it would be easier just to kill the old man and leave it at that. "That's not really what you want, doll." I didn't realize I said the words aloud. Fuck, these are some good drugs. I feel great and horrible all at once. That's probably why I don't do drugs. This feeling is weird.

"Just rest for now. We'll get it all figured out. I have to check in with the guys, but I'll stay close." He waits until I close my eyes again to walk away. I know that I'm safe here with the doctor and nurses, and my guys nearby. But more than anything, I just want to go home.

I take a deep breath and relax into the sleep that pulls at me. I vaguely notice the nurses taking my vitals and the doctor checking his work on my shoulder. Mostly I just let myself sleep and wake as my body desires. Fuck. Desires. I need to ask the doc when I'll be able to enjoy my men again. I don't want to give that up.

"I'll make sure they know how long you need to wait. Don't worry about anything, Vanessa. They'll know how to take care of you. I'm giving them all the instructions, and they'll call me if you need anything."

JAREK

I overhear Ness asking Jim when we can service her sexually and I laugh. At least she's feeling better. He tells us that he expects a full recovery, so there's nothing really to do except wait it out. Once her father is taken care of, we'll get her home and start babying her.

I was terrified that I was going to lose her like Terri. My mind goes back to the day I lost her, along with the rest of my pack. A not-yet-bonded, cocky, twenty-one-year-old alpha who underestimated the lengths my father's enemies would go to take me out. I believed that I was invincible. If only I had listened to my father when he said we needed to be more careful. It was too late for that now.

That had been the worst pain of my life, and I wasn't looking forward to repeating it. Hopefully that never happens. There is no sense dwelling on the past. I have to move forward and prevent it from repeating itself.

"I'm sure you heard her question. I'm going to have to advise that you wait at least a few days—three to four—just to be on the safe side. Try to keep her distracted other ways. I want to make sure the wound doesn't get infected. And there's always the risk that she'll rip out a stitch. Call me if you have any questions or need anything." Jim shook my hand as his men tear down the makeshift surgery tent and pack everything away.

"Thanks, man. I owe you one." There are no words for how much I appreciate him coming down here to treat Ness instead of making us take her to a hospital where there would be questions and press.

"You'll get my bill. You may not thank me so much when you see what I'm charging you," he laughs as he gets into his car and leaves. I don't care what he charges, I'll pay it. I'd probably pay triple to make sure she's okay.

Raf and Milo are still guarding Dragonetti and his bodyguard. I walk over and check things out. Their ties are still secure. "You want to go talk to Ness?" I ask Raf, taking his spot in front of the old man. He nods his thanks at me and walks away.

"She's going to be fine, by the way. Not that you care about your own daughter, but I figure you should know. I'll make sure she's taken care of. Especially since you're going to prison.

For the rest of your pathetic life." I spit the words at him, knowing I shouldn't because he's not worth it.

"We'll see about that. My lawyers will get me out in no time," he barks back.

Milo laughs. "Even with your ledger? Because Ness has been translating it. The book is pretty good reading, listing every contact and deal you've done in the last five years. I think that will be plenty for them to use to put you away for life. It even has a section on hits you put out and who did them for you. Do you really think your lawyer can explain that away?"

"What the fuck? I've been searching for that book for nearly a year, and you have it?" I can't hold back my reaction.

"I told you, didn't I? Or did I tell Raf? I had no idea you were looking for it. But yeah, Ness has it. She's got a large chunk of it translated already." He seems apologetic for the slight, but I'm still annoyed that I had no idea that he had what I was looking for.

"Well, fuck. I spent so long looking for it, I'm not sure what to do now that we have it. I was planning on using it to blackmail the old man into paying me for silence. I guess that's out now. I'll have to settle for putting him away." I can't really stay mad at Milo for having the book I've been looking for. It's not like I told him or Ness that it was a book, or even gave them details about what I'd been doing.

A wave of relief washed over me at Dragonetti's reaction to Milo mentioning the book. He turns pale and starts to stutter.

"What? How? When did you take it? Have you been working against me this whole time?"

"It really sucks to find out someone you trusted betrayed you, doesn't it?" he asks the old man. I laugh again.

"I can't wait to see how this turns out," I reply as Raf comes back.

"Milo, you're up. She's gonna ask you to do things...just don't. She's definitely not up for them yet," he warns as Milo shakes his head and walks over to Ness. Jim settled her into the SUV when he packed up, so she's protected and comfortable.

"Did you know that Milo had the ledger?" I ask my cousin, worried about what his answer would be.

"I don't know. Maybe? He might have said something about a book, but I don't think I knew it was the one we've been looking for. Makes sense, though. I thought he managed to find us for a reason. And not just Ness." Raf's words play around in my mind. Is he right? Was all of this fate?

"I wonder if the Feds are coming to get them, or if we're going to have to figure out how to drop them off ourselves," I say, thinking aloud.

"Milo said Jackson isn't answering. How long do you want to wait?"

"We can give them a little longer, since Ness is patched up. I'm anxious to get her home, though," I admit.

"Same. But we have to take care of these guys first. I could just put a bullet in their skulls. Then we could leave them here and go home," Raf offers.

Dragonetti balks at the thinly veiled threat. "You can't do that!"

CHAPTER EIGHTEEN

GETTING THE FEDS INVOLVED

MILO

I hate waiting. Especially when there are better things I could be doing. After checking on Ness, who is sleeping peacefully in the back seat of the car, I pull out my phone and call Jackson again. This time he answers. "Man, I've been calling. Where are you?"

"Trying to get everyone moving. The chief wants nothing to do with anything you're involved in, so I had to go above her head. We'll be there in ten," he says, disconnecting the call. Well, at least I know they're coming. That's a relief.

I check on Ness again, then walk back over to Jarek and Raf. "Jackson says they're on the way. Ten minutes," I explain, hoping that my former partner is right about how long it will take them to get here. I'm ready to be done with this.

"Good. Let's move the car over here, so we can keep a closer eye on Ness and these two." I nod at Jarek's suggestion and pull the SUV over, parking across from the columns where our prisoners are tied up. I stay in the car for a minute, listening to Ness' soft breathing.

My heart still hasn't recovered from the thought that we nearly lost her today. I need to be close to her to make sure she's okay. I know the surgeon took care of her shoulder, but my heart and brain don't agree that she's going to be fine. What if this experience makes her want out of the mate bond with us? I would never recover from that.

I drop my head in my hands for a minute and take a few deep breaths to calm down. I need to be in control when the Feds get here. I have to convince them that we're the victims here. Dragonetti says he has so many people in his pocket. Is Jackson one of them?

At one point, I thought that I would know if someone else was working for him, since I was. But now, I'm not so sure. I hope that I'm right in trusting Jackson, but I won't know until they get here. And by then, it may be too late. If we all end up in jail with Dragonetti, I'm pretty sure Raf and Jarek will kick my ass. To be fair, I would deserve it for making a poor judgement call. Please let me be right about Jackson. I send the words up like a small prayer, hoping for the best.

Has it been ten minutes yet? Either way, I should get out of the car and let Ness rest more. I climb out and carefully close the door behind me. I notice that Jarek and Raf look rough, like they're wearing down. I'm sure I look just as bad. This has been the longest day, and it's not going to end any time soon. A thought occurs to me, and I can't resist spitting it out.

"You guys could leave, you know. You could take Ness and go back home. I can sort all of this out and meet you there when I'm done. It would keep you from having to deal with the Feds and answer questions," I make the offer, wondering why I hadn't thought of it before.

Jarek shakes his head. "Not gonna happen. We're family."

"And family sticks together," Raf finishes the thought. It's sappy and sweet, and touches me more than I think it should. Knowing that these men have accepted me feels like going home. This is exactly where I need to be. And we're doing this together.

"Okay. I can handle that," I reply. Dragonetti glares daggers at me from the ground. "They'll be here soon to get you." I can't help but smirk at him and his sour face.

"You know, Milo, your brother never would have betrayed me like this. He wouldn't have stolen from me either. It's too bad he had to be the one to die," the old man snarls with his words. I can feel the venom of his hate for me.

There was a time when I would have been upset that he thought less of me. I tried so hard to be what he wanted. I would have done anything to make him proud of me, to be like my brother. I think the only reason I wanted to be like him was so I would finally feel like I belonged somewhere. But I have that now with D'Angelo. With my family.

"Dragonetti, you can't intimidate me anymore. I'm not scared of you. I don't need your approval. I have a family, and a place where I belong. And none of it happened because of you." I stop to consider that for a minute. "Or did it? Maybe all of this is because of you. If that's the case, thank you." You'd think I told him to fuck off instead of saying thanks with his reaction to my words. Either way, it was really satisfying to tell him exactly what I thought. No matter how much I miss my brother, revenge would not bring him back, and that was what I have to remember.

Moments later, flashing lights on top of unmarked cars fly into the garage. I'm glad I moved the car closer, because it blocked us from most of the headlights and flashing lights. When they stopped, we were surrounded. For a second, fear grips my chest. This is it. We will either go to jail, or we will go free. I'm not sure which one it will be.

Jackson climbs out of one of the cars and walks toward me. "I'm gonna need you to put the guns down, fellas." He has his own pulled and is aiming it at Jarek and Raf.

"Wait, Jackson, those two are with me. We caught Dragonetti together." I turn to Raf and Jarek. "You can put the guns down. Probably better to put them on the ground, so Jackson knows we're not causing trouble."

VANESSA

I hear a commotion, and it pulls me from the deep sleep I've been in. Looking out the window, I realize that the SUV is in a different place than it was a little while ago. Hmm. I wonder what happened. There are flashing red and blue lights, and men with guns surround us.

I debate jumping out of the car, but decide it may be safer to stay inside. I know my guys would prefer to keep me as far away from all of this as they can. "Okay, for now, I'll stay put." I decide that if it looks like my guys are getting arrested, I'll step out. For now, I'll just watch.

I notice that someone has rolled the windows down a little more than they were earlier. I can actually hear what the Feds are saying.

"Thanks, Milo, but I'm going to need you to drop your weapon too." That must be Jackson. He seems like a stand-up guy. I wonder if they're friends, or if they were just work acquaintances.

"Sorry, man. Here." Milo puts his gun on the ground and scoots it toward the man, then nods at Jarek and Raf to do the same. They exchange a look, then do as the man asks. Good, we need to cooperate. I even see them taking hidden weapons out and putting them on the ground. Damn, I hadn't realized just how many knives and guns these three had brought with us today.

"That's good. Now, go stand by the SUV. Martinez will keep an eye on you for now." The man, who I've decided is Jackson, walks over to my father with cuffs in his hand. "As for you, we have a special cell waiting for you. I can't wait to see how long you get once we have all the evidence ready." Hmm, he seems to have a vendetta against my father just like the rest of us. Good.

Another agent cuffs daddy dearest's bodyguard and takes him away. I wonder what they're going to do with us. It seems like they should ask some questions, but I don't know if they'll do that here or at the station. I don't really want to go to the police station, but I know that we may not have a choice.

"Is there anyone else here?" Jackson asks. Milo grabs the door handle and opens it to reveal me.

I wave tentatively, barely moving my hand. I'm sure I look a mess, even with a clean shirt on. "Hi."

"Wait, is that—" he looks at Milo then continues, "Vanessa Dragonetti?"

I shake my head. "No, Vanessa Dragonetti is dead. I'm Ness D'Angelo." I watch Jarek's face as I introduce myself to the agent.

Milo laughs. "It's her, but she's right. She isn't a Dragonetti anymore. Just like I'm not a Spezia. We're D'Angelos now."

"Holy fuck, Milo! You finally found a pack? Dude, that's awesome." Jackson shakes Milo's hand. "We still have to take you all to the station and ask a ton of questions to sort all of this out. I'm sorry. I know you've been through a lot today already."

"Is there any way we could answer questions somewhere a little more comfortable than the police station? I got shot today, and I'd really like to rest," I admit. The agent looks at me, shock crossing his face.

"You got shot? And you still look that amazing. Wow, Milo, you got a good one for sure." He slaps Milo on the back. "Let me see what we can do. I'm sure you don't want us coming to your home, but maybe we can compromise and use a hotel nearby."

I've never heard of the FBI questioning suspects in hotels, but maybe I just don't know these things. It sounds to me like Jackson doesn't suspect us of any wrongdoing. I keep my guard up just in case. I don't want to get surprised by a sudden arrest.

"Let me call this in really quick and see what we can do." He walks away, and my men descend on me. Milo hugs me gently, kissing my cheek, then passes me to Raf, who does the same. Jarek doesn't wait for Raf to be done, pulling me away from him and wrapping his arms around me protectively. I'm surprised that none of them look upset about it.

"You'll really take my name when this is over?" Jarek asks me quietly. I nod, wiping a single tear from my eye.

"It sounds like Milo is too," I offer, trying to shift his focus from me. Jarek is intense, and it's a lot right now.

"Well, hell, if everyone else is doing it, I am too," Raf chimes in. Jarek laughs, and it's contagious.

"That's settled then. I figured we'd end up with some strange hybrid name where we took so many letters from each last name and mixed them up," he admits.

"We respect our head alpha too much to do that," I say with a smile. I know that's what it boils down to, and there's no reason to hide the truth. After what he did for me today, I will happily take his last name. Especially if it gets me further away from my father.

"Thank you. All of you. This means a lot to me. We'll get the paperwork filled out tomorrow, then see about submitting it as soon as possible. Unless you want to wait for all of this to blow over?" The offer pains him, but he seems determined not to push for anything I'm not ready for.

"Not at all. I want it done as soon as possible. I want the world to know that I'm yours."

Raf and Milo nod in agreement. Thank goodness. Forming a pack can be one of the hardest parts of being an omega. These three have made it fairly easy, minus the whole faking my death thing.

RAFAEL

It seems like today is going to be the day for settling everything. I don't mind changing my name. Especially since it means I have an official pack to call my own. I'm excited about our easy agreement, but worried about the publicity of a trial for Dragonetti. I wonder what people will say about Ness choosing us.

Will it hurt the case? Or will it help? There's no way to know. I guess there's no point in stressing over it. We'll just go along with whatever happens and see how it turns out. Which is not the way I like to do things.

Jackson comes back and makes an announcement. "My boss will let us do the interviews at the hotel across the street, but only if you all agree to be hooked up to a lie detector machine while we talk."

Shit, this could get ugly. What if they ask something we don't want to answer? There may be prison time ahead of us after all. I can't see a way out of this.

Jarek steps forward. "Are you planning to ask us about our business ventures, or just what happened here today?"

Jackson clears his throat. "I don't think we need to discuss your business ventures. Unless they pertain to this incident or to how you know what you've shared about Dragonetti." He steps closer to Jarek and whispers. "I'm not after you or your family. Milo is like a brother to me, so I'll do whatever I can to protect you guys. And that's strictly off the record."

Jarek nods. "We'll do your lie detector, then. Thank you for understanding my need to protect the family."

I can tell that Jackson will easily become one of our allies in the future. We load up in the SUV, with Jackson at the wheel, and head across the street to the cozy hotel. Jarek lets Jackson book a room, and we follow him upstairs.

After settling Ness into one of the double queen beds, we watch as Jackson's team sets up the lie detector machine. I'm surprised when he dismisses them as soon as it's done. "No, I don't need anything else. It will be better for the witnesses to do this without a crowd." One of them tries to argue, but he holds up a hand. "It's fine. If anything comes down about it, it'll be on me."

With that assurance, they file out the door and leave. When it's just the five of us, he motions to Milo to sit across from him. "You wanna get us started, Milo?"

I watch as Milo gets hooked up to the machine and settles into the chair. I know a few methods for beating these things, but I'm not sure I'll need them. I listen as Jackson goes through a basic list of questions and Milo supplies his answers.

The whole thing is over faster than I think it should be. After Milo gives his account of what happened at the garage, Jackson glosses over the whole issue of how many guys we killed. He states that it was obviously self-defense, and there would be no charges for it.

When he's finished with Milo, it's my turn. He must be saving Jarek or Ness for last. I let Milo help strap me into the contraption, then sit. I can feel my heart hammering in my chest. I'm concerned, but not scared. I don't want this whole thing to go sideways, but I still feel like I'm waiting for the other shoe to drop.

Jackson starts with easy questions, my name, my relationship with the other people in this room, and how I know Dragonetti. This one is a little harder to explain. I decide to stick as close to the truth as I can.

"I worked for him as security for his daughter for almost a year. That was how I learned of his plot to have her killed for the insurance money."

Jackson's jaw drops. "During your employment with Dragonetti, did you witness any illegal activities?" Ah, so the questions would get a little more in depth for me.

"I did. I actually have a thumb drive with names, dates, and other pertinent information. I'd be happy to provide it to you later today or tomorrow." He stops paying attention to the machine and focuses on me.

"How much intel do you have?" he asks. I have to remember that this entire conversation is being recorded, and I'm trying not to implicate myself. Although it looks as if I'll get blanket immunity at this point. This guy is salivating hard over taking Dragonetti down. And I am here for it.

"It's a year worth of records. I kept track of everything. Even jobs that weren't mine. I noted everything I saw and heard. I know where the drug manufacturing is done, who's in charge of distribution, and where they launder the money. I was actually collecting it to hand over to you guys in the future." I know it might make me look kind of suspicious, but it's actually true. Jarek and I had a plan to take Dragonetti down one way or another.

If legal means didn't work out, we would have used the intel to blackmail him and convince him to bow out of different areas of his business. Then when we had the chance, we would have killed him to remove him completely.

"That's a lot of intel. Is there anything else you need to tell me?" I shake my head at his question, not sure what else I could say. The records will speak for themselves, especially when combined with the ledger that Milo found.

Jackson seems especially interested in all the records. I guess that's because it can all be used as evidence. Everything they get will add to the case against the old man. The more they have on paper, the better.

He finishes up with some random questions that don't seem relevant, then moves on to Ness.

VANESSA

When Jackson finishes with Raf, I volunteer to go next. He insists on bringing everything to me, so that I can remain in the bed resting. It's a sweet gesture, and I appreciate it. I'm still exhausted, and really just want to go home.

Once I'm strapped in, he starts asking questions. "What's your full name?"

"Vanessa Elizabeth Dragonetti D'Angelo. But I'll be dropping my father's last name as soon as the paperwork is completed." I answer with an air of authority. I will not fear this man. Even though he could take my entire family away in a moment.

"Good to know. How did you end up at the garage today for the meeting with your father?"

"That, sir, is a long story. Do you want the whole thing? Or just the summary?"

He chuckles at my statement. "If you don't mind, start at the beginning."

Somehow, I expect this from him. I spend the next half an hour explaining how Raf was my bodyguard and we overheard a plan to kill me. Then Raf and Jarek took me and faked my death. I also mention that I lost a few memories along the way because a couple of their guys roughed me up a bit. I leave out the way those guys were taken care of.

Jackson doesn't ask, but I'm sure he understands what happened. I continue my story, explaining that I didn't expect to fall in love with my captors, but the more I got to know them, the more right everything felt. When I found evidence that my father had been the one to order the hit on me, some of my memories came back. I tell him everything, leaving out any illegal activities any of us were involved in.

"So, you see, the men who love me simply wanted to give my father a chance to apologize and explain himself," I finish my tale and lay back against the pillow.

"I'm sorry to make you go through all of that again, Ms. Dragonetti," he offers. I wince at the name. "Sorry, Ms. D'Angelo."

"Thank you," I reply. "But I know I'm going to have to go into even more detail when my father goes to trial. I'm not looking forward to it, but it has to be done. He has to pay for the people he's hurt. He needs to be held accountable for his actions." It seems kind of hypocritical of me to want my father to be punished when I refuse to admit any of the illegal things that my family has done to protect me.

But I don't care. I will fight to protect these men. To the death if necessary. I will not back down or give up. They are mine, and no one can take them from me. "I'm feeling a little nauseated. Is there anyway we could get some food up here? Getting shot takes a lot out of you."

He nods his understanding and calls down for room service. He doesn't ask what we'd like until he has the chef on the phone. We each give our order and he orders food for himself too. I wonder how much longer this is going to take.

He goes over my story again while we wait for the food, asking more questions that flesh out details I missed the first time. "That makes more sense. I understand why you did what you did today, but it was dangerous. I hope you all know that taking the law into your own hands should not ever be done."

"Yes, sir. I understand that we should have simply turned our evidence over to you. We wanted to, but I was worried that my father would leave town and disappear before you could catch him. I didn't want to take that chance. I'm sorry for the inconvenience. This was all my fault." I glance over at Jarek as I speak.

He shakes his head at me. "Not your fault. It was a group decision, Jackson. We all had a hand in it." It's sweet the way Jarek won't let me take the blame for everything.

"It's okay. Everything is settled now. I just need your word that you won't do something like this in the future. If you discover more evidence against someone, you should bring it to our attention and let us take care of it. Understood?" He's trying to be authoritative, but it comes across as more friendly than anything.

I wonder if we would have been friends in another life. More likely than not. But being on opposite sides of the law tends to prohibit those types of friendships. What Milo and I have is a fluke. He should have never let my father get away with the things he did. He should have turned the whole family in and watched the fallout.

I wasn't guilty of anything until after I got mixed up with Jarek, but that doesn't matter now. I am mixed up in it, and I wouldn't have it any other way. I close my eyes for a minute and relax. I hear a knock on the door and smell the food as it's wheeled in.

Jackson announces that we'll take a break to eat, then Jarek will give his account of today's events. I feel like he's giving our head alpha more time to get his story figured out than he should. But I appreciate the allowance.

Milo sets a plate in my lap, and I stare at the food. "I know I need to eat, but I'm so tired." He holds a french fry up to my lips and I take it from him. It tastes like heaven, and I decide that I need them to take turns feeding me from now on. "A girl could get used to this, you know," I admit as he feeds me before turning to his own food.

With my belly as full as I can stand, I doze off, and no one stops me.

JAREK

When Ness falls asleep, I know it's my turn to answer questions. I don't want to, but I understand that Jackson is just doing his job. I let Milo strap me into the machine, then settle in the chair next to where Ness is resting. I won't leave her side.

After the usual beginning questions, name, occupation, and what not, Jackson asks about the meeting today. "Why were you meeting with Dragonetti?"

"To let him know that his daughter is alive and that she's been claimed by my pack. I thought her mother deserved to know that the child she's been grieving isn't dead." It is half the truth, and I wonder if it will be enough.

"That sounds plausible enough. Why that parking garage? Couldn't you have met him at his home or at a restaurant?" He seems genuinely curious, so I figure why not just answer.

"Well, you see, Dragonetti and I are, let's just say, not so friendly. We have competing business ventures and he doesn't exactly like me. I expected it to go about as well as it did, considering. And I just figured that an abandoned parking garage was safer than the middle of main street, where there could be civilian casualties." I watch Jackson's face as he watches the output of the machine.

"Wow. I don't know what to say about that."

"You could start with, 'I understand, and I'm not taking you to jail.' That would be nice to hear." I know that he said he's on our side, but he's also an officer of the law, and has certain obligations to uphold said law.

"Oh, I meant what I said earlier. I'm not taking you guys in. As far as my report will show, everything you did was in self-defense. I just needed to know for my own peace of mind that you weren't lying to me. None of what you say here would even be admissible."

"Then why—" Milo starts, but Jackson holds up a hand.

"I have to have interview notes, yes. I don't have to tell them everything that's said. I had to make sure I was the one to do this interview, instead of someone else. That's why I sent the rest of my team away. They'll be able to tell if the machine isn't used, so I had to hook each of you up to it. And I did record the parts of your answers that didn't implicate you." He looks up at Milo and smirks.

"You'd do this for us?" he asks.

Jackson nods. "I would. Family is important. And protecting that family has no boundaries."

"Thank you," I offer my hand along with the words. He shakes it.

"There is something I don't understand, though." He makes sure we see him checking the recording to be sure it's off. "Don't worry, strictly off the record. Why not just kill him? Why have him arrested and risk him getting out?"

"Because of her. He's her father. A horrible one, but that's beside the point. What kind of alpha would I be if I killed my mate's father? Honestly, if you guys hadn't shown up when you did, I might have. He was testing my patience more than anything ever has. I thought I was going to lose it and snap his neck. And we'd already had to pull Milo off of him twice. I wasn't sure Raf could keep us both away." I look at my cousin as I speak. I need him to know how close I was to going off plan.

He nods at me. "I would have found a way. But if we're being honest, I wanted to kill the bastard myself."

"Okay, that makes a lot more sense. I couldn't figure out exactly what the deal was, and it bothered me. I felt like there was more in play here. But with him in jail, his daughter can take over his assets, unless he has a wife?"

I nod. "He does, but Ness is pretty sure she'll just sign it all over to her. Her mom's a typical omega. She doesn't want responsibility. She just wants to be taken care of. Ness wants to be in control, so it would make sense for her to take over the business."

With all that settled, Jackson starts packing up the equipment. Milo unhooks the harness from around my chest and hands it to his former partner. "Thank you," I say again.

"No problem. You guys stay here and let her rest for a while. I rented the room for the night. Stay as long as you need to. Take care of her. I'm sure we'll need her testimony against her father." Jackson shakes everyone's hands, making sure to stay quiet and not wake Ness.

After he leaves, I look at Raf and Milo. "I feel like that was close. I know he kept saying he wouldn't arrest us, but I feel like he wavered on that a few times. If we'd given him any more detail, things may have ended differently."

"I know him pretty well," Milo says. "And that was definitely out of character for him. He's always been completely by the book with no exceptions. Maybe something about Ness being our mate convinced him to be lenient."

I guess that's possible, but I wonder if it has more to do with getting us to testify against Dragonetti. They need us or they can't take him down. The thought amuses me. "Well, brothers, I guess we should settle in and get some rest while our girl recovers."

I kick back on the second bed where I can keep an eye on Ness and the door. I don't want to take any chances, and I think Raf agrees. He walks over, locks the door, and puts a chair under the handle.

"Now we can rest," he says.

CHAPTER NINETEEN

ESCAPE OR NOT

VANESSA

The next few weeks are filled with questions and interviews. All I want is to be left alone to enjoy my mates, but we can't catch a break. We had to move twice in one week because reporters found Jarek's hideout and blasted it on the nightly news. The same thing happened with the second one. I don't want to move again. I'm at the point where I hate the police for dragging us into all of this.

I know that my father's trial is set to start in just a few days, and I'm not sure that I'm mentally ready. I have to tell the judge and jury everything, even if it incriminates my loves. Jackson claims we have blanket immunity, but I'm still scared I'll lose everything.

I have no idea why Raf and Jarek trust him, but I guess it's okay. "Do we have to do another interview today?" Raf asks, sounding as annoyed as I feel.

Jarek laughs at him. "Yeah, every day this week. Trial starts next week. The prosecutor told you that. They need to know how we're going to answer all of their questions before they ask them. That way they can avoid asking certain things. It's to help us out, actually."

It's the third time this week that Jarek has explained this to us. I roll my eyes as I walk away to get ready. I'm still living out of suitcases, because I refuse to officially move in until we know that we're staying here. The house is nice, but it's not the same as the building where we fell in love. I miss that place.

There's no sense dwelling on that, because we can't go back. I know, I've asked. It's not safe. And that sucks. I know that Jarek will find us a permanent home as soon as all of this is over. How long will that be? I have no idea. The sooner, the better, for everyone involved.

Once I'm dressed and ready, I meet my loves and leave for the precinct. When we pull up to the building, there's a crowd of reporters waiting for us. We fight our way through the crowd, the four of us linking hands and letting Jarek pull us through the fray.

"You guys really should do something about that," he says to the officer who holds the door open for us.

"We keep trying. It's not doing any good. I'm sorry you have to deal with this chaos, Mr. D'Angelo." I'm surprised at the respect the officer shows us. I guess being star witnesses will do that for you, though.

"No problem, Steve. You didn't call them and tell them we were gonna be here, did you?" Is Jarek actually joking with this guy? Wow, he's really mellowing out since my father is no longer an issue. I kinda like it, but I'll miss my growly beast if he stays this way.

A reporter rushes through the doors and I realize I have nothing to worry about. The man approaches Jarek, who turns and growls at him. I almost feel sorry for the little guy, but they have all been warned. The poor guy does an about-face and runs out of the building.

I can't help but laugh at how comical the whole thing was. Jarek glares at me, then winks. At least he's not really mad. It's just frustrating that they think they can hound us constantly. I don't know how many times I've said 'no comment' over the past few weeks. But we're almost done.

We're escorted to our usual interview room and wait for Jackson to get here. I sit in Milo's lap, mostly because it drives the other two crazy. He holds me protectively, as if he'll pounce on anyone who tries to take me away.

The interviews are the same as they were yesterday, and the same as they will be tomorrow. The prosecutor is a thin woman in a smart suit, with short, mousy brown hair that's cut to her shoulders. She reminds me of that television lawyer from forever ago, but I can't remember the name of the show—Ally something or other. It was a great show, but I'm not sure she's the right attorney for the job.

She is flexible on doing our interviews together. Most people would have insisted that we be split up, but she just takes turns talking to each of us and explaining what will happen when we're called to testify. We go along with everything, and just when I think we're done, she asks my guys to give us a minute, woman to woman.

I raise an eyebrow and shrug when Jarek looks at me. What could she possibly want to talk to me about alone? It seems strange since we've never done one-on-one interviews since this started. I know I'm safe here, so I nod that it's okay, and Jarek leads the other two out of the room. When it's just me and the lawyer, she turns to me.

"Are you being held against your will? Do you need help to get away from these men? It's okay to admit that you're in over your head here. I can help you if you tell me about it."

I laugh so hard that I double over. "This is what you wanted to talk to me about?"

She nods, clearly serious. That fact sobers me up instantly.

"I'm sorry, I thought you were joking. Thank you for your concern. These men are my mates, they're my alphas, my pack, my family. They have never hurt me. The only thing they've ever done is protect me and take care of me."

I watch as her expression changes. She really thought I was a prisoner. I feel bad for her, because as a beta, she'll never understand what it's like to be an omega.

"I'm going to go now. Thank you again, Claire, for your concern. We'll see you tomorrow."

JAREK

"What was that all about?" I ask Ness as soon as she leaves the interrogation room.

She laughs and threads her fingers through mine. I kiss her left hand, just below the two-carat princess cut blue diamond on her third finger. I'm impressed that the three of us agreed that the ring was meant to be hers. Each of us got bands to match, and we had a very private ceremony where we exchanged them.

"Claire thinks you're holding me hostage. She obviously isn't very observant," she retorts.

"What? I should talk to her," I offer.

"And leave me to go to dinner with your parents without you? I don't think so."

Since our pack was officially formed, we're all D'Angelos now. Which meant that all of us were now required to attend my mother's weekly dinners. "You wouldn't be alone. Raf and Milo have to go too," I tease. I've nearly forgotten about the appointment with all the fuss about interviews and such.

We head back to the safehouse to change for dinner. I would prefer to wear what I have on, but I know how upset my father would be if we weren't dressed for dinner. It was one of his many stipulations in signing off on our pack formation request. Since he is my head alpha, I had to have his permission to create my own pack. The whole system is archaic and ridiculous, but it's tradition.

Once we're suitably dressed, we climb back into the car and head over to the estate outside of the city. It's private and will allow us some much needed down time. Perhaps Ness will even get to forget for a little while that she has to testify against her father. I can't help staring at her as Raf drives us down the gravel road leading to the main house.

Ness is wearing a knee-length pale blue satin dress. It's casual and dressy at the same time. The color so closely matches her eyes that a person would think the dress was made for her. In reality, we stumbled across it online and I surprised her with it. The bodice is tight but modest, and the skirt flares out a little.

She catches me staring as Raf parks the car. "What? Do I look bad?" I can hear the panic in her voice.

"No, my love, you're gorgeous. Don't worry; you already know that my parents love you," I reassure her. I understand her nerves, though. Milo seems to be having the same problem. I put my hand on his shoulder from the back seat. He turns to see what I want, and I press my lips to his. I never expected to have this kind of relationship, but I have to admit, I enjoy being with Milo and Ness at the same time.

His cheeks redden from my kiss, but it appears to calm him enough that he can get out of the car. Raf opens Ness' door, and I capture her lips with mine before he can whisk her away from me. I revel in the fact that she can taste Milo on me. Her approving hum is all I need to get through tonight. While my parents have accepted our new pack, they aren't always as kind to me as they are to the rest of my little family.

I'm expecting my father to chew me out about anything he can come up with today. I want to be wrong, but so far, I haven't been. He's used our weekly dinners as an excuse to have private meetings with me every time we've been so far.

We enter the house and are escorted to the dining room. This is the formal dining area, and not the casual one we usually use. There are name cards, telling us which seats are ours, and informing us that we will not be dining alone with my parents this evening.

Why would they invite the District Attorney and the Attorney General to dinner? That doesn't make sense. Before I can leave to find my mother and ask, the doors open, and our guests are escorted inside. From that moment until my parents arrive, we're playing hosts. They keep us busy with small talk and questions about our upcoming trial. I'm surprised when they ask about our safety and how we're staying hidden.

My parents make an entrance, being sure to be just a bit late to give everyone a chance to be in the room for it. Of course, Mother looks beautiful in her silver gown, and Father is dressed just as nicely in his suit that matches a little too well. Mother always enjoyed everyone matching. It's probably why I refuse to let Raf or Milo have suits that look just like mine.

Once everyone is settled at the table, I give my mother a questioning look. She simply smiles and shrugs. She knows something but doesn't want to tell me. I'm starting to feel like we're being ambushed here.

"Good evening, everyone. Welcome to my home," my father begins his speech as the first course is brought out. I could care less about the food at this point. I want answers. What are all of us doing here tonight?

"I'm sure you're all wondering why I invited you here tonight," he says, smirking at me. Can the old man actually read my mind? I hope not. "Well, I'll tell you. Dragonetti's lawyer reached out to me today with a business proposal, and I wanted to discuss it with you all before I respond."

"A business proposal? What does he possibly have to offer you now? He's going to prison, and Ness is taking over his legitimate businesses. Everything else is being shut down." Or so the lawyers need to believe. In reality, I'm absorbing them into my own illegal dealings.

"Yes, son. A business proposal. He wants you and your pack to recant your statements to the DA. If you do, he's giving me everything."

MILO

"We can't do that, sir. With all due respect, you have to know that we cannot let him back out into the free world." I know that I shouldn't speak my mind here, but I can't resist.

D'Angelo stares daggers at me. "Jarek, get your pack in line. This isn't your decision or theirs. It's mine. And you will do as I tell you."

"Except we won't," Ness insists. "I will not recant anything, and I refuse to let my father's empire be handed off to anyone but myself. I understand how difficult that is for you to understand, since you and my father share a lot of the same ideals. But that is the way of it. The empire is mine. End of discussion."

Fuck, our girl is hot. I can't believe the way she's standing up to Jarek's father. It's dangerous, and she knows it. But she doesn't let that stop her. She stands up at her seat as if daring him to tell her no.

"Young lady, you are an omega. You are not fit to run an empire. I will be taking over, and you will go back to playing house with my son. Do not test me here." His words seem final, as if he's laying down the law, and we have no say in any of it.

Ness starts to argue, but Jarek holds up a hand. Then he gets to his feet. "Ness, please, let me handle this," he says to her. She sits down, pouting because he's basically agreed with his father.

"First of all, Father, you will not ever speak to my omega that way again. She is free to express herself as she sees fit. You will not stifle that. Second, if one of my packmates has an opinion about something you've said, he is free to express that. I do not control my family. Instead, I support them and ensure they have what they need to be successful."

Ness' jaw drops at Jarek's words. My eyes go wide. I wasn't expecting that to be what he said in response to his father's orders.

"Jarek, you will not be disrespectful to me. You are still my son, and still fall under my rule as your head alpha." D'Angelo is clearly getting pissed. His face is red, and the vein in his forehead is bulging. I'm a little worried about what he's going to do to punish us.

"You're wrong there, Father. The pack formation paperwork that you signed, allowing us to form this pack? That paperwork gives me full autonomy over my own pack. It also releases me from your hold as head alpha. I am the head alpha of my pack now, the same as you are of your own. You can tell them what to do, but not me. And before you even make the threat, I have my own money. I don't need yours." I can see Jarek shaking slightly. I'm sure he's not used to standing up to his father this way.

Pride fills my heart at his words. I watched him pour over that documentation for days, but he refused to tell us what he was looking for. Because it was these clauses he's citing now. He wanted to be sure he could legally tell his father where to stick it before he did. I can't stop the smile that tugs at my lips. I love this man almost as much as I love Ness.

She's smiling now too, and I notice a small smirk on Jarek's mother's face. She must have known this would happen. I look at Raf to see how he's holding up. This is his uncle, and I can't imagine it's an easy situation for him to process.

He's smiling at Jarek, too, though. I can see the pride filling his eyes as well. D'Angelo sputters and tries to come up with some threat that will work, but Jarek shoots everything down. He's not backing down on this, and the old man knows it. Looks like we're going to be in competition with Jarek's patriarch now, but I think we're up for the challenge.

"You will not disobey me, boy," his father yells. Raf makes a subtle motion for me to grab Ness and move toward the door. Things are definitely going sideways here, and it doesn't look good. I don't want to abandon Jarek, but I have to trust Raf to have this handled. I take Ness' hand and we slowly move to get out of our seats.

Jarek's dad sees us, though, and grabs Ness' other arm. She cries out in pain and Jarek pounces on him. Raf moves over as if he's going to restrain Jarek, but instead, he keeps anyone from pulling his cousin off. I work to get the old man's hand off of our girl. As soon as I can peel his fingers back, I put myself between them. I'm not going to let him touch her again, but I'm not going to let anyone stop Jarek either.

His father puts up a fight, and I see the glint of something metallic. Is that a gun or a knife? "Watch out, Jarek, he has a weapon!" I shout just as D'Angelo sinks the knife into Jarek's side. I expect to see our head alpha fall, but adrenaline kicks in and he simply pulls the knife from his side and sinks it into his father's throat.

D'Angelo's eyes go wide, and he starts to choke on the blood that's pouring from the wound. Jarek rips the knife out and stands up, putting some distance between himself and his father. Ness runs to him, pulling his jacket and shirt off to tend to his stab wound.

I turn to the DA and Attorney General. "You saw that, right? It was self-defense. There was nothing else he could have done. He probably even saved your lives."

They nod in understanding. "Agreed. There will be no charges. It was self-defense. Let's get Jarek's wound taken care of."

RAFAEL

Well, family dinner takes a weird turn. The moment my uncle grabs Ness' arm, I know it's all over. Jarek will beat him to death. And in front of the Attorney General and the District Attorney, none the less. That's unfortunate.

What happens next shocks me, though. Everyone steps back and lets Jarek do it. It's like D'Angelo's bodyguards just decide to take a break. I step forward to stop them from intervening, but no one even tries. Then I realize that's because the old man has a knife. Milo shouts a warning, but I'm not quick enough to get there.

The knife is buried to the hilt in Jarek's side, but he just seems annoyed. He pulls it out and sticks it into his father's jugular. Now we're all covered in blood. His mother screams before she faints. I barely get to her in time to keep her from smashing her head on the table. I ease her to the floor a few feet away from the mess her husband is making as his life leaves his body.

No one makes a move to help him, either. Did they have this all planned out? It just doesn't make sense. And why would Uncle think he could order us to recant our testimony against Dragonetti? He hates, I mean, hated that man. None of this little dinner party makes any sense.

Ness runs to Jarek and takes his jacket off, then rips his shirt off to check the stab wound. The knife wasn't that big, but it was buried to the hilt in his side. He'll be lucky if it didn't get his lung. I pull out my phone to call for an ambulance just as I hear sirens heading this way.

I turn to Milo. He shrugs. The DA looks at me and says, "I texted the precinct as soon as things started happening. No one is coming after Jarek. It was just a precaution in case something like this happened. It's medical response only, no cops."

I nod and walk over to Aunt Janie. She's still unconscious, and I wonder how she'll take the news when she comes to and realizes that her son just killed her husband. The EMTs race in and I gesture to her first. "She fainted but hasn't come to yet. She'll be in shock and probably panic when she learns what just happened."

A second EMT team comes in after the first starts loading my aunt onto a gurney. The second team heads straight for Jarek and I have to pull Ness out of the way. "They need to take a look at it. He's gonna be okay. We have to let them work." I have to convince her to come with me so that we're out of the way.

I hear them asking him questions about what happened, and he goes over the whole story. One of the EMTs comes to check Ness' wrist where Uncle had grabbed her. It's starting to bruise, but they don't think it's broken. We'll get x-rays to be sure, though. Jarek will insist on it. If he doesn't, I will.

The EMTs take statements from all of us, just to be sure they don't miss anything. They also check everyone for shock and other injuries. Satisfied that it's just Jarek, his mom, and Ness that need attention, they load up the ambulances and head back to the city. Ness goes with Jarek. "Milo and I will meet you at Memorial as soon as the coroner comes to pick up the body," I tell Ness as I kiss her goodbye. I know she's scared and doesn't want to be alone.

I hope they'll keep her with Jarek until we get there, but if he needs surgery, there won't be any way for that to happen. I'm debating our options when a hearse suddenly rolls up the drive. When it stops, a uniformed officer and the coroner get out. So much for no cops.

I escort them inside and explain everything again. For some reason, Uncle's bodyguards have disappeared. I guess they're worried about being blamed for not stepping in. I expect the officer to ask us to come to the station to answer questions, but he doesn't. Instead, he busies himself helping the coroner extract the body and get it loaded up.

Once that's taken care of, we head to the hospital. "I'm driving as fast as I can, Raf," Milo tells me.

"What?" I ask, not understanding why he would say that.

"You keep saying 'come on, come on' like I can drive faster. There's too much traffic and we aren't close enough to the ambulance to go any faster than this." I didn't realize I spoke my thoughts aloud.

"I know, man. I'm sorry. I'm just anxious. All of this seems strange. What happened to Uncle tonight? I don't get why he acted that way. It was completely out of character." It isn't an excuse, and I hope that Milo understands.

"I had the same questions. It didn't seem like anything he would do. I just figured maybe I didn't know him as well as you guys did," he replies as he weaves in and out of traffic.

When we arrive at the hospital, we're taken back to Ness' room immediately. "We had to sedate her. She'll come out of it in just a little while. But she got hysterical when we had to take Mr. D'Angelo to surgery. And I thought he was going to get up off the table and take our orderlies out when they made her leave." The nurse explains everything to us as she closes the door to Ness' room.

"Have you been able to do any tests on her wrist yet?" I ask, knowing that we got here right after the ambulance did.

"Not yet. I don't think it's broken though; with the way she was beating on the orderly to let her go. I'll be back in just a minute."

VANESSA

I don't want Raf and Milo to stay behind when Jarek and I go to the hospital. I know that Jarek is going to have to have surgery, and I'm not sure that I can stand to be away from him. The EMTs take us inside the emergency room and try to split us up. Jarek and I hold hands, refusing to let them escort me away without him.

When two big orderlies physically separate us, I think Jarek is going to tear the restraints off and fight them for me. I know he has to have surgery, but I'm scared. I don't want to leave him, even though I have no choice. The orderlies carry me away and a nurse jabs me in the shoulder with a needle. It must be a sedative, because everything gets blurry just before it all goes dark.

I wake to Raf and Milo pacing the floor. "What happened?" I ask, pushing myself up in the bed. I want to get up, but I notice that I'm strapped in much like Jarek was.

"They had to sedate you so they could take Jarek to surgery. And since you were out cold, they strapped you down. I'll get the nurse and see if we can get things moving. They need to x-ray your wrist," Milo explains before dashing out of the room.

"Any word on Jarek?"

Raf's eyes meet mine, and for just a moment, fear creeps up my spine. He's taking too long to answer, and I start to panic. My heart races and my hands suddenly feel cold and clammy. "Nothing yet, but the doc said he'll call me when they're done."

"Okay," I sigh, sinking back into the mattress. The restraints loosen a little since I'm no longer fighting against them.

"I was so scared that I was going to lose you both. Jarek is more than a cousin to me. He's always been like the big brother I didn't have. And I love you so much. I couldn't stand to lose either of you." His admission makes me cry. He unfastens the restraints and pulls me into his arms, sitting on the edge of the bed and holding me close.

"What happens now?"

"Jarek will be okay, and you will too. We'll get through your father's trial, and then things will finally go back to normal." I wish I could believe Raf's words, but it just seems like too much to ask for. I don't know if we'll ever have normal.

Milo comes back into the room wearing a strange expression. "Ness, I have news."

I instantly tense. "Is Jarek okay?"

"As far as I know, he's fine. The nurse gave me a message for you before she went to get the x-ray set up. Apparently, your parents are still listed as your next of kin for the hospital to contact. They called your mom to let her know that you're here." Milo swallows hard, his eyes never leaving mine.

"And?" Raf asks when I don't respond.

"And they found Dragonetti dead an hour ago. It looks like a rival crew took him out, hoping to gain favor with us. It happened right after word got out about D'Angelo. I'm sorry, Ness. Your father is dead." Milo says the words, but I'm not sure I believe them.

"I need to see him. I can't believe it if I don't see the body myself. We'll always be looking over our shoulders, wondering when he'll attack again." Panic takes hold now, and I start to hyperventilate. My hands feel like ice, except they're coated in sweat. I feel a trickle drip down my spine. What if this is all a trick? What if he's not really dead? What if he is?

"I'll make some calls. I heard it was pretty violent, though. Are you sure you want to see him?" he asks. I nod. Milo excuses himself again to call whoever he knows that could get us access. A few minutes later, he comes back with a uniformed officer.

"Smith is going to escort us to the morgue so you can officially identify the body. Then you're coming back up here for your x-ray," Milo tells me. I can't respond. Raf carries me and follows the cop and Milo to the elevator. We descend floors until we're in the basement. It's dark and creepy, even with the fluorescent lights glaring above us.

We go into the morgue, and the coroner greets us. My eyes are filled with tears, and I'm not sure I can handle this after all. "You don't have to do this, love. We can go back upstairs if you want," Raf whispers against my ear.

"No, I can do it," I answer, my voice cracking. He sets me on my feet and takes my hand. Milo steps over and gently takes my injured hand. Sandwiched between them, I feel stronger. I nod to the coroner and she grabs the sheet.

"I have to warn you, it's bad. They sent him to me in pieces." After that, she pulls the sheet back. My father's head stares back at me, his lifeless eyes meet mine. The first thing I notice is that his head is not attached to his body. She wasn't kidding when she said he was in pieces. His arms and legs have been severed as well, and his torso is cut in half. It's gory and disgusting, and I know that I should feel sick.

"That's definitely him," I say, laughter bubbling up through me.

"What's so funny?" the coroner asks.

"He tortured her mentally and physically for years. This is kind of cathartic for her, I'm sure. There's no more reason to be scared of him. Besides that, we were preparing to testify against him next week." Raf's explanation makes me laugh even harder. I'm doubled over and start struggling to breathe again.

Chapter Twenty

EPILOGUE

VANESSA

After verifying that my father is indeed dead, Raf manages to calm me down while Milo talks to the coroner. They have no idea exactly who killed him. Apparently, several different gangs have claimed responsibility. Given his list of enemies, I understand why it's so difficult.

Fast forward six months, and my mother still won't speak to me, although Jarek's mom calls every day. I expected her to be upset about what happened between her husband and son, but she's not. She even insists that we call her Mom, the same as Jarek. It's strange really. Until we get the certified letter from D'Angelo himself.

Jarek refuses to open it. "It's a trick. It can't be from him. That would be like saying he knew exactly what was going to happen and planned it out. There's no way."

"It's postmarked after his death. That is kind of suspicious."

I open the letter and pull out the carefully written pages. I can't wrap my head around what I read, going over my dead father-in-law's words so many times before I finally hand the pages to Milo.

"I don't understand," he says as he reads.

"That was my problem. But it makes perfect sense. He was a proud man, who'd made many enemies, just like my father. I can't imagine either of them wanted to grow old and suffer."

Jarek looks at us and holds out his hand. Good, he needs to read it for himself.

My dear boy,

I know that if you're reading this, I'm gone. Most likely it happened by your hands. And for that, I must say thank you.

I've done things in my life that I'm not proud of. I've stolen, trafficked drugs, taken lives, and for what? To build an empire that will be passed down to the next generation? It looks that way. All I ever wanted was for you to be happy. And I see you have that with your beautiful omega. Please take good care of Vanessa. She's good for you.

I cannot ask for forgiveness for the things I've done, but I hope that you'll understand that I did them for you. By now, you know that Dragonetti is dead too. I ordered the hit, and had Francesco make sure it got paid. I didn't do it because I hated him. I did it because he asked me to. Like me, he saw his own mortality staring him in the face, and didn't like it.

Unlike me, he was healthy as a horse when he died. I asked your mother to keep this from you, and hopefully she did. I was sick, Jarek. I knew that my time was close, and I didn't want you or your mother to watch me suffer at the end. I wanted to go out swinging.

That was why I devised the plan that led to the weekly dinners. And I made sure there were witnesses to prove that you took my life in self-defense. At least I hope that's how it happened. Because that was my intent.

Don't mourn me too hard, boy. I'm not in pain anymore. And I have plenty of time to think about my actions while I wait for your mother to join me wherever I end up.

Love,

Dad

His explanation of everything is insane, but makes perfect sense at the same time. It helps me to know that he wasn't intentionally trying to break my wrist. He just had to make it look real enough for Jarek to attack him. In his defense, it was a solid plan, and it worked. I understand him not wanting to suffer through a terminal illness, but wish he'd been able to talk to us about it.

I hadn't known him well. That was the one thing I had wished could be different. Of course, he and my father ended up being more alike than we knew. How had my father contacted him to make that request? Was the thought of going to trial just too much for him? Or was he secretly ill like Mr. D'Angelo? I'll never know.

What I do know is that my mother blames me for his death. She told me as much at his funeral, where she also informed me that she has no daughter and wants nothing to do with me or the Dragonetti empire ever again. Funny, she wants nothing to do with it, but she sure took that settlement we offered. I don't pretend to understand her, or her motives. I wish things could have been different, but there's no point in living in the past.

"You should put that away. Your mom will be here for lunch soon. We don't want to upset her," I say, gesturing to the letter. Jarek folds it and slides the pages back into the envelope before tucking it into his copy of Her Personal Demons by Ginna Moran. There's no way his mom will pick that book up, so it's safe there.

Milo kisses me before he goes to the kitchen to help Raf with lunch. I stare out the window, finally understanding why Jarek's mom insisted that we take this property. At first, I thought it was because it was the site where her husband was killed and she couldn't handle that. Now I see that it was what he wanted. Not for us to think of his death every day, but for us to have the space for our family and pack to grow.

Jarek slips his hands around my growing belly from behind me, laying his chin on my shoulder. "Are you okay?" he asks as he presses a kiss to my neck.

I rub the mound that holds our child. "I think so. I hate that he felt like that was what had to be done. But I understand why he did it. All of it, even killing my father at his request. Does that make us monsters? Because we can relate to why they did it all."

"No, Ness, that makes us human. Being able to relate to others is not a bad thing. It keeps us from doing things that would hurt people."

"Unless they need to be hurt. Then we take them to the dungeon," I reply, thinking about the two men who are locked up now. No one knows we have a dungeon here, and no one will ever find out. We will continue to do what we have to in order to keep this family safe.

"My little blood thirsty queen. You know how much I love that, but the doctor said you need to start taking it a little easier. You've been doing too much getting the house taken care of." He kisses my neck again, clearly trying to distract me from my thoughts. It's starting to work.

I can't wait to meet our little one, but I want to make sure that she's as healthy and ready as she can be before her debut. That's actually why Janie is coming to lunch today. We're planning a baby shower. I don't have many friends since everything came out about my father. Most of them were only using me to get to him. That doesn't matter now. I have my family, and that's what's important.

I'm looking forward to filling this house with love and babies. I know that my guys are on board. I've never seen men so excited about a baby before. I think I've definitely unlocked a daddy kink in a couple of them, and a breeding kink in all three. We'll start interviewing nannies in a few weeks, then prepare for our little one to come. I should have a few months with her before my heat hits again.

Then the cycle will start all over. I'm sure Jarek, Raf, and Milo will all fight to be the one who knocks me up, especially when they finally find out which one of them is the biological father to the baby. They won't treat her any different, but they definitely want bragging rights as the one who knocked me up first.

I'll never admit it, but I kind of hope it's Raf. Those baby blues with his dark hair would make an adorable daughter. But I'll be happy with whatever she looks like, as long as she's healthy. The rest is just details.

I know that the three of them will have to start going back to the city for work soon. I don't want to think about it. There's still so much to do to get ready for our little one. I want them all to stay home with me. It's easier to get things done that way. Besides, when one of them is around, I don't have to walk anywhere. It's kind of nice to be carried around like you weigh nothing when you're hugely pregnant. Makes a girl feel skinny.

"She's here," I say, seeing Janie's car pulling up the long driveway. Before I can move, Jarek scoops me up and carries me out to the porch to meet her. I swat his arm playfully as she parks the car. "Put me down."

Jarek lowers me to my feet, but doesn't let go. His arms stay wrapped around me, with his palms on either side of my belly. Janie can barely contain her excitement as she gets out of the car and rushes up to hug us. I return her embrace just as tightly, enjoying being in the middle of this hug.

"We have a lot of planning to do. You boys had better make yourselves scarce. This party is for the mama, not the daddies," Janie orders her son as she steps back and looks at me. "But first, you need to get Ness a snack. She looks as if she's about to fall over. I swear, if you boys don't start taking better care of my girl, I'm going to take her home with me."

It's the same threat she makes every time she sees me. She tells them that I'm too thin to be this far along, and that they have to start feeding me. Then at some point tonight, she'll end up in the kitchen making a giant pot of spaghetti for me. It's so sweet, especially if she decides to make brownies too.

My stomach growls and she laughs. "You see? She's hungry." Janie shoos Jarek away and puts her arm around me. "Come on, lovebug, let's get you and that baby taken care of." Jarek disappears, understanding that his mom and I need this. Since my mom refused to ever go against my father, she wasn't anything like his mom. All of my guys have agreed to let Janie pamper and baby me when she's here.

All I have to do is sit back and enjoy it. I make a mental note to buy her a special gift when the baby comes to celebrate her first grandchild. I hate that she's moved in to the city, but she claims that it's better there. She has her penthouse and it's close to her friends. At least she comes to visit.

We walk into the kitchen, where Raf is making lunch. "At least one of you boys is trying to take care of my girl. Where's that other one? I want to talk to him. And when will food be done?"

Raf gives her a kiss on the cheek and hugs her tight. "Aunt Janie, Milo ran to the store to pick up some fresh fruit for your girl. He'll be back in just a bit. As for food, it's almost done. We're having tomato soup and grilled cheese sandwiches."

My stomach growls again and he laughs. "Don't worry, love, it's almost done. I'll get you some chips to tide you over." He kisses my cheek and turns to the cabinet to find the nacho cheese tortilla chips I love.

I let Janie settle me at the table as he brings them over. I know that I can eat the whole bag if I want, but I'd rather have the soup and sandwich. Raf makes the best grilled cheese. And I think he's lying about what Milo is doing, but I have no reason to question him.

MILO

I pull up to the precinct, hoping that Raf is able to distract Ness enough that she doesn't realize I'm gone for a while. I don't want to be here, but when your former boss calls and insists, you can't exactly say no.

I walk into the building where the police chief and the director of the FBI meet me. "Milo, it's good to see you." I'm hesitant, but shake the director's hand.

"You too. But why am I here?" I don't waste time. There's too much to do for me to stand here and wait for them to tell me what's going on.

"We want you to come back to work for us. You'd be leading the anti-terrorist task force based here in the city. There would be very little travel involved, and you would have an entire team at your disposal."

My jaw drops at the offer. A year ago, I would have jumped at this. It was my dream job. Back then, that is. Now, I'm not so sure. "Can I think about it?"

"Sure, for about five minutes. If you have to think about it, then you don't really want it. What could you possibly have lined up that's more important than this?"

"Ness is pregnant. My pack has several business ventures that I can head up. We don't need the money. Then there's the way you all treated me after her 'death,' or did you think that this offer would just make all of that go away?"

The embarrassed and pissed stares that I get back tell me that I'm not far off. I helped take down one of the biggest threats to the city, and now they want my help. It's kind of ridiculous. I can't help but laugh at the fact that they thought I could be used and bought that way.

"Milo, you know that isn't what we're saying," the police chief says, trying to smooth things over.

I shake my head. "No. My answer is no. I have more important responsibilities." I can see that they're offended by my refusal. "Look, I appreciate the offer, but this isn't what I want anymore. If that changes, I'll let you know. But for now, I belong with my pack; with my family. They need me, and that is the best feeling in the world."

Jackson walks up and shakes my hand. "I told you he'd say no."

"You should promote him, instead," I tell them before turning and walking away. I have to get to the store and grab some fresh fruit so I can get back to home before Ness realizes I've taken off. It's probably too late already.

JAREK

While Mom has Ness occupied, I make some calls and take care of business I've been putting off. With Dragonetti out of the way, the D'Angelo family runs the city now. There are certain responsibilities that come with that. I have to be ready with a strong crew to handle any threats. Since my father's death, I've taken over his operations, and Ness has given me most of her father's businesses as well. The combined empire is a lot, and I'm glad I have Raf and Milo to help me run it.

We've pretty much split everything up as far as what we're responsible for. I'm handling all the illegal stuff, because that will keep Milo's hands clean. Raf will help me if I need it, but I prefer to keep him out of that as well, if I can. Our kids need good, strong, moral role models to look up to. I'm going to do my best to keep them away from those dealings too. I don't think it will be easy, but at least I have help.

Although I know it's only a matter of time before the FBI begs Milo to come back, because he was instrumental in taking down Dragonetti. He was the one who found the ledger and he was the one who came up with the plan before he realized that I had Ness. He'd make an amazing director, but I know they won't give him that. At least not right away.

After I make some calls, I head upstairs to the nursery. I have some painting to finish, and I'd like to get it done while Ness is busy. I'm painting the walls a pale pink, with a rainbow accent wall. The whole thing is coming together nicely. I don't mind doing the work myself. Raf is building the bassinet, and Milo has taken responsibility for stocking everything we'll need.

I let my mind wander as I transform the walls of the room that I grew up in. It's nice to think we're going to fill this house with children. My childhood here was happy, and I like to think theirs will be too. And thinking about babies gets me thinking about my omega.

She's so strong and stubborn. I love her determination. She wants to stay home with the kids, but also plans to run a couple of above-board charity organizations, one to help omegas who are mistreated and one that would help underprivileged kids. Her heart is bigger than anyone I've ever known. It's one of the things I love about her.

I can't wait to finish this room so she can see it. I hope that my choices meet her approval. I guess if they don't, she'll make me repaint everything. It's not like I'd complain. She's my omega, and I want her to be happy. No matter what it takes.

I continue to paint until Raf yells that lunch is ready, then I head downstairs to enjoy my family.

RAFAEL

Watching Aunt Janie take care of Ness while I cook lunch is the sweetest thing ever. It's such a relief to see her back to her old self again. She had gotten much more timid and quiet the past few years after Uncle's health issues were discovered. Of course, she was the only one besides him that knew about those. We just thought the old man was becoming an asshole.

Turns out, he had a reason for it. Not that there's any excuse for grabbing an omega the way he did Ness. Knowing that he did it intentionally to get Jarek to kill him doesn't make saying goodbye any easier. And I know that Jarek is struggling with that now that he knows what happened. He felt guilty before, but knowing that his dad was sick makes it worse.

If only Uncle had talked to us and let us know what was going on beforehand. But that wasn't his way. Just like him taking Dragonetti out before the trial. That was the way men from their era took care of things. There was a weird kind of code between those men. They hated each other, but somehow still respected each other as well. While it was nice to have the competition taken care of, it made me nervous that someone new would come onto the scene and try to compete.

Now that we've combined everything, we have enough legal businesses to keep the three of us busy. Add to that, Jarek handling the not so savory dealings, and it's almost too much for us. We'll find a way to make it work, I'm sure.

For now, I set the table and carry lunch over to it. After I yell for Jarek, I serve soup and sandwiches to everyone. Milo comes in just as I finish.

"How did it go?" I ask, not thinking that he didn't want Ness to know what he was doing.

"Fuck, Raf," he says, glaring at me. Oops. Too late now. I shrug and sit down.

"What's he talking about?" Ness asks pointedly. I get another hateful look from Milo, but then he explains that the director of the FBI had called and asked to meet him.

"They offered me a task force. More than just my old job back. This would be a promotion and everything I'd dreamed of," he explains.

Ness nods, "Okay. I think we can make that work, can't we?" She looks at Jarek who nods as well.

Milo holds up a hand. "I turned it down."

"What?" Jarek's jaw drops. "What do you mean, you turned it down?"

"I mean, that's not what I want anymore, so I turned it down. I'd rather be here with you guys, unless you don't want me."

Ness smiles so big that I think her face is going to break. "That's the best surprise ever. Thank you."

Jarek shakes his hand and I squeeze his shoulder. "It's good to know that you're all in, Milo."

VANESSA

Milo's little secret should piss me off. I wish he'd told me he was going to meet his former boss, but I understand why he didn't. And if he'd decided to go back to the FBI, we would have figured it out. As it stands, Jarek is trying to limit the shady stuff a bit. I know there's no way to make it all go away, but it would be nice to have jobs we can tell our kids about. I don't want them to be ashamed of their parents.

I don't ever want them to feel the way I did growing up. This little girl growing inside of me will know that she is loved and wanted, no matter what her designation is. And hopefully in just a few years, there will be half a dozen more, filling this house with love.

It's hard to believe that all of this started with a plot to take my father's empire down. I guess in a way, it worked. There is no Dragonetti empire anymore, because there is no Dragonetti. We're all D'Angelos now, and I couldn't be happier about it.

I've been working on the charity organizations, and feel like they're coming along nicely. I know things will get harder once the baby comes, but I'm preparing for that. Janie has already offered to help, and most of what I need to do can be done from home while the little one sleeps.

I'm so relieved that Milo refused the FBI job. I know that Jarek and Raf have too much to worry about without having to cover what Milo has agreed to handle. And there would be no way for him to do both. It's nice to know that my men value family as much as I do. The universe put us together for a reason.

Lunch is filled with talking and laughing. We continue talks of renovations that we'd like to do to the property and things that need to be done before the baby comes. But mostly we just enjoy each other. This time with family is exactly what we all needed. Once we're all finished eating, Janie starts talking about the baby shower, finally relenting and letting Jarek, Raf, and Milo stick around for the planning.

She even gives each of them jobs to handle for the party. It all seems like a lot, and I'm glad that my only responsibility is taking care of my own needs. I know that's selfish of me, but I am nurturing the next generation here. And if my family wants to spoil me a bit, who am I to argue?

When the planning is done, Janie has to go. I'm sad to see her leave, but I know that she'll be back in just a few days. We all wave to her as she drives away. Then I stop my loves before they can run off to handle their chores. I pull each of them in for a kiss, and we stare out at the land that is our home.

ABOUT THE AUTHOR

M.P. Starkweather is a wife, mother, author, poet, casual online gamer, self-proclaimed fan-girl, and full-time nerd. She writes free-form poetry, paranormal romance, sci-fi romance, reverse harem romance, omegaverse romance, and is branching out into contemporary romance. In her free time, she enjoys writing, reading, Dungeons & Dragons, table top games with her husband and friends, and playing with her son. M.P. also enjoys tv, movies, and music across various genres.

To get the most up-to-date information about her latest releases and book signings, check out www.mpstarkweather.

com or follow her on your favorite social media site.

ALSO BY M.P. STARKWEATHER

Standalones – Contemporary RH

Finding Fiona
Standalones - Contemporary RH OV

Forsaken Omega – free with newsletter signup

Cold Princes

Knot My Valentine
The Pack Next Door – Contemporary RH OV series

Princess or Knot

Fiancée or Knot

Queen or Knot

<u>The Pack Next Door: The Original Trilogy</u>

<u>Christmas or Knot</u>
Standalones – Paranormal RH

<u>The Wayward Girl</u>
The Cursed Blade Series – Paranormal w/ different pairings

<u>Digital Blade</u> – RH
Elemental Blade – RH
Vampires at Midnight - Paranormal RH series
<u>Blood Moon</u>

<u>Blood Lost</u>

<u>Blood War</u>

<u>Vampires at Midnight: The Complete Trilogy</u>
VaM/HoF Crossover Novella - Paranormal RH

<u>Blood Wolf</u>— free with newsletter signup
Hunters of the Forest - Paranormal RH series

<u>Wolf Bane</u>

<u>Wolf Caged</u>

<u>Wolf Moon</u>

<u>Hunters of the Forest: The Complete Trilogy</u>
Forged by Magic - Sci-fi/Fantasy M/F series

<u>Hidden</u>

<u>Betrayed</u>

<u>Saved</u>

<u>Forged by Magic: The Complete Trilogy</u>
Daydreams and Sunsets - a collection of poetry

<u>Daydreams and Sunsets</u>

www.ingramcontent.com/pod-product-compliance
Lightning Source LLC
Chambersburg PA
CBHW031155310726
48969CB00001B/96